Prais
Fantasy
Jeann
and *Ba*
Shad

"A book that's a real book, rather than just a TV tie-in knockoff . . . Absorbing and affecting . . . Excellent."

—Andy Lane, author of *The Babylon File*

"From the explosive opening . . . to the chilling ending, *The Shadow Within* fires on all cylinders. . . . Ms. Cavelos does a wonderful job of deepening the layers of the *Babylon 5* universe. . . . A highly enjoyable reading experience with a powerful and chilling ending. Best of the B5 media novels."

—*The Zocalo*

"One of the best TV tie-in novels ever written."

—*Dreamwatch* magazine

"Most satisfying . . . [I] devoured this flashback book (which takes place before the first episode) cover to cover. The plot involves realistic political intrigue, a sparkling interstellar mystery and a sense of doom so thick you can smell it on the pages. Still, the sharply defined characters display so much wit, intelligence and warmth that you root for them to change history anyway. . . . This is no by-the-numbers knockoff. . . . Perhaps the best TV tie-in novel ever."

—Captain Comics, *The Sunday Telegraph*

Published by Ballantine Books:

CREATING BABYLON 5 by David Bassom

Babylon 5 Season-by-Season Guides by Jane Killick
SIGNS AND PORTENTS
THE COMING OF SHADOWS
POINT OF NO RETURN
NO SURRENDER, NO RETREAT
THE WHEEL OF FIRE

BABYLON 5 SECURITY MANUAL

BABYLON 5: IN THE BEGINNING by Peter David
BABYLON 5: THIRDSPACE by Peter David
BABYLON 5: A CALL TO ARMS by Robert Sheckley

The Psi Corps Trilogy by J. Gregory Keyes
BABYLON 5: DARK GENESIS
BABYLON 5: DEADLY RELATIONS
BABYLON 5: FINAL RECKONING

Legions of Fire by Peter David
BABYLON 5: THE LONG NIGHT OF CENTAURI PRIME
BABYLON 5: ARMIES OF LIGHT AND DARK
BABYLON 5: OUT OF THE DARKNESS

The Passing of the Techno-Mages by Jeanne Cavelos
BABYLON 5: CASTING SHADOWS
BABYLON 5: SUMMONING LIGHT*

**forthcoming*

BABYLON 5™

Book I of The Passing of the Techno-Mages

Casting Shadows

By Jeanne Cavelos

Based on an original outline by J. Michael Straczynski

™

A Del Rey® Book
THE BALLANTINE PUBLISHING GROUP • NEW YORK

A Del Rey® Book
Published by The Ballantine Publishing Group
 Published in the United States by The Ballantine Publishing Group, a division of Random House, Inc., New York, and simultaneously in Canada by Random House of Canada Limited, Toronto.

www.randomhouse.com/delrey/

Library of Congress Catalog Card Number: 00-108231

ISBN 0-345-42721-1

Manufactured in the United States of America

First Edition: March 2001

10 9 8 7 6 5 4 3 2

To Leo F. Ferris
who first showed me
magic

— acknowledgments —

Thanks very much to J. Michael Straczynski for again allowing me to come and play in his fascinating universe. Thanks also to Fiona Avery at Babylonian Productions for helping me remain consistent with that universe, and to Skye Herzog and Paula Allen at Warner Bros.

Thanks to my editor, Steve Saffel, for all his support, and to my agent, Lori Perkins, for her tireless efforts.

Grateful thanks to my group of science experts, who applied their genius and expertise to bizarre and complex questions: Tom Thatcher, Dr. Charles Lurio, Dr. Korey Moeller, M. Mitchell Marmel, Dr. Stuart Penn, Dr. Dennis C. Hwang, Bruce Goatly, Megan Gentry, Dr. David Loffredo, Jim Batka, Dr. Gary Day, Elizabeth Bartosz, Dr. Stephanie Ross, Reed Riddle, Dr. Michael Blumlein, Beth Dibble, Dr. Gail Dolbear, Dr. John Schilling, Britta Serog, and Dr. Paul Viscuso.

Thanks to my group of *Babylon 5* experts, who generously shared their incredible store of knowledge with me: Karen Hayes, K. Waldo Ricke, Merryl Gross, Don Kinney, Alec Ecyler, Penny Rothkopf, William (Pete) Pettit, John Donigan, Patricia Jackson, Marty Gingras, Allen Wilkins, Terry Jones, Bill Hartman, Michael A. Burstein, and Nomi Burstein.

Thanks to all the people who read pieces of this book in manuscript form and gave invaluable feedback: Laurie and Mike Hilyard, Keith Demanche, Barnaby Rapoport, Susan Shell Winston, JoAnn Forgit, Martha Adams, Stephen Chambers, Marty Hiller, Troy Ehlers, Elaine Isaak, Margo Cavelos, David Lowrey, George Williams, and Roxanne Hutton.

Thanks to my research assistant, Keith Maxwell, for finding exactly what I needed exactly when I needed it.

Thanks to James George Frazer and Orson Scott Card for saying things worthy of a techno-mage, and to James Randi.

Thanks to Ben Dibble for the loan of a laptop, without which this book wouldn't have gotten finished in time.

Thanks to Mark Purington, Sue Gagnon, and the rest of the staff at Saint Anselm College's Geisel Library.

A special thanks to my husband, Michael Flint, for his unending help and understanding, and for telling me of the lonely command of Confederate General Cadmus Wilcox, who held his own against superior forces at Chancellorsville.

And in the "No thanks" department, a dishonorable mention to Igmoe, my iguana, whose constant attempts to mate with me throughout the writing of this book were enough to drive me to distraction, though they did keep the days exciting. And I was flattered. I do love you, Igmoe, just not in that way.

WHO ARE YOU?

"Many a man has seen himself first in a dream."
—Anonymous

November 2258

— chapter 1 —

Soon the war would come.

With a cry of joy Anna swooped toward the barren moon, her sisters behind her. As her sleek body cut through the invigorating vacuum of space, she surveyed the training site eagerly, hungry for challenge. The Eye had specified the coordinates to be attacked. This exercise was to be at close range, surgical, precise.

Anna loved training, exploring her abilities, honing her skills. She had learned the dizzying delight of movement, the exhilarating leap to hyperspace, the grace of flexion, the joy of the war cry. She had learned to deliver from their confinement great balls of destruction; to calculate the most efficient patterns of attack; to engage and never break off, not until the enemy was utterly destroyed.

This would be the first time she uttered her war cry. As she wheeled toward the target, Anna held her body in perfect control. She felt tireless, invulnerable. The machine was so beautiful, so elegant. Perfect grace, perfect control, form and function integrated into the circuitry of the unbroken loop, the closed universe. All systems of the machine passed through her; she was its heart; she was its brain; she was the machine. She kept the neurons firing in harmony. She synchronized the cleansing and circulation in sublime synergy. She beat out a flawless march with the complex, multileveled systems. The skin of the machine was her skin; its bones and blood, her bones and blood. She and the machine were one: a great engine of chaos and destruction.

The rocky brown surface of the moon grew closer, taking

on definition, detail. She located the seven targets, boulders within a wide, shallow crater. She and her six sisters were each to destroy one. She narrowed her focus to her assigned target, coordinated her speed with her course. Excitement gathered in her throat. She plunged into the crater and shrieked out her war cry. Her body rushed with an ecstasy of fire. Energy blasted from her mouth in a brilliant red torrent. The boulder was vaporized.

Around her, her sisters fell upon the targets, their mouths screaming destruction.

Chaos through warfare, the Eye said. *Evolution through bloodshed. Perfection through victory.*

One of the targets was not completely destroyed. A fragment remained. Anna pounced on it, eager to shriek again. She targeted it, screamed out chaos. The exhilaration shot through her. The fragment was obliterated, a hole scorched into the surface below.

Excited by the activity, her sisters fell upon the vanquished target, shrieking out a cacophony of chaos. Particles of rock flew up as they blasted a great hole into the moon, firing again and again. Anna drew energy up into her mouth, screamed it out in blazing red.

The greatest excitement is the thrill of battle, the Eye said. *The greatest joy is the ecstasy of victory.*

Anna's greatest desire was to feel it. And she knew she would soon.

For soon the war would come.

The ship sang of the beauty of order, of perfect symmetry and ultimate peace. It glided through the calm blackness of space, absorbing it. Energy circulated through its petals in a regular rhythm. The serenity of its silent passage, the unity of its functioning, the satisfaction of service wove through its melody.

Ahead, a blue-and-white orb glowed in the blackness, the goal of the journey. The ship slipped through the stillness toward it, following Kosh's direction eagerly. Obedience was its greatest joy.

Within the song, Kosh slowed the ship's speed, directing it to stop a safe distance from the planet, which was known to its inhabitants as Soom. Although most of the planet's inhabitants had little technology, two lived among them and served as guardians, two fabulists, who would detect his presence if he went too close.

Soon more would come as the fabulists gathered for their assemblage. Long had Kosh watched them, for three hundred and thirty and three such assemblages. He had watched as different races had become dominant within the group, the most recent being Humans. He had watched as the fabulists gradually transformed from anarchy to order. They had achieved some admirable goals, had created fleeting moments of great beauty.

But now the universe was gathering itself for a great conflagration. The forces of chaos had returned to their ancient home and had begun to build their resources for war. The Vorlons, Kosh among them, likewise prepared. The fabulists did not know the danger of their position. They carried great power. They could be the pivot on which the great war turned.

Many among the Vorlons thought the time for action was now. They did not trust the fabulists. Yet Kosh felt they must watch just a while longer. The fabulists faced a difficult decision, and they should be allowed to make it. If they chose wrongly, then they would die. But let them first choose. Great power carried both great danger and great possibility.

Kosh altered the ship's song, directing the ship to extrude several buoys, which would take up positions around the planet and observe it. Then he would return to Babylon 5. And he would watch this one, last assemblage.

Galen closed his eyes and focused on the equation. He thought of all his spells as equations, though they weren't anything like traditional scientific ones. The terms of his equations were complex and bizarre, impenetrable and irreducible. Yet to him they represented actions and properties, and if he could form an image in his mind of a particular equation, he could conjure the thing it represented.

Like most spells, this one had many terms: several to generate a pinkish translucent sphere three inches across, another to generate energy within it, yet more to give that energy the appearance of a delicate flame. He'd done this one many times.

Taking a deep breath, he imagined his mind as a blank screen, visualized the equation written upon it. The chrysalis, fastened to his head and spine, acknowledged the equation by echoing it back to him. Galen opened his eyes. The ball of energy floated in front of him.

"Around the hall," Elric ordered from behind him, gripping the tail-like section of the chrysalis that ran down his spine.

His teacher's voice, deep and rich, carried a power that had at first intimidated Galen. Later, when Elric taught him the techno-mage techniques of voice modulation, Elric's voice and the skill with which he used it amazed Galen. By extending certain sounds, pausing at specific places, and modulating his intonation to almost hypnotic effect, everything he said took on heightened power and importance.

Holding the image of the original equation firmly in his mind's eye, Galen added another, a spell for movement. One equation took the ball of energy from the center of the modest training hall, where it hovered before him, to the hall's stone wall. Another equation sent the ball into a circular course around the hall. The ball circulated a few feet below the thatched ceiling, where several of Elric's light globes floated for illumination.

"A second ball," Elric commanded.

Holding the original equation and the equation for circular movement in his mind's eye, Galen conjured a second ball. The chrysalis echoed the spell, reflecting his thought.

"Change the flames to flowers," Elric said.

Galen concentrated on the equation for the second ball, specifically on the terms that generated the flames. Below them, he visualized the terms necessary to create an image of white kwa blossoms. Then he moved the new set of terms up, replacing the old. The flames changed to flowers.

"Triple speed first ball."

With intense focus, Galen kept the two equations for the two balls firmly in his mind, and at the same time altered the equation of motion, tripling the velocity of the first ball's circular course. The effort caused his breath to come faster now.

"Second ball up and down."

Maintaining the images of his three spells on the imaginary screen, Galen formed an equation that sent the second ball up to the thatched ceiling, then a new equation to send it back and forth between the ceiling and the woven grass mat that covered the floor. The ball of flowers began to zip up and down.

"Third ball with a piece of lint in it."

Galen held his focus. Elric tried to use odd requests to throw him off, to make him lose concentration. But he would not. He formed an equation for the third ball, giving it a dark interior so that the image of a tiny fleck of white lint inside would be visible. The third ball appeared. Galen was breathing even harder; this was the farthest he'd ever gotten.

"Circle around your head."

Holding the three equations for the three balls and the two equations for motion in his mind, Galen began to formulate an equation of motion for the third ball. As he calculated its circular course around his head, though, his mind *slipped*. Like patting his head and rubbing his stomach, the multiple signals crossed in his mind. Control slipped away as the equations became entangled. Galen cursed himself.

The lint ball popped out of existence. The first ball raced down the side of the hall and slammed into the rock wall with a burst of flame; the second bounced off the thatched ceiling at an angle and came screaming toward them.

Galen frantically formulated the quenching spell that would dissipate the energy of the ball, unmake it. But the spell had to be matched with the position of the object, which was now shooting past his face and heading straight for Elric. Why didn't Elric override his control of the chrysalis, as he always did when things went awry?

Galen focused desperately on the ball's position, inserted

the position into the equation. About two inches from Elric's eye, the ball's pinkish surface flashed in a glittering wave and abruptly dissolved.

Galen looked away, breathing hard, exhausted from the exertion. Beneath his black robe, his skin ran with sweat. Elric released his hold on the chrysalis so Galen could turn to face him. Reluctantly, Galen turned.

Elric's figure, as always, was severe: plain black robe with high collar, scalp scoured hairless in honor of the Code, lips in a thin straight line. His posture was erect, his hands at his sides.

His gestures, when he made them, were as controlled and powerful as his words. His face generally showed one of two expressions: disappointment or grave disappointment. The difference was the number of frown lines between his eyebrows.

Disappointment had two; grave disappointment, three.

He had three.

"Why didn't you—shut me down?" Galen asked, still breathless. The chrysalis was designed so that a full techno-mage could override its functions at any time, erase all active spells instantly and completely. A mage held onto the taillike section of the chrysalis, which ran down the apprentice's spine, the sensors in the mage's fingertips making contact with the chrysalis tech. This allowed the teacher to break the connection between apprentice and chrysalis if necessary. The apprentice himself could dissolve or end a spell—assuming he could conjure the correct quenching spell in time—but he did not have the instant override capability his teacher did.

"In two days' time," Elric said, "no mage will be able to shut you down. You'll have to deal with your own mistakes then."

In two days' time, Galen was to be initiated and receive the implants that would make him a techno-mage. It was what he most wanted. And yet here he was, still failing to control his conjuries, still failing Elric. He was not ready. He was not fit.

His skills were nowhere near Elric's, and he didn't know if they ever would be.

"You focus on knowledge and understanding," Elric said. "These are the highest goals to which a mage can aspire. Yet underlying all that we stand for, all that we do, is one cardinal requirement: control. You must master the tech. It must do what you direct. And you must direct what it does. Under any circumstance. Despite any distraction."

Galen nodded. He knew that Elric was constantly engaged in multiple spells, accessing data from the many probes he had planted on Soom, reinforcing spells of protection, performing various services he had promised to the inhabitants. Yet Elric never appeared distracted. Elric never *slipped.*

"Tell me the other weaknesses in your work," Elric said, lingering over the word *weaknesses*. It was one of Elric's favorite topics.

"Presentation."

"Why?" Elric walked over to the rough wooden table in the corner, where Galen had placed a jug of water and two mugs. Other than a long wooden bench along one wall, this was the only furniture in the stone hall.

Galen followed, the chrysalis clinging to the top of his head and his spine, pulling at his skin as he walked. "I concentrate on the spells rather than on the effects they have on others. My focus is inward, not outward."

"You must control people's perceptions," Elric said, pouring two mugs of water and handing one to Galen. "The greatest of us—Wierden, Gali-Gali, Kell—have so perfectly controlled the perceptions of others that in many cases those others never knew technomancy had been employed. They never even knew a mage had walked among them."

Galen noticed a tiny black bug floating on the surface of his water, its legs gesticulating.

"A public act of technomancy is a competition of wits between the mage and all onlookers. The mage must connect with those onlookers, observe and evaluate their reactions, misdirect and manipulate them."

"I've been studying the techniques," Galen said. "But I

still don't understand why people's perceptions can be so easily manipulated." He glanced back down into his mug. He realized the tiny black object floating there wasn't really a bug, as he'd thought, but just a piece of dirt whose shape suggested a bug.

"Most intelligent beings aren't comfortable living in a state of uncertainty. Their brains automatically revise what they see, filling in details that were never there. They make events fit into patterns they understand."

Galen reached into the mug to pick out the piece of dirt and realized he'd been right the first time; it was a bug. He could clearly see the legs moving. He pinched at it and was startled to feel a flutter. Tiny wings opened and the bug flew away.

It landed on Elric's open palm. Elric closed his hand around it. "Rather than accept uncertainty, people will discount the input of their own senses." He raised his eyebrows. "Would you like some water in that?"

Galen looked down at his mug. It was empty.

After gulping down some water, Galen prepared to face his greatest weakness. "Originality," Galen said, as Elric resumed his hold on the chrysalis.

Galen had been struggling with this issue for months. Each mage cultivated his own distinctive style, specific types of spells that he cast and characteristic flourishes that appeared in those spells. Elric had taught him that a mage's conjuries should reveal, express, and complete him.

Yet Galen had thus far failed to develop his own style, his own set of flourishes. He much preferred to reproduce the spells of others rather than create his own. He wasn't terribly good at inventing his own spells, and when he did manage to think of one, he often discovered it had been conjured before. It wasn't original. The few times that he had thought of something new, he'd discarded it, having decided the spell was unworthy and foolish compared to those of the greats. And although that was accurate, it was not the whole truth. Something else made him hesitant to develop his own spells. The idea of displaying something that had come from within him, something original to him, made Galen very uncomfortable. He found he did not want to reveal himself.

He had searched for some solution that would satisfy Elric and help lead him toward his own style. At last he had settled on a tribute to Wierden.

So he closed his eyes a moment, clearing his thoughts, and again visualized a blank screen on which he might write equations. Then he opened his eyes, determined to give a better presentation.

He extended an arm. From his five fingertips he conjured five brilliant points of light that rose upward, spreading to form a circle three feet across. In the center he created a foot-tall image of Wierden, who had formed the techno-mages into a cohesive group one thousand years ago. She was one of an ancient, extinct race called the Taratimude, with great stiff wings that hung in folds from her arms, and long, tapered fingers. In the image she wore a sleeveless black robe, her golden wings draped over it. She spoke in the ancient language of the Taratimude the words that every mage knew. "Our five wisest will form the Circle, which will guide and rule the techno-mages. Five is the number of balance." Her voice, which he had reconstructed from the ancient recordings, was high yet resonant.

Galen stretched the five points of light taller and wider, until the image became a circle of seven standing stones glowing with inner light, Wierden still at their center. Each stone was imprinted with a different brilliant blue rune in the language of the Taratimude. Galen rotated the image, so Elric could see the rune on each stone. Wierden said, "Above all will rule the Code, the seven principles of technomancy: solidarity, secrecy, mystery, magic, science, knowledge, good." Galen saw with satisfaction that he had correctly coordinated the motion of the stones so that Elric saw the rune representing each principle as Wierden named it. "Seven is the number of understanding."

The standing stones stretched longer, arcing inward at top and bottom to form a large sphere of light. Inside appeared the face of Wierden, with her wise, lined cheeks, the dark skin around her eyes that had always struck him as sad. "Let this begin an age of unity for the techno-mages. And let none violate the Code."

Galen squeezed the sphere into a narrow cylinder of brilliant light, sent the light streaming up to the thatched ceiling. He had worked painstakingly to create the visual impression that the light was flowing through the thatch and continuing upward, into the heavens, though it actually stopped there.

Galen dissolved the final spell with relief. It was the most elaborate conjuring he had ever done. He swayed a bit as Elric released him.

"Dissociate," Elric said.

Galen nodded, breathless, and focused on the equation that terminated the connection between his chrysalis and the implant at the base of his skull. The implant—much simpler than those of a full techno-mage—had been inserted three years ago, when he had entered chrysalis stage. While the connection between the chrysalis and his implant was active, the chrysalis remained bound to his body, clamped onto his head and sealed to his spine with the thin layer of his robe trapped between them. The chrysalis was drawn to him by the kindred implant that had originally been a piece of it.

He successfully broke the connection, feeling a familiar relief as the pressure against his body lessened. The device relaxed with a squelching sound, and Elric lifted it off. Wearing the chrysalis always provided an underlying sense of energy, a subliminal vibration or resonance. Now he felt the accompanying drop in energy. The cool air prickled over his hot skin. He ran a hand through his short hair, which was plastered to his scalp.

Galen followed Elric to the bench, where Elric lowered the chrysalis into its clear canister. Floating in the liquid, it looked somewhat like a terrestrial jellyfish. The umbrella-shaped top that clung to his head resembled the bell of a jellyfish, while the extension that ran down his spinal cord looked like one of its long oral arms.

The chrysalis had grown thicker and wider in the three years he'd been training with it, and its translucent skin had gained a silvery sheen. Elric had explained that it had been only partially formed when Galen had begun to work with it. That was why the first year of chrysalis-stage training had involved only the visualization of different spells, and no casting. The chrysalis had been adapting to him, adjusting itself to his patterns of thought, in a way almost mirroring him.

The process had continued even after he'd begun to cast spells. That was why the echo from the chrysalis had grown progressively stronger. As Galen was being trained, so was the chrysalis.

Galen was struck again by the brilliance of the Taratimude. They had developed a technology that could read one's very desires and out of nothing, conjure them. Their scientific understanding had been incredibly advanced, their sense of beauty, of magic, unequaled. What spells Wierden's people may have conjured, the mages would never know. When nearly all of them had died in a great cataclysm, most of their knowledge had been destroyed. The few survivors, Wierden among them, had decided to share what tech they had, and the secret of replicating it, with other species.

Wierden had formed the Circle and established the Code, and the techno-mages in their current form had been born. Yet their understanding of the brilliant science that had designed the tech had been lost. Galen feared the mages would never again be the equal of their predecessors.

"You honor the work of Wierden through your conjury," Elric said, closing the canister.

"Yes."

"Well and good, but what is *your* work?"

Galen didn't know. His parents, both mages, had died when he was ten. After that, he'd wanted to be a healer. That desire had remained with him all the way to age eighteen, the time of the last convocation. At that gathering, he'd entered chrysalis stage and taken the name of Galen, an ancient Greek physician and philosopher.

But in the three years since then, he'd realized he had no aptitude for healing. His work as a healer was ineffective at worst, incompetent at best.

He now felt the answer to Elric's question might lay in the work of the ancients, which fascinated him, but he didn't know how he could contribute to that great work. His conjury had simply paid tribute to the accomplishments of Wierden, without showing how his own work would relate to them. He had failed to create something original. He stared at the floor. "I'm not sure," he answered finally.

Elric headed for the door. "Good technique and precision on that," he said quickly.

Galen jerked his head up. Elric had sworn always to speak truth to him, and in the eleven years Elric had trained him, Galen had received praise only twice before.

Elric paused beside the door. "Have you considered the question I posed yesterday?" His voice had returned to its deep, measured tones.

The question—*Why are you a techno-mage?*—was one that all chrysalis-stage apprentices would have to answer as part of the initiation ceremonies. The response often helped to define a mage's work. If he could answer that question, then all his conjuring would have a direction.

"I've thought of little else," Galen said.

"And have you thought of an answer?"

"To study the work of the ancients, to further their work where I can."

"To further *their* work."

"It seems so much more worthy than any work I can think of."

"It is worthy. But you must make it your own." He grasped the door latch, said the password. "Archimedes." Elric's containment field around the hall kept others out, and held any wild energies within. "You will show me something original tomorrow morning." Elric strode out.

Galen picked up the canister and followed. He had nothing more to show Elric. He had put all his expertise into the tribute for Wierden. He could think of nothing truly original, nothing to equal the work he admired.

Outside, the sun was high and the mist was thin, adding a hazy, brilliant overlay to the surroundings. The brisk sea breeze cooled Galen's sweat-soaked body. He took in the sharp sea air. The mak, the huge plain of moss-covered rock on which they stood, was a brilliant lime green today. About a hundred feet away, swathed in mist, stood the edge of the great stone circle that marked Elric's place of power. The seven stones, marked by the seven runes of the Code, stood over twenty feet high. With their moss shrouds, they appeared almost like outgrowths of the planet. Beneath the circle, in a chamber hollowed out of the rock, was Elric's place of power, which augmented and enhanced his abilities and connected him to the planet itself.

Elric was looking toward the area where the convocation was to be held, beside the cliffs that overlooked the sea. Over the last several days, Elric and Galen had set up an extensive network of interconnected white domed tents where different meetings would be held, Elric marking them with glowing runes and symbols to indicate their various purposes. Once the tents had been set up, the two of them had supervised as supplies and workers had arrived.

Elric kept the preparations as simple as possible. Most of the workers he drew from the local town of Lok, though large supplies of food and a few specialists had to be brought in from the city of Tain. Keeping five hundred techno-mages happy for a thirty-five-day convocation would be no easy task.

Although Galen could see only hints of movement among the mist-shrouded tents, he knew they must be busy with activity. As of this morning, everything had been going according to schedule, but Galen knew Elric was anxious. The sites of the convocations rotated among the homes of the five members of the great Circle. This was the first to be held on Elric's home planet. Of course, that didn't mean Elric would cancel a practice session—even though the mages were expected to begin arriving in a few hours.

Elric turned his stern gaze on Galen. "As a group we seek wisdom. As individuals we can be eccentric, peevish, perverse, opinionated—apt to take offense upon small occasions. Act with restraint. Be courteous. We get along best at great distances from one another.

"Every convocation has its confrontations, its challenges. You've been sheltered in the past. Once you're initiated as a full mage, you won't be under my protection any longer. Others may challenge you, to test your powers or prove their own. Do not rise to the fool's challenge to be a fool yourself." Elric straightened. "Your friend is coming."

Galen turned. Behind them, a scrap of orange flashed through the mist. Orange was Fa's favorite color; she wore it almost all the time. Her orange jumper emerged first from the white mist. Then her limbs and face, covered in curly wisps of white hair. Her legs were small and delicate—she had only eight cycles of the sun, or ten years Earth standard—yet she traversed the uneven rocky plain nimbly with her broad feet. Externally, her species, the Soom, appeared surprisingly humanoid. The most striking difference was that at midleg, the knee joint bent back rather than forward, as was the case with many of the species on the planet. Galen had spent so long here that his own legs sometimes struck him as odd.

Fa ran across the mak toward them. She waved—a gesture she had learned from him and used with tireless enthusiasm. "Gale! Gale!"

"Would you like me to check on the preparations?" he asked Elric.

"Don't you think we should see what your friend has to say?"

Galen sighed.

Fa became hesitant as she approached them. She was always nervous around Elric.

"Good day, Fa," Elric said in the language of the Soom. Both Elric and Galen knew the language well; Galen had lived there eleven years, Elric over thirty.

Fa straightened—she was proud of how much she'd grown, the top of her head now above Galen's waist—and gave a quick nod of her head, a sign of respect. "Good day, Honored El," she said. Her eyes shifted back and forth between Galen and Elric, and then her self-consciousness seemed to evaporate and the news burst forth. "There's a big fight in town. Farmer Jae and Farmer Nee may kill each other. You must come. They told me to bring you as fast as I could."

The town of Lok was about one-quarter mile away. From their position, the mak extended another hundred yards or so inland, then gradually changed into rising grass upland. Elric could easily perform an exotic propulsion incantation and conjure a flying platform, but there was no big rush to reach the dispute; Farmer Jae and Farmer Nee fought regularly, and the most violent thing they had ever done was toss clods of excrement into each other's fields. And Galen knew Elric wouldn't conjure a platform. Elric didn't like to display his powers before the people of Lok. He had designed his house and the training hall to look as much like their structures as possible. In front of them, he limited himself to just a handful of spells. He said he didn't want them to fear him or worship him.

As it was, they considered him a wise man and turned to him to settle disputes. And at times of celebration, they enjoyed his ability to entertain with delightful illusions.

Holding back in the presence of the Soom was the one issue on which Galen disagreed with Elric. Elric had spent his entire life developing and perfecting his powers. Why not use them? And why not let the people respect him for what he was? Not only a techno-mage, but one of the great Circle.

"We will hurry," Elric said, starting for town.

"I must come! I must come!" Fa cried.

"You can run all that distance?" Elric asked.

Galen knew what was coming.

Fa turned to him, raising her arms. "Gale could carry me."

"Galen will carry you," Elric said, his stern face preempting any argument. He took the canister from Galen.

Fa leapt onto Galen, locking her arms and legs around him so he could hardly breathe. She was growing too big to be carried. Elric began to run across the lime green carpet of moss. Galen followed.

"How was your training?" Fa asked, her head bouncing

against his ear, the white hair tickling his skin. "Did you show him the lights of Wierden? Did he like them?"

"He said to work harder." Galen felt foolish; he couldn't keep the disappointment out of his voice.

Fa licked his cheek, and he jerked his head away in irritation. "He loves you, Gale. He wants you to learn well."

"I know," Galen said. She didn't understand. He didn't think he could do what Elric asked.

"You'll do better tomorrow."

Galen nodded. He adjusted his grip, pressing her more tightly to him, and they ran through the mist.

"I warned you to keep that cursed Jab off my land," Farmer Jae yelled.

Galen rounded Farmer Jae's barn and made his way through the crowd that had gathered at the common border of Farmer Jae's and Farmer Nee's properties. Weighed down with Fa, he'd had to slow to a walk near the outskirts of Lok, so Elric had arrived ahead of him.

"My Jab wouldn't have your filthy swug if she was crazy drunk," Farmer Nee said.

Galen reached the front of the crowd, and Fa squirmed out of his grip, dropping to stand beside him. Jae and Elric stood on the near side of the low stone boundary wall, Nee on the far side. The differences between the properties were dramatic. The yard surrounding Jae's barn and outbuildings was clean, his equipment lined up neatly for use in the grassfields. Nee's yard was cluttered with discarded, rusted tools, the dead remnants of failed gardens, and the elaborate contraption that was his livelihood: his still. Apparently the clod-throwing had escalated to a higher level this time, because both farmers were marked with large olive-colored splotches. Small pieces of excrement clung to their coveralls, and a fairly large piece hung from the curly white hair on Farmer Nee's cheek in apparent defiance of gravity.

Elric turned, his hands raised. "And now we have silence. That is good. Farmer Jae will tell his side."

Farmer Nee mumbled in protest; a look from Elric silenced him.

"Honored El." Farmer Jae smacked his lips as he gathered himself to speak. "I went in to feed Des today at highsun. He was lying on his side and wouldn't get up. He hadn't eaten his morning meal." Farmer Jae's prizewinning swug, Des, was the cause of many disputes. Jae cared for him with fanatical devotion, feeding him the finest sea spree four times a day, bathing his flabby bulk in sea water, and rubbing kwa blossoms into his bumpy skin to bring out its sought-after mottled coloration. As the villagers said, Farmer Jae cared for Des as if he had moss growing out of his head. He was convinced that any unusual activity in the vicinity was designed to upset Des, a conspiracy by those jealous of the swug's prizewinning stature. "He hasn't eaten anything for the past three days. He always eats. He's starting to lose his color. The judging is only two months away. I know what's behind this. Four days ago, I had to chase that cursed Jab out of my barn. I know she stung Des." Jae pointed at Nee. "He ruined my Des!"

Jab stood at Nee's feet, straining eagerly at the rope leash to cross over to Jae's property. She had a long cylindrical body and muscular legs that held her low to the ground. Scaly pink skin was perpetually covered by a layer of dirt. Her needle-sharp sting, the source of much of the trouble, was retracted into her forehead now.

Jab was a notorious creature in the town of Lok. Farmer Nee, busy fermenting moss into alcohol, let her roam wherever she pleased, and wherever she pleased tended to be a source of trouble. Galen couldn't imagine how Elric could waste his expertise on another one of Jab's misadventures, yet he knew that Elric actually enjoyed these escapades, since he would often recount them with the townspeople, and those were among the rare times Galen had actually seen Elric smile or laugh.

Jae took a threatening step toward Nee. "You shouldn't be allowed to keep that animal. You don't control her. She's a menace to the town!"

Elric blocked his path. "Thank you, Farmer Jae. We will now hear Farmer Nee's side."

"He has no side," Jae yelled. He stabbed a finger at Nee. "Incompetence! Laziness! Jealousy!"

Nee had been craftily holding one final clot of excrement behind his back, and he now flung it at Jae. It hit Elric in the side with a loud smack. The clot tumbled to the ground, leaving a splotch on Elric's robe. Galen gasped as the crowd around him yelled insults at Nee and laughed. Elric lowered his head, but Galen could tell he was smiling.

Galen didn't understand it.

Nee gave a short nod. "My apologies, Honored El."

When Elric raised his head, Galen was glad to see the look of grave disappointment. "You will deliver three casks of your finest for the festival in two months' time."

Nee's face contorted at the thought. At last he gave a reluctant nod, and the crowd laughed.

"Have you a side, Farmer Nee?"

"My Jab didn't sting his Des. Wouldn't want to."

"Well said. Now we will examine Des." With a flourish he extended an arm toward Farmer Jae's barn.

The crowd parted, and Elric proceeded into the stone barn, followed by Galen, Farmer Jae, and most of the town. There was some controversy about Farmer Nee entering; he was forced to leave Jab outside. They crouched around the swug, who lay on his side in a bed of freshly cut kew grasses. A suffocating putrid odor suffused the air. Elric conjured a few small balls of light. The townspeople had seen him create light displays in the night sky, so this was little more than a curiosity. What most interested them, Galen knew, was who was right, how Elric would discover this, and how the farmers would react. This day would be a hot topic for months to come.

Elric bent over the vast expanse of swug. He placed his hands high on her mottled side, stepped them down slowly and methodically as he made his examination. If Jab had stung Des, that meant the swug would have tiny jabs growing beneath his skin. Jab reproduced by injecting her fertilized eggs into a host. Galen had done one of his earliest research projects on this. The eggs developed within the host, feeding off of it until they hatched into tiny larvae and popped back out through the skin.

As unappealing as that was, it wasn't fatal. But Jab inserted something else along with her eggs, a virus that incapacitated the host's immune system, preventing it from killing the invading eggs. As far as Galen knew, a swug had never been stung by a jab, so any effect the virus would have was unknown. Jabs generally chose other animals as hosts, but Jab was a renegade and a bit sting-happy. She'd stung several townspeople in her day, triggering days of vomiting and diarrhea, and startling outbreaks of larvae.

Elric's eyes found Galen, and his hand extended in a practiced gesture to indicate Des' right front leg. Galen lifted the fleshy limb, exposing the pale, bumpy belly. Elric palpated the expansive surface thoroughly, then gestured again to the swug. Clearly, he intended for Galen to turn Des onto his other side. Galen didn't have the first idea how to go about this. He took hold of two of the front legs and pulled. Des twisted a bit, but his bulk didn't budge. Galen let go of one of the front legs and took one of the back instead, pulled again. The legs stretched toward him, but the swug stayed put. Galen tried bracing a foot against Des as a lever. He caught Farmer Jae hiding a laugh behind his hand.

Farmer Jae licked his lips and cleared his throat. "Well then." Jae picked up Des' tail and began hauling him over. The townspeople, apparently ready to move on to the next stage of fun, pitched in and pushed the swug over. He fell with a ponderous thump.

Elric examined Des once more, including the head, neck, and back. He waved a hand over Des. "He has not been stung."

Farmer Jae pulled unhappily on his facial hair.

"I knew it," Nee said. "My little Jab wouldn't have that fat carcass."

The townspeople quieted him, anxious to hear what Elric would say next.

Elric had surely known Jab's innocence since the beginning of the argument. One of the many probes Elric maintained on Soom was attached to Jab. She had such a nose for trouble, Elric had said she gave him more useful information than all his other probes combined. The microelectronic device transmitted images and other data to Elric's place of power, where he could access them as needed. If Jab had violated Des, Elric would have a record of the crime. But if Jab was innocent, then what was wrong with Des?

Elric stood. "You have changed his food."

"No," Jae said. "I feed him only the best. Sea spree gathered from the caves." Jae had asserted this with pride many times.

Elric produced a large bowl from his robes, making the townspeople gasp. "This is not sea spree." The heavy earthen bowl was filled with a foul-smelling glop. "This comes from the city."

Galen was angry at himself for not anticipating Elric's action. He was supposed to know by now how a mage worked: information, preparation, control. He played back events, trying to figure out when Elric had concealed the bowl in his robes. He had arrived before Galen. He must have gone into the barn first to examine Des, found the odd food, and placed it near the barn door, where he could easily grab it and conceal it when he led the group inside. A quick chemical analysis could tell him the food's composition, and he could cross-reference that with information on the care of swugs. His sensors could reveal any intestinal upset or blockage.

Jae appealed to the assembled crowd. "I bought it from a trader. He said all the prizewinners in the city eat this. Gives them better color."

"This food has made Des sick."

"No." The hair on Farmer Jae's head stood up on end. He was horrified.

"You endangered his life to win a prize. You did not know this stranger, yet you trusted him. You know your neighbor, yet you accuse him."

Farmer Jae crouched beside Des, cradling the swug's head in his hands. "Will he live?"

"You must feed him only the chal root for three days. Then he will stand. And for each of those three days, you must sit with Farmer Nee and drink three mugs of his brew."

Farmer Jae licked Des' cheek. "My boy. You'll be all right. My large flower." The townspeople laughed. Farmer Jae noticed Elric's stern gaze still on him. He stood and approached Farmer Nee. "I wrongly accused. It is a mark against my own name. I apologize."

Nee had retrieved Jab from outside. He pointed down to the animal. Stiffly, Jae crouched, and his voice quivered. "I wrongly accused. It is a mark against my own name. I apologize."

Jab's nostrils widened, and her head lowered. Galen knew that look. Jab's sting shot out to full extension, and with her powerful legs she lunged at Jae. Galen grabbed Jae's arm, yanking him back. He stumbled and fell, Jab's sting passing only an inch from his leg. Galen pinwheeled his arm for balance, but it was too late. He was pulled down with Jae. He landed on Des, eliciting a sonorous belch.

Jab made aborted lunges at the end of her leash while Nee held her just out of reach of Jae, a satisfied smile on his face. Farmer Jae raised his head. It had landed in the bowl of foul-smelling glop.

"We erase the mark," Nee said. He turned and dragged Jab out. The townspeople began to follow, stopping to give Elric a nod of respect.

"Look!" Fa cried. Galen had lost track of her. She stood in the doorway of the barn, pointing upward. "Wonders fall from the sky!"

Galen worked his way off the swug and threaded through the crowd, burst outside. The mist had cleared—the work of Elric, of course. The sun was low, and against the clear backdrop of pale blue, he saw what appeared to be a long red streamer coursing and twirling downward. Above that, a winged horse glided down in a lazy spiral. The mages were beginning to arrive.

Elric laid a hand on his shoulder. "We will meet them." He had only one frown line between his eyebrows, and his thin lips were raised in a slight smile.

Galen had looked toward this convocation with a mixture of excitement and dread. It brought the chance to renew old friendships, the chance to learn from the wisest and most skilled. It also brought his initiation, when he would become a techno-mage, as he had hoped since he could remember.

But in truth he did not believe he was ready. He did not yet deserve to become one of their number. He had not produced anything truly original for Elric.

"You have set me a task for tomorrow," Galen said. Fa grabbed hold of his hand and tugged him in the direction of the landing ships.

A second line appeared between Elric's eyebrows. "You need time to prepare."

Galen knew he should greet the mages with Elric. Elric had impressed on him that he, too, was a host of this convocation. But he needed time. "I don't want to disappoint you."

"You will not disappoint me." The intonation was somewhere between a reassurance and a threat. "Go," Elric said.

Galen bent toward Fa. "Stop. I'm not going with you. I have work. Go with Elric."

She released him reluctantly, and he ran toward home.

Angels, dragons, and shooting stars rained from the sky.

chapter 2

Mages arrived steadily now, as the sun set. Elric stood before the tents on the mak. As always, he stood not only in this place but in many places; he saw not just one thing but many things. All around him, the planet lived and breathed. Magma circulated; volcanoes exhaled; water nourished; life grew. He had given himself to Soom, sunk his bones deep into this planet. As it lived, he lived.

His place of power was just a few hundred feet away, below the great circle of standing stones. A part of him was always there, within that silent chamber of rock, within Soom itself, connected to it, giving it living spirit. The connection arose from a large section of the chrysalis with which he had long ago trained. It sat at the heart of his sanctum, and over the years it had grown, sending threads deep underground. It was a part of his extended body, as was the planet. Intertwined with a variety of other devices, it formed his place of power, allowing him not only spiritual union with his home, but increased abilities and powers.

Within the datasystems of the place, he held his knowledge of the planet, its history, evolution, and development. Through the place, he coordinated the many devices that he had developed and deployed over the years, devices that controlled the planet's weather, that directed the course of rivers, that diffused the force of earthquakes, that sensed changes in the universe about him and helped further his scientific studies.

From the place, he accessed the faster-than-light relay in orbit about Soom, a part of the vast network of relays mages had established around their homes and other locations that drew their attention, allowing them to communicate with one another across vast distances. With the energy of the place, generated by his chrysalis, he maintained spells over the course of days and months and years, and recorded data from millions of microscopic probes he had planted across Soom. He monitored those probes constantly, nourishing his relationship with this world and everything on it.

On the far side of the planet, a herd of wild tak trotted toward the Lang River, the sunrise shining through their voluminous hair.

Across the continent, the desert city of Drel baked under the high sun. Deep below it, the stress in the planet's crust had been safely dissipated, preventing a disastrous earthquake.

Closer by, the coastal city of Tain was fading into dusk. Tain was one of the largest Soom cities, an unplanned patchwork that served as a center for trade, mainly by sea, but in a modest way, also by space. The sole spaceport on the planet was quiet, a single row of small trading ships parked out on the grassy field. The corrupt leader of this city, the Rook of Tain—His Exaltedness, as he liked to be called—appeared particularly thoughtful as he chewed energetically on his dinner, a swugskin soufflé.

In nearby Lok, the town Elric had made his home, the streets were quiet and the air was clear. Elric had altered the weather patterns so the arrival of the mages would not be obscured by mist. Many of the townspeople had come down to the mak to watch the wondrous display in the sky, and the landing of the ships. They were welcome for this opening night of the convocation. After that, the proceedings would be closed to them.

Behind Elric, Fa watched from the shelter of a tent flap. Though Elric had placed no probes in the tents, out of respect for the mages' privacy, he knew that within, cooks, attendants, and cleaners, hired from Lok and the city of Tain, were finishing preparations for the welcoming feast.

All this he knew at once, and all this he watched at once. Yet one vision in particular held his heart and mind, and before it all others faded into the background. He terminated his connection to the various probes, allowing himself to focus on the beauty of the here and now.

Each ship, as it approached the landing site, was disguised in a different, beautiful illusion. A silver fish wound among the evening stars, singing a haunting aria. A golden dragon breathed bouquets of flowers. A sailing ship rode the air currents. A giant model of an atom made a stately descent. A pinwheel of fire spiraled through the night. They were dreamers and shapers, singers and makers.

Once they had been greater in number. Yet in the past, more had been drawn to them for power than for understanding. Now they were five hundred, dedicated to learning, sharing the beauty of magic, doing good. For once no mage was in serious violation of the Code, and no feuds between mages seemed likely to erupt into violence. They were far from perfect, to be sure—eccentric, opinionated, intense, quick to anger—but Elric had never been more proud of them.

When he had been elected to the Circle nine years earlier, his feelings toward the mages had subtly changed. Before that, they had been his colleagues, his order, his clan, his family. Now they were also his responsibility. Joining the Circle had been a great honor, yet it was also a great burden, in ways he could never have anticipated. The mages' past, and their future, lay in his trust. It was his charge to keep them safe and whole and focused on the Code. He felt that responsibility keenly now.

The convocations were critical times of bonding and affirmation, and this one perhaps more than any other. The signs were uncertain, yet he felt a growing sense that things were changing, quietly but irrevocably, not only here on Soom but everywhere. A darkness was growing. The mages had to be unified in purpose and spirit, prepared for any danger that might threaten.

And if no danger threatened, he would gladly laugh at the fool he had been.

As the various shapes landed they shed their illusions, revealing the sleek, triangular techno-mage ships beneath.

Using his sensors, Elric scanned the three ultraviolet frequencies in which mages hid signs. Signals sent on each of the three frequencies had to be correctly combined for a complete sign to be revealed. This allowed mages to mark various objects, such as their ships, with signs that no one else could see. Each ship was marked with the rune representing its owner.

The mages began to emerge from their ships, and they crossed the mak to greet him, walking beneath his globes of conjured light.

Elric greeted them each in turn. First came Kell, the greatest of them. Kell was of the line of Wierden. They shared no genetic connection, but Wierden had passed her wisdom to her apprentice, and those teachings had continued along a chain from mage to apprentice. That chain had led to Kell, and now to Kell's apprentices. Though each member of the Circle was meant to be equal, Kell's opinions were given the greatest weight; his plans were most often approved. He was the Circle's unofficial leader, the one who had guided them, during his nearly fifty years in the Circle, into this period of focus and relative equanimity.

Elric was dismayed to note that Kell had further weakened. In his prime, he had been strong of body and mind, a master techno-mage with a vibrant, charismatic personality, filled with energy, driven by commitment, and illuminated by wisdom. But he was now one hundred Earth years old, and over the last six years, Elric had observed signs of decline. Kell's stride, once long and quick, was now shorter and slower. His shoulders had become hunched, his lined face tensed with the effort to understand events that would have previously required no effort. Kell's powers of technomancy must have suffered a similar decline, though Elric had seen no evidence of it. Kell's falling star had burned as brightly as ever as it had made its way to the planet's surface.

Kell always used that symbol at convocations, as did many others in his honor. Kell believed the falling star embodied the concepts of magic and science for every intelligent race. What intelligent species did not look up in wonder at the sight of a mysterious, brilliant object streaking through the night sky, or later seek to explain its nature?

Kell wore a plain black robe with a short, white fur cape over it, and carried an intricately carved ivory staff. The cape had been awarded to him several years earlier by the Shan of Zafran 7, to whom Kell served as adviser. Kell kept his dark scalp hairless, in respect of the Code, though he always wore a goatee scoured into the complex pattern of the rune for knowledge. It had gone white in recent years.

Behind Kell followed his two apprentices, Elizar and Razeel. They, along with Galen, were part of the group of fifteen chrysalis-stage apprentices to be initiated into magehood at the convocation. Elizar and Razeel were brother and sister, both dark haired and fair skinned. Kell had received them as babies in exchange for services, as many apprentices were obtained. They wore rather more ostentatious clothing than Elric would have approved for apprentices, rich with velvets, gold chains, and lace. Yet they lived on a different world and were more involved in galactic events. Not everyone chose to live as he did.

Kell embraced Elric. "A joy to see you. An auspicious time for us both, is it not, finally gaining our freedom from this unruly rabble?" He indicated Elizar and Razeel with a masterful flourish of his hand. His voice was strong, vibrant. "But where is Galen? You don't have him counting the atoms on the head of a pin, do you?"

"Something not dissimilar," Elric said.

"The air here. What a wonderful smell." He turned to Elizar. "You smell that? That's fresh air."

"Don't you want to tell him about the boxes?" Elizar's tone carried a hint of challenge.

Kell showed no reaction to it. "Oh, yes," he said, turning back to Elric. "I brought some refreshments to contribute to the festivities. They're in my ship when you want them."

"Thank you," Elric said, knowing well what the boxes contained. "We're laying a banquet inside, if you would like to relax."

"I have some wonderful stories for you," Kell said.

"And I for you," Elric responded.

Kell embraced him again. "We will talk soon." He strode toward the tents, Elizar and Razeel following. His steps were slower than they once would have been.

Elric dreaded the day Kell would pass to the other side, not only for his own loss, but for fear of what would happen to the techno-mages. Kell was the one who held them together, who kept their squabbles and political differences from overwhelming them. They did not fracture because they all wanted to be a part of the order that included Kell. None of the other members of the Circle had that attractive power, including Elric. Losing Kell would pose a serious threat to their solidarity when it occurred; Elric feared they might break permanently into differing factions, and the authority of the Circle and the Code would be lost. Similar breaks had occurred in the past, though the rifts had always healed.

Elric hoped that he worried needlessly. Kell might yet live and serve many years, and in that time, perhaps Elizar would grow to fill Kell's place.

Behind them came the other members of the Circle. At almost two hundred, Ing-Radi was the oldest. She was elderly even for a Kaitay, yet she showed little sign of aging. Ing-Radi extended her four orange hands, palms up, laid them one on top of the other, and bowed her head. Then she bent to gather Elric in her four-armed embrace. A sense of comfort radiated from her orange skin, even through her robe. She was their best healer, and Elric often felt she was the most skilled of them. She healed even where there seemed to be no wound.

"Welcome," Elric said.

"Relax. Here." She touched the back of his neck. Muscles relaxed that he hadn't known were tense. Her slit pupils regarded him. "You are busy. We will speak later."

"I would enjoy that."

The slash of her mouth smiled down at him. "I'm glad to see your home at last. It is much like you." She gave another slight bow and moved on.

Herazade was next, with her apprentice Federico. She was

the most liberal of the Circle, and it was reflected in her dress. She wore an elegant sari, and had let her thick black hair grow long. As they exchanged greetings, a golden dragon swooped out of the sky, racing over their heads. Elric admired the well-defined scales on the belly, the nicely curved toenails. Alwyn had made some improvements.

When he looked down, Blaylock stood before him. "It seems your friend has arrived," Blaylock said.

"It seems he has." Alwyn never failed to irritate Blaylock, on many levels. Chief among them was Alwyn's notorious love for wine, women, and song.

Blaylock was the one mage who could make Elric feel like a hedonist. Second in influence only to Kell, Blaylock believed an ascetic lifestyle was the only one appropriate for techno-mages. Blaylock's body was scoured completely of hair, including eyebrows, which gave his pale face and high forehead a dramatic starkness against the black skullcap he wore. The skullcap was made of felt and fit tightly, tracing out the line that hair would have made. Blaylock felt that keeping the body scoured was a sign of respect for the Code, but that displaying the head was a sign of arrogance. His gaunt figure in a plain black robe somehow always seemed vaguely accusatory.

Blaylock believed that mages could find true unity with the tech implanted in their bodies only if they foreswore all physical pleasures, focusing on the inner life rather than the outer one. He fostered the idea that the mages should cloister themselves in an austere environment. While waiting for the rest of the mages to see the light, he and his many followers had learned how to cast spells that would deactivate different sensory centers in their own brains: taste, smell, touch, hearing, and even sight. Before eating, they would deactivate taste and smell. In the presence of beauty, they would deactivate sight. Blaylock told his followers that the tech was a blessing that tapped into the basic powers of the universe. The goal of all mages, according to Blaylock, should be to attain a complete, spiritual union with the tech, and so with the universe.

Elric respected his abilities, but felt that knowledge could never be attained by cutting oneself off from life. Self-denial was unnecessary. Discipline and the Code were enough.

"The blessing of Wierden upon you," Blaylock said, bowing. The words were echoed by his apprentice, Gowen.

"Welcome, Blaylock. I trust the surroundings are not attractive enough to cause distress."

"It's less the place that will cause distress, I think, than the people," Blaylock said.

"If only we could close our eyes and make them go away," Elric said.

"I await your instruction on that matter." Blaylock bowed and withdrew, his apprentice quickly following.

A stream of mages followed. Djadjamonkh floated through the air with crossed legs, the ends of his turban dancing above his head like snakes. Maskelyne changed faces and bodies every few seconds, conjuring full-body illusions that disguised her true appearance. A group of Blaylock's followers came in an orderly, solemn procession. Circe, in a tall, pointed hat, presented Elric with a new variety of microelectronic probe that she would be offering to the mages, and invited him to her talk on the subject. She seemed intent on explaining the improvements she had made, though this was clearly not the time for extended conversation.

The Kinetic Grimlis appeared in a flash of lightning, wearing glowing purple tunics and long white feather capes. They were the only long-standing group within the techno-mages. Since Elric had last seen them, several of their members had quit in disputes, and new members had joined. One of them jumped into the air and performed a succession of somersaults, continuing over the top of the tents and out of sight. The others launched into a dizzying series of acrobatics. The Grimlis made the ships used by all the mages. They were motion crazy but brilliant. After the initiation, they would give the new initiates their ships and train them in their operation.

Elric greeted many others, some in elaborate outfits, some in simple robes, some with staffs or wands or talismans, some with heads bare, some with apprentices of varying ages. The night filled with color and activity, energy and fire.

At the height of activity, an outsider, a Human of compact build and dark hair, inserted himself between mages. "I'm sorry to bother you at such a busy time. Are you Elric?" At Elric's nod, he gave a short bow, his hands folded in front of him. "I bring you greetings from His Exaltedness, the Rook of Tain. He has asked me to convey his great pleasure that your esteemed group has chosen his home for your gathering."

"Yes, yes," Elric said, watching as one of the spinning Grimlis barely missed an attendant carrying a basket piled high with pastries. He had little patience for the Rook.

"He has asked me to officially welcome you all, and to say that the hospitality of the Rook is extended to you. He sends you the fifty finest pects of Tain." The man handed Elric a sealed letter and gestured toward a group of Soom with crates on their shoulders. They were wandering in amongst the mages, generally increasing the chaos.

To Elric's annoyance, one dropped his crate and pects spilled out, squawking and running in circles. "Take those to the tents," he yelled in their language. "Get out of the way here."

"If there is anything that His Exaltedness can do to improve your gathering, I am directed to do it." His voice was smooth, with uncommon control for a nonmage.

Elric's gaze focused for a moment on the man. He wore a dark, well-tailored suit, and a dark stone hung on a chain around his neck. His manner was meant to be deferential, but something about it was disturbing. More than that, Elric knew well what went on in Tain, and the Rook had no Human adviser or ambassador. He opened the letter quickly and skimmed over the obsequious prose, which he well recognized. "And who are you to the Rook?"

"I am his special envoy." The man bowed again and smiled. "Mr. Morden."

Elric found the date at the bottom of the letter—just two days past—accessed his place of power and directed it to search the record of the probe in the Rook's office for that day, looking for Morden's figure. The record was quickly found, and Elric saw Morden in a meeting with the Rook. Clearly the Rook was trying to expand his power by including a Human in his group of corrupt supporters.

And now the Rook was currying favor with the mages, no doubt in preparation to ask something of them. His last request, five years earlier, had been to lay a curse of impotence on an enemy. Elric had declined in memorable fashion. He hadn't expected the Rook to regain his nerve for several more years.

A pect jumped into the air, and a Grimli spun right into him, feathers flying. One of the young apprentices burst out crying.

"Get your people to the tents, Mr. Morden," Elric said, wading in to clean up the mess.

After the pects had at last been secured, and the Grimlis banished to the far side of the tents, Alwyn approached. He wore a multicolored robe with a long black cape over it. His silvery hair had begun to recede since Elric had last seen him, and the lines beneath his eyes had deepened.

"Nice work on the dragon's claws," Elric said.

"You think so? I was inspired by a female of my recent acquaintance. Beautiful creature, but oh, the talons." Alwyn leaned close. "Anyone do anything foolish yet?"

"They've shown admirable restraint."

"Give them another hour. Give them a few drinks—except Blaylock, of course. He's someone I'd really like to see drunk. Let his hair down, so to speak."

Elric smiled. "I think you may find this convocation lacking in controversy and excitement. I'm determined that no crises will erupt."

"And for your next act, Almighty One?"

Alwyn's apprentice, a Centauri named Carvin, ran up, breathless. Alwyn had given her the slip again. She gave a harried bow, her ponytail bouncing down over her face and back. The bags below Alwyn's eyes wrinkled as he suppressed a smile. Elric knew he took great pride in Carvin, and great joy in teasing her. As a child, she had caught his attention with her quick mind while Alwyn visited Centauri Prime. He had taken her from her home planet, where as a female, she would have had no status or opportunity. Now she was in chrysalis stage, like Galen.

"Going to join me in some rabble-rousing this time?" Alwyn asked Elric.

"I don't think you need any help." Elric wondered again why he and Alwyn were friends. Alwyn had been a friend of Galen's father and an eccentric uncle figure to Galen. Once Galen had come to live with Elric, Alwyn began to visit, he and Carvin adding a sense of family to their austere existence. Elric disagreed with Alwyn on most things, yet at the same time respected him. Alwyn had a great devotion to his adopted home of Regula 4, similar to Elric's attachment to Soom. Alwyn also had an unerring ability to sense any hypocrisy within the techno-mages or the Circle, and he cared enough to call them on it, repeatedly and publicly.

Alwyn turned back toward the field of ships. "Ah, the trouble begins apace." He rubbed his palms together.

A procession marched from between the ships toward Elric. They came in two columns of fifty each, Human males, muscular, oiled, and completely naked. Most of them carried poles topped by magical light. Four in the center carried an ornate sedan chair on their shoulders. In it rode Burell. She wore a dress of golden scales that Cleopatra would have envied. Her nonexistent hair was done up in a dark cascade incorporating golden fish and starbursts. Her eyes were accented by strong black lines of kohl, in the ancient Egyptian fashion. She waved to them as if to throngs of admirers.

Elric found the craftsmanship exceptional. The ability to create realistic illusions fell off rapidly with distance, as did many techno-mage powers. A full-body illusion overlaid on the mage's skin could be so realistic that it could withstand even careful scrutiny. Yet the greater the distance from the mage, the cruder and more artificial-looking the illusions became. The slave men at the front of the line, a good fifty yards away from Burell, looked fairly convincing, with well-formed muscles and glistening skin. He saw just a hint of the sharp angular planes and shiny, artificial texture that characterized most work conjured at that distance.

Alwyn looked over Elric's shoulder. "I hope Blaylock is seeing this." He turned back, his mouth falling open in fascination. "What is she thinking? Presenting herself with such grandeur. This is going to inflame her enemies even further."

Elric said nothing. Burell was already a very divisive figure, supported by some and condemned by others for her scientific research into the tech.

In addition to the controversy, Burell carried mystery as well. Although she was only in middle age, she had been ill for almost four years now, so ill she had missed the last convocation. Mages suffered few illnesses, since their implants automatically generated microscopic organelles that served as agents of healing. While the mages didn't know how the organelles worked, they knew that the microscopic healers worked much better on injuries than on long-term illness. Yet Burell's incapacity had been sudden and severe. It was most strange.

Elric knew that Ing-Radi had offered to try to heal Burell's illness, but Burell had declined. When he had heard she intended to attend this convocation, he had assumed she had recovered, at least partially. It was clear to him now that she was even worse. Although she had always been partial to the occasional naked slave man, this ostentatious display was far beyond anything she had done before. It had obviously been created to camouflage her condition. She was unable to walk.

The slave men at the front of the procession passed by Elric and Alwyn, curving off toward the side of the tents. When Burell arrived in front of Elric, the slaves stopped and lowered her sedan chair to the ground. She planted her palms flat on the arms of the chair in preparation to rise. Elric dropped to his knees to preempt her. "My queen." He took her hand, kissed it. Burell had her pride, and perhaps something more.

Her eyes widened. "If I'd known this is what it took to get

a reaction from you, I'd have done it twenty years ago," she said.

"If I'd known you'd wanted a reaction from me, you would have gotten a reaction from me." Elric resisted the urge to use his sensors to examine her condition. It was improper for one mage to secretly use his powers on another. Without that basic etiquette, the mages would never agree to meet.

Burell noted the crowd that had gathered around them and withdrew her hand, keeping her voice low. "Privacy would best serve what I have to tell you." Her hands were now clenched in her lap. "I know you are busy, but it is a grave matter."

"I will come to you as soon as I am able." Elric stood, concerned.

Burell raised her voice. "You may not remember my apprentice, Isabelle."

A young woman had appeared beside Burell. She had reddish blond hair, thin upslanted brows, and slender hands, which held a package. Isabelle was Burell's daughter through a sexual liaison with a nonmage, which was the other common method of obtaining an apprentice. Since neither Burell nor Isabelle had attended the previous convocation, Isabelle had grown up since Elric had last seen her. He remembered Burell looking similar when she had been initiated, a few years after him. She had touched off a number of fights between male techno-mages in those days.

"Yes, I remember," Elric said. "A pleasure to see you again."

Isabelle bowed. "I am honored. I deeply admire your work." She took a breath. Her voice control seemed competent, but she was obviously quite nervous. "I made you this. I wanted to thank you for hosting the convocation that will bring me to mage-hood." She thrust the package at him. "Within it are woven the hyperspace currents you mapped out in your last talk."

Elric accepted the package with a bow. "Thank you for your generous gift."

Isabelle nodded with obvious relief. Burell signaled to the

nonexistent slaves to lift her chair, and the procession continued. She sent most of them around the side of the tent, where they could vanish without destroying the illusion. With just the four that carried her, she proceeded into the tent. Other mages followed, drawn in by the controversy.

Elric was left with Carvin, Alwyn's apprentice. She turned around suddenly, finding Alwyn gone. "Damn," she said. Then, to him, "Sorry." Elric had lost track of Alwyn himself as he spoke to Burell. Carvin's eyes narrowed on the slave men retreating around the side of the tent. "Got him." She ran after them.

Elric found himself alone. He looked out at the field of ships. From the tents, laughter and booming voices washed over him in ephemeral, ghostly waves, carried on the currents of the sea breeze. Someone conjured music, and the bass line echoed out into the night.

Outside, all was still. The air remained clear, and the sky was brilliant with stars. The conjured globes of light cast the ships' gentle shadows on the moss. To his right, his stone circle stood tall in the dark—solid, certain, his link to this place he loved.

He took a deep breath of the sea breeze. The temperature was brisk, just as he liked it. The night seemed infinitely precious, a transient bit of time out of the endless eons of eternity, on this tiny planet lost in the vastness of space. As insignificant as it might be in the course of the universe, this night would come only once, and for him it carried great value.

One had to enjoy life where one could, he thought. It was, truly, a great blessing. In his stress of discipline and control, he had failed to teach Galen that. Enjoy life. Enjoy it while he could.

Galen sat in his bedroom hunched over his screen, a fistful of hair gripped in one hand, rocking back and forth. The spells on the screen had turned to nonsense. His brain had stopped functioning several hours ago. All he could think of was that look of grave disappointment he was going to see on Elric's face in the morning.

In the nearly one thousand years since Wierden had established the Circle, all the spells that were worth doing, and were possible, had already been done. For the last several hundred years, spells were built upon, intertwined, varied with great creativity and ingenuity. Mages altered their presentation, generating different effects. They added ever more complicated flourishes, reflecting their unique identity and power.

Yet these increasingly complex spells didn't seem truly original. The truly original he found as he moved further and further back in the history of the techno-mages: Gali-Gali's discovery of the unfolded shield, Maju's leap from electron incantations to healing spells. A truly original spell would have to be on a par with those of the greats, and that task was beyond him.

He'd studied those great spells extensively. One difficulty every mage faced, though, was translating the work of other mages into his own spell language. Each mage had to discover and develop his own spell language, because a spell that worked for one mage would not work for another. Elric had explained that the tech was so intimately connected with one's body and mind that conjuring became shaped by the individual. Since each person's mind worked differently, mages achieved the best results in different ways. An apprentice trained to achieve clarity of thought, and his preferred method of thought formed his spell language. His chrysalis learned to respond to the spell language, and when he received his implants, this knowledge was passed to them through the old implant at the base of his skull.

Galen's spell language was that of equations. Elric had been concerned at first as Galen's language had developed. Most spell languages were more instinctive, less rigid, less rational. But Galen wasn't a holistic, lateral thinker who jumped from one track to another, drawing instinctive connections. His thoughts plodded straight ahead, each leading logically and inexorably to the next. Elric had expressed fear that Galen's language would be cumbersome and inflexible. Yet as Elric had worked with Galen on the language and seen how many spells Galen had been able to translate, his reservations had seemed to fade.

Translation was one of the most difficult tasks facing any mage. It was only after looking at many spells that Galen was able to understand how another mage's spell language related to his, then translate those conjuries. He had managed to translate most of Wierden's and Gali-Gali's spells, as well as many spells of other mages. With different levels of success, he had translated spells to create illusions, to make flying platforms, to conjure defensive shields, to generate fireballs, to send messages to other mages, to control the sensors that would soon be implanted into him, to access and manipulate data internally, to access external databases, and much more.

He had memorized them all.

But since each spell language possessed its own inherent strengths and weaknesses, he found it impossible to translate some spells, such as those for healing. Others, such as the spells used to generate defensive shields, he believed he had translated correctly, yet when he cast them, the results he achieved were weak, inferior.

Galen wondered, and not for the first time, if his spell language hampered his attempt to conjure something original. As his thoughts plodded straight ahead, so did his spells, equation after orderly equation. In his language, it made no sense to simply make up a spell. An equation must be sensible in order to work; all the terms must possess established identities and properties. So how could he discover an equation that somehow reflected him, revealed him? He had been uncomfortable with the idea of revealing himself, but now that hesitance faded to insignificance beside the undeniable necessity: he could not disappoint Elric.

Galen brought up a different section of text on the screen, his translations of some of the spells of Wierden. They varied in complexity and involved many different terms, some of which were used in multiple spells, others used only once. Again it seemed to him that there could be no truly original spells, only more complicated ones. Frustrated, Galen started to reorder the spells on the screen, from simplest to most complex. As he did, he noticed that some of the spells formed a progression. A spell with two terms conjured a translucent globe. A spell with those same two terms, and one more, conjured a globe with energy inside. A spell with those same three terms, and yet another, conjured a globe with the energy given the form of light. Add another term, and it conjured a globe filled with light and heat. And on it went.

Several of Gali-Gali's spells furthered the complexity. If he could work his way to the last spell in the progression, could he think of one that would go beyond it?

But wasn't this just what others were doing, building ever more elaborate spells without really creating something new? He didn't know if the other mages thought of it this way; since they didn't formulate their spells as equations, their spells didn't have multiple terms in them. Elric, he knew, simply visualized what he wanted to happen, and if it was within his power, it happened. One simple visualization for any spell.

Galen's eyes went back to the top of the list, to the spell containing only two terms. Why was there no spell with only one term? No such spell existed in Wierden's work, or, as he thought about it, in any of the mages' conjuries he'd yet translated. Most of them had many, many terms. In fact, he couldn't even remember another equation with only two.

Perhaps spells *had* to have more than one term. But why? He stared at the two terms that began the progression. If there was an initial spell in the series, a spell with only one term, which term was it?

The first of the two terms was common, used in this progression and elsewhere. Galen had come to think of it as a sort of cleanup term, necessary for everything to balance, but having negligible impact.

The second term, on the other hand, existed only within the spells of this progression. As far as he knew, at least. That seemed very odd. Surely it could have other uses.

That second term, then, seemed the defining characteristic

of the progression, and the obvious choice for the first equation in it. But what would the term do when used alone?

Perhaps it would have the same effect as the second equation, conjuring a translucent sphere. If the cleanup term truly was negligible, that's what would happen. The sphere itself, as he'd discussed it with Elric, was an odd construct, not a force field as it first had seemed. It didn't really hold things in, or keep things out. It simply demarcated a space within which something would be done.

If removing the cleanup term did have an effect, what might it be? Perhaps the sphere wouldn't form at all. Perhaps it would be opaque or have some other property. Or perhaps it would be deformed in some way. In any case, it wouldn't be very impressive.

Galen forced himself to take a break. He released his screen, stretched tight muscles. Outside the circle of light cast by the lamp on his worktable, his room had fallen into darkness. The walls of stacked stones had lost definition in the dim light. His rough wooden wardrobe, night table, and bed were vague, indefinite shapes.

On the wall above his worktable, four long shelves hung in shadow. Galen organized all his projects and materials there. Each item was neatly in place. Galen had found he couldn't concentrate when items were left out on the worktable, or in any disarray. Items on the bottom shelf related to his recent research projects: microscopic probes that he had made, probes made by Elric and Circe for comparison, data crystals containing his latest translations of spells, props he had developed for a variety of minor illusions. On the second shelf he kept objects left over from previous projects: powders and potions, crystals and microchips, loose components and curious novelties. The top two shelves held older projects and other materials for which he was not sure he would find a use: his medical research, various primitive inventions, an identikit that could produce replicas of the identicards issued by twenty-three of the major governments, a keycard Alwyn had given him for his last birthday. Alwyn had promised that it would open any door.

A burst of light from outside drew his attention. He got up from the rough wood table and went to the window.

A great golden shower of light rained down over the mak. As that vanished, a long red snake climbed up the starry sky. It was the convocation's opening-night celebration. Galen rested his palms against the cold stone wall on either side of the window.

Could he be one of them? Did he have the skill? The snake nudged a star with its nose, and the star arced downward. Then the serpent curled into a circle and took its tail in its mouth. The symbol of death in life, of renewal. It shrank smaller and smaller. Across the sky, one star after another burst open into a brilliant flower.

A dark shape appeared in his window.

He jumped back. "Fa!"

She waved vigorously and climbed in. "You are missing everything! They came down from the sky. Creatures and lights and ribbons. Pretty pictures. They are all like Honored El. They can make the dreams of light." She turned to look out the window beside him. In the glow from outside, he studied her face. Her eyes were wide, mouth open. Her tongue was just touching her upper lip. She was enchanted. Yet like most of the Soom, she had no understanding of the true power and knowledge of the mages. She considered them wise, perhaps, and clever, but she had no idea of the discipline and study, of the efforts and works of incredible genius that allowed them to do what they did.

"Look!" she said, pointing to a braided rainbow arcing overhead.

"I have to work," he said, and returned to his table. He stared down at his screen without seeing it. Respect for the techno-mages seemed to be lacking not only here, but everywhere.

Elizar, who traveled much more widely as Kell's apprentice, had told him at the last convocation that on some worlds, techno-mages had been completely forgotten. On others, memory remained only in legend, as a superstition or a story told to children. Little to nothing was known of their noble history, of Wierden bringing order to the early mages; of Gali-Gali defeating the menace of the Zrad and serving at the right hand of the Empress Nare for one hundred years of peace; of Maju's sealing of the Lau hyperspatial rift that threatened billions of lives, at the price of his own.

Techno-mages had been advisers to great leaders, and sometimes great leaders themselves. They had stood at the center of important events. They had been generals, inventors, masterminds, heroes. In those days, convocations were times when nonmages would honor mages, thanking them for service. Whole planets would celebrate and honor them.

Now they met alone, their praises unsung.

Galen had been glad to find someone who shared his concern at the last convocation, and he and Elizar had become friends as they entered chrysalis stage. Since then, they had sent messages to each other regularly, sharing a desire for the mages to take a greater part in galactic events and regain the prominence and respect they once had. If they could not hope to regain the lost scientific knowledge of the Taratimude, at least they could hope for that.

Elizar seemed to have a vision for the future of the mages, a vision that Galen hoped he would be able to bring to pass. Over the last year, though, Elizar's messages had become more and more infrequent. Galen hadn't heard from him at all for the past four months. Elizar was busy, Galen knew; he looked forward to talking with his friend during the convocation.

Fa stuck her head under his arm. "What are you doing?"

"I told you. I'm working."

She climbed with damp feet up onto his lap, and then onto the table, squatting there. He moved the lamp to the other side. She had the ring on again.

"I told you not to play with that," he said.

She was wearing it on her smallest finger, which was thick enough that the ring of Galen's father fit perfectly. The stone was ragged and perfectly black, set in a heavy band of silver that held to the stone with sharp claws. Somehow, in her many explorations of his room, she always fixed on the ring, the one thing he wished never to face again. Galen didn't like to see it, didn't like to think about it.

"I won't break it," she said, tilting her hand back and forth. "What's that?" She pointed at the equations on the screen.

"Work I have to do for tomorrow," Galen said.

"Those aren't letters."

"No, they're symbols that represent different elements in the spells we cast."

"That's a spell?"

"Yes, for me it is." Maybe if she saw how complicated the spells were, she'd have more respect for the mages. "You see how this spell has two elements, and this one has the same two but one more." He explained the progression to her as she turned her head back and forth over the screen.

"What comes next?" she asked, after he had led her to the most complex equation.

"I don't know. But I think the more interesting question is, what comes first? Why is there no spell with only one term?"

"Why?"

"I don't know." Perhaps because it would do nothing, in which case Elric wouldn't be terribly impressed. He saved his work on the screen and turned it off. "Shouldn't you be in bed?"

She smiled. "Shouldn't you be working?"

He picked her up off the table and dropped her to the floor. "Go on. Get out of here."

She ran to the window, turned. "Gale, will you move away from here? Once you are"—she struggled with the foreign word—"initiated?"

He hadn't really thought of that. All his efforts had been concentrated on reaching this point. He still couldn't believe he would be a techno-mage. But even if he did become a mage, he still had three years as an initiate, during which Elric would continue to supervise him. "No, I won't leave. Not for a while, at least. Now go home."

She held up her hand and wriggled the fingers, flashing the ring at him. Galen held out his hand. She pulled the ring off, held it up, then dropped it into the large pocket on the front of her orange jumper. She held up her empty hands. "Nothing here. But what's that behind your ear?" She reached up to Galen's ear, revealed the ring in her hand. "Odd place to keep it."

Her thick fingers made the sleight of hand difficult, but she'd gotten much better. She'd been practicing. "Better," Galen said, taking the ring from her with a flourish to misdirect her attention. "But what's that behind your ear?"

"What!" Fa said, turning her head from side to side as if that would help her see.

Galen reached behind her ear, producing a small, smooth rock. He kept a cache of such items in a tiny sack fastened to the underside of his table. She grabbed at it, but he closed his hand, and when he opened it, the rock was gone, pinched behind two of his fingers. He closed his hand again, waved the other over it to distract her, and then opened it to reveal the rock again on his palm. She snatched it away this time. With a cheer of triumph she ran to the window and climbed out. She gave a furious wave good-bye, then ran off.

Galen forced his clenched hand to open. On his palm sat the ring.

He had watched his mother make it, building microscopic circuitry into the silver band, creating the natural-looking black stone with layer after layer of crystals deposited in precise patterns. His parents had been powerful mages, highly respected, working at the right and left hand of a corporate president who had risen to great influence. Although his father had been his teacher, his mother had taught him that day.

The ring had been a birthday present for Galen's father, a gift that would allow him to copy the contents of any data crystal with which it came into contact. The ring had gleamed on his father's finger as his parents went for a birthday space cruise through the midnight lights, leaving Galen with a visiting Elric.

Elric emerged from the fire of the accident with a protective full-body shield close around him, clinging like a second skin. It gave his face a cool bluish cast. With his black robe and severe demeanor, he looked like death itself. Behind him floated two supine figures shrouded in sheets, which his shield had stretched to enclose. The shapes beneath the sheets were irregular, uneven, too small. Elric stopped before Galen and extended his hand. On it sat the ring.

Galen closed it in his hand. He often felt as if his life had begun when Elric walked out of that fire, the bodies of his parents behind him. Galen preferred not to think of them alive. He had turned his back on the memories, and had only the sense of their pressure pushing on him, an ever-weakening force he hoped would vanish forever before he had to face it.

He went to his night table, jammed the ring into its woven grass box. He didn't want to see it, didn't want to think about it.

Galen heard Elric close the front door. The lights in the sky had died. It was late. He didn't know what the spell he'd discovered would do. He didn't know if it would do anything. He didn't want to disappoint Elric. Yet as a chrysalis-stage apprentice, he was forbidden to perform any magic without his teacher present. He wouldn't know what the spell did until tomorrow.

At least he thought the spell was original; not only original in the sense of something that hadn't been done before—as far as he knew—but also in the sense of being the origin of the progression, something fundamental to the powers of the techno-mages, a basic postulate.

Elric would have to acknowledge that, even if the attempt to conjure it was foolish.

Yet Galen didn't see how the spell could do what Elric expected—reveal, express, and complete him. The spell had not developed out of some fancy. It had been deduced through simple, objective logic. Perhaps his spell language was too mechanical to reveal anything about him. Galen knew it was limited, knew he was limited. He wished, for Elric's sake, that he could have been a better apprentice.

In any event, he had tried elaborate complications; the tribute to Wierden had failed to satisfy Elric's requirements. Galen could think of no other option.

— chapter 3 —

Galen woke to find the chrysalis in its canister on his table. It hung motionless in the clear liquid, translucent silvery skin catching the sunlight. He crouched before it. This would be the last time he would wear it. He had never been allowed to wear it outside Elric's presence, but now, for the last day and night before initiation, he was to wear it to symbolize his status. It would be removed by Elric tomorrow morning, at the ceremony. Today was a day of fasting and preparation.

Galen realized with alarm that he had overslept. He had much work to do, and his training session with Elric came first. He dressed quickly in a light black robe and boots. He put a sensor-pad in his pocket—in case he found anything to study. Then he opened the canister.

Usually Elric held the chrysalis up to Galen as he visualized the association command. This time Galen scooped the limp chrysalis gently from the liquid. He brought the bell-shaped section to the top of his head, letting the extension trail down his back. He visualized the equation.

The chrysalis leapt from his hands and seized his head and spine in a powerful grip. Its body rippled against his, adjusting itself quickly to his curves and contours to maximize contact. The connection echoed through him, creating a subtle vibration of energy. He wiped the liquid from his forehead.

As he rushed through the thick, brilliant white mist toward the hall, it crossed his mind that with the chrysalis, he could try out the new spell he'd discovered before facing Elric. Then he would know what it did. Casting spells without his teacher was forbidden, though. And surely giving apprentices the ability to do so before initiation was a test, a temptation. He would not fail. Besides, what good would it do to see what the spell did? He had nothing else to offer.

And he was late.

Galen was surprised to find a number of mages and apprentices standing outside the hall. Then he realized all the apprentices must be using the hall to train this morning. More would be inside. That meant his session with Elric wouldn't be private, as he had expected. Galen stopped, imagining his spell failing while everyone watched. The chrysalis returned a faint echo of his anxiety.

Federico, Herazade's apprentice, approached. "Hey. You look like you just swallowed a rock." As Galen tried to erase the anxiety from his face, Fed jerked a thumb over his shoulder at the others. "Nothing like a little pressure, eh?"

Though Galen knew Federico liked to be called Fed, he was uncomfortable with the familiarity of the diminutive, especially because Fed always seemed so familiar with him. Galen's awkwardness around people made him sound more distant than he intended. "Federico. Good to see you." Galen was always afraid that people—especially mages—were seeing things in him that he did not intend to show. In his attempt to prevent that, his behavior around others became strained or overly formal. At least until he knew them well. "You arrived last night?"

Fed nodded. For some reason, Fed's chrysalis seemed canted to one side, like a jaunty cap. His thick, wiry hair stuck out from it, mixing with his unkempt beard. He looked like a wild man. "Elric is inside, if that's who you're looking for."

"Yes," Galen said, forcing himself forward toward the hall.

"Where were you last night? You missed some manic action."

"I had to work."

"All work and no play, Galen. Speaking of which, Gowen went first this morning. That is one strange guy. Of course can you blame him, with Blaylock as his teacher. I'd bug out in a day." Galen greeted various mages as he and Fed passed. He was glad Elric had made him review all their names. "Anyway, he did this weird illusion—he had the heavens opening up, this choir singing, and a hand came down and put the chrysalis on his head. Truly freaky."

They reached the door all too quickly. But then, if it was sealed as usual, they wouldn't be able to get in. "How have people been getting inside?"

"Elric set it to open when there's no conjuring being done." Fed grabbed the latch and opened the door. They entered.

Along the front stone wall, a strip about six feet wide had been set up as a rectangular gallery from which the training could be watched. Mages and apprentices were packed into it, separated from the training area by a blue-tinged defensive shield that would protect them from any stray energies. The two worked their way toward the shield to get a better view. They came up behind the long wooden bench, which had been pulled up to the shield and was filled with spectators.

In the training area, Alwyn was preparing to work with his Centauri apprentice, Carvin. Alwyn glanced his way and smiled at Galen. Galen raised a hand in response. After Elric, Alwyn was the mage to whom Galen felt closest. Alwyn visited often, and had helped Galen learn the runic language of the Taratimude. They shared an interest in that ancient race. Alwyn's teaching techniques were unconventional, as Galen had experienced a bit himself, and he'd heard much more from Carvin. Alwyn would hide from her, or play the same trick on her over and over, until she figured it out. She was expected to play tricks on him as well. Galen couldn't imagine doing that with Elric.

During Alwyn's visits, Galen would study with Carvin. She was a dedicated student, in part because she was the only Centauri currently working toward mage-hood. The previous one, Tilar, had failed initiation at the last convocation and been cast away, his chrysalis taken from him and destroyed.

Carvin shared Galen's commitment to master the ways of technomancy, yet somehow she was able to combine discipline with a great joy for life. To Galen she had always seemed strangely fearless—passionate, outgoing, open.

Carvin held up her hands, requesting silence from the gallery. She was a strong showman, and her multicolored Centauri silks drew the eyes, an asset for misdirection. She began by asking Alwyn to remove his boots. Alwyn's eyes crinkled in pleasure at the unexpected request. He bent to remove the cracked, discolored things. "I can't vouch for the smell."

When he had handed over the boots and taken hold of her chrysalis, she began to juggle them in one hand. It was pure hand-eye coordination; something at which Galen had never excelled. With a flourish of her hand, she conjured the illusion of a ballet slipper, added it into her juggling. Carvin's spell language was that of the body; specific, precise movements and their accompanying mental impulses comprised her spells.

With a slightly different flourish of her hand she conjured a sandal, then a buckled shoe. She was now juggling with two hands. Then she seemed to run out of objects to juggle, as the collection of real and fake shoes refused to descend. They had collected in a line over her head, tapping and twisting. It was a great combination of reality and illusion. She could move the illusory shoes easily with a spell. But the real shoes had to be held aloft with transparent flying platforms, which were difficult to conjure at any distance.

Under one of Alwyn's boots, Galen could make out a rippling distortion about an inch thick. The distortion shifted slightly as the flying platform tilted and twisted, so that the boot resting on it seemed to move.

Carvin extended her arms to the right and swung them around to her left. The shoes began to move in a circle around her and Alwyn. As they did, she waved one out to arc overhead and rejoin the circle on the other side, then another. Soon she had the shoes moving in a complex pattern, her body swaying and her arms tracing out intricate spells. In her multicolored silks, her movement itself became a part of the magic.

At last all the shoes came back to Carvin's hands to be juggled. One by one she dissolved the illusions, until all she juggled were the two boots. Then she dissolved those illusions as well. No shoes were left. Alwyn coughed in surprise at that; she'd gotten him. The onlookers clapped, including Galen and Fed. Carvin gave a playful bow.

Alwyn released her. "Am I expected to walk in that muck—I mean mak—with no shoes on?"

Carvin took his hand and turned him around. There, lined up neatly against the wall, were his boots. At some point she had switched the real ones for illusions, and Galen hadn't known the difference. Alwyn's eyes crinkled up as he nodded in appreciation. "I raised a genius."

Galen caught sight of Elric down the gallery. He was wearing a robe Galen had never seen before. It had the high collar Elric favored, but on the chest, silver and copper cords glittered in an elaborate pattern against the black fabric. Such ornamentation was quite unlike Elric; Galen wondered where he had gotten the robe and why he wore it.

Elric was in conversation with Circe, and Galen couldn't catch his eye. It was unnecessary anyway. Elric would know he was here; Elric almost always knew where he was. Galen realized they would simply have to wait their turn for training. He would rather have gotten it over quickly. Nothing to do but wait.

The shield dissolved. Herazade appeared beside them, wearing a deep blue sari. She greeted Galen and put a hand on Fed's back, pushing him around the bench and into the training area. "Let's see what you can do."

Fed flashed a panicked expression over his shoulder. Alwyn and Carvin approached.

"We missed you last night," Alwyn said, embracing Galen. Though it was just a friendly greeting, the close contact made Galen uncomfortable. He and Elric did not embrace. The shield came back up. Alwyn released him.

"It's good to see you," Galen said. "Congratulations, Carvin. That was perfect. Seamless."

"Don't say that," Alwyn said. "She'll get a swelled head. And who knows what item of my clothing she'll make disappear next time."

"Now there's an idea," Carvin said.

"Have you trained yet, Galen?" Alwyn asked.

Galen shook his head.

"I need to get some of that delicious local brew. I'll try to get back to see you."

"Don't rush on my account," Galen said.

Alwyn smiled. "You'll do fine. Elric wouldn't allow any less." He turned to Carvin. "Think you can keep up with me all the way to the tents?"

Carvin ran for the door, and Alwyn followed.

On the other side of the shield, Fed levitated himself and Herazade off the floor with a flying platform. From the slight distortion, Galen could tell it was a rectangle of typical size, about two feet by three feet. Fed was already notorious for his platform stunts, which, it was said, had once landed Herazade flat on her back in a mud puddle. Since the platform was, in a sense, an extension of the mage who generated it, he had an instinctive ability to keep his balance through various maneuvers. Those instincts could also be improved by practice, as he commanded different accelerations and decelerations and learned to compensate for them, the way an experienced tube rider could.

Of course a platform could be conjured in shapes that were more secure, such as a chair, a chariot, or a scooter, but the tradition of the plain rectangular platform was strong. Any passenger on the platform, though, had to either hold tight to the mage or hope for a gentle ride. Herazade had one hand on Fed's chrysalis. As the platform began to spin, she clamped her free arm about his waist.

Galen admired Fed's talent, but he felt fairly confident in using a platform and wanted to see who else was in the hall. So he turned toward the gallery. Elric had taught him to study everything around him. Observation yielded knowledge and understanding. Knowledge and understanding were necessary to use the tech wisely.

While he felt fairly adept at observing most phenomena and drawing scientific conclusions, he had trouble understanding intelligent beings. Their motivations and feelings were often impenetrable mysteries.

Circe was speaking to Blaylock. She had conjured a schematic in the air between them, and as she pointed to different areas, she looked to see his reaction, apparently anxious for his approval. Blaylock, on the other hand, betrayed no emotion, wearing a fixed, dour expression. Galen couldn't tell if he approved or disapproved of what she said.

Beyond them stood Kell, with his apprentices Elizar and Razeel. Though he spoke softly in a gallery filled with talk, his masterful voice sent a deep vibration through the space. Kell's large frame and precisely formulated gestures embodied power and control. With his dark skin and brilliant white goatee scoured into the shape of the rune for knowledge, he presented a dramatic figure. His accomplishments over his long life were legendary, particularly his feeding of the drought victims on Viscus 4 and his great deception of the Drazi.

Galen had never yet said a word to Kell, though he had sensed the mage, at previous convocations, watching him. He supposed Kell had to take an interest in all of them. Elric and Alwyn had discussed Kell's increasing age with concern, but Galen thought Kell was still the best of them.

Elizar and Razeel were now receiving Kell's wisdom, the wisdom of Wierden, which Galen envied when he thought about it. But he wouldn't have traded Elric for any other teacher. Besides, he wasn't cut out to be a leader, which was what Kell's apprentice needed to be. Elizar fit that role. Something in the tilt of his head made his silvery chrysalis look like an ancient helm. With his long maroon velvet coat and gold-patterned vest beneath, he looked regal. He had even grown a dark goatee to mirror Kell's, his shaped into the rune for magic.

Today, though, Elizar seemed distracted. He was looking around at the other mages, his right hand curled inward, his thumb running in circles around his fingertips. Razeel's eyes were aimed down, as if her focus were inward. Elric would never have let Galen get away with something like that. He demanded full attention at all times. Yet Kell simply kept talking, as if he didn't notice.

Elizar glanced over and saw Galen. He excused himself from Kell and started across the gallery, stopping to exchange greetings with other mages as he passed by. Something was different in Elizar's manner. As before, his long stride was assured, his angular face tilted upward. Yet anxiety clung to him. It was something in the way he leaned in for an embrace, in the intensity he put into each greeting, as if he feared losing the goodwill and affection of the mages. As Elizar's thumb returned again and again to circle his fingertips, Galen realized that Elizar's attention wasn't on the other mages at all.

Elizar extended his arms. "Galen, good friend. It's been too long." Elizar embraced him. "Sorry I fell out of touch." Keeping one arm over Galen's shoulders, Elizar steered them away from the shield.

"I didn't mean to interrupt your conversation with Kell," Galen said.

"It's of no consequence."

Galen was shocked that Elizar would speak this way of Kell, and apparently he showed it, for Elizar quickly added, "He was merely offering encouragement. Razeel needs it much more than I."

That was more like Elizar. Confidence had never been one of his problems. "I read the memoir of Gali-Gali that you recommended," Galen said. "Thank you for telling me of it. He was a brilliant thinker, more than I even knew. His strategy in the war against the Zrad was genius."

Elizar smiled. "I'd forgotten all about that. He had an amazing life. I loved that story about his initiation, about the challenge and what it meant to him." They stopped in a quiet corner, and Elizar finally removed his arm.

"You're ready then, for the initiation?" Galen asked.

"Undoubtedly. Unlike those poor sods." Elizar gave a quick tilt to his head, indicating a trio of chrysalis-stage apprentices a few feet away. "Kane and his crew of fools don't even deserve to be initiated. Their great dream is to settle down on some stone-age planet and dazzle the natives with fireballs. How bold. And they're about as imaginative as they are skilled." His eyes scanned the hall. "Carvin—she might succeed as a stage magician. Perhaps Rebo and Zooty are in need of an assistant."

Elizar tended to dismiss any apprentice whose teacher wasn't one of the Circle. Galen was used to his attitude, and though he disagreed with it, he felt that perhaps in comparison to Elizar, who was of the line of Wierden, the rest of them were inferior.

"You and I, Galen, and a handful of the other apprentices—the future of the techno-mages is going to depend on us, once we're initiated." Elizar's thumb resumed its course around his fingertips. "A lot of decisions to be made after that. What we're going to make of ourselves."

"I haven't given it much thought, I'm afraid," Galen said. "I would like, someday, when my skills are great enough, to do the things we've talked about—to do good, to make a difference, and to help restore the glory of the techno-mages."

"Life doesn't always give us the time we need."

Something was bothering his friend. "I suppose not."

Elizar stepped closer, lowering his voice. His dark blue eyes fastened on Galen. "I have a great weight upon me, Galen. You may not understand. I'm expected to assume Kell's place and lead us forward. But forward into what? We've become obsessed with technique, with flourishes and phantasms, rather than with impact." His fist hit his palm. "We entertain, we enlighten, but what power do we truly possess? The mages of old, the Taratimude, they had power. And they used it wisely, decisively. They knew how to make the tech, and how to use it. We've lost so much. And of what little we have retained, I believe key pieces are kept from us by the Circle. I think, perhaps, the Circle is custodian of secrets far beyond what most would suspect."

Galen was shocked by his friend's accusation. Elizar might have complained in the past that the Circle was overly conservative, but he had always respected their wisdom and leadership. "What kind of secrets?" he asked.

"I'm not sure. Secrets of power, almost certainly. Of abilities we don't know we have. But the most serious . . ." Elizar glanced behind him, leaned over Galen. "Imagine a threat coming, Galen. A threat not only to us, but to everyone. A threat that could end our order forever. And the knowledge of it kept from us."

"By the Circle? Why would they do that?"

"I think they are afraid. Things have grown quiet, things have grown safe. They have grown complacent. I think they are frozen to inaction by what they know. They're not prepared to do what has to be done." Laughter burst from the mages; apparently Fed was clowning again.

Galen couldn't believe Elric would ever withhold information about a threat to the mages, or to those they protected. "If that is so," he said, "then we would make our case to the Circle."

"The Circle would deny."

"Then we would make our case to the mages themselves."

"They wouldn't believe us."

"What evidence do you have?"

Elizar glanced toward Kell. "We must discuss this later. But I tell you Kell is neither willing nor able to deal with what is coming. New leadership will be required."

There were many with greater experience and wisdom than Elizar; it seemed presumptuous of him to think he was the only solution. His time to be elected to the Circle was many years off. Yet why was Elizar the only one to suspect this threat? Galen didn't know what to say. "It will be many years before Kell leaves the Circle."

"He is old. You don't know, Galen. He's not what he once was. The Circle has always included one of the line of Wierden. If not Kell, that would mean Razeel or I, and . . ." He shrugged, dismissing Razeel.

"But the youngest ever to be elected to the Circle was Elric, when he was fifty." And a new member could not be elected until a current member died or resigned, with resignation usually taking place very close to death.

"Kell waited too long to take apprentices. He should have

done so many years ago. And he should have taken only one. But he believed himself infallible. I cannot help the fact that I'm young. And I cannot use that fact as an excuse to stand by and do nothing. Drastic action must be taken. I happen to be the only one in a position to take that action. I hope that, when the time comes, you will support me."

"What kind of action?"

"The secrets"—he wiped a hand across his mouth—"must be uncovered. Power must be restored to us. The survival of the mages will depend on it." His mouth hung open at a crooked angle, and his eyes drifted to the side, as if watching the future he contemplated. Like an apprentice about to cast his first spell, he seemed simultaneously terrified and excited. Then his eyes returned to Galen, and he laid a hand on Galen's shoulder. "Wish me success. And speak of this to no one."

Galen nodded.

Then Elizar was moving on, greeting others and giving embraces with that same anxious intensity.

Elizar had to be mistaken, Galen thought. Elric would have told him of any danger. And if there were a danger, the Circle would be doing their best to prepare them to face it.

He moved toward the shield. Razeel was training now, under the supervision of Kell. Galen didn't have much of a memory of her from previous convocations. She had followed Elizar around a lot, a pale shadow of her brother. The thing Galen remembered most was that at each convocation she dressed in a different fashion, her hair dyed a new color, her clothes reflecting a particular subculture of a particular historical period on a particular planet. It was as if she were trying on different identities. Yet whatever the identity, she always seemed lost.

This time, her hair was its natural dark brown, and her velvet dress matched Elizar's in style. Perhaps she had found who she was, or perhaps this time she had acquiesced to their requests. Yet the velvet dress hung shapelessly on her petite, slender form, too large. Even this identity didn't fit.

Kell towered behind her. Razeel's eyes were downcast, her

arms hanging at her side. Galen couldn't recall the sound of her voice; didn't know if he'd ever heard her speak. Yet her small lips were moving now, in silent incantation.

The globes of light floating within the training area faded to blackness. A mist began to leak from the woven grass mat on the floor around her. The area quickly filled with it, and the dark figures of Razeel and Kell were lost. Seemingly deep within the mist, a light began to strobe on and off. Vague, dark shapes appeared in the intermittent light, their positions jumping between one flash of light and another. They looked a bit like the holodemons Alwyn occasionally conjured, but there was something different about them, something disturbing. With each flash their shapes seemed slightly changed, transformed. Yet each had at its center a constant hole of complete blackness: a mouth.

In a rapid series of jumps the shapes raced toward the shield, and within each the black mouth swelled. Galen took a step back. As the shapes swallowed themselves, they released a tortured, screeching cry.

Then the light of the globes returned, and Razeel and Kell were standing in an empty mist. With a final movement of Razeel's lips, the mist slowly retreated into the carpet.

There was scattered applause from the mages. Something hit Galen on the back, and he jumped. It was Fed. "Does our group of initiates seem weirder than normal, or is it just me?"

The last thing Galen wanted to do was make small talk. He had to figure out what Elizar had been talking about, and he had to prepare for his own training session. It would be his turn soon.

The shield came down, and mages came and went from the hall. Galen saw an open space on the bench. "I'm going to sit down," he said to Fed.

Fed followed. "You know what Razeel told Carvin? She said her chrysalis talks to her."

Galen tried to judge whether Fed was joking or not, thought maybe he wasn't. "Does she mean it echoes her thoughts?"

"She said it actually tells her stuff. I'm not sure what. Of course Gowen thinks the tech is a gift from God, so if she can hear it, maybe she can get the winning New Vegas lottery numbers from it."

Galen sat in the empty space on the bench.

Fed squeezed in on his left. "I've been thinking of doing a study of lottery numbers, nonrandom factors in random number generation, get a drop on those losers who play."

Fed was always thinking of different research projects. As far as Galen knew, he hadn't yet completed any.

"There should be some sort of payoff for all the work we've gone through, don't you think? And the pain. I hear the initiation hurts a lot. I'm warning you right now, I may scream like a girl. But if it were painless, then everyone would want to do it, right?"

"I suppose."

Fed kept talking. Kell called Elizar into the training area, and the shield went back up. It made a faint hum, almost below the level of hearing. Elizar began with some simple exercises. Whatever Elizar thought the Circle was withholding, he wouldn't do anything to jeopardize his initiation.

With the shield just in front of him, Galen studied it for the first time. It was uniform, solid, well constructed. He had met with only mediocre success in creating shields. He'd managed a few times to conjure the simplest type, one that mimicked the contours of his body like a second skin. It had been only weakly protective, though, and unstable. After a few minutes, the energy in his floppy shield had streamed down to pool along the floor. He'd never been able to perform more advanced tasks, such as unfolding the shield from around his body and sustaining it at a distance. This one might teach him something.

He took out his sensor-pad, magnified his view of the shield by ten thousand. At this scale, he ought to be able to see the shield structure, its level of integrity, and any irregularities. At this scale Galen's shield—before it collapsed—looked like a rigid blue grid with fairly large square openings in it. The screen on the pad, though, showed a solid, blue field.

Amazed, he magnified by another one hundred. The bluish

surface was still solid, yet he could see now that it was made up of tiny threads of energy. They were woven together, warp and woof, so tightly as to leave no opening. The strength and elegance of it, the simplicity, awed him. The woven shield was self-contained, complete, a work of art. He had no idea how it had been conjured, but the concept now made sense to him in a way it hadn't before.

Using the sensor-pad, Galen searched for a connection between the shield and its maker. Perhaps he could receive further guidance from whichever master had made it. He found a tiny thread of energy extending from the shield, followed it carefully. It led to the intertwined hands of the person sitting to his right. The strong, slender fingers made slight movements, maintaining the shield with diligent care. The mage wore a black robe, and Galen was amazed to see she had a chrysalis. She was an apprentice like him. Yet he didn't recognize her. Long strawberry-blond hair was tucked behind her ear, which stuck out at an odd angle. A muscle traced the line of her neck. She turned to him, a curious expression on her face. "Hello," she said.

Suddenly he wanted to know everything about her, about the spells she performed, how she had learned to do them, what she liked to eat, what shapes she saw in the stars, whether she'd ever been in love, and why she wanted to be a techno-mage. He was filled with a great care and tenderness toward her, for her jug ears, her warm gray eyes, her strong, slender hands. He didn't want her spell to fail because of his interruption.

His stomach defied anatomy and moved into his throat. He was falling. "Hello," he said.

"You must be Galen."

"Can you talk?"

"I do it quite often, actually." She smiled, her lips pressed together in a mysterious, delightful way. He got the feeling she knew everything about him, but for some reason it didn't bother him. What she knew, she seemed to like.

"I meant—the shield."

"Oh, yes. If you don't mind me being slightly preoccupied. It's kind of like knitting."

"It's beautiful work."

"Thank you. Shields are my specialty. I'm trying to get over it."

He should have studied the list of mages more carefully. "I'm sorry. I don't recognize you."

"Isabelle. Burell's apprentice."

Of course. How could he have been so stupid? He was such an incompetent around people.

"I missed the last convocation," she continued. "Burell was ill, so we stayed home. Kell came with Elizar and Razeel, and"—she paused to concentrate on the spell—"he performed a special ceremony to bring me into chrysalis stage. The last time I saw you, I was fifteen. I preferred to stay with the younger girls."

Her image finally came to him. "You were always knitting!"

She gave that mysterious, closed-lip smile again. "Yes. And you were always reading."

"Yes." Strange thoughts tumbled through his head. Could she possibly ever feel anything for him? And if they both became mages, could it ever endure? In the last two hundred years, only one pair of techno-mages had maintained a long-term relationship. And that had been cut short.

"Will you train soon?" she asked.

"Inevitably." He realized Isabelle was conjuring without her teacher. He looked around for Burell, didn't see her. "How is it you're allowed to work without Burell?"

"She was here this morning. Got me started. She wasn't feeling well, so she made an arrangement with Elric. He was comfortable with my ability to make the shield. I'm not allowed to do more without supervision."

Her voice had risen as a buzzing filled the room. Galen turned toward the training area. Elizar stood at the center of a circling swarm. He bent slightly forward and brought his cupped hands to his mouth, as if to warm them. With a jerk of his body he cried out, releasing a long, sustained syllable. A thin dark spike emerged from his hands and began to sail around the room, joining the rest of the swarm. The spikes made a fierce metallic buzzing. With one cry of power after another, Elizar generated spike after spike, until they formed a whirlwind surrounding him.

Kell spoke into Elizar's ear, and Elizar shook his head. His chest was heaving, sweat running down his pale, angular face.

Elizar released a deeper syllable, drawing it out. The fluctuating volume created a momentary ringing in Galen's ears. As Elizar terminated the sound he jerked his body. With one movement the spikes surged outward, as if alive.

Three sides of the training area were enclosed by the stone walls of the hall, which were reinforced with Elric's containment spell. The spikes struck them and became stuck, like darts in a dartboard. Slowly they were sucked inward and disappeared, their energy absorbed by Elric's spell.

The fourth side of the training area was enclosed by Isabelle's shield. The spikes had been stopped by it as well, but tiny pinpricks of the shield were being pushed outward. Elizar loosed another harsh syllable, and the spikes spun like tiny drills, pressing their advantage. Galen turned to Isabelle. Her eyes were closed, her face flushed, fingers moving rapidly. The spikes pushed farther into the shield.

But Elizar was tiring. His yells were hoarse, the jerking of his body weak. He had begun fighting both Elric and Isabelle, and he had little energy left to sustain the contest with Isabelle. Elric had warned that some would test their strength against others, and Galen had seen many such contests at previous convocations. But Galen didn't understand why Elizar was doing this, or why the result seemed so important to him. Was he trying to prepare for the threat of which he'd spoken? He was still in the chrysalis; his power could never be as great as Elric's.

One of the spikes near Galen popped out of existence. Then another, then another. Elizar was losing his focus. Galen thought the contest might be over. Then Isabelle's shield began to vibrate. He glanced down and saw the sensor-pad still in his hand. The screen showed that the threads of energy were breaking, tiny holes opening up. The shield was unraveling.

Elizar gave one last, guttural shout, doubling over. The spikes vanished.

Isabelle made one final motion with her fingers, dissolving the shield, then laid her palms flat against her legs. With one great heaving breath, she straightened and fixed her gaze on Elizar.

The mages broke into applause.

"A contest well fought," Kell said. "Congratulations to you both."

Elizar ran the back of his hand over his face. He gave a short bow, extending a hand toward Isabelle. She nodded. As Elizar left the training area, his eyes met Isabelle's. Galen thought he might see anger in Elizar's gaze, or frustration, but he sensed instead an intense interest.

Elric stepped into the training area.

Galen stood, his dread returning full force. After everything that everyone had done thus far, was he to conjure a misshapen sphere? Isabelle took the sensor-pad from his hand.

"Excuse me," Galen said, and entered the training area.

Kell took Galen's seat on the bench and exchanged a few words with Isabelle. She nodded, and he generated the shield in her place.

Elric took hold of Galen's chrysalis. "Control. Presentation. Originality."

Galen focused inward, slowing his breathing, relaxing his muscles, straightening his posture. He closed his eyes, picturing his mind as a blank screen on which equations could be written.

He did some warm-ups first with balls of fire. He maintained control, although Kell was sitting right in front of him, his intense dark gaze distracting.

Galen tried to ignore him and went on to conjure his tribute to Wierden. He knew Elric would be impatient, but he wanted to show Kell—and Isabelle—that he could do something. Isabelle held the sensor-pad up to study his work. The tribute came off perfectly. Isabelle and a few others clapped; Kell showed no reaction.

Elric cleared his throat impatiently. Galen could visualize him with the three frown lines between his eyebrows. No point delaying further; it was time to try the equation he'd discovered, the one with the single term.

He didn't bother with any fancy gestures. If the spell did nothing, he'd look even more foolish. He closed his eyes, saw the blank screen. On it, he imposed the simple equation.

He expected the faint echo of confirmation from the chrysalis. Instead, the instant he visualized the equation, energy surged up around him in a massive, overwhelming wave. It seemed to gather itself, for a moment. Then it fell upon him, layer upon layer upon layer, the energy crushing him with suffocating concentration. He gasped, his eyes snapping open.

The molecules of the air had somehow become impossibly distant. He couldn't feel the floor beneath his feet, nor even the weight of his body.

With a great rush the energy shot out from him, pushing him back against Elric. Once again he could feel the weight of his body. He stumbled to regain his balance. As the energy concentrated around the coordinates he'd specified, a spherical area began to redden and darken.

Yet his body still did not feel normal, and more than that, the hall did not feel normal. The air felt charged, and time itself felt wrong, as if it had become sluggish, distorted. As the spherical area darkened, the faces of Kell and Isabelle on the far side of it became oddly distorted, as if he were seeing them through a soap bubble. He felt distorted as well, his left arm longer than his right, his left eye bulging outward, as if his body had become ductile. Something was deforming space and time.

This wasn't the translucent globe conjured by the two-term equation. This wasn't some magical dream made manifest through ancient technology. This was something misshapen, something horribly dangerous. His thoughts seemed fuzzy, out of focus. He had to stop it, he realized. This was his responsibility. His creation. Yet a quenching spell could unmake something only after it had been made. With the strange distortion of time, this spell was still taking shape, still making itself. What it was making itself, he didn't know.

He focused desperately, visualized the equation to access the sensors built into the chrysalis. The left side of his head seemed to be expanding. Finally the chrysalis echoed the equation, and the sensors became available. They revealed massive energy, massive instability all around.

The interior of the sphere had darkened to a reddish gray; he could no longer see Kell and Isabelle. It was as if they no longer existed.

Elric must stop the spell, Galen thought desperately. Only he could stop it while it was still in the making. He could erase it. But Galen wondered if Elric was even still there, behind him, or whether he had become twisted into something beyond recognition.

Then the dark boundary of the sphere began to contract, and the grayness within it to fade. As the sphere began to shrink, time snapped back to its normal pace. The sphere was collapsing in on itself, vanishing, and as his body drew back to its normal shape, he suddenly felt as if he could breathe.

As he sucked in a breath, Galen was pulled up short. For a moment he felt completely disoriented. Part of his mind, part of his body, seemed out of reach, as if he'd had a stroke. An iron grip held him apart. The equation in his mind was wiped away. The power associated with it drained out of him.

The sensation was different from dissociating. He wasn't separated from the chrysalis; it was still a part of him, yet that part of him was paralyzed. Galen had felt the sensation a number of times before, and it always made him sick.

Elric had shut down the tech.

A thunderclap shook the hall as the energy that formed the sphere dissipated as quickly as it had come.

Galen's sense of balance failed, and he fell to the floor, gasping. Elric moved with him, maintaining the override on the chrysalis. "Don't fight it," Elric said.

Galen couldn't make his body work. His heart sped ahead. He gagged on saliva.

Behind the shield, the mages stood in silent ranks, their faces caught in immediate, transparent reaction. They stared at him as if he was a stranger, as if he had, for the first time, revealed himself, as if they now saw the basic truth of him and realized that he was not like them, that he was something terribly different.

In the center of them sat Kell, his dark eyes studying Galen.

— chapter 4 —

Galen sat at the rough wood table in the main room of their house, his face pale, his hands in his lap. Elric observed him closely. Galen's respiration was only slightly above normal now, as was his heartbeat. Yet his eyes remained fixed on the middle distance, caught in a place where Elric could not follow. Elric knew he was shaken by the huge destructive force he had conjured.

Elric had brought him from the hall as quickly as possible, knowing that he would need time to recover from the disorientation of the override. It was always a difficult experience. And Galen's spell was something that had to be discussed privately.

Galen was nearly recovered from the override, but he seemed trapped within his thoughts, overwhelmed by them. When Galen was very upset, Elric had noticed, he always became still. In the days following his parents' funeral, he had sat on a stool by the fire with his hands folded, not moving for hours.

At that time, Elric had felt inadequate to the task of caring for Galen. He had long lived alone, and had accepted solitude as his natural condition. The roles of teacher and parent were foreign to him. He had no affinity for children, who struck him generally as irritating, unpredictable, and undisciplined. In his visits to Galen's parents on mage matters, Elric had come to find Galen somewhat less objectionable than other children. Yet he had felt uneasy in taking Galen on as his apprentice, afraid that he would be unequal to the task.

Elric had been surprised to find their natures quite suited

to each other, and somehow, Galen had developed into a promising apprentice. Sometimes, though, Elric wondered if Galen might have been better served by a teacher who could have been more of a parent.

Elric set a mug of water on the table in front of Galen, which at last brought him to life. He looked up at Elric with large, hungry eyes. "What was it?" he asked.

"I do not know."

"It was dangerous."

"So it seemed. With a power greater than any I've sensed from a conjury."

"I didn't lose control."

"That," Elric said, "is the most troubling aspect of it." At the beginning of their training, chrysalis-stage apprentices often lost control and generated violent bursts of energy. But that wasn't what Elric had observed today. Galen's spell had been focused, controlled. This hadn't been some outburst of undisciplined violence. It had been a carefully crafted, directed, outpouring of huge power. Elric had barely been able to stop it in time.

Galen shook his head. "I didn't know . . . what it would do."

"I realize that. Tell me how you arrived at this spell."

Galen brought his screen from his bedroom and led Elric through a progression of equations that he had derived from translating the works of Wierden and Gali-Gali. As Galen spoke, Elric was glad to see him become more animated.

"I realized there was no first equation in the progression, with only one term. That is what I conjured."

Elric sat beside him. "The idea of a first equation in the progression. It makes perfect sense in your spell language. Yet there is no equivalent in mine." Galen was a genius for coming up with it. Although Elric had helped Galen formulate and develop his spell language, it was vastly different from Elric's: much more complex, much more regimented. Elric had thought this would limit Galen's abilities; he had never imagined it would lead to new discoveries.

"I thought it might be a fluke of my language, that it might do nothing. But it did . . . do something."

A spell like this might explain some of the mysteries in techno-mage history. But the implications disturbed Elric. "It gathered great energy and instability."

Galen's hands tightened around the screen. He was still troubled about what he had done, and how he had come to do it. "The second term must stabilize the first. Perhaps it creates an opposing force of some kind."

"The result of the spell could not have been anticipated," Elric said.

Galen turned to him, brilliant blue eyes needy, unblinking. "How is it that my spell language led to this?"

"The same way that the study of the atom led to the atomic bomb, or the study of light to the laser. The potential was there. You discovered it."

"I intended no harm," Galen said.

"And you must make sure you never do." Through his discovery, Galen had imposed a great burden on himself. Elric wished Galen did not have to bear it, did not know if he *could* bear it. If Elric had not taught him, had not pushed him, harshly and relentlessly, Galen might never have had to bear it. But knowledge, once gained, could not be willfully forgotten. Elric stood, holding Galen's gaze. "You have a grave responsibility now, a burden that you must bear for the rest of your life. You understand, you must never conjure that spell again."

Galen put the screen down. "Yes."

"Under any circumstance. For any reason."

"Yes."

"We do not know what the effects would be, or how widespread they would be."

"Yes."

"A mage is sworn to use his powers for good, not for death or destruction."

"Yes."

"And you must never tell anyone how you arrived at the spell."

"Yes."

Elric gave a single nod. Galen had spoken with determination, but he did not yet understand what the burden meant. Elric did not fully understand it himself. All mages had great powers, and they had to learn to control those powers so that they followed the Code and did only good. They not only had to control the tech, but to control themselves, their own impulses. It required constant discipline.

Many mages, unfortunately, lost control at one time or another. Fights broke out, fireballs were cast, but usually, no permanent harm was done. Apologies could be said, and the slip could be forgotten.

But Galen could allow himself no slips. Elric had taught him discipline and control. Galen had learned better than he knew. Yet no mage had perfect control. If, in a moment of anger, he cast the spell, it could have vast, destructive consequences. Elric did not know what the spell would have done if he had not stopped it.

At least the spell had been cast in training, which meant it remained a matter between teacher and apprentice, and the Circle would not become formally involved. With them Galen would face many questions and many doubts. Elric had no doubts where Galen was concerned. He knew that Galen would devote all his efforts to obeying Elric's commands and following the Code. He was a dedicated, skilled apprentice, and he would become an exceptional mage.

The Circle would certainly want to hear informally from Elric, and some might even question whether Galen should be initiated. But Galen had done nothing wrong, and so Galen would be initiated. Elric would see to it.

Galen had taken his screen back to his bedroom, and now he returned. He tilted his head, as he did when he was about to ask a question. "It seems likely that someone would have discovered this spell before me. Is that possible? Might the knowledge be kept for safety by the Circle?"

It wasn't like Galen to question the Circle. "I know of no such discovery. I think you fail to recognize the uniqueness of your language, and what it has shown you. But if the spell was found in the past, the user might have been killed in the conjury.

"Although many outside the Circle would like to believe we are omniscient, and many within would like to appear so, our records are far from complete. Mages contribute to our archives only the knowledge they wish to share, and while in recent years that has often meant the majority of what they know, in the past many mages preferred to pass their knowledge on privately, to those of their choosing."

Galen nodded. Although the incident obviously still troubled him, he looked better. The color had come back into his face, and he seemed to have come back to himself.

"I must return to the convocation," Elric said. "You are fit?"

"Yes."

"Good. I need you to set up the Becoming."

They left the house behind and headed out across the mak. The mist had thinned since morning, and the sun was bright. In the distance Elric could see activity around the tents. Through his place of power, he accessed various probes to see what needed his attention. One probe, on the side of the tents that faced the sea, showed a group of chrysalis-stage apprentices looking out over the cliff. They reminded Elric of a topic he had long postponed discussing with Galen. He found the topic even more difficult than the one they had just discussed. But he had known, when he had seen that expression on Galen's face this morning, that he must not delay. Perhaps the change of subject would do Galen good.

"At these convocations," Elric said, "you are around Humans of your own age, including females. And now, as you are an adult, you may find a certain excitement in this. Many times, mages begin relationships with each other. These are almost always short-lived. As you know, we found long ago that mages do not do well in relationships with other mages. They are too opinionated, too intense. Disputes arise, feelings are hurt. Any attempt to create something of depth or duration ends unfortunately." He looked at Galen. "I say this merely as a precaution."

"Her shield was outstanding," Galen said.

"That it was. But there are many here with exceptional skill."

They walked in silence for a time. Galen's head lowered, and Elric could sense him falling back into worry. Yet after a minute or so he seemed to make an effort to fight it off, taking a deep breath and looking across the mak.

"Did you hear Elizar has his own ship?" Galen asked.

Elric had been anticipating those words from Galen since last night. "I saw it."

"Kell must have believed he was ready to have it."

"Apparently so."

Galen tilted his head curiously, and after a moment Elric saw him realize the argument was no longer one worth fighting. Elric had made it clear he could get his ship and begin working with it after he was initiated. Since that was only a day away, the fact that Elizar had received his ship early was not an issue.

"Where did you get that robe?" Galen asked.

"One of the apprentices gave it to me. A gift for hosting the initiation."

Galen walked backward, studying it, and Elric admired the robe again. Curving silver and copper cords adorned the front in a bold pattern, while within the fabric itself was woven a more intricate, subtle pattern.

"The hyperspace currents," Galen said.

"A fairly nice job in just two dimensions."

"Isabelle."

Elric nodded, and Galen fell into step beside him. Elric wasn't one for adornment, but the gift was a thoughtful one—it even had the high collar he favored—and he felt an unaccustomed pleasure in wearing it. He would not be pleased, however, to see Galen fall into a relationship with another mage. Galen was defenseless in matters of love, as he was in so much. His life here had been demanding, perhaps lacking in the warmth of a family, but he had been sheltered, safe. His large eyes, taught to observe, hungry to learn, were open to the world, vulnerable.

With the initiation, Elric would lose his ability to protect

Galen. Perhaps he had done Galen a disservice in protecting him too well until now. Galen would have to face the trials of life and maintain discipline, control. In his initiate stage, he would begin to travel, to choose his own goals, to find his own place. Soon enough, he would be completely independent. He would no longer be the attentive pupil shadowing Elric's every move.

And Elric would be alone.

Gowen laid the grass mats on the mak one at a time, forming a circle. He always made Galen think of a monk, for some reason—something about his serene round face, his reverent attitude toward the tech. Gowen was becoming a good healer; Galen tried to be happy for him.

Galen had a pile of mats of his own, and he laid out the other half of the circle of fifteen. He had felt better after talking to Elric, but he'd been reluctant to return to the convocation and face the others. Gowen and Carvin, at least, were treating him normally. When he had first approached them, Carvin had made a quick, sympathetic comment about training-session disasters, and then they had dropped the subject. He was grateful for that.

Still, Galen felt uneasy and self-conscious. He had thought his spell would conjure a simple globe, at most. Instead, the energies and instabilities generated had been so great, the spell could well have killed them all. He had considered that the one-term equation might be unstable, but never that it would carry such great power. He was just thankful Elric had stopped it in time, overriding his control and erasing the spell.

The mages had stared down at him as if he'd revealed something about himself, something horrible. Perhaps Galen's memory was inaccurate. The conjury had been so startling, intense, and the override so disorienting, that he might have a distorted view of their expressions.

Nonetheless, the spell had arisen out of his language, his way of thought. Did it in some way reveal him?

It was a foolish idea. The spell had been logically derived.

And as Elric had said, the power had been there. Galen had just discovered it.

Apparently a spell needed at least two terms to be stable. The spells of other mages always translated into multiterm equations. The one-term spell was an idiosyncrasy of his language, Galen had decided, not ever meant to be conjured.

Elric had compared Galen's discovery to the discovery of the atomic bomb. Perhaps, as the atomic bomb had been created by splitting an atom, the great dark sphere of energy in the training hall had been created by splitting a spell.

Galen had no idea what exactly had been forming there. The energy had been directed, gathering into the sphere, growing darker, then fading. Whether it would have lost all coherence and degenerated into wild energies, or whether it might have ultimately formed into a stable construct of some kind, like a black hole or something more exotic, he didn't know.

If only the mages had not lost the scientific knowledge of the Taratimude. They would know what had happened.

Galen laid down the last of his mats.

"How is that?" Gowen asked.

Hands on hips, Carvin appraised the situation. "That one"—she pointed at the last mat Galen had placed—"out just a little more."

Galen crouched, the chrysalis pulling at him, and adjusted the mat.

"Stop," Carvin said. "Perfect."

"The brazier is off center now," Gowen said.

Galen stepped over the mats into the center of the circle and wrestled the brazier around until Carvin and Gowen were satisfied that it was centered. Then everything was perfect.

They had set up the Becoming on the far side of the tents from the ships, near the cliffs that overlooked the sea. The echo of the waves carried up the rocks through the clouds and mist. It was a beautiful setting, and they'd found a natural depression in the mak, forming a shallow circular bowl that was perfect for the ceremony. Tonight the fifteen chrysalis-stage apprentices would sit in a circle around a conjured fire, and each would affirm his identity as a techno-mage.

Galen stepped back out over the mats. Razeel stood silently at the cliff's edge. The wind billowed through her oversized dress, swirled her thin, dark hair over her face. The others avoided her, as perhaps, some might now like to avoid him.

Galen came up beside her and looked out over the cliff. As the shrouded sun descended toward the sea, the mist was growing dark. It formed a heavy blanket below. "I've only been able to see straight down to the sea once," he said.

"Sight is illusion," she said, her voice richer and deeper than he would have expected. "The reality is sound."

"The few times I've been away from here, I've missed that sound."

"It is the sound of death," she said.

Galen didn't know how to respond. "Would you like to go into the tents? The sound will be muted there."

"No."

Galen wondered if she really could hear the tech, as Fed had said. If it did speak, what wonders would it say, what secrets would it share? Such communication would be a sign of the true fusion between mage and tech, to which Blaylock aspired, but none had yet achieved. More likely Razeel just heard herself, the echo of her own thoughts.

Elric had told Galen to check on the mages in the tent after setting up the fire circle, to see if they needed anything. The chefs and servers had been sent away for the night, all outsiders banned until the initiation in the morning was complete.

"I must go," he said. "Excuse me."

She gave no response, her face lost in windblown hair. Galen turned back to the fire circle. Fed had arrived—now that the work was done—and he stood with Carvin and Gowen.

The last thing Galen wanted was for Fed to recount what had happened in the hall. Galen waved to them. "I have to go inside."

Carvin nodded.

Galen headed into the maze of tents. On the periphery, great tables of food and drink were laid out, meant to suffice until the chefs and workers returned the next day at highsun. The food looked plentiful and well prepared, and with such variety as Galen had only seen at previous convocations. Galen's mouth watered as he counted the hours until tomorrow, when he could break his fast.

He headed deeper into the tents. The mages had adapted the tents to their needs, labeling different areas with runes and other signs. There were seminars on a variety of scientific topics, workshops on engineering techniques, roundtables on sleight of hand and other more traditional magicks, and lectures on arcane skills. Galen stopped in each tent chamber to see if anything was needed.

What Galen remembered most from previous convocations were the unscheduled sessions that ran late into the night. As tankards were repeatedly filled and emptied, and the air grew thick with spent energies, mages who seemed so stern and disciplined by day laughed at their errors, argued over technique, and told the most outrageous stories of their exploits. Most of these sessions were supposed to be private, of course, so mages would create shields or illusions of walls to keep others away. Though it was only early evening, some of these sessions had already begun. Galen talked his way into as many of them as he could to check on the participants, fetching local brew or fried chitwings when asked.

But Galen now found himself becoming quite turned around by the conjured walls and altered structure of the tents. He reached a dead end in one direction, went back in the other, only to find that, too, was now a dead end.

A single conjured globe of light illuminated the truncated passage. He reached into his pockets for his sensor-pad to get a better idea of what he was facing. It was gone. He'd left it with Isabelle.

"Hello," he called to the newly formed tent wall. It gave off a faint hum. "I'm here to see if you want anything. You've sealed me in. I need to get through." He brought his fingers to the tent fabric. The surface was hard, slippery. A shield. "Hello?"

They didn't want to be disturbed. They may have even blocked out all sound, so they wouldn't hear him no matter how loudly he yelled. He decided to search the passage more carefully. Some of the walls must be real tent flaps, and those that were could be opened up or squeezed under. Working his way down the passage, he found what appeared to be a flap. He unfastened it.

"Hello? I wonder if you need anything."

"I don't need anything," a high voice called.

Galen bent and slipped through the opening. "I don't mean to intrude," he said. "I seem to be trapped."

The room was small and irregularly shaped, an overlooked spot within the shifting structure of the tents. One person sat on the damp ground, shrouded in a cape and hood. The only light leaked through from the passage behind him.

"I can get you a better room to work," Galen said.

The figure looked up, the hood fell back. Isabelle gave him that lips-pressed-together smile. "You're trapped, and you're going to find me a better room?" She'd been disguising her voice at first.

He was glad that she still smiled at him. "The passage outside seems to have turned into quite a nice room, for now."

"I like my privacy."

"I am sorry. I'll be out in a minute." Galen ran his hands over the walls, searching for another way out. He felt like a clumsy fool.

After an awkward minute of silence, Isabelle spoke. "Burell is on our ship. Elizar has been following me everywhere I go. I thought this place seemed safe."

"Safe for what?" Another silence followed. At last she continued.

"Do you believe that what we do can be explained scientifically?" Her deliberate tone betrayed the importance of the question to her. Galen stopped his examination of the tent but kept his back to her, afraid she might turn silent if he faced her.

"Not by us. Not yet."

"But someday, do you believe it may be possible for us to understand the tech scientifically, as its inventors did?"

"Someday, yes."

"And what of the effort to achieve that understanding? Is it a mistake to examine that which we have received?"

Galen believed the knowledge far beyond their reach, and so had not considered studying how the tech worked. He knew that he had a great deal to learn before he could even attempt it. Right now he was focused on mastering the discipline of its use, on understanding and expanding his spell language. Even if he was able to master it, he would know only how to control the tech. He would know nothing of its workings. Yet to understand its workings was a noble goal, and scientific exploration was a critical part of a mage's life. "It is never a mistake to seek understanding. It has been said that the tech is too far beyond us. That we have lost so much knowledge we must work our way step-by-step back to understanding."

Suddenly she stood beside him. She carried the scents of moisture and moss, and more than that, of a subtle combination of oils and perspiration, her unique essence. She held up a screen with an image on it. "Do you know what this is?"

The image appeared to be under extreme magnification. Galen recognized the pyramid-shaped cell bodies of neurons. The cell bodies were a light tan. Overlying them was a forest of dark dendrites, the branching projections that connected neurons to each other. These neurons were densely interconnected. The image didn't look terribly different from images he had seen of the brains of different creatures, except for one thing. These cell bodies were unusually uniform, all nearly the same size and shape, and they were arranged in a uniform pattern, a pyramid pointing up followed by a pyramid pointing down followed by a pyramid pointing up. They seemed arranged to fit the most cell bodies into the most compact space. "Is this some tissue you grew?" he asked.

"It's a piece of a chrysalis."

He touched his hand to the image, surprised that he had

failed to recognize something with which he'd been so intimately connected. "I know that some of the others don't approve of this type of research, but you don't need to hide."

"Burell has forbidden me to research the tech. She has been criticized for years for her research. Kell and Elizar have ridiculed her. Blaylock has condemned her. The Circle even reprimanded her. She learned too late to keep her research to herself. She's lost her influence. She's lost her health. She doesn't want the same to happen to me." Isabelle sat back on the ground, the screen on her lap, her head bowed. Galen sat beside her.

He knew that some of the mages—Blaylock and his followers included—drew a line between scientific research of the rest of the universe, and scientific research of the tech. They argued that the tech was so incredibly advanced that its workings not only *seemed* like magic, they were indistinguishable from magic and so *were* magic, and somehow transcendent.

For them, dissecting the tech was sacrilege, tantamount to doing a DNA test on the Host at a Catholic Mass to see if it had actually transformed from bread to flesh. In any case, those who had tried in the past to understand the tech had failed. Most of the mages felt that the only path to understanding was to work toward a better understanding of the rest of the universe first. As long as the Circle knew the secret of replicating the tech so that new mages could be created, they could live with the frustrating lack of knowledge.

"Have you been able to understand anything of its workings?" he asked.

She looked up at him, her face soft in shadow. "Not much. Not yet. But Burell has. I've managed to read a few of her notes. She's discovered that the tech accesses a mage's own energy in order to sustain itself, but for conjuries it uses the zero-point energy of space itself as a nearly limitless energy supply. It's just the tip of the iceberg. But it's a beginning."

"How does she obtain tech to study?" The Circle guarded the tech and held the secret of its replication, so that rogue mages could not be created. When a mage died, the tech was cremated by magical fire, along with the mage.

"She has used my chrysalis, as have I." She leaned toward him, the light from the passage outside painting a line down her cheek. "I have a plan to get more, though. The Well of Forever." She spoke the name with a special reverence.

"You plan to find it?" Many had tried; all had failed. The Well was the legendary burial place of the earliest techno-mages, perhaps even Wierden. It was a focal point of immense power, a repository of great knowledge—and of tech. Its location—if the Well was even real—had been lost long ago.

She raised her eyebrows, her voice gaining intensity. "I *will* find it. And when I do, I'll have enough tech, and enough of the ancient knowledge, to understand it all."

The boldness of her dreams and the intensity of her commitment captivated him and humbled him. She knew who she was, what she wanted, why she would be a techno-mage. He was still struggling with those questions.

Suddenly he thought of the Becoming, where he would have to answer those questions. It would start in less than an hour. He shot to his feet. Elric would kill him. "I have to go. I'm sorry. Do you have my sensor-pad? That would help me find the quickest way out of here."

Isabelle stood and pulled the sensor-pad from her pocket. "How could I have lost track of time? I need to check on Burell. Here. I was using that during your training session today. I recorded some energy readings from your last spell. You're not going to believe them."

Galen stuck his head out into the passage, found it was no longer a dead end. He stumbled out through the tent flap, and Isabelle followed.

"I'm going this way," Galen said, starting right.

"I'm going that way," Isabelle said, starting left.

"Meet you at the Becoming," Galen said, jogging backward.

Isabelle gave a little spin and waved back at him.

He watched until she turned out of sight, his chrysalis

echoing the pounding of his heart. He felt as if he had just come to life.

Ten minutes later, he thought he must be getting close to the outside. He recognized a few of the meeting rooms, though they were now all empty. The apprentices had the Becoming to attend; the mages had the Being.

He ran around a corner and thought he had turned that corner before, possibly several times. The passage beyond was darker than the others, lit only by the rune for science glowing on the far tent wall. Something moved in front of that light, blocking it out, and Galen stopped short. The head and shoulders of a man were barely visible in dark silhouette. "Can I help you?" Galen asked.

"Can I help *you*?" the man replied, walking closer. He wasn't a mage, for his voice was untrained, yet it carried a smooth, threatening power. As the man approached, the light from behind Galen illuminated more of him. He was a compact man, with dark hair, wearing a dark, tailored suit. A silver chain at his neck caught the light. His right hand was in his pocket, his left arm bent at the elbow, hand extended.

"Are you looking for something?" Galen asked.

"Are *you* looking for something?" the man replied.

Galen expelled a breath. He didn't have time for this. "What do you want?"

The man smiled, revealing a row of perfect white teeth. "That's just what I was going to ask you."

Elric climbed into the darkness of Burell's ship. As the air lock closed behind him, the interior flooded with light, transforming itself into a vast portico decorated with sheer hanging linens. Egyptian hieroglyphs were chiseled in the stone floor. As he looked down the ranks of stone columns, Elric could see in the distance the vibrant blue sky of a late Egyptian afternoon. A breeze ran past him, and Elric appreciated the scents of myrrh, cinnamon, and sesame. It was a lovely illusion.

Burell was stretched out on a lounge in a tightly wrapped

gown of deep cranberry, dark hair piled on her head and accented with small golden starbursts. Slave men covered by the scantiest of shentis formed a semicircle behind her, two cooling her with fans of feathers, one feeding her grapes.

Elric sat in an ornate chair at her side. "I thank you for dressing the slave men."

"A token of my appreciation for your visit." She waved the slave with the grapes away. "I apologize for taking you away from the convocation. I realize this must be a very demanding time."

"You have something you need to discuss."

"Yes."

Elric saw her take a deep breath, gathering her energy. She was not doing well. Perhaps she had changed her mind about receiving healing.

"It's about my home," Burell said, surprising him. "I've noticed some disturbing activity around the spaceport on Zafran 8. We don't get much traffic there—at least we haven't in the past—for two reasons. We're on a marginal hyperspace route that connects systems off the beaten track. And what trade does come through our jumpgate uses the spaceport on Zafran 7, which is a much better facility. We get the shadier trade on Zafran 8. The port is corrupt and poorly run. It's easy to pass through without answering a lot of questions, or with falsified documentation."

Elric nodded. At least in her younger days, Burell had enjoyed the wild, anything-goes atmosphere of her adopted home. Perhaps now she sought something quieter.

"Only Kell can speak to the activity on Zafran 7, but what I've noticed is a dramatic increase in traffic through 8. We're now getting five times the number of ships passing through that we usually do. And it's not just the numbers. Ships are coming through with unfamiliar designs. Those they carry are of races that haven't been seen in a hundred years or more. Drakh, Streib, Wurt. Even poor records and falsified documents can't hide something of this scope: a mass migration of intelligent beings and resources toward the last jumpgate on our route, the one closest to the rim."

Elric and the Circle had been hearing rumors, seeing signs for the last two years. But the signs had been vague, unsubstantiated. Most of the Circle had dismissed them as unimportant. Elric had hoped his fears were unfounded, or if not unfounded, at least premature.

Burell put her palms flat against the arms of the lounge and pushed herself up straighter. "Where they go from there, I can't be sure. But my probes and my sources bring me talk, talk of a world on the rim known in legend as a dark place. Z'ha'dum.

"I know its existence has never been confirmed, but the writings of the ancients support the existence of Z'ha'dum, and of its inhabitants, the Shadows." Burell clasped his hand. Hers was cold. "Dark forces are at work on Zafran 8, Elric. And this can only be the beginning. History tells us what to expect—'a time of death and chaos.' We must gather information. We must be ready to fight."

Elric remembered his first day as a member of the Circle, the honor of serving as so many great techno-mages had served. Knowing of the many times of strife throughout their history, he had been glad he was serving in a time of relative calm. In calm he could do good, in calm he could build a future for the techno-mages. Yet mixed with his pride and honor had been an unexpected feeling of terror. It would be his responsibility—along with the rest of the Circle—to lead the mages through any crisis that might occur. They would depend on him for wisdom, for answers. His one hope had been that no great crisis would arise during his tenure. "If the Shadows are returning, it will mean a galactic war. Everything that has been built will be torn asunder."

"I am not well liked in the Circle," Burell said with dry understatement. "If I come to them with this evidence, I fear they may discount it because of the source. I don't know if others have seen similar signs, but I know what I have seen, and I know we must take action. I need your support to convince the Circle."

"They are never easily convinced of anything. Only if

there is clear, compelling evidence will a majority endorse action."

"Here is what I know."

Elric's implants informed him he had received a message. It was from Burell. In his mind's eye, he opened it. The message contained all the evidence she had compiled. Elric scanned it quickly. Accounts of ships, passengers, equipment. Hyperspace routes. Covert activities. He didn't know if the others would be convinced, but for him, the fear of the last two years at last took certain form, manifesting itself in substance and shape—the substance of darkness, and the shape of the Shadow. "I will go with you to the Circle."

"Thank you, Elric." She drew her hand back, shifting uncomfortably.

"We can meet with them after the initiation tomorrow. For now, it is time for the Being. Are you prepared?" The Being was central to each convocation. But it was a time for truth, not illusion. Elric didn't know if Burell would attend.

Burell lowered her legs over the side of the lounge with great deliberateness, as if she had to concentrate to make them respond. Pushing herself up with the arms of the lounge, she managed to stand. Elric joined her. Suddenly they stood beneath a single globe of light in a small, dark room. Burell's cranberry gown had become a plain black robe. Her coiffed hair had vanished to reveal a bare head. Her shoulders were hunched, her body held at an angle, as if it had lost its symmetry. Her face also carried a hint of asymmetry, as if all the pieces didn't quite fit together. Elric wondered again what illness had struck her.

Burell reached into the darkness and found her staff. She planted it firmly on the floor to support her weight. Elric offered his arm for further support. She took it, leaning heavily on him, and they walked out into the dusk.

The chrysalis-stage apprentices were gathering for the Becoming. Galen stood beside the circle of grass mats, awaiting the arrival of Kell, who would conjure a fire in their brazier. Elric had told Galen that he must act as host for this event.

Once Kell had conjured the fire, he would join the other mages around their own circle for the Being, and the chrysalis-stage apprentices would be left to carry on by themselves. The muscles in Galen's legs were still burning from his marathon run through the tents. He looked around anxiously. The mist was thin, the night illuminated by globes of light. Several of the apprentices had not yet arrived, and they were due to start within a few minutes. He saw Fa crouching in the shadows by the side of the tents. Galen went over to her. Her fists were jammed under her chin. She looked as if she'd been there for some time.

"You have to go back to town. This is a private time for the mages. You can't be here."

She did not look up at him. "You will be—initiated?"

"This is the start of it. Go home now. Go on." He shooed her away, and she ran back toward Lok. Galen was about to return to the fire circle when he saw Elizar and Isabelle standing farther around the curve of the tents. They were on the wide strip of land between the tents and the cliff that overlooked the sea. Elric and Galen had set it up as a scenic walk illuminated by globes of light, though it was empty now save for Isabelle and Elizar. Against the blackness of the land's end, their figures seemed almost to glow.

Isabelle had her back to him, as if she were heading toward the ships and Burell. It seemed as if she had never reached her destination. Elizar was leaning toward her. He gestured in a sharp chopping motion.

Galen approached them. This afternoon, Isabelle had said Elizar was following her. Was Elizar trying to gain her support as well? Or was his interest related to the training session today? Galen was suddenly overcome with the fear that Elizar was attracted to Isabelle.

"A shield cannot carry that kind of power." Elizar's hand again chopped down through the air, his tone argumentative. "Not any shield that we know." He was so intent on Isabelle that he didn't notice Galen until Galen came up beside them.

Isabelle's face was flushed and her eyes wide. Her hands were clenched together in front of her. "I don't know what else to say. I'm not keeping any great secret from you. My shield has no greater power than others."

Elizar flung his arms wide, pacing out a small circle. "Then my weapons should have been successful. Projectiles of that size and energy should have been able to break through."

Galen's heart jumped to a more rapid beat. They were both agitated. Galen felt he should say something to calm them, but he didn't know what to say. A sickening sense of dread came over him, a feeling from the past.

Isabelle glanced at Galen. "My weave is very tight. Perhaps that's the difference. With most shields a tiny projectile can slip through."

"That's it," Galen said. "I was watching on my sensor-pad"—he took it from his pocket—"and the energies were woven so tightly together the spikes couldn't find a way through. It wasn't the power of the shield that stopped you. It was the integrity. Your strategy would have worked well on most shields, but with Isabelle's, the best attack would be one with all the energy concentrated at a single point. If that energy is greater than the energy of the shield, it will have to fail."

Elizar straightened, his hands falling to his sides. "You haven't found a secret for a more powerful shield, then."

"No," Isabelle said. "I wish I had."

Elizar's voice was soft. "I wish you had too."

Galen released a breath, relieved that the argument seemed to be over. "We should go to the fire circle."

Elizar's gaze fell on the sensor-pad in Galen's hand. "You took some readings when Galen was training, didn't you?" he said to Isabelle.

"A few," she said. "I haven't had time to look at them yet."

She was lying, Galen knew. Why? There was no way the readings could be used to derive the spell that had generated them. The spell hadn't even fully formed. Yet the readings must be so alarming that Isabelle felt they should not be shared.

But would the lie work? Although Elizar wasn't supposed to use his chrysalis without Kell present, perhaps, if he was upset enough, he would. A skilled mage could detect lies through his sensors, monitoring heartbeat, respiration, blood flow to the skin, pupil size, voice stress. Some mages could regulate these functions, and so mask their lies. Galen had failed at this thus far; he didn't know the extent of Isabelle's skills. Yet for Elizar even to be monitoring her—for one mage to suspect another of lying—would show how far the conversation had deteriorated. And he didn't understand why.

Elizar's hand curled inward; his thumb began its circular course around his fingertips. "You and Burell are quite the pair. You claim to have the ability to understand the tech through scientific inquiry, yet what have you found? By the time you discover anything useful, it will be too late."

Elizar knew of a threat—*a threat not only to us, but to everyone,* he had said—and he was desperate to find some weapon to fight it. But his urgency did not make sense.

He acted as if the threat were here, now. Yet if that were so, the other mages would have to know about it. Galen found himself breathing hard, his system racing. The chrysalis echoed his anxiety.

Elizar's angular face turned toward Galen. "What spell did you conjure this morning in the training hall?"

Galen wanted to help his friend, but he couldn't. The spell was too destructive. It could never be used. Galen shook his head. "I . . . I don't really know."

"That's impossible, Galen!" Elizar yelled. "You always know. I told you this very morning of secrets being kept from us. Now you are keeping one of those secrets. Why would you do that? Why are you both keeping secrets from me?" Elizar looked from Galen to Isabelle, his chest heaving, mouth open, caught between fear and anger.

A surge of adrenaline shot through Galen. His heart pounded, and the pounding echoed back to him from the chrysalis with anticipation and readiness.

"Let me see the readings," Elizar said, extending his hand. "Perhaps *I* can find the time to look at them."

Galen took a step back.

"What's this?" Elizar's voice broke.

"It's too dangerous," Galen said.

Elizar gave a truncated laugh, throwing up his arms with a flourish. "Too dangerous. You have no idea what's going on. Most of them don't. They do their petty stage-magician tricks and pat themselves on the back. They have no idea what our true potential is." He leaned over Galen, enunciating his words with frightening intensity. "We have greater powers, Galen, than we know. If we are to survive what comes, if we are to make a difference, if we are to restore the glory of the techno-mages, we must know the full extent of that power. We must learn the secrets of the tech. If we don't find out . . ."

Elizar's hand clenched into a fist. "When I discovered the Circle—and Kell—withholding such information . . . I felt as if I had lost my parents. And now you. I've no one to trust here. No one at all." He strode away, stopped, turned back to face them, a pale figure against the darkness. "You want power for yourselves, is that it?"

"No," Galen said.

Elizar's eyes narrowed. "Of course not, how could you. You haven't the ambition, or the imagination. You are a technician," he spat at Galen. "You," he said to Isabelle, "a frustrated scientist. You bury your noses in study and play at being wizards. You keep your secrets. You do what the Circle tells you. You crawl when you could fly. But you know what happens to those who crawl? They are crushed."

Elizar cupped his hands around his mouth. A sustained syllable emerged from deep in his throat.

"No," Isabelle said.

Galen felt his chrysalis echoing the spell before he even realized he'd intended to cast it. His action had been instinctive, immediate. He had to stop the attack, to protect himself and Isabelle, and to do so his mind had jumped to the equation he'd conjured today, the first spell in the progression. The chrysalis, in an adrenaline-heightened state, responded instantly.

Energy suffocated him with its crushing pressure and then shot outward. Galen stumbled, jerking his head up toward

Elizar, immediately realizing his great mistake. A spherical area surrounding Elizar began to redden and darken.

Galen could cast a quenching spell, but it would not begin to dissolve the sphere until it had fully formed. That would be too late. But if he could not dissolve the spell, perhaps he could alter it. Galen desperately visualized adding the second term to the equation.

Time turned sluggish, distorted, and Galen's arm was suddenly long enough for the hand holding the sensor-pad to hit the ground. Within the reddening sphere, Elizar's body deformed, as if Galen saw him through a distorting lens. His head and hands stretched tall, his fingers rippling. Then something emerged from Elizar's cupped hands. It was not a spike at all but an image, a malformed image that expanded to float and undulate in the air: Elric's circle of moss-covered standing stones, crumbling to dust.

The chrysalis echoed Galen's new command, but the echo was distorted, a smeared superposition of the one-term and two-term equations. A ringing dissonance racked the air, and the sphere surrounding Elizar rippled. Elizar took his hands from his mouth, revealing an opening that had once been a mouth but could be called one no longer, the dark cavity twisting and stretching and curving back on itself in some abstract pattern that no longer looked Human.

The vibration built until Galen thought space itself would be ripped apart, and all of them with it. Then the right side of the sphere bloomed open like a dark flower. And with a great crack the orifice exploded in a stream of fire.

Time and space snapped back to normality, and Galen found himself flying back through the air. As he hit the mak and tumbled backward, he saw Elizar screaming, covered in flame.

— chapter 5 —

Galen ran toward Elizar and Elric. To his left, Isabelle sat in darkness near the cliff, where she had been thrown, her legs splayed out in front of her. To his right, fire roared through the tents.

Within seconds of the explosion, Elric had arrived on a flying platform. He knelt over Elizar. Galen stopped behind him. The smell of charred meat passed on the air. Without turning, Elric reached back, grabbed Galen's arm, and pulled him to his knees beside Elizar. Galen was shocked to see that Elizar only looked stunned. His eyes were fixed on some point in the sky, and his mouth released short, rapid breaths.

"Have I taught you nothing?" Elric whispered.

Elric's head was bowed, and Galen followed his gaze down to Elizar's left arm, which lay before them. It was black. At first he didn't understand what he was looking at. Then he realized that the jacket sleeve had been burned away. What remained of Elizar's arm was thin, almost skeletal, with a leathery, black surface. Elizar's hand was a petrified claw. It gleamed in the firelight with an unnatural shininess.

Here was the source of the charred-meat smell.

Others swooped down around them. Ing-Radi immediately came to Elizar's side. With only a glance of her slit pupils at Galen, she extended her four orange hands toward Elizar.

"No," Elric whispered. "Galen must do it."

Elric's face, for the first time in Galen's experience, had lost its sternness. Even when Elric was in a good mood, his face always carried a tension to it, a sense of discipline, as if he were always examining, evaluating. Yet now it was completely relaxed—no lines between the eyebrows, no stern compression of lips. It was as if he had lost control of it, as if he was so far away from Galen, and from this moment, that he had left his body behind.

Galen realized he had destroyed any chance he had of becoming a techno-mage, that he had gone against everything the mages stood for. He couldn't even fulfill this one last task Elric had set him. "I can't," Galen said.

That brought the sternness back to Elric's face. "You will." Elric laid his hands on Elizar's arm, sending a fleet of microscopic organelles from his body into Elizar's. From his pocket, he brought a crystal hanging from a silver chain. He laid it in Galen's hand. Then Elric stood and took his place behind Galen, taking hold of the chrysalis.

Elizar's good arm rose a few inches, flopped back down. "I can"—each syllable came out with a panting exhalation—"do it myself." His face had gone white.

Elizar was in no shape to heal himself. Galen had no choice but to try. He closed his eyes and visualized the equation to access the crystal and the organelles with which it communicated. The crystal requested Elric's key, the secret symbol that would allow Galen control. Elric used the same key on all the probes and devices to which he wanted Galen to have access. Galen visualized it, and the crystal's systems became available to him.

He held the crystal by the end of its chain over Elizar's arm. The organelles had very weak transmitters, and so could not transmit information from one body to another without some mechanism to boost their signal. The crystal had been designed and built by the mages to serve that purpose.

In his mind's eye he received images and data from the organelles, as they moved through the injured area. The skin had been completely burned away. Great masses of dead fat and muscle tissue dominated the layers near the surface, looking very much like cooked meat. In some places the fat had protected the muscle beneath; in others, such as the hand, the burn had penetrated deep into muscle. Nerves were dead or overloaded with conflicting signals. Capillaries were broken, clogged, melted.

Farther below, healthy cells did survive. New tissue could grow. With traditional medical treatment, over time, Elizar would heal, though he would never regain full use of his limb.

From Galen's early years of study, before he'd realized he had no aptitude for healing, he had an idea of what needed to be done. First, nerve impulses to the burn area had to be blocked. Then healthy skin cells at the edge of the burn needed to be stimulated to grow skin over the arm. This would keep moisture in and microorganisms out. At the same time, blood vessels at the edge of the burn would need to send out capillaries to provide blood flow to the new skin. All dead tissue had to be liquefied and drained from beneath this new skin, and then within that underlying space the necessary muscles, nerves, arteries, veins, and tissue must grow. Finally, the nerve block had to be removed.

The problem was that healing didn't work this way. There was no spell to block nerve signals, or to stimulate the growth of skin over an area. In all the reading Galen had done, in all the discussions he'd had with Elric, Ing-Radi, and others, he'd never found a concrete link between the healing tasks that needed to be done and the spells that were cast. And so he'd been unable to successfully translate any healing spells into his language of equations. Healing spells were the most complex of any used by mages. In Ing-Radi's case they were songs she hummed with barely any variation in volume or pitch. Her explanation for how they worked was equally obscure. *You must understand the damage. You must find the shape of what needs to be done. And you must become that shape.* In her case, the shape was the shape of sound.

Galen could accomplish the first step, understanding the damage. But he didn't know how the necessary healing actions could comprise a "shape," or how he could become that "shape."

In the past, when he had tried his uncertain translations of healing spells, none had any significant effect. If this was to be his last act as an apprentice mage, he would try his best to do what was required, to at least in some small way undo the horrible wrong he had done.

He took a deep breath and cleared his mind. He visualized Elizar's arm, the damage the organelles had shown him within it. He visualized the healing that needed to occur—the nerves, the skin, the capillaries. He searched for a shape to the healing, a sound, a word, an equation. He imagined the microscopic organelles moving about. Like the chrysalis, like the implanted tech, they were organic technology, a hybrid of the biological and the electronic. He visualized them providing chemicals to block neuronal signals, stimulating particular cells to divide, gathering and liquefying dead cells. He felt no echo within the chrysalis, no sense of an order being received and carried out.

He was simply breaking the healing down into tasks again, rather than viewing it in some holistic way as a shape. He tried again, blanking his mind, praying for some insight, some way to help. He had lost his parents to fire, had determined to become a healer to undo such damage. Instead, he had become the source of fire.

He could find no "shape" to the healing. Perhaps that was the most important lesson of his apprenticeship. He had wanted to be a healer, and he had failed. He had injured his friend, and now he could not help him.

Before him on the mak, Elizar's arm lay black and shiny. His chest continued to flutter in rapid, shallow pants. His gaze was fixed on Galen.

"I'm sorry," Galen said. "I'm sorry. I'm sorry I hurt you. I'm sorry I can't fix it. I don't know how."

Galen felt Elric release the chrysalis, turned to see him walking away.

Ing-Radi leaned across Elizar's body and laid her hands on his arm. She wore her crystal on a long chain, and it hung over his body as she worked. After a few seconds, she closed her eyes and began to hum. Elizar's breathing began to slow, and some color returned to his face. Galen tried to follow the slight variations in pitch, in volume. The sound carried hints of patterns upon patterns upon patterns, overlapping and interfering with each other in such complexity that any overall pattern was lost. The humming seemed tuneless, shapeless, yet Galen found himself caught in it. He realized he had no idea how long he'd been listening to it.

Pale, hairless skin began to grow down from the shoulder over the charred arm, like a sleeve. Ing-Radi was not only stimulating the right types of cells to divide, but guiding them into the right pattern, an impossibly complex task. The skin spread down over the elbow, the forearm, the wrist, the fixed claw of the hand, closing itself around the fingers.

For a time after that, there was little external change. Then a tiny slit appeared in the skin just above Elizar's elbow, and yellow-brown pus began to stream out of it. Several other slits appeared up and down the arm, releasing more of the liquefied tissue. It smelled like rancid fat. As the ruined tissue drained away, the new skin became baggy and wrinkled, hanging on the remnant of the arm.

At last the pus stopped draining, and the tiny slits healed. The structures beneath were now being rebuilt, nerve fibers growing along their old pathways, tracks of collagen forming to act as the foundation for tendons, muscles being reconstructed from what had been undamaged. The arm began to regain its shape, and the skin was pushed outward, wrinkles smoothing out. The arm gained a slightly pinkish tone. Finally, the hand opened, relaxed.

Ing-Radi at last straightened, and her humming stopped. The arm had an odd look to it, too uniform, too soft, yet it appeared restored. Elizar was asleep, his breathing calm, his color good.

Isabelle gasped as Ing-Radi fell over into her arms. "Are you all right?" Isabelle asked. "Do you need anything?"

"I am fine," Ing-Radi said. But her skin had gone from its normal intense orange to a paler shade, and she seemed unable to straighten.

"She needs rest," Kell said. "Blaylock, if you please."

Blaylock gave a short nod and knelt beside Ing-Radi, taking her from Isabelle.

Galen realized that his legs below the knees had gone

numb, and the rest of his body was stiff. Many hours had passed since Ing-Radi had begun her healing. He'd somehow been caught in her song and lost track of time. At some point most of the mages had left or been sent away. All that remained now were the members of the Circle—save Elric—and he and Isabelle.

Blaylock conjured a flying platform for himself and Ing-Radi and guided them toward her ship.

Kell conjured a platform below Elizar, raised him several feet off the ground. Although Kell's face was in shadow, Galen sensed Kell's dark eyes studying him. From the darkness came a heavy sigh. "You are not injured?" he asked.

"No," Galen said, and Isabelle echoed him.

"We will discuss this in the morning," he said. His steps were heavy as he walked away with Elizar and Herazade.

Galen felt no desire to stand. He felt no desire to move, ever again.

"I thought he was going to attack us too," Isabelle said. "He was so angry. I had my hands ready to conjure a shield the entire time we were talking."

Galen remembered her hands clenched together in front of her, remembered the tiny movements that had generated the shield back in the hall. He realized now that she had thrown up a shield, in the middle of everything. He hadn't needed to act at all.

"You walked in on the middle of it," Isabelle said. "You weren't as prepared as I was."

"It never occurred to me that he would attack us, until he brought his hands to his mouth. Then it was just instinct," Galen said. "Somehow it was just my first reaction. My first reaction to kill him. I don't know why."

"But—you did something, didn't you? Something to stop it. It wasn't the same as in the hall."

"I tried to make it harmless. It was too late."

They remained in silence for a few minutes. Then Isabelle extended her hand. She held the sensor-pad. "You dropped this. In the explosion."

Galen took it. He was out of words.

"I better go. Burell will be worried."

Galen nodded. Her dark figure vanished into the mist.

He couldn't go home now, couldn't face Elric. He would leave tomorrow, after he made sure Isabelle and Elizar were not blamed for what had happened. He would go to the city, find a job. Give up any dreams of being just a little bit in control of events around him, of manipulating power and using it for good.

Better to do no harm.

The wind had calmed, and the night was quiet, except for the susurration of the sea. *The sound of death,* Razeel had called it.

Galen looked absently at the sensor-pad, pressed its buttons without thought, called up the record of what he had done in the hall. It had recorded the same great energies, the same great instabilities that his sensors had found. Yet it recorded other details as well. It not only had a sophisticated array of sensors built into it, but it gathered information from sensors Elric had in place all about the planet.

Galen had thought perhaps the sphere was a black hole, based on the distortion of time and space. Yet a black hole would have pulled them all toward it, and this did not. Some of the readings suggested a wormhole or jump point, yet those would have radiated energy, and the sphere did not. According to the data, the energy he had first sensed all around him had gathered itself in the membrane of the sphere. As the sphere formed, it seemed to seal itself off more and more from the surrounding hall. The images of Kell and Isabelle standing on the far side of the sphere, which had at first been visible through the sphere, had later been blocked by it. The light that had been contained within the spherical area when the spell was cast found it harder and harder to escape, so that the sphere seemed to darken. The reddening of the light suggested a Doppler shift, as if the sphere were moving rapidly away from them.

Just before Elric had interrupted the spell, the sphere had begun to fade and collapse. The energy readings had begun to drop back to a more normal range, as if the membrane and what was contained within it were simply vanishing.

Yet energy didn't simply disappear. It went elsewhere. As he thought about it, the fading was the last logical step in the sphere's process of sealing itself off. It had not only sealed itself off from the light and energy in the hall, but from the space and time in the hall. The sphere had pinched itself off into a separate universe.

Although he couldn't be sure, that would explain the fading, the return to normality. But why had the sphere begun to shrink at the end? The gravitational waves recorded by the sensor-pad indicated major instabilities. The universe created seemed inherently unstable, in a state of collapse.

The second term of the equation must be the one to stabilize the sphere, to make conditions within it consistent with those without, and to allow the passage of energy, space, and time in and out of the sphere. In the absence of that second term, the sphere tried to seal itself off from everything, and in so doing, destroyed itself.

The image returned to him—the sphere reddening and darkening around Elizar. How could he have cast that spell against his friend? If he hadn't altered the spell, would Elizar have been sealed into his own universe, a collapsing universe that would have crushed him to nothingness?

He could not be sure. He still hadn't seen the final result of the spell. Perhaps the membrane holding the unstable universe would fail, its energies flying out like a miniature big bang. The contents of the two universes would mix, and if the physical constants, the physical laws governing them differed, it could trigger a huge chain reaction of destruction.

Other mages fought, yes, but it was sound and fury, fireballs and shields, contests like Elizar and Isabelle had fought in the hall. No mage had died of anything but old age in hundreds of years.

Gradually Galen became aware of a sound beneath the steady murmur of the sea, a quiet sobbing. He searched for the source, found a dark silhouette in the mist. He climbed awkwardly to his feet. His legs refused to move at first, until the blood circulation returned. As his legs began to tingle he moved toward the sound, dragging his feet ahead step by step.

He stopped a short distance away from the figure, still unsteady. "Fa." He had told her to go home.

"That man went on fire."

He could barely see her in the dark, in the mist. She was crouching on the ground. "Yes."

"Why did he do that?"

"He didn't," Galen said. "I did."

She wiped at her eyes. "I don't want to see any more people on fire."

"Then you better go home." He realized how late it was, how tired and scared she must be. He bent and opened his arms. "I'll carry you."

She skittered away from him. "No. I can go myself." He had wanted her to respect the power of the mages. Now she did. She was terrified of him.

"I won't hurt you."

She popped to her feet and ran into the night.

Then he was alone.

He felt the worst for Elric. Elric hadn't been able to choose his own apprentice, instead being saddled with Galen. He'd dedicated eleven years of his life to teaching Galen, only to have his undeserving student fail so miserably on the night before initiation. Galen wanted everyone to know it wasn't Elric's fault. Elric had been the best teacher an apprentice could have.

The fault was in him. Galen hauled the sensor-pad back and threw it over the cliff. It disappeared in silence.

Elric raced across the mak on a flying platform, late for the meeting of the Circle. He was not himself. He'd lost track of the time, sitting up all night, and had nearly forgotten to scour his head.

His place of power informed him of the various tasks it had performed and the latest data it had collected, as it did every morning. It alerted him to situations he had been monitoring; it summarized the images collected by the probes; it presented him with options he commonly accessed in the morning. Each morning—as each night—he liked to access probes across the planet, checking on this place of which he had made himself a part, to keep their bond strong, to help the planet and its inhabitants as needed.

This morning, though, he had to neglect that part of himself. He had no time for the beauty of the morning, for the sun, the mist, or the sea breeze. His mind refused to focus, save on one thing.

Elric flew into the tents and headed toward the chamber where the Circle was to meet. Unlike the vast chamber he originally had set aside for the Circle, this one was small, only twenty feet in diameter. About a third of the tents had been lost last night to the fire. The remainder he had reorganized after the fire had at last been stopped. They would be short on space. They would require replacements of supplies. He would make do.

He dissolved his platform outside the chamber, pulled aside the tent flap, entered. The other four members of the Circle were already there.

"My apologies for the delay," Elric said.

As usual, Ing-Radi had created the illusion of the great stone amphitheater at which, legend had it, Wierden and the original Circle had met. The mak on which he stood formed the floor of the amphitheater, and around it in a circle rose tier upon tier of stone levels, a vast dome of blue-green sky and a pale yellow sun visible at the top. The diameter of the amphitheater was smaller than usual, to fit within the constraints of the chamber, but still the illusion gave the sense of a much greater space than the one in which they actually stood.

The nonexistent sunlight shone down at an angle, illuminating the ground and the lower levels of the far side of the amphitheater. The air even felt drier, as if he had stepped onto another planet. Around the bottom level of stone glowed the seven runes representing the seven principles of the Code.

The setting reminded them all of the history of the Circle, and of the responsibility each held as a member of it. It was a responsibility Elric took very seriously, and it was a responsibility that, for the first time, demanded of him something he did not think he could do.

He visualized a flying platform that resembled in shape and color a large stone chair. It appeared, and he sat down on it, then raised the chair eight feet to give the illusion that it rested on the first tier of the amphitheater, along with the others. They were spaced out in a semicircle, Kell in the center, Ing-Radi and Elric to his left, Blaylock and Herazade to his right.

Kell pushed himself up from his seat with the support of his ivory staff. He looked tired, his shoulders more hunched than usual, the creases around his eyes deeper. The incident had upset him deeply. He began the meeting as was customary, and his vibrant voice carried a slight echo, part of Ing-Radi's illusion. "We of the Circle meet to uphold solidarity, secrecy, mystery, magic, science, knowledge, and good."

Kell had loved Elizar from his infancy, delighting in his first step, his first word, just as a father would with a son. But Kell had also been proud of Elizar, as a teacher was with a pupil. He took great pains to make Elizar into a leader who could think independently, act decisively, and one day guide the techno-mages. He noted each of Elizar's accomplishments with great joy. Kell had once confided in Elric that he saw something in Elizar, some hint of future greatness.

For himself, Elric found Elizar's most admirable quality his passion for the history and accomplishments of the mages. That had drawn Galen to him. Yet in Elric's opinion, Elizar took his future leadership a bit too much for granted. He had shown signs of arrogance. Although this trait was not rare among techno-mages, it was a poor quality in a leader. And Elizar's behavior last night, which Elric had later observed through a probe's recording, was extremely troubling.

Still, Elric hoped that somehow Kell was right, and that Elizar would be the great leader to take his place. He knew how much Elizar meant to Kell. Almost as much as Galen meant to him.

Kell asked Ing-Radi to report on Elizar's health, and then he sat.

Ing-Radi laid her hands, palms up, one on top of the other, and bowed her head. She returned her hands to the four arms of her chair. Her movements were graceful, hypnotic. "The burns were severe. Some scarring remains, both internally and externally. He can retrain himself to use the rebuilt muscles. He can retrain himself to understand the sensory input of the regrown nerves. He can work to regain his muscle tone. In a short time, he should have partial use of the arm. He will never recover its full use, though."

Kell leaned forward in his chair. "When he receives the implants—will they not further the healing?"

"All that can be done, I have done. I am sorry."

The three apprentices were called in. Although Elric had shared his probe's recording with the rest of the Circle, so that all knew what had happened, those involved must be questioned to see if they would give an accurate accounting.

Galen's cheeks were dark with stubble, and his robe hung heavy with moisture. He must have sat out on the mak all night. His chrysalis even seemed slightly discolored, with hints of yellow among the silver. He took his place with the others before the Circle and stood completely still, head bowed. He expected to be cast away, Elric realized. And could there be any other possible outcome?

Isabelle's robe was wrinkled, but she looked clearheaded and determined. Elric accessed his sensors. Her heartbeat and respiration were high, signs of nervousness most likely.

Elizar actually looked the best of the three of them. He was dressed in a clean outfit of blue velvet, which meant he had removed his chrysalis temporarily, in violation of custom. His left arm hung limply at his side. Elric knew he must be exhausted; the healing process put a great strain on the body. Yet he carried himself proudly.

"We would know what happened last night between the three of you," Kell said. In a precise gesture, he extended two fingers toward Isabelle. "Speak."

Isabelle bowed her head. As she began to recount what had happened, Elric found himself thinking of Tilar, who had been cast away by the Circle three years ago, on the eve of his initiation. This was rare, since most unfit apprentices were weeded out long before that point. Tilar had been a student of Regana, who was a good mage, though perhaps she had blinded herself to the flaws of her student.

Now Regana seemed a ghost of her former self, lacking in energy, will, joy. The failure of Tilar, after she had devoted so much of her life to him, had devastated her. Maintaining any relationship with him was forbidden, once he had been cast away. Elric wondered, for the first time, what had become of him.

"Elizar insisted that my shield had some special power," Isabelle continued. "He pressed me to tell him its secret. I told him there was no secret, but he would not accept that. He became very agitated. I was alarmed by his vehemence, his insistence. Something serious has been troubling him. He believes the mages are under a threat of some kind. I don't—"

"If Elizar has such concerns," Kell said, "he can bring them before the Circle." He ran his index finger over his goatee, one of the few gestures Kell made that was not precisely formulated, controlled. Elric had seen him do it only a handful of times before, all when he was deeply upset. "Please focus on the incident."

It struck Elric suddenly that more had occurred yesterday than a fight between two poorly disciplined mages. Elizar had been speaking of a danger, a threat to their survival. But what danger could so frighten him? Did he have evidence that the Shadows were returning? And if he knew, and Kell knew, why would Kell try to keep this knowledge from the rest of the Circle?

As with everything involving the mages, nothing was just what it seemed. There were layers on layers, circles within circles. And as with Carvin's well-crafted conjury involving Alwyn's boots, there was always misdirection.

Isabelle took a breath, clearly frustrated that she couldn't speak of Elizar's concerns. Then she continued. "As I said, Elizar was extremely agitated. I believed he might attack me, and I was prepared to conjure a shield."

Kell revealed nothing, yet Elric knew he must be disappointed with Elizar.

"I was relieved when Galen joined us. Galen convinced Elizar that my shield had no special power. But then Elizar began to question Galen about the spell he'd done in the hall. Elizar wanted to know how it had been accomplished." Isabelle's voice strengthened, and she enunciated deliberately. "He seemed to feel an urgent need for this information. He accused us of wanting power for ourselves, of withholding information at the behest of the Circle. He said we wanted to crawl when we could fly, and those who crawled were crushed."

Blaylock made a disapproving grunt.

"Then he brought his hands to his mouth, as he had done in the hall, and I was certain he was going to attack. I had been prepared to throw up a shield, and so I did. Galen, I think, was more shocked, and instinctively cast a counterattack. I thought I recognized the same effect he'd created in the hall. A sphere formed around Elizar and began to darken. But then it changed, distorting and releasing a plume of fire. Galen told me later he had tried to change the spell, to neutralize it, but apparently that was only partially successful."

Elric had been occupied elsewhere, preparing the Being, when all this had transpired. He'd been flipping through images from his probes, searching for some tardy mages, when he'd checked the probe on the side of the tents that faced the sea. He had seen only the very end of the confrontation, and had sped toward them immediately, terrified Galen would be injured.

Later, Elric had accessed the probe's record, stored in his place of power. It was then he saw the full confrontation, as Isabelle had described it, Elizar's extreme agitation and Galen's precipitous attack. He had watched it over and over through the night, haunted by memories. Galen's instincts were wrong, as seemed true in so many mages. In this case, vastly, dangerously wrong.

It had been perhaps his one hundredth viewing when Elric noticed an abrupt dip in the energy generated by Galen as he cast his spell. Elric isolated the second in which the spell was cast, accessed energy readings every tenth of a second, then every hundredth, every thousandth. There he found Galen's attempt to alter the spell, the energy vibrating wildly out of control. Galen had tried to stop the destruction, to reverse his error. But the attempt had come too late.

Isabelle's gaze met each member of the Circle in turn. "I should have gone to Burell or someone else when Elizar first confronted me, rather than considering the use of my chrysalis, which is forbidden. I blame myself for the escalation of events."

Burell had raised a truly outstanding mage. Isabelle had skill, determination, and honor.

"We thank you for your truthful accounting," Kell said. "Galen, have you anything to add?"

Galen raised his head. His eyes were hollow, the planes of his stubbled cheeks drawn. "Yes. Isabelle is wrong. What happened was my fault alone. I misread the situation, and I reacted prematurely and violently." His gaze remained focused on Kell, avoiding Elric. "Elric had forbidden me ever to use that spell again. We both realized that it carried the possibility of great destruction. I violated Elric's instruction. I violated the Code. I injured Elizar, I endangered the lives of all the mages, and more than that, I endangered the lives of all." It was an unqualified admission, as Elric had taught him to make. Galen bowed his head, unable to look at any of them any longer.

"Elizar," Kell said, "what have you to say?"

Elizar had been studying Galen intently, and it took him a moment to realize he'd been addressed. He turned to face the Circle and gave a deep bow, his left arm dangling. "Esteemed mages. I desired only to learn from my fellow apprentices. I apologize that my desire was so strong it somehow caused anxiety. I take very seriously the charge to 'know all that can be known.' I was disappointed at their failure to share information, and I acted improperly, using my chrysalis to conjure an image that I hoped might remind them of the necessity for solidarity and cooperation.

"At no time did I intend an attack upon Isabelle or Galen." He hesitated a moment, then raised his good hand, palm upward. "I would like to request lenience toward both Galen and Isabelle. As the injured party, I hold no ill will toward them. We are all young; we were all unwise. We all regret what has happened. Galen and Isabelle are both great assets to us and should not be cast away. For that I humbly beg you." Elizar bowed again.

He was full of surprises, Elric thought. To harass Galen and Isabelle for secrets of power, to accuse them of seeking power for themselves. And then, when attacked, to request leniency for them. Perhaps Elizar felt more regret than he revealed. Of course, if Galen and Isabelle were cast away, Elizar would never be able to learn their secrets.

"Does the Circle require any further information?" Kell asked.

If all went as usual, Blaylock would present some challenge or complication. Blaylock and Kell were often at odds, and Elric learned much from their disputes while revealing nothing himself. Elric hoped Blaylock's instincts would not fail him this time.

Blaylock stood, a severe figure with his black skullcap and gaunt face. His pale skin, scoured of all hair, including eyebrows, had an almost waxy sheen. Blaylock did not need to stand to speak—Elric stood only when he had something of particular import to convey—yet Blaylock always stood, claiming the floor and discouraging interruptions, even if he had only a single word to say. "Isabelle spoke of a threat to the mages," Blaylock said, dependably resurrecting the topic Kell had tried to bury. "Elizar, what threat is this?"

Elizar's heart rate jumped, and his right hand curled closed, his thumb running nervously around his fingertips. He bowed, stalling for time. He couldn't lie without risking discovery, yet for the clever, there were ways around lying. "You may find my comments presumptuous, but I believe the techno-mages are threatened by decay. Our numbers have been declining, our accomplishments lessening, our reputation fading. I fear the galaxy is leaving us behind. Instead of putting our energy into clever magic tricks, we should use our power to its greatest extent, to influence peoples and planets, to make lives better, and to earn respect through our actions."

Blaylock nodded with narrowed eyes, the way he did when he had a victim in his sights. "And to fight this threat of decay, to make lives better, you need Galen's spell of destruction."

Another jump in heart rate, accompanied by a jump in respiration. "We need mastery of our tech. Galen's spell reveals potential previously untapped."

It was clear that Elizar was withholding something. A threat that required a weapon to fight it was a threat from without, not within.

Yet both Kell and Elizar were trying to suppress this information. If the threat truly was the Shadows, what reason could they have for hiding it? Did they believe someone within the Circle couldn't be trusted? The secrecy was too clumsy, in that case. In the past, Kell had proven himself extremely skilled at secrecy and misdirection. If there was something Kell didn't want the Circle to know, then they would not know it until he deemed them ready.

Elizar was the weak link here, having revealed the threat to Isabelle and Galen. How could Kell trust such dangerous information to an apprentice? Had he begun to lose his judgment? Elric had seen no evidence of that.

Perhaps the threat Elizar spoke of was not the Shadows at all. Perhaps Elric was seeing their hand where it did not exist.

"Are there any further questions?" Kell asked.

The only questions Elric had were for Kell himself, and those would not be answered.

"You will await our decision," Kell said.

The three left the amphitheater, Galen last, his head low. Would today be the last day Elric would ever see him?

Kell sealed the chamber and asked first for their judgment on Isabelle. They decided quickly on a mild rebuke, with the standard wording for a chrysalis-stage apprentice who has cast a spell without her teacher present but caused no serious harm.

Then they turned to Elizar.

"I propose a mild rebuke for him as well," Kell said. "He should not have used his chrysalis, yet he did no harm with it. And his forgiveness toward Galen and Isabelle is commendable."

Herazade spoke next. She had exchanged her usual sari for a black robe, and her thick black hair was piled on top of her head. "I agree. However, I found his comments about the future of the techno-mages offensive and wrongheaded. A return to the old desire for power and glory is a step backward, not forward. Yet we do not punish mages for foolish opinions. If we did, we would be a very small group indeed. On the issue of his actions, Elizar deserves a mild rebuke."

Herazade had been in the Circle only two years, yet Elric had a hard time believing she could be as narrow-minded as she seemed. This was but one of many instances in which she seemed so focused on her own agenda—moving the mages toward a more people-friendly, social services role—that she completely missed the point.

Blaylock had been tapping the arm of his chair the entire time Herazade spoke. As soon as she finished, he stood again. His voice was harsh and certain. "This is idiocy. Elizar's behavior is erratic and overly emotional. He claims there is a threat to the mages. He uses this claim to try to acquire secrets of power and destruction. Yet when we ask him of this threat, he evades the question.

"He seeks power for himself. He seeks a weapon for himself. My belief is that he fabricated this threat. If not, there can be only one reason he does not tell us of it: he seeks to use it to his own advantage. *He* is a threat to the mages, the greatest threat, perhaps, that we have faced in many years. That some of you cannot see this frightens me even more." Blaylock paused for effect, a tall, thin specter. "We must cast Elizar away." He sat.

Kell's eyes flared in alarm. "Your conclusions have no basis. Elizar has done nothing to endanger the mages."

Elric stood. It all came down to one's faith in Kell. What Blaylock said could be true. Yet it didn't explain why Kell was supporting Elizar, why he sought to suppress the discussion. That suggested Kell possessed some additional knowledge, knowledge that for some reason he felt couldn't be shared with the Circle at this time. Blaylock had strong philosophical differences with Kell, though, and so could not accept on faith that Kell knew best. Elric, however, knew that sometimes secrecy was necessary. And he believed in Kell. "I vote for a mild rebuke," he said, and sat.

Ing-Radi bowed her head. The oldest of them, she had formed her views in an earlier time, and they didn't fall neatly into any segment of the current political spectrum. Yet she tended to be cautious and compassionate. "I agree," she said.

Following the will of the majority, the Circle would rebuke Elizar.

Elric found he had received a message. In his mind's eye, he opened it. The message was in simple text. From Blaylock, of course. *You have your own reservations about Elizar. Why didn't you vote with me?*

It was inappropriate to send messages during a meeting of the Circle. But Blaylock was not one to be put off.

Elric visualized a blank message screen. *I trust Kell. That is all.* He visualized the message being broken into bits of information, traveling through the air to Blaylock, reassembling itself.

Kell spoke again. "Now we must discuss the fate of Galen. Elric, tell us what you know of Galen's spell."

Elric reviewed what Galen had told him about deriving the spell from a progression, and then described what he himself had deduced from studying the readings of his own sensors and probes. "These huge energies and instabilities seem to coalesce in the creation of a new, unstable universe. A spherical area of our own universe is pinched off to create another. In the training hall, as this pocket universe formed, it also began to collapse. But the collapse occurred while I was working to erase the spell. I'm uncertain whether the collapse was due to my interference, or whether it was part of the spell."

"The second time he cast the spell," Kell said, "he altered it, so we still do not know its ultimate consequences."

"Yes. The new universe could form completely, separating and vanishing from our own and having no further effect upon it, other than removing a small piece of our universe. Or the integrity of the membrane separating our universe from this new one could fail, loosing wild energies whose destructive extent is unknown, but potentially vast."

"Are there any limits to the size of the sphere?"

A curious question, Elric thought. The spheres of energy that mages commonly conjured were limited to about twelve feet in diameter, and Elric's guess would be that Galen's sphere was similarly limited. But if not, could it then pinch off an entire fleet of ships, or an entire planet? Elric found it hard to believe such destructive capability might be within the province of a techno-mage; most of a mage's powers were confined to limited sizes and short distances. But it interested him that Kell would think along such lines. "That could only be determined with experimentation, I believe."

Kell dismissed the issue with a casual wave of his hand. "What is your recommendation, then, for Galen?"

This was the question that had dominated his every thought since he had seen Elizar's burned arm. When Galen had conjured the spell in the training hall, Elric had recognized the danger. Yet he had hoped Galen would be able to maintain lifelong control. With the burden of power Galen carried, there was no choice. His hope had been, perhaps, unrealistic. Yet without it, he would have been forced to recommend that the Circle cast him away.

Now, what hope could he have in Galen's control? The chrysalis-stage apprentices were given their chrysalises to wear a full day before initiation. It was a test of control. Over the years, a fair number had failed the test, as had Isabelle and Elizar. Nonetheless, most were given a mild rebuke and went on to be fine mages.

But Galen could not be held to the same standard. Galen had not only failed to maintain control. He had attacked, in violation of the Code. And he had attacked with a weapon of potentially vast destruction.

Elric gathered himself. It was his duty, as one of the Circle, to speak. "Galen is guilty of everything he said. Mages have fought in the past, and will do so in the future. Yet no chrysalis-stage apprentice has ever attacked with a weapon of such power. We do not know how he will behave as a full mage. We dare not—" Elric found he could not continue. He could not say the words to cast Galen away. "I will not vote in this matter."

"If I may," Ing-Radi said. "Has Galen ever reacted with violence before?" she asked Elric.

"No, he has not."

"To cast away after one incident seems premature."

Herazade brought her palms flat against each other. "Perhaps he has never been in circumstances that would bring out his violence. Elric, has Galen ever felt threatened before?"

"No, he has not."

Herazade hated violence, Elric knew, even when it was justified. She could vote to cast away. Blaylock would likely do the same. Kell had devoted his life to making the Code more than something the mages paid lip service, but something many of them actually believed and followed. He had worked to change their focus from power and feuds to learning, beauty, and good. He did this partly through force of personality, partly through his own considerable power, partly through a vigorous weeding-out of unfit apprentices, and partly through harsh punishments. During his time in the Circle, he had turned many violators into examples.

It was time for an example, Elric knew. With three votes, Galen would be cast away.

Blaylock stood. "The very purpose of having apprentices is to discover whether they are worthy to become one of our number. An apprentice who violates the Code does not deserve to become a mage." His gaze met Elric's, and Elric knew that behind his severe expression, Blaylock regretted what he had to do. "I can vote no other way." He sat.

Kell stroked his goatee. "I would argue thus," he said, speaking slowly. "With great power comes great potential. We should cast away such potential only if we are sure it will be used for ill. I have watched Galen as he has developed, and

I have found him to be skilled, disciplined, and dedicated to the Code. His spell language is unique, and now leads him down avenues it may be none have trodden before. To cast away someone with Galen's great ability, unless we are absolutely sure he is unfit, would be unwise."

Elric knew then for certain that Burell's deductions were true. The Shadows were returning, and Kell knew of it. He knew, and he was frightened. If they were to become involved in war, Kell wanted a weapon. He wanted Galen.

"If the Circle agrees," Kell said with a practiced flourish of his hand, "I will personally oversee Galen's initiation. It will be a test of personality, and a lesson. For his first act as a mage, we will then set him a trial, a task that will put him in harm's way and test his reaction.

"His attack on Elizar was a serious error in judgment. We must know if he will make such an error again. If he uses the weapon forbidden to him or reacts with inappropriate violence, then he will be flayed."

Elric shivered, and was startled at his loss of control. To be flayed meant that the techno-mage implants would be removed. But once inserted, the implants quickly intertwined and connected with the mage's own body, so that they could not be removed without also removing fair portions of the body's natural systems, particularly the brain and spinal cord. If done soon after implantation, the mage would become a brain-damaged husk at best. A month or two later, death was certain.

Perhaps, Elric thought, it would be better to have Galen cast away. In time he could find a new life, new pursuits. He would not have to bear the burden of his discovery, nor the trial of the Circle. But Elric knew that to be cast away would destroy Galen. The lore of the mages was already a part of him; to be cut off from it would be almost as bad as flaying.

"He must not know of the trial," Ing-Radi said. "Else he will modify his actions."

"The trial must be faced as soon as he has recovered from initiation," Herazade said, "so that the danger is not prolonged."

"Yes," Kell said. "And he will be reprimanded, in the strongest terms."

Kell, Ing-Radi, and Herazade agreed on the plan. As they debated the wording of the reprimand, Elric felt a strange combination of relief and fear. Galen would not be cast away. He would be initiated, into a world of Shadows, trials, and destruction. He would carry his burden of power. And he would either learn to control it, or he would be flayed. He alone could master his impulses. Yet if there was any other way in which Galen could be aided, Elric would do all that could be done.

Across the chamber, Blaylock gave him a slight nod.

— chapter 6 —

Galen sat cross-legged on the mak within the small tent chamber, his hands on his knees. He breathed deeply, going through the mind-focusing techniques Elric had taught him. Visualize each letter of the alphabet appearing on a screen in sequence, and hold them all in your mind at once. Go through the prime numbers from one to one thousand. Create a mnemonic tree of one hundred objects and repeat them backward, forward, every third one, every prime one, every one containing the letter *T*, every one that matches with your heartbeat.

Still, he could not hide from the truth. He would soon be cast away.

Elizar returned from the next chamber, where the Circle met. The energy he'd shown earlier, during the inquiry, had vanished. His mouth hung open, and his good arm was crossed over his chest, holding his injured arm to his side. "I was rebuked," he said.

Galen stood. "I'm sorry. It was my fault."

Elizar's dark blue gaze fixed on him. "I have behaved erratically. I should not have spoken—as I did."

"I would like to understand. I would like to help."

"I know things, Galen, that I should not know and that I cannot share." Elizar glanced back at the tent flap. "If you knew what I know, if you had the opportunity I have, you would do the same as I."

"What are you doing?"

Elizar shrugged, looking away. "Trying to save us all."

The rune representing Galen's name appeared in fire over

the tent flap. Galen went to it. "It's my turn. Whatever they decide, thank you for asking for leniency. It was generous of you."

Elizar's back was to him. "Do you remember how we used to dream of going on great quests, of doing great deeds?"

"We were to go as partners."

"I realize now, Galen, that some quests seek not to bring about some great new good. They seek merely to save as much as can be saved before all is lost. And some quests, one must go on alone. I had hoped it would not be so." Elizar sighed and turned to face him. "I'm sorry for calling you a technician. I know you don't seek power for yourself. I—" He shook his head. "It doesn't matter. It doesn't matter." He left through the far opening, his footsteps heavy.

Galen passed beneath the rune of fire to face the Circle. He again found himself in the great amphitheater, the place of origin of the Circle. The runes of the Code burned from the walls around him. Tier upon tier of stone stretched up into shadow. He felt great awe at being in this great place, before these great mages. He felt shame at the reason he stood before them. He had failed to live up to the Code.

The Circle was arrayed above him, Elric on the far right. Galen forced himself to meet Elric's eyes, and the eyes of the others: Ing-Radi, Kell, Blaylock, Herazade. These five were the best of them. They had done great deeds, discovered deep truths, led the mages to peace and learning. He was not fit to be among them.

Galen could read no emotions on their faces. He focused on his voice, striving for control, evenness of tone. "I would like to speak, if it may be permitted." Once they cast him away, they would not let him speak.

"We will hear no pleas for mercy," Kell said.

"I have no pleas to offer. I will be brief."

Kell nodded. "Very well then."

"I apologize to the techno-mages and to the Circle for failing to live up to their Code. The techno-mages are noble and good, bringers of beauty and mystery; I am unfit to remain in their company. I apologize for the time this matter has taken from the Circle, and appreciate the wisdom you have dedicated to the resolution of it. I am grateful to receive your judgment. I apologize most deeply to my teacher, Elric, who has given me everything an apprentice"—*or a son*—"could ask." He drew a deep breath, struggling for voice control, and met Elric's gaze. "I wish I had been a more worthy apprentice. I wish I had not failed you. What I have done reflects only on myself. If I could give the time back to you that I have taken away, I would." Galen bowed, then forced himself to stand very, very still. He would hear their judgment, and he would leave.

Elric's face was stern; perhaps he thought Galen's words inappropriate.

Kell pushed himself to his feet. Though he was aged, his dark skin lined, shoulders hunched, he still had the bearing of a great leader. His large frame seemed imbued with power, and the short white fur cape over his robe added to his stature. His voice was vibrant. "The first word of the techno-mage Code is solidarity. In solidarity we meet, connected by a common dedication, common ideals, a common purpose. We seek to understand, we seek to generate beauty and mystery, we seek to do good. If our solidarity is violated, if we strike at each other, our purpose is lost in anarchy.

"You struck at a mage without knowing what he intended. You struck out of fear, not out of control. A mage must be master of his tech, his power. He must control it at all times. Only in control can you do good, the last word of the Code. And if you do not do good, then what are you?" Kell's intense gaze seemed to see right into Galen, to know things about him that he himself did not know. The sensation was extremely uncomfortable.

"You have behaved recklessly," Kell continued. "You have used your chrysalis without supervision. You have attacked another mage without provocation. You have conjured a spell that you were ordered not to use. You have injured a mage. You have violated the Code.

"The damage you caused might have been much, much worse. The endpoint of the spell you conjured remains unknown, but its destructive power is potentially vast. You might have destroyed all of us, all of everything, with your one impulsive attack.

"You are forbidden from using your spell of destruction. You are forbidden from telling anyone outside the Circle how this spell was done.

"If we find any further evidence of this behavior, we will act without debate or delay. You will be flayed." Kell paused, allowing the words their importance.

"Do you understand?"

He wasn't going to be cast away. He couldn't believe it. They were giving him another chance. Another chance to be a mage.

Elric was giving him a stern look.

"Yes," Galen said, "I understand."

"For your behavior, we, the Circle, reprimand you. You have fallen in our eyes. You are diminished. We are disappointed by your blatant violation of the Code and angered by your recklessness. Do not again earn our wrath."

Galen felt as if his life had been handed back to him. He marveled at the Circle's generosity, and vowed to be worthy of it. "I won't," Galen said. "No matter what happens, I will never fail you again."

Galen felt as if he were floating, disembodied, in the night mist. He was exhausted, light-headed from two days of fasting. But he was here, at the Becoming, the moment he had been working toward all his life.

They sat in a circle around the conjured fire, apprentices poised to become techno-mages. The light caught their faces—hopeful, determined, frightened, inspired. Tonight they would go around the circle, each asking questions of the next, questions that would define who they were as techno-mages.

The sea murmured quietly as Elizar said he would begin. He turned to his left, to Galen. "Who are you?"

"Galen." Galen carefully visualized the equation, felt the echo of the chrysalis. He raised his hand and drew in the air the fiery rune that represented his name.

"What are you?"

"I am a techno-mage." He transformed his rune into the rune that symbolized the mages.

"What is a techno-mage?"

He had recited the given answer many times over the years. "One who can alchemize science into magic. One who knows all that can be known. One who does not destroy. One who maintains the illusion, who keeps the secret. A breed apart, an ancient fellowship conceived in wonder, fired in discipline, proven in technomancy."

"Why are you a techno-mage?"

This was the one question each individual must answer for himself, the question with which Galen had struggled. Elric had objected to the answer he'd come up with—to further the work of the ancients—saying that Galen must find his own work. But Galen's attempt to be original had ended in failure. He had no other answer. "To revere and keep alive the traditions of the ancients. To devote my life to study and strive to further their work. To master control of the tech. To do good where I can."

He turned to his left, to Isabelle. She flashed a nervous smile. "Who are you?" asked Galen.

He went through the questions, and she gave the correct responses. He was curious to see how she would answer the final question. "Why are you a techno-mage?"

Isabelle straightened with conviction, her eyebrows rising. "To penetrate the mysteries of magic, to see it whole and unadorned, and to reveal that the emperor need not wear magical clothes to inspire loyalty and devotion."

The questions passed, and each declared his reason for being a mage.

Carvin smiled. "To create joy and wonder, mystery and revelation."

Gowen brought his hands to his heart and bowed his head. "To be a keeper of the great blessing of the Taratimude. To revere their name and protect their benefaction."

Fed scanned the circle and shrugged. "To make the rest of you look good, obviously." Gowen grunted his displeasure, just as Galen had heard his teacher Blaylock do.

Razeel closed her eyes. "To assuage the needs of the tech."

Elizar wiped his mouth and stared deep into the fire. "To make a difference in the coming dark times. To reveal the true power of the techno-mages and help lead them to an age of greater acclaim."

Within the great stone circle marking Elric's place of power, the mages stood, five hundred of them, arranged in a spiral. Though there was no formal order, the most junior of them stood along the outer sections of the spiral, while the eldest stood near the center. Ring upon ring, working steadily inward, each affirmed his identity in a loud voice, the rest listening silently. Again they answered the questions they were constantly forced to confront, questions whose answers life constantly revised.

Standing near the center, Elric thought of Galen, in a similar circle, and his heart was filled with pride. In the morning, Galen would be a mage.

At last, Blaylock asked the questions of Elric, and he answered, looking out over the group that formed his extended family, his colleagues, his faith, his nation, his species. "To use my power for good, at my own discretion. To deny those who would use me for ill. To safeguard the knowledge of the techno-mages and to support this fellowship that has given me a place and a purpose."

Beside him stood Alwyn, whose answers never failed to entertain. "To help those who deserve it, to knock sense into those who ask for it, to punish those who demand it. To fool those who are fools, to confuse those who are confused, to right those who are righteous, and to generally be a pain in the neck to all."

The very last, Kell's answers boomed out over the mages in a vibrant voice. "To give heart, and mind, and soul, and tech to the service of our great fellowship. To pursue knowledge through a universe of mystery. To follow the Code, above all. And to see us safely into the future."

That last sentence, Elric realized, was new.

* * *

Galen sat at the cliff edge in a cocoon of mist, his palms flat on his legs. Behind him, Elric's light globes cast a faint illumination, glinting off the moisture on the moss, the bare rock of the land's end. Pale, ghostly shapes of mist drifted before his eyes.

After the apprentices had answered their questions, they had each gone alone into the night, to meditate and wait. A mage would come to each, take hold of the apprentice's chrysalis, and impose a challenge. Elric would tell him nothing of these challenges, so Galen had no idea what to expect. He had heard only that they were not tests of power, but lessons of character. Alwyn had said they often served to focus a mage on his future and his purpose. Few had ever "failed" a challenge. In fact, the only one Galen knew of was Tilar, who had then been cast away. But after his failure with Elizar, Galen didn't want to make the slightest mistake.

His anxiety was muted by fatigue, though, and after a brief mind-focusing exercise, he fell quickly into a meditative state. He followed the shifting shapes of the mist, the regular rhythm of the sea. The mist sparkled in the dim light, almost as if trying to communicate with him. Then it parted, and a table stood before him. On it sat a black, rectangular comp-pad. A message glowed in yellow on its screen. The comp-pad seemed weighted with import, as if it carried some great secret. Its secret both frightened and drew him. It was a secret about himself. It would change everything.

At the same time that Galen felt the profound truth of this, he realized what was being done to him. The mage challenging him was stimulating the temporal lobes of his brain. Stimulation of the temporal lobes caused extremely intense visions, weighted with emotional import. Galen had read about a spell that did this, and at his request, Elric had performed it briefly on him. Galen recognized the heightened reality, the dreamlike sense of significance. Yet knowing the cause didn't make the vision any less compelling.

He approached the table, picked up the comp-pad. The yellow glow of the words burned into his mind. "To hide from others is magery. To hide from oneself is folly."

The words were a revelation. They carried the wisdom he had avoided all his life. He hid from himself. He did not know if he had always been this way, but it was true of him since he could remember. He read, he studied, he trained. He did as he was told. He focused on each day, avoiding the past, avoiding the future, avoiding the big picture that might be revealed if he stepped back from the canvas.

At times he would become upset, or afraid, but these emotions were like messages from a distant galaxy, faint hints of the unexplored territory that lay deep within. He preferred to keep his eye close to the canvas, to tune out those distant signals, to keep still until they passed. He kept still so they would not find him, these signals sent from himself to himself. He did not want to hear them.

He hid from himself.

The comp-pad hit the table. It had been in his hands, and it had fallen through his hands, passing through his fingers as if he were a ghost. As he brought his hands closer, his flesh faded to white, dispersed in the mist. He had no body, no substance.

Galen screamed, but he had no voice, no mouth. He had hidden from himself too well. He was lost.

Beyond the table stretched a long grey corridor. He sped down it, searching for his body. The corridor ended at a T, offering him two alternatives. The intersection was marked with the rune signifying ignorance. Galen took the right branch, rushed ahead. The next intersection offered three choices, the next four. Galen chose randomly, racing ahead, becoming absorbed in the complex maze. As he swept around a curve he caught a glimpse of a hooded, robed figure ahead. The figure turned a corner. Galen bolted forward, but when he reached the corner, the figure had vanished down the corridor. He dashed after it, searching for another glimpse.

The corridors grew more and more intricate, the branches more and more numerous, leading not only in different directions on a single plane, but leading up and down to different levels. As he twisted around a turn, again he caught sight of the black-robed figure, only to lose him again at the next turn.

Galen forced himself to stop, controlling his waves of panic. Reason told him he would never catch the robed figure. Not like this. If he had no substance, then the maze could not hold him. He raced upward, through the countless levels of the maze and out the top of it. As he soared upward, he realized what lay below him: a microchip. The corridors of the maze were the pathways of the chip's circuitry. Somehow, he could see through the chip's many grey layers to the passageways etched within, which glowed with a golden light. In one of those passages he saw the tiny black figure, running.

He, too, was lost, Galen realized. And afraid. They could hide from each other no longer.

With the inexplicable knowledge of a dream, Galen suddenly understood that he could manipulate the passageways in the chip. He blocked off the corridor ahead of the robed figure, and as it turned back, he blocked off the corridor behind. Then he shot down into the chip and through the many layers to the corridor where it stood.

Confronted, the figure removed its hood. It was Kell, though he was Galen's age, and not yet shorn of his hair. His dark eyes pierced through Galen. "You are not like us." His words resonated with significance.

Galen found he now could speak, though he had neither body nor voice. "My skills are weak. I lack control. I lack originality. I will never be your equal."

"A mage's conjuries should be an extension of himself. They should reveal, express, and complete him. You have hidden behind your conjurings. You have aligned them in regimented rows to prevent any of yourself from contaminating them. Likewise, you have aligned your thoughts in these rows, keeping them safe and contained. You have hidden so well that any more you might have been is lost. You have become these regimented paths, and the places to which they lead. Yet you do not know it. You do not know who you are, and so you do not know what you are or why you are." Kell took a step toward him, his body growing taller, broader. "Who are you, Galen?"

Galen felt a great emptiness where the answer should be.

The question reverberated within that emptiness. He had to fill it. "I am a student. I study—"

"But tomorrow you are no longer a student. Tomorrow you are initiated. Tomorrow you no longer study life, but live it. Then who are you?"

"I am a techno-mage."

Kell took another step toward him, his body now huge, dwarfing Galen. "A role."

"I am Galen."

"A name." Kell came closer, his dissatisfied face filling Galen's field of vision.

"I am one who wanted to be a healer and failed."

Kell nodded. "And who are you now?" His voice rang through the corridor.

"I am a seeker."

"And what have you found?"

Galen couldn't think. "Many things."

"What have you found?"

"I have studied the ways of Wierden."

"What have you found?" The question tolled again.

"I have learned the control of spheres."

"What have you found?"

"I have discovered a progression of spells."

"And what have you found?"

The knowledge fell upon him like a curse. He had found only one thing of import. One thing that now overshadowed all else in his life. "I have found the secret of destruction."

"And who has it made you?" Kell's voice rang. "Who are you?"

"I am the techno-mage who carries the secret of destruction. The secret that must never be used."

Kell's body paled and dissolved into mist, and Galen looked down to find his body coalescing out of that mist, his hands white, then gaining color, substance. Kell's voice pealed through the corridor. "Write that across your soul, boy."

Galen found himself standing in a large circle with the other apprentices. He knew he had not been asleep, but he did not know how he came to be here. From the expressions of some of the others—Elizar, Razeel, Carvin, Gowen, Fed, Isabelle—he knew they felt the same.

Their group stood within Elric's great circle of stones. A band of brilliant moss-green energy connected the stones. Behind each apprentice stood his teacher. Galen recognized Elric's firm grip on his chrysalis. Galen checked to see if all fifteen apprentices had made it to this moment. They were all there.

Somehow, he knew the time had come to speak the words of the Code. They spoke together.

"Solidarity."

He closed his eyes and visualized the equation, created the rune that in the language of the Taratimude represented solidarity. The fiery rune blazed in the air before him.

He sent it into the center of the circle to join the runes of the other apprentices.

"Secrecy."

Again he created the rune, sent it to the center.

"Mystery."

The runes intertwined with one another, creating a tangled ball of energy.

"Magic."

The orange-red light from the runes grew intense. Galen had to squint.

"Science."

The far side of the circle was lost behind a blinding ball of flame. Galen's heart raced.

"Knowledge."

The beauty of being a mage, of living by the Code, raced through him in a surge of adrenaline. He could want nothing more. Nothing more than to be worthy of them.

"Good."

Though he was perhaps one of only a few to know, his study of the language of the Taratimude had told him there was no rune for good. The rune the mages used to symbolize good actually meant useful. Galen generated the rune, projected it to the center.

The light was too intense; he had to close his eyes.

Through his eyelids he saw the tangled ball of light rise overhead. Kell had taken control of it.

"Dissociate," Elric said to him.

Galen visualized the equation that terminated the connection between himself and the chrysalis. The chrysalis echoed the command, then went silent. Elric removed it.

After two days of wearing it, Galen's body felt incomplete without it, as if a limb or an organ had been removed. Galen squinted his eyes open to watch Elric and the other teachers carry the chrysalises out of the circle. The green band of energy connecting the stones opened a portal for them, closed it behind them.

And now it was time to be purified by the Code that they had chosen. Again they spoke the words.

"Solidarity."

An umbrella of fire shot out from the ball overhead to envelop them. It rushed down over Galen's body like living lava, searing him. Galen gasped. Several screamed out. Galen found it had burned away his clothes, his boots. No trace of them remained. He steeled himself.

"Secrecy."

A second umbrella of flame fell upon them. The heat crawled down over him, consuming the hair from his head, his body. He panted.

"Mystery."

The outer layer of his skin was scoured away. Someone released a ragged cry.

"Magic."

Fire raked through his remaining skin, scalded it.

"Science."

Several cried out at once. Galen's raw flesh quivered.

"Knowledge."

There were no cries now, or perhaps Galen could no longer hear them. He focused on staying upright, on forcing his burning lips to form the final word.

"Good."

The last of the fire fell upon them.

A portal opened again in the ring of green fire. The apprentices moved toward it, falling into a line. Once through the portal, Galen found himself on a path lined on both sides by mages. The path led to a tent standing separate from the others, a tent he hadn't seen before. That was where his transformation would take place.

The interior was dark, and as Galen entered, he found himself somehow alone. No one seemed to be in front of him or behind him. A globe of light appeared farther inside the tent. It hovered over a table of dark crystal.

In the faint light, Galen noticed that to the side of the entryway were several stacks of canisters. The canisters were smaller than the ones that held the chrysalises, about two feet high and one foot across, and they were covered in an opaque outer layer that was ornate, carved with runes. This must be how the Circle stored the implants, once they made them. Galen marveled that something so intricate and so powerful could be so small.

Galen approached the table and rested a hand on it. The cold surface stung his raw skin. Obviously he was meant to lie on it. He eased himself down onto the crystal table. As soon as he was supine, a great force—like an invisible hand—slammed down on him. He was pinned flat against the cold surface. His breath came in short gasps. He couldn't move. His lungs couldn't fully inflate against the pressure.

The light above him went out. All was silent except for the panting of his breath. A line of fire cut through the darkness above him, curled itself into the rune for solidarity. The rune descended until it hovered just above him, the same size as his body. The heat of it awakened more pain in his skin. He tried to turn his head to the side to escape from it, but he could not move.

Then the rune began to unravel. The line of fire whipped out and down, driving into the flesh of his shoulder. Galen screamed.

Fire burned like a microthin wire shot down his arm. It split into three parts as it reached his hand, running down his thumb, index, and middle fingers and exiting out the tips. The three lines of fire rose and turned back toward him, plunged into the fingertips of his other hand and blazed up his arm, joining and popping out at the shoulder. Galen's breathing grew harder, faster. The fire ran up into the darkness and vanished.

He lay in blackness, the line of fire an afterimage above him, anticipating the appearance of the next rune. He didn't know if he could stand six more of them. He remembered Fed joking nervously, *If it were painless, then everyone would want to do it, right?* Fed was going through the same thing.

If Fed could do it, then he could do it.

As he lay in the dark, though, something glided over his raw shoulder, faint as a whisper. He started, but the jerk of his muscles had no effect against the force holding him down. Something thin and cold and wet pushed into the tiny hole burned by the fire. It wormed inside him, deeper and deeper, generating a dull tingling that spread like goose bumps down his arm. On his shoulder, the length of its body followed into the hole, contracting and relaxing, contracting and relaxing. Its head passed his biceps and continued toward his elbow, drawing a line of coldness with it.

At the other shoulder a second invader stirred, wriggling its way inside. This was not the way it had felt when he'd entered chrysalis stage. One implant had been inserted at the base of his skull. He'd been asleep during the procedure, and he'd awoken only with a vague headache. He'd never had the feeling of something inside him, something other.

These new implants would connect to that original one, accessing all the information that had been gathered and stored while he trained with the chrysalis. Yet they felt different. These things moving inside him that were not him were wrong. They did not belong.

At last, as they each split into three and pushed into his fingertips, the movement slowed, stopped. His hands and arms tingled, infused with the cold. The tech was inside him now, waiting.

Above him, a line of fire appeared and twisted into the rune for secrecy.

The pressure holding him down suddenly vanished. Galen's gasp turned into a huge ragged inhalation. The desire to run was nearly overwhelming, though he felt too weak to move. Were they giving him a chance to leave? Was this another test?

The rune descended and unraveled, the end of the line of fire raised, poised to strike. Galen realized what was wanted of him. With numb fingers he turned himself onto his stomach. The pressure returned, and with it, the fire.

The pattern was repeated for each of the seven runes of the Code as Galen watched the lines of fire reflected in the table and panted against its surface. Twin tunnels were burned across the back of his shoulders, one down each side of his spine, and four from the base of his skull up into his brain.

Each time the formation of the tunnel was followed by the insinuation of the tech, cold, thin, and wet, contracting and relaxing, pushing inside him, stretching the skin of his back, sending prickles like tiny needles down his spine, driving the cold in intricate coils through his brain and settling there, making his body its home.

He sensed something then, like an echo of an echo of an echo, the faintest hint of what he had felt with the chrysalis. The echo carried his revulsion back to him.

The pressure lifted, and Galen's head fell to the side in relief. Numbness spread through his body.

He was not who he had been. He was not himself anymore. He was something that was part himself and part other.

He was a techno-mage.

December 2258

— chapter 7 —

Galen sat in his room hunched over his screen. He rocked back and forth, his hand uneasily rubbing his bare head. He had never realized how strange the lack of hair would feel, not only on his head but all over his body. He felt naked, vulnerable. The touch of his robe against his skin was a constant irritant. Perhaps part of it was the residual rawness from the initiation.

The deepest of his injuries had been healed by the Circle following the implantation of the tech. The remainder were healing quickly with the help of the organelles that were now being produced within him by the tech. The hair, it was said, would begin to grow back after a few more days. He planned to scour it regularly from his scalp as a sign of the initiation he had undergone and the Code that it embodied. Yet he would be glad to have the hair on the rest of his body restored.

Even then, though, he feared he would not feel as he had before. His body had become foreign to him since the initiation. He had thought the implants would only be involved in the casting of spells. Yet every task—breathing, walking, chewing—had been altered in some way he couldn't describe. His body felt as if it had been changed and an agitating undercurrent of energy churned deep inside him. It was disorienting, unsettling. Although he was fit, he had not yet left the house. He didn't feel in control. He knew his system was adapting, but he was uncomfortable with the process, uncomfortable with the sensations he remembered from the initiation, the tech invading him, burrowing deep into his body.

The invasion reminded him of the stab of Jab's needle-sharp sting, releasing its eggs and the virus accompanying them. Now, as he imagined it, the virus was multiplying, infecting him, and the eggs had begun to hatch, releasing wriggling larvae that raced through his system.

Galen looked at the canister on his worktable. The chrysalis floated within, silver with hints of yellow. It seemed, more than anything else, to be waiting. The chrysalis had become attuned to his system. It would now serve as his source of external tech, connecting his body to various other systems built from lesser technology, such as a ship, a place of power, a staff. It was as if an organ had been removed from his body, yet the connection remained. Wherever it was, he would be too.

And something new had been inserted into his body. From the data stored in the old implant at the base of his skull, the tech knew his body systems, his thoughts, his spell language. It was growing, intertwining itself with his systems, combining itself with him, making itself part of him. The tech couldn't be taken off and stored in a jar. It wasn't something he would access only while safely under Elric's supervision. It was with him now and for the rest of his life, ready to respond to any command he might give at any moment. Elric had spoken to him of this, but Galen hadn't truly understood until now.

He retrieved a small square mirror from his shelf, lowered his robe from one shoulder. As the tech developed, discolorations would appear along his shoulder blades and spine, where the tech came nearest the surface of his skin. Galen had seen Elric's; they formed an intricate brown, stippled pattern that looked like nothing more than an elaborate tattoo. Galen held the mirror behind him, twisting his neck to catch sight of his spine. The discoloration was faint, but an elaborate pattern had already formed. He tilted the mirror, finding that the pattern ran the entire length of his spine.

He had cast no spells since receiving the tech. He told himself he had no need, but the truth was he felt reluctant to rouse it.

Oddly, Elric had not pushed him to use the tech or to return to the convocation. If Galen didn't know better, he would think Elric had given up on teaching him. Galen had been afraid—after his attack on Elizar—that his relationship with Elric had been ruined. Although the Circle had given him another chance, Galen knew he had disappointed Elric deeply. He hadn't known whether Elric might still find him worthy of teaching, or worthy of care.

Yet Elric had overseen his recovery as if nothing had changed. Late each night, after satisfying the demands of the convocation, Elric drove him relentlessly through hours of mind-focusing exercises designed to sharpen his mental discipline and control.

During the day, Elric surprised him with tests, checking his ability to control his impulses in various disconcerting ways, such as by throwing objects at him—some illusory, some not—and seeing how he would react. The rigorous training brought Galen a great sense of reassurance. Elric still wanted to teach him. Elric was giving him another chance. Galen was determined not to disappoint him again.

To prove himself worthy of this second chance, he must never use the spell of destruction again. After conjuring it in the training hall, Galen had never imagined that he would. He had thought common sense would prevent him from doing anything so foolish. Yet common sense didn't operate in a fraction of a second. Only instinct.

Galen had thought the spell was unrelated to him, that it had been derived through objective logic. Yet what Kell had said was true, and Galen could not hide from it, much as he might want. His thoughts ran in narrow, regimented pathways. His methodical spell language reflected those pathways, reflected him. The spell derived from that spell language reflected him. And his use of the spell had, finally, revealed who he was. Someone who would attack a friend. Someone who would strike with overwhelming force. Someone whose first, most basic instinct was to kill.

The restless energy of the tech churned inside him. Galen returned to his worktable and his screen and tried to ignore it, to work on translating some new spells. But the agitating undercurrent would not allow him to concentrate. The tech was growing.

After a few moments, he became aware that Fa was peeking into his window. He felt relieved at the distraction. Keeping his eyes on the screen, he snuck a hand under the table, into the tiny sack he kept fastened there, and took out a small bauble. "Do you know what happens to someone who stands outside a techno-mage's window?"

"She gets invited in."

Galen turned and gave her a reassuring nod. She remained outside, her thick fingers clenched on the windowsill. This was the first time he'd seen her since his attack on Elizar. She was still frightened of him. Yet at least she'd come.

He walked to the window and crouched in the sunlight. With every motion, his body felt strange, no longer his own. "What do you have there?" He reached behind her ear, produced the bauble.

"Oh!"

"That's pretty," he said, as if seeing it for the first time. He handed it to her.

She stared at his bald head, and he saw a tightness in her face, a dismay, that he'd never seen before.

"That man—Elizar—who was burned," Galen said. "He's going to be all right. I wish I hadn't hurt him. I told him I was sorry."

Fa looked down, nodded. It struck Galen that he should have visited Elizar before now. When they'd last had a chance to talk, Galen had been certain he was going to be cast away. Now that he was not, Galen thought he should make sure the rift between them was healed. He would like to have his friend back, and if there truly was some threat to the mages, perhaps Elizar would confide in him. Perhaps Galen could help.

First, though, he had to repair his relationship with Fa. The corner of a book bound in tak hide stuck out of the large pocket on the front of her orange jumper. "Shall we read your book?" he asked.

She tugged it out, handed it to him. The book was *Mirm, the Extremely Mottled Swug*, her favorite. He knew it by heart. He opened the worn, hand-tooled cover and propped the book on the windowsill between them. He flipped past the title page, with its hand-tinted engraving of Mirm, to the beginning of the story. "Mirm was the largest and most mottled swug in all the land. His skin was as colorful as—"

"Gale!" Fa tugged at his sleeve. She was pointing into the mist.

Gliding toward them on a flying platform came Isabelle. She sat cross-legged, holding a basket. The platform was larger than usual—about four feet by five feet—and had the appearance of a flying tapestry, black with gold designs woven into it. The edges rippled in the wind. Galen couldn't tell if it was real or illusion. He laid the book on the windowsill. The fact that she had already accessed her tech amazed him.

She stopped outside his window, floating there. "Good day," she said to Fa. "My name is Isabelle."

Galen translated Isabelle's words for Fa. Fa seemed mesmerized by the tapestry, so Galen replied for her. "This is Fa."

Isabelle nodded. She looked beautiful without hair. Her scoured head emphasized her striking grey eyes, her protruding ears, which he found charming. She seemed completely recovered from the initiation. "I happen to know that you haven't yet left the house. It's been far too long for that, so I'm here to invite you—and Fa—on a picnic."

Galen was relieved that his attack against Elizar hadn't kept her away. She seemed comfortable with him. He wished he could put aside his awkwardness and feel as comfortable with her. And more than anything, he wished he could go with her. "Thank you for the kind invitation. But I must visit Elizar first. I must offer him my help."

"Elizar has left," Isabelle said. "This morning. He told Kell he could better recover from his injuries at home, and asked leave to depart early."

Galen couldn't believe it. Elizar hadn't yet faced the mages and been formally accepted as one of their number. "But the welcoming ceremony."

"I know. Kell gave Elizar the staff he had made as a welcoming gift. And he sent Razeel with Elizar, in case Elizar grew too fatigued to pilot the ship."

Galen had hidden in his house, and now his opportunity was lost. Had Elizar left in anger? Or had he left because of the danger of which he spoke? Did he intend to face it alone?

"I borrowed some very greasy chitwings for this picnic," she continued. "The last ten they had. I suggest you don't refuse."

Although Fa couldn't understand Isabelle's words, she clearly had picked up the general topic. She looked hopefully from Isabelle to Galen.

"You have to leave the house sometime," Isabelle said.

Galen motioned Fa aside and began to climb out. The tech made each movement feel ponderous, awkward. "I don't know. Everyone I want to see comes to my window."

Galen hoisted Fa up onto the tapestry, then climbed on himself. He ran his hand over the black-and-gold design of flaming suns. He could feel the texture of the weave; this was no illusion. Gali-Gali had been the first to combine a conjured platform with an ordinary carpet. It elicited a greater feeling of magic.

Isabelle conveyed them at a gentle pace, remaining only a few feet off the ground, so Fa would not be afraid. Fa stood in a half crouch and held her face up, her curly wisps of hair blowing in the breeze. Through Galen, Isabelle asked Fa for a good place to picnic, and Fa led them off the mak to a field of flowers and high grasses. The tapestry settled onto the ground, the invisible platform below it dissolving, and shortly Isabelle began to distribute the food.

The mist was thick, the sun reflecting within it to create a brilliant white glow. The sea breeze ruffled through the grasses.

Fa ate only a few bites, repeatedly running her hand over the tapestry, then looking up at Isabelle. After a few minutes she ran off to pick flowers, her orange jumper dissolving into the mist.

"She's a lovely girl," Isabelle said.

"Quite an effective irritant as well," Galen said.

"She has several older siblings, doesn't she?"

Galen frowned. "Yes. But how did you know?"

She gave him that mysterious smile, her lips pressed together. "I'm always right. Except for the times I'm not, of course." Isabelle raised her eyebrows. "Why haven't you used the tech yet?"

Galen smiled, trying to cover his unease. "Have you been talking to Elric?"

"We only exchanged greetings as he came to take Burell to a meeting of the Circle."

"She has business with the Circle?"

Isabelle nodded. "Misdirection—very nice. But you won't get me off the subject so easily."

"What?"

"Why you're not using the tech."

While Galen would have preferred a different topic, he loved talking with her, could talk with her forever. He still felt self-conscious and awkward, but it was an awkwardness he would gladly suffer. "I've been studying."

"Ah."

"What?"

"So that's what a lie looks like. The tech's sensors are much more powerful and varied than those in the chrysalis. Your heart rate jumped, blood flow to your skin increased, and your voice stress was a dead giveaway. You should try it."

"Lying?"

"The tech." She smiled, the conversation firmly back on her point.

He found a smile of his own forming. "Tell me more about that image you showed me of the chrysalis. The neurons. Is that what the tech is made of?"

She gave him a pointed look, then nodded. "I'm not sure about the implants, because what I used for study was my own chrysalis. Its structure changed as I used it more and more. The image I showed you was recent, after it had become fully developed. When I first received the chrysalis, it had fewer neurons and more of a different kind of cell, a generalized type. I believe they're something like stem cells. As the chrysalis is used, these generalized cells differentiate into different types of cells, but particularly into neurons."

Galen knew a fair amount about stem cells from his time studying medicine. Stem cells were the most generic cells, the precursors from which all others came to be. Embryos began as stem cells, and as they divided to produce more cells, some remained stem cells, while the majority took on different roles in the body, becoming, in Humans, more than two hundred different types of cells: nerve cells, muscle cells, blood cells, and more. "What controls their development?" he asked.

"I'm not sure. The cells in my chrysalis contain my DNA, but additional DNA as well. The DNA must guide the development of the chrysalis, just as our DNA guides our development. Yet the training clearly also plays a part, otherwise the chrysalis would develop fully before we begin to train with it. As we visualize different spells, I believe the neurons in the chrysalis make connections between each other, creating and strengthening pathways that reflect our ways of thinking.

"In addition to the neurons, there are muscles that allow the chrysalis to hold on to the apprentice. And a blood circulation system. The chrysalis seems in ways to be similar to a brain. Something that receives and echoes our thoughts, and then . . ." She shrugged. "I'm vastly oversimplifying. There are many layers of technology intertwined with this structure. I haven't had a chance to make heads or tails of them. And I still don't have a clue about how the whole thing works."

"What you've found is fascinating. I would think the tech must be designed in a similar way." Thinking of the tech as stem cells containing—at least in part—his own DNA made it feel less threatening, less like an invading life form. But it had seemed to have a will, a will to penetrate his body. The Circle must somehow program certain desires and directives into it. He wondered how much they understood of what they made.

"So why haven't you tried it?" Isabelle asked.

Fa ran up with flowers stuck into the hair of her head, arms, and legs.

Isabelle laughed, a light, musical sound. "She looks like a bouquet."

Galen translated for Fa.

"She laughs," Fa said.

"Yes?" Galen said.

"I thought you weren't allowed."

Isabelle was looking between Galen and Fa. "What did she say?"

Galen was uncomfortable relaying the comment. "Fa is surprised that you laughed. She thought mages were not allowed."

At that, Isabelle laughed even harder. "With you and Elric her only examples"—her laughter trailed off—"well, I can imagine how she might have gotten that impression."

The restless energy of the tech amplified Galen's unease. He began to think that coming out for the picnic had been a mistake. Fa moved shyly toward him, and she put her hand into her pocket in a move Galen recognized as preparation for sleight of hand. He had to teach her to do that sooner; she was giving away her intentions.

"What's that behind your ear?" she asked him.

"What?" He turned his head from side to side, feigning irritation. He was glad for the distraction.

She reached to his ear and revealed a yellow blossom in her hand.

"How did that get there?" he said.

She handed it to him. "Odd place to keep a flower." Her hand darting quickly into her pocket, she moved hesitantly to Isabelle. She raised both her hands. "Nothing here." Galen translated for her. "But what's that behind your ear?"

She reached behind Isabelle's ear, produced a blue flower.

"Oh!" Isabelle clapped. "That's lovely. Thank you. How smart you are!" Isabelle accepted the blue flower and gave Fa a hug. Fa, startled, licked Isabelle's cheek.

Galen realized he had never hugged Fa, in all the years he had known her. He had never been good with people. He had always told himself it was a skill he lacked, but perhaps the truth was that he always held back, hiding not only from them, but from himself. He did not want them to see what he did not want to see. He did not know why he was like this, but it was ingrained in him. Long ago he had formed a hiding place deep inside and had secreted himself within it.

Even now that the spell of destruction had revealed who he was, and Kell had forced him to face it, still he hid. He hid in his room. He hid from the tech. It was an instinct, just like the instinct to kill.

But he had to face the tech, and more than that, he had to face the reason he hadn't yet tried it. For in truth, he was reluctant to awaken the tech not because he didn't trust it, but because he didn't trust himself. Yet the Circle had given him another chance. Elric had given him another chance. They must believe in his ability to control himself.

And he must believe in himself. While he didn't believe instincts could be changed, they could, perhaps, be controlled. He had been unprepared before. Now that he fully understood the danger, he would be on guard, and he would cast no spell without careful thought. That he swore to himself, and that he must believe. For if he could not trust himself, he had no right to be a techno-mage.

He closed his eyes, visualized a blank screen. Upon it, he imposed the equation to create a message. The echo from the tech was strong, instantaneous. No sphere of destruction formed. No flames spouted over the field. There was no sense of independent will from the tech, no sense of anything alien stirring within him.

Thank you for the picnic, he wrote in the message. He debated saying more, decided against it. He visualized the equation to send the message. The tech obeyed, much like the chrysalis, but more quickly and efficiently. Casting the spell barely required any effort. Suddenly he was eager to work with the tech, to begin exploring its abilities and bounds.

Isabelle had begun packing up the food, and she hesitated as she received the message. Galen saw her face contract with concentration.

She resumed her packing, and Galen was startled to find that he had received a response. He opened it.

You're welcome.

Elric stood beside Burell in the center of the Circle's amphitheater. It had fallen to him to prove to the Circle what their leader already knew, but refused to say: that the Shadows had returned.

It was the irony of being a techno-mage. Elric did not want to disrupt Kell's plan, but at the same time Kell needed to be informed that he had kept his secret long enough, that now was the time for him to share his knowledge.

"Previously," Elric said, "our evidence has been uncertain, unconfirmed. But as you have seen, this latest evidence is confirmed and compelling. It strongly suggests the Shadows are returning to Z'ha'dum and gathering resources for war."

Burell's data was strong. One with an open mind could not dispute it. Yet the Circle's minds were not always open, and this, more than anything, they would resist. They did not want to believe their peaceful times would be brought to an end, that a war would come to overshadow all plans, all accomplishments, all desires in their lives. Everything would change, and much that they had built would likely be destroyed. They would no longer be making history, but would be made by it, overwhelmed by it.

Elric hadn't wanted to accept it either. But if the Shadows had come, that far-advanced race would pose the greatest challenge the mages had ever faced. Although the mages preferred to channel their abilities into scientific pursuits and magical displays, they were among the most powerful beings currently alive. With the exception of the Vorlons, who were arrogant and undependable, the mages stood the best chance of fighting the Shadows.

And the Shadows, of course, knew this.

Burell nodded to him, encouraging him to continue. They had both agreed she would speak as little as possible, to avoid introducing her reputation into the discussion. She had even brought herself unadorned to the Circle. She stood with her staff planted to her left, her legs braced to form an uneven tripod for support. The sense of asymmetry about her body had increased, as if pieces of it were drifting out of alignment. Her lips drooped on the right side of her face. She looked even worse than the last time she had dropped her veil of illusion, at the Being.

Traveling away from one's place of power was taxing for any mage; for her, coming to this convocation might be a strain from which she would not recover. Elric was determined to help her accomplish everything she could.

"The techno-mages were but in their infancy during the last Shadow war," he continued, "so we have few of our own records for study. But the return of the Shadows has been prophesied by the Minbari, the Narns, the Pak'ma'ra, and many others. The most ancient sources reveal that the Shadows come in cycles. They have manifested themselves in chaos many times over the history of this galaxy.

"We know all that can be known, and so we knew this: the Shadows would someday return. That day has come. We must inform the mages. We must create a great intelligence-gathering network. We must make plans and build alliances. We must act. Or else death and chaos may engulf all." Elric scanned the Circle. He had their rapt attention, except for Kell, who was deep in thought.

Herazade leaned forward. Elric could think of no reason why she would oppose, but he assumed she would find one and would enlighten him. "Surely this cannot be true," she said. "The Shadows were defeated in a war one thousand years ago. I see no reason why they should ever return, and no evidence that they have done so. It appears that some new settlements are growing on the rim. I find no justification for concluding anything further. I see no need for action."

Burell shifted, and Elric sensed she was about to erupt. He sent a quick message. *Say nothing. Anger will lose our cause.*

Burell's response was swift. *She cultivates ignorance like the rest of us cultivate knowledge. How is it, in all these meetings, you haven't killed her?*

She's been in the Circle only two years, Elric responded.

Blaylock stood, his face tight. "You bring dire news, Elric. The Shadows are returning. Yet your recommendations are misdirected. We cannot put ourselves on the front lines of this war, if war there must be. We are but a few, devoted to learning and study. We have worked hard among us to create peace. We carry a sacred blessing and are charged with the task of becoming one with it. We are not meant to be soldiers. Violence and bloodshed, politics and warfare, will serve as distractions, drawing us away from the path. We cannot let our blessing become corrupted." He sat.

Ing-Radi laid her four orange hands, palms up, on top of each other and bowed her head. "I am not yet certain that the Shadows are returning. I would support a very small, very subtle investigation. To gain more information from Burell's home, Zafran 8. Nothing more. We must proceed with caution."

She was afraid. They were all afraid. They did not want to come out as enemies of the Shadows. But how long could neutrality be maintained? And how could ignorance and inaction serve them?

Kell rose. Elric hoped that he would reveal now what he knew. With his leadership, they would put aside their reluctance and accept the obvious. They could begin to form a plan of action.

He straightened his massive frame. His eyes squinted with age, yet his voice was resonant, strong. "Burell, you have done us a great service in gathering this information. Thank you for your efforts, and my appreciation to Elric for bringing your information before us.

"I am deeply troubled by this news. If it is true that the Shadows have returned and are preparing for war, we will be sought after by both sides. Our ships are among the fastest, our powers offer possibilities no others have. He who we will not make our ally, will make himself our enemy. And while we are powerful, such enemies as the Shadows would destroy us. I agree with Ing-Radi that caution, above all, should be our watchword. Before we can take any action, we must know, for certain, that the Shadows have returned. I support a small covert mission, as Ing-Radi has suggested, to further explore the situation on Zafran 8 and obtain evidence that leaves no doubt."

Kell would not share what he knew. He had a plan in motion. And he wanted more time before the rest of the mages became involved.

"I would support you in this," Herazade said, making a majority.

They would confirm what they already knew, what Burell's evidence clearly revealed. Anything to delay the truth.

Blaylock's eyes narrowed. He was even more unhappy with Kell's response than was Elric. Though Kell remained standing, Blaylock stood, challenging him. "Kell, you live on Zafran 7, neighbor to Burell's planet. Have you seen no signs of activity on your home? Surely such massive movements would affect Zafran 7 as well. Could it be that the Shadows are the threat of which Elizar spoke?"

Kell spared Blaylock only a glance. "I have heard talk." A flourish of his hand dismissed it. "But I have seen no evidence."

Elric found himself monitoring Kell's body functions, which he had never done before. Kell, of course, would maintain control of his body and reveal nothing. But the very fact that Elric would do this revealed his growing uncertainty. The possibility of the Shadows' return was already creating distrust and turmoil among them. And the chaos was just beginning.

"As for Elizar," Kell said, "he has spoken for himself to this assembly."

Slowly, Blaylock sat.

Kell's gaze swept over them. "We must now decide the nature of this mission to Zafran 8, and who will be sent. Elric and Burell, you brought us this information. Have you any recommendations?" Kell sat.

Recommend me, Burell's message read.

Elric knew the Circle would never agree, despite the fact that, even with her ill health, Burell was the best one to do the job. She was too controversial a figure to be chosen by the

Circle. In addition, choosing Burell would make even clearer the redundancy in the mission. Why send her to collect evidence that she had already collected? Yet he had to plead her case, or she would do it herself.

"Burell would gladly continue her investigation for the Circle. Zafran 8 is her place of power. She has extensive connections to it, probes in all the areas of interest, useful sources of information. Her presence there is expected and so would draw no attention."

"I feel we have asked enough of Burell," Ing-Radi said, her slit pupils avoiding both Burell and Elric. "I join with Kell in thanking her for her efforts. Perhaps more evidence can be gained by approaching the problem in a different style."

"The use of Isabelle, however, would be wise," Kell said. "She would draw no attention."

An inexperienced mage would also take longer to find any convincing evidence, Elric realized.

I don't want her involved! Burell's message read.

I will do what I can, Elric responded.

Elric considered volunteering, but knew he was an unacceptable choice. A member of the Circle, or any powerful mage, would draw the suspicions of any who might be watching.

"She will need assistance, of course," Ing-Radi said.

"I offer Elizar," Kell said. "Since he lives nearby, a friendly visit will not seem out of place."

Kell's body functions showed no particular fluctuation, but Elric was suddenly afraid, in a way he hadn't been in years. Kell wanted to control the evidence that reached the Circle. Elric had told Blaylock, *I trust Kell. That is all.* Was he wrong to do so? Was the vision of the universe on which he had based his life flawed?

Blaylock stood. "Elizar is injured and needs time to recover." His tone left no room for disagreement. "We are overlooking the obvious candidate. Galen. He was to be set a task after initiation, a task that would place him in danger and test his reaction. This seems the perfect opportunity." His unyielding face turned to Elric. Blaylock had wanted Galen to be cast away. Now that Galen was a mage, Blaylock would have him be the first casualty of the war. "He can visit as a friend of Isabelle's as easily as Elizar. We can even let it be known that Burell is ill, and that Galen has come to help with her care."

Ing-Radi nodded. "I agree. If the second mage is a peer of Isabelle's, it will draw less suspicion. And if Galen is to be a danger to the mages, we should know it now. Before he is fully come into his powers."

Elric could see that Herazade was about to throw her hat in with the others. She thought the mission unnecessary; it made no difference to her who went. It made no difference to her if Galen was the first to face the Shadows. It made no difference to her if Galen was lost.

"Wait." Elric stepped forward. "This may be the most important issue that has faced the mages in a thousand years. We need not send beginners where experts are required. I can go to Zafran 8 in disguise. No one need discover I'm a mage. I know the evidence. I can find out what we need, quickly and quietly. We will risk no discovery."

Ing-Radi bowed her head, and in the slash of her mouth, Elric read pity. "If there is a Shadow presence there, they may well be able to penetrate your disguise. Then they will discover a member of the Circle investigating them, deceiving them. That we dare not risk."

"I agree with the proposal to send Galen and Isabelle," Herazade said, making a majority.

They've got both of our babies now, Burell wrote.

"Let them be sent now," Blaylock said, "before the convocation is ended. We can say that Burell was taken ill and had to return to her place of power."

Herazade and Ing-Radi agreed.

"Very well then," Kell said. "Elric, will you explain to Galen and Isabelle their task?"

Galen would have no more time to become accustomed to the implants. He would have no more time to improve his control before facing danger. Elric nodded.

"We shall see what they find."

As the Circle went through the motions to end the meeting, Elric received a message from Blaylock. *You cannot spare Galen his trial.*

Elric quickly composed a response. *You would send him just out of the chrysalis against the Shadows.*

He is well able to defend himself.

And if he does so, you will flay him.

If he reacts with violence when none is needed, or uses the spell forbidden to him, yes. The trial is a fair one. Do you believe he will fail?

Elric took Burell's arm and helped her from the chamber. Burell leaned into him and hissed under her breath. "They are bastards, all. Bastards."

"The nights are cold there," Elric said. "Do you have your coat?"

Galen cast a glance over his shoulder as he packed the valise. Elric was acting strangely. "Yes." He had a coat, robes, pants, shirt, underclothes, and toiletries; he had his screen and a pouchful of data crystals; he had props for various minor illusions; he had the keycard Alwyn had given him that was supposed to open any door; he had the microscopic probes he'd made and additional probes made by Circe in case his didn't work well; and he had a lot of loose components, just in case. On top of that, he had loaded every program he thought might be remotely useful directly into his tech, so he could access it easily. Galen was bringing way too much. And instead of pointing out the error, as was Elric's custom, he was encouraging Galen to bring even more.

The agitating undercurrent of energy from the implants made Galen feel itchy all over. He looked around his room. Aside from the chrysalis, what remained were the remnants of old projects, primitive inventions, and various components and raw chemicals he couldn't imagine needing. The small woven grass box lay on the bottom shelf in the corner. He retrieved it, put it into the valise.

"You're taking the ring?" Elric asked.

"I inserted one of my probes into it. I thought I might be

able to use it." After Elric had told him that the Circle had selected him for an important task, Galen had found himself last night staring uneasily at the ring. Made by his mother, worn by his father. It embodied a part of himself from which he hid. He was now a mage as they had been. Although he would have preferred never to see it again, perhaps it was time to stop hiding.

He had visualized various equations, sending different commands to the ring, commands that would allow him to perform the tasks his father had performed, to access the data his father had stored. But the ring had refused to respond. Just as Elric's probes were keyed to respond only to him and those who knew his code, the ring was keyed to respond only to its owner, his father. With an odd sense of relief, Galen had at last given up and had added his own probe, which only he could access.

The mages had learned to make probes very small and very smart. They required none of the tech of the Taratimude within them. Yet as a probe that would covertly observe and record its surroundings, the ring was a rather awkward device. A probe could be made now as small as a grain of dust, and those made by Circe and some of the other mages would cling to any surface, or move to a well-lighted location, or follow other directives. A ring was much more conspicuous and impractical. Yet perhaps he could find some use for it.

He forced the overstuffed valise closed and sealed it.

"You need one more thing," Elric said.

"I can't fit another thing," Galen said, turning to face Elric.

Across his open palms, Elric held a staff. Given during the welcoming ceremonies that ended the convocation, a staff or other gift of magic was a teacher's acknowledgment that his apprentice had become a mage. Elric nodded.

Over four feet long, the staff was a lustrous black, with golden etchings of circuits in finest filigree. It fit perfectly into Galen's hand, warm and smooth and balanced, as if a new limb had sprouted there.

"Associate," Elric said.

Galen looked to the chrysalis on his table, found that it was missing a small piece from the end of its "tail." Elric had incorporated it into the staff, making the staff a part of Galen, an extension of him. The staff was a combination of the advanced tech of the Taratimude, which powered the staff and connected it to him, and the technology currently within the power of the mages, with which various tools had been built into the staff.

Galen closed his eyes and focused on it, visualized the equation for association.

It awoke, echoing his equation. A subtle vibration of energy slipped into him. The vibration was echoed back by the implants, echoed again by the staff. The echoes came faster, growing stronger and sharper, reflecting back and forth like the ringing of a bell in a bell tower, swelling in rapid reverberation. His mind raced. He didn't know if he could control it. Wild energies could escape. Elric could be injured. Elric could be disappointed. Galen must figure out how to prevent that. Galen must not allow that. But what if he couldn't perform the task set for him by the Circle? What if he failed? He had already failed once. Isabelle certainly didn't love him. How could she love him? How would he cope with that?

And what was happening to him?

The energy from the chrysalis had combined with the undercurrent from the implants to produce a surge of nervous anticipation, as if he'd been injected with adrenaline. He'd read of this effect—parallelism, they called it—and knew that mages became accustomed to it, over time.

He recited the prime numbers, silently, deliberately. The orderly progression echoed back to him, calming him. The vibration remained, yet its intensity lessened.

The staff was now a part of him, a new limb. A menu of options appeared in his mind's eye, reflecting the more traditional part of the staff's technology. He studied the possibilities. It could control, hold, and channel energies. It could observe; it could record. It could destroy itself, if he deemed it necessary.

He closed his eyes, carefully visualizing the equation to

dissociate. The connection broke, the vibration died. His limb went to sleep.

Yet the undercurrent of energy from the implants felt stronger than ever. Galen realized he had begun to grow accustomed to it. Now that he was attuned to it, he began to realize how truly strong it was, a resonance more intimate and subtle than that with the chrysalis, one that was quickly becoming a part of him. It was restless and powerful, quick to respond. No wonder mages got in so many fights. He must control it, always.

"In time, you will feel more comfortable with the staff," Elric said.

Galen nodded, holding the smooth, sleeping surface away from his body. "Thank you."

"You will find it unnecessary under most circumstances. Yet it can be helpful when a sophisticated channeling of energy is needed." The familiar tension was there in Elric's face, but something else as well. As he spoke, his teeth barely moved, clenched. Galen had seen this in Elric before, when he was angry. But Elric was not angry now—at least Galen didn't think so.

It seemed suddenly odd to Galen that Elric, who was so strict about process, who had insisted Galen could not begin work on his ship until he had become a mage, would give him his staff early, as Kell had given to Elizar.

"Are you trying to spoil me?" Galen said.

"I can take it back if you like."

"No, no." Galen picked up his valise and glanced toward the window.

"Your friend wanted to say good-bye."

"I told her when I had to leave."

"She is on her way. She can meet us at the ship. We should not delay."

Galen took a last look around his room, nodded. He should be back in a few weeks, hopefully before the convocation concluded at the end of the Earth year. But he would return as an initiate mage, not an apprentice. Then he would have to begin the process of breaking away from Elric, finding his own life and his own place of power. This trip, he supposed, was the first step, his first time away from Elric since Elric had brought him here to live, eleven years ago. Everything was changing.

Galen followed Elric from the house, and as they set out across the mak, Galen periodically looked back, the modest stone house slowly dissolving into the mist. "I reviewed Burell's findings. They seem quite convincing."

Elric frowned. "Clear-cut evidence is needed. Evidence beyond doubt. Evidence that proves the hand behind the migration, behind the gathering of resources on the rim, is the hand of the Shadows. Because if doubt remains an option, some will stubbornly cling to it."

"I will find proof. I will not fail the Circle." *I will not fail you,* Galen thought.

"You have read some of the ancient texts. The Shadows prefer to work secretly, invisibly. They find others to do their bidding. They have hidden themselves so well that we know very little about them, or their abilities." Elric glanced at him. "All we know of their powers is that they are great. They may be able to detect the presence of a mage, or the energies of his spells. They may even be able to defend against your spells."

"But you think it's possible to find proof."

"Possible, yes. For one who is very clever, and very subtle. You must follow the strings from puppet to puppet master."

Galen knew his own weaknesses well. While he was intelligent, his thinking was methodical, unswerving. Cleverness and subtlety were not among his strengths, as Elric was well aware. "You said that for this task the Circle wanted a contemporary of Isabelle's, someone who would not draw attention. But you failed to say why the Circle chose me."

"The Circle's deliberations are its own affair." Again Galen saw the clenched teeth, the anger. It was not directed at him, though, but at the Circle.

They arrived at Burell's ship. Galen set down his staff and valise. He saw a hint of orange flash in the distance, moving toward them. Elric faced him, and the anger was gone. His eyes were wide, his lips pressed into a thin, straight line.

"Remember that the wisest mage takes without anyone knowing anything was taken. Prepare for every possibility. Manipulate the perceptions of others. Maintain control of the situation at all times. Be cautious. And be wary."

Galen nodded, uncertain how to react to Elric's concern. "I will." Elric did not want him to go, Galen realized. Elric did not think he could succeed.

Then Fa was calling out to him. "Gale! Gale!"

Elric turned away, going to meet Isabelle, who had come out of the ship.

Fa arrived before him, breathless. "I thought you would be gone."

"Not yet," Galen said. "I will only be gone for a short time, anyway. I will come back soon."

"When is soon?"

Galen gazed after Elric. "Soon is after today and before long."

"But when?"

"Expect me," Galen said, looking down at her, "when you see me."

She frowned briefly. "What's that behind your ear?" Fa pointed, and Galen crouched so she could reach him.

She brought her hand to the side of his face and opened her palm to reveal a woven grass star. "Odd place to keep a star," she said, and handed it to him. He hadn't even seen her reach into her pocket this time.

"Thank you," he said. He had nothing for her. And he realized, now, that he should. She did not trust that he would return. She would worry each night, watch each day. She would feel better if she had something of his, something to hold against his return. Then he knew what to give. As he thought of the object, Galen was relieved. With Fa was where it belonged. He felt uneasy with its custody. He had faced the ring last night; he would not be hiding from himself now if he gave it away. And it seemed fitting that, as he left, they should reverse the ritual they had performed so many times. Instead of her giving him the ring, he would give it to her.

He palmed the star, visualized the equation to create an

image of it, then set the image snaking up into the air. "It's blowing away. Catch it, Fa."

She ran after it, and he sent it behind Elric and Isabelle. Quickly he unsealed the valise, retrieved the ring from its grass box, and resealed the valise. He cast the spell to access the ring's probe through the tiny transceiver built into it. He added a new program to the ring. Cupping it in his hand, he drew the illusion of the star back toward him. Fa followed, arms extended upward. The star suddenly toppled downward, and Galen reached out and appeared to grab it.

Fa regarded him skeptically. "Odd wind."

"An object of great magic must not be abused," Galen said, keeping his fist extended in front of him. "It must only be used in great need."

Fa was looking at his hand with great interest now.

"One who controls such an object must be wise. She must not call on it lightly."

Fa came close to his hand, her eyes shifting from it to Galen's face.

"If she does not abuse it, it will watch over her always. And if ever she is in great need, she may call my name three times, and I will come."

Fa looked at him with such hope, such dreams. While her attention was on his face, he dropped the ring into her pocket, quickly reclosing his fist.

"Say the words now, and never say them again unless such need comes." He activated the recording device in the probe.

"Gale! Gale! Gale!" she cried. Elric looked toward them.

Galen inserted the sound of her words into the program, so that he would be informed if ever she said them. "You will care for it."

"Yes. Yes."

"You will not abuse it."

"Yes!"

He opened his hand. It was empty.

"Ah!" she cried.

"What?" he said. "Where is it?" He patted himself down.

Fa watched him, half excited, half worried. "Do you have it?" Galen asked.

Fa began patting herself down, stopped, her hand on her pocket. Wonder lit up her face. She reached inside, pulled out the ring. "Oh!" As his mother had given it to his father, he gave it to Fa. It was a great relief, finally, to be free of it.

Galen stood, picked up the staff and valise. Fa looked up at him, then at the valise, and her face fell. She bolted across the mak. He watched as her orange jumper faded into the mist.

Galen approached Elric and Isabelle. Isabelle was wearing a small golden amulet, an eye surrounded by the curving flames of a corona. On each flame was engraved a scientific symbol. He wondered if it had been a gift from Burell, as his staff from Elric.

"Burell is inside," Elric said. "She is ready."

Galen nodded, and Isabelle started up the ramp into the ship.

"Contact me daily," Elric said. "I will relay your findings to the Circle."

"I know."

As Galen was about to start up the ramp, Elric seized him in an embrace. Galen took an awkward step to keep his balance, his hands holding staff and valise in midair. The close contact made him uncomfortable. He could not remember Elric ever holding him, not even at the deaths of his parents. He'd received no more over the years than the occasional hand on the shoulder. He'd grown accustomed to seeing little emotion, and to showing little. It was what he preferred.

Elric embraced the other mages in greeting, of course, or in departure. But those were like friendly handshakes. This embrace was more than those, Galen thought, and it threatened to bring up emotions whose acquaintance he did not wish to make.

Elric spoke softly. "Remember the reprimand of the Circle."

Galen pulled back, startled. Why would Elric say that here, now? Elric knew that he had vowed to obey the Circle, to maintain control, to hold the spell of destruction uncast within him. Galen had thought the Circle, and Elric, had given him another chance because they believed he could succeed. Did Elric fear that he would fail?

Galen stepped away and lowered his arms to his sides. "I shall," he said.

Elric nodded. Galen turned and climbed up the ramp into the ship. Isabelle showed him a seat in the plain, dark interior, and within a minute they had begun to shoot up through the atmosphere. It felt strange, leaving Soom without Elric for the first time. As if he had forgotten that which he needed most.

Galen visualized the equation to access one of the probes to which Elric had given him the key. It was on the west side of one of the great stones that marked Elric's place of power. The probe requested the key, and he gave it. An image appeared in his mind's eye. The mak stretched toward the sea, the mist brilliant in the morning light.

And there on the open plain, a shadow shrouded in mist, stood Elric, alone.

— chapter 8 —

"Before I let you in," Burell said at the doorway, "I need your assurance."

"My assurance," Galen said.

"I didn't know that I'd be bringing a guest home. I could make you stay elsewhere, but that would be highly inconvenient, and I'd worry about you constantly."

Galen nodded, hoping an explanation would come.

She sighed, realizing he still didn't understand. "I have—things—inside that are not intended for anyone else to see. You must give me your word that you will tell no one what you find."

Her research, he realized. She must be doing even more than the mages knew, work that many would condemn if they discovered it. "I give you my assurance. No one will know."

"Good." She extended her hand, and the door to the penthouse apartment opened. "Welcome."

Burell entered first, in the wheelchair illusion she had created after she'd parked her ship in a private hangar at the spaceport. She had agreed to the deception that Galen had come back with them because she was in ill health. But she had refused to let the people between the spaceport and her apartment see her true condition. Galen had still not seen it himself, though he understood from Isabelle that Burell was very ill. The trip to Soom had made her much worse; Isabelle hoped that returning to Burell's place of power would improve her health.

At the spaceport, Burell had altered her usual, glamorous image to create a greyish pallor, lank greasy hair, and a quite unpleasant odor. The odor sold the illusion, Galen could see as they passed through customs. The officials left her alone, speaking in hushed voices with Isabelle. Burell acted the role with gusto. On the tube ride home, she had gone into a fit of wet, phlegm-filled coughs that made it sound as if she might drop dead right there.

Galen followed Burell inside, Isabelle coming last and closing the door behind them. Galen was relieved to find Burell's odor immediately vanished. The pallor and greasy hair went as well. She appeared healthy, wearing a tight-fitting red dress, dark hair in a short, sophisticated style. The wheelchair was replaced with a yellow armchair that floated a few feet off the ground.

"Sorry about the mess," Burell said, moving toward a screen on the far wall.

The apartment was about as different from Elric's simple, Spartan house as it could be. The living room/kitchen was large but crowded. An overstuffed couch and several armchairs were scattered about the room, covered with boxes, newspapers and magazines, electronics, tubes, and other unidentifiable items. Jammed in among the normal living room furniture were various pieces of sophisticated scientific equipment. He recognized a muon microscope, an image processor, a genetic sequencer, a portable magnetic resonance imager, gain amplifiers, and a compact particle accelerator. Boxes and piles of materials had encroached onto the floor, so that Galen had to follow a circuitous path to get from one end of the room to the other. The one hint that anything had once been done to decorate the room came from the colorful tapestries hanging on the walls. Galen realized Isabelle must have woven them, as she must have made the tapestry on which they'd picnicked and the robe for Elric.

Galen always kept his room in perfect order. He was uncomfortable with the disorder. The restless energy of the implants increased his unease.

Isabelle came up behind him. "You'll stay in my room. It's the first door." She pointed toward a narrow hall to their left. Galen found a path that led to the hall. Isabelle followed.

The room was a small island of order amongst the chaos. A loom took up the far half of the room. A simple bed covered by a knit afghan ran along the wall to the right, and along the side wall were several shelves with skeins of different colors and materials. The arrangement of the threads held some kind of symmetry he couldn't quite identify. A tapestry hung on each wall, and a woven carpet lay on the floor.

Isabelle opened the closet, which contained a row of drawers on the right. She took a couple of sweaters from the top drawer, pushed them into the bottom. "You can put some things in here, and then hang up what you need." Along the bar hung several plain black robes and a couple of simple dresses.

He had never stayed in anyone else's home. When he traveled with Elric, they usually slept aboard the ship. Or when they couldn't, in a hotel. It seemed a terrible invasion of her privacy.

"I could stay in the ship," Galen said.

Isabelle's eyebrows had begun to grow back during the few days' trip, and now they contracted in a frown. "It's safer if we all stay together. Besides, this apartment is strongly tied to Burell's place of power, which lies below. We have best access here to events everywhere on Zafran 8."

She seemed a bit irritated, and Galen realized he'd said something wrong. "I hate to put you from your room."

"It's all right. I will stay with Burell. She often needs me during the night, and with the stress the trip has put on her, I'll feel better staying near her." As she looked toward the living room, her fingers intertwined nervously. Galen tried to imagine what it would be like if Elric were seriously ill. It was hard to envision, since Elric had always been healthy. Yet there would come a time, many years in the future, when age would cause major decay that the organelles would not repair.

Galen tried to take her mind from her worries. "Your amulet. Can you associate with it?"

She smiled, touching it. "Yes. Like your staff, I suppose. Burell made it for me." And so the worry returned to her face. "You can leave your things in here," she said, and went out into the living room. Galen set down his valise and leaned his staff into the corner, then followed.

"Are you ready to get to work?" Burell asked. "I've a few secret weapons to share with you." Her yellow chair hovered in front of a large screen built into one wall. The screen was divided into twenty rectangles, each showing a different image. Isabelle stood to one side, and Galen stepped through the clutter to end up beside her. The tiny hairs that had sprouted on her head accented the graceful curve of her skull, her slender neck. He brushed against a basket of data crystals, nearly upsetting it.

Burell turned her head toward them, though it turned only a few degrees, as if its movement was restricted. Burell caught Galen in the corner of her eye. "As Isabelle well knows, I guard my secrets carefully. But you've already seen the evidence I have gathered. Since you are to continue that work, I'll share with you some of my methods for obtaining it."

Over the next few minutes, Burell shared a wealth of information. She gave them the key to access certain of her information systems. She led them through her extensive network of probes, planted in places both public and private, reputable and disreputable. She had probes throughout the spaceport. She had probes in the home of the planetary governor, and she had probes in the home of the planetary governor's mistress. She had probes in warehouses and industrial plants; she had probes in bars and gambling houses. She had a probe in the jewel in the navel of the port's most popular belly dancer.

She pointed out those that might be of most use, then reviewed what records the port kept of spacecraft traffic, passengers, and cargo. She gave them the names of people who provided useful information, knowingly or unknowingly.

"Last but not least, let me introduce you, Galen, to a little computer demon I conjured. He's been the one to sneak his way into the spaceport records and retrieve all their information. He'll be very useful for you. He's quite a hard worker, and easy on the eyes too. Johnny?"

The large screen went black, and in the center appeared a

male figure. He fell to one knee, bowed his head. "I live to serve, Enchantress." He stood. He wore a skimpy red bathing suit and nothing more. His physique was that of a bodybuilder, with huge biceps and quadriceps, and rippling abdominals. "Greetings, Daughter of Enchantress."

Isabelle nodded, a slight smile playing across her face.

"What have you found, Johnny?" Burell asked.

"The ship *Khatkhata* arrived yesterday. According to port records, it's bound for the last jumpgate on our route, near the rim. It's got a four-day layover in port before continuing its journey. The crew is Narn, and they're staying at the Strauss Hotel. The *Khatkhata* is a cargo ship, carrying several heavy pieces of demolition and construction equipment. But at least some of the cargo is passengers. I haven't been able to get any information on them. They aren't leaving the ship."

Johnny's face and voice seemed familiar somehow. Galen studied the figure and found that the head and body didn't quite go together. The head had a more normal amount of body fat in its cheeks, and a slightly lighter skin tone.

Johnny went through some additional information on ships that had arrived or departed while Burell was away. When he was finished, he lowered himself again to one knee.

"Thank you, Johnny," Burell said.

"It is my great pleasure, Enchantress."

"Good-bye, Johnny," Isabelle said.

Johnny vanished, and the other images returned to the screen.

"His face . . ." Galen said.

"Yes, he is a beauty, isn't he? The body is Tidor Puentes, Human bodybuilding champion. The face and voice belong to a military man from the newsfeeds who caught my fancy. EarthForce Captain John Sheridan."

The newsfeeds had called him the hero of the Earth-Minbari War. Galen remembered Elric saying he was "a noble man fighting an ignoble war." And Burell had grafted his head onto the torso of a bodybuilder. Galen must have looked shocked, because Burell let out a sharp laugh.

"Even older women need to have their fun."

"Burell," Isabelle said, "why don't you show him the Strauss Hotel?"

"Yes, yes." The images on the screen changed. "Isabelle and I used to visit the Strauss often. Most of their guests are ships' crews or those doing trade with the ships. For a while I even did some fortune-telling in their lounge. It was a great way to pick up information." Different images showed the hotel's lobby, lounge, restaurant, and various guest rooms. They changed quickly as Burell flipped through them. "These days I mainly work from here, watching through the probes and receiving gossip from the manager, Cadmus Wilcox. Cadmus is a bit of a ninny, but he has a good eye for detail. He's one of the few who have realized that something has changed in the last several months."

Burell pressed her palms against the arms of the chair and pushed herself up, readjusting her position. "He contacted me just a few weeks before the convocation and begged me to put a spell of protection on the hotel. He was afraid of some of the dangerous-looking clientele checking in. I sent Isabelle down to plant probes, sensors, and sonic generators throughout the hotel. We told Cadmus she had to go through every room as part of the spell, of course.

"The system is set up so that the blast of a PPG or any other sophisticated weapon will set off the sonic generators, whose sound waves are strong enough to vibrate the internal organs of most intelligent species, stunning them, causing spasms, or liquefying their bowels. Of course Cadmus is probably overreacting; I don't think his guests want to draw any attention to themselves. But he sleeps better at night, and I have a much more complete intelligence-gathering system in place."

Isabelle pointed to one section of the screen. "There's a Narn."

The Narn was standing in one of the guest rooms, staring at herself in the mirror. She looked grim. A pale scar ran across the middle of her nose.

"I wonder what she's thinking," Isabelle said.

Within seconds Burell had retrieved her record from the Narn Transport Organization and displayed it beside the picture on the screen. Her name was G'Leel, and she was second-in-command on the *Khatkhata*.

"Interesting," Burell said, tapping her upraised index finger against her lips.

Isabelle read from G'Leel's record. "She's been crewing on cargo ships for seven years. Six months ago she switched to a non-Narn shipping company. Based on Stabota 5. Where is that?"

"I've run into this company before," Burell said. "They've been involved in several of the other shipments I followed. Stabota 5 makes us look centrally located. The only thing there is a colony of nudist Drazi. The shipping facility is nothing but a communications relay. I haven't been able to trace it to its true source, which suggests some very sophisticated technology is involved."

Isabelle continued reading from the record. "Her base pay tripled, not counting bonuses. Closest relatives are two parents living on the Narn homeworld. They are the beneficiaries of her life insurance policy."

G'Leel went to the door of her hotel room. Several Narns stood outside, in a jovial mood. Burell added sound to the image. A brief exchange followed in Narn, and G'Leel left with them.

"Do you speak Narn?" Burell asked.

"No," Galen said.

"You should learn. But until you do, you should at least be able to translate. Isabelle, give him the program."

Isabelle's strong, slender hands came together, and her fingers moved slightly. Galen found he had a message. It was a few words in Narn, and attached was the translation program. He accessed the program, translated the message. *I can't speak Narn either,* she had written.

He'd spent the journey from Soom studying all they knew of the Shadows, and information that Isabelle and Burell had provided about Zafran 8. He hadn't thought learning Narn would be a priority.

With the translation program, he could have text or conversations translated, with the translation appearing in his mind's eye. It wasn't as good as learning the language, but he hoped it would be enough.

Accessing various probes, Burell followed the Narns down to the lounge. They were a rough-looking group, dressed in dark leathers with weapons openly displayed. They pushed other guests out of the way to make room for themselves at the bar. It looked like they were in for a night of drinking.

Burell swiveled her chair to face Galen and Isabelle. Even with the illusion of health, her face appeared drawn, fatigued. "I have given you all I can. Now it's your job to find the evidence the Circle requires. It's not my place to do more, unless my help is absolutely necessary."

She pressed her palms against the arms of the chair again, shifted her body. "The Shadows are the greatest danger the universe has to offer. Take great care in everything you do." She looked from Isabelle to Galen, her brows raised in an expression he recognized from Isabelle. "Now you need a plan."

They exited the tube, and Isabelle led the way through the port city to the Strauss Hotel. The back of her head was bare of stubble today. She had scoured it that morning for the first time since the initiation.

Galen had done the same, independent of her, after rising to find his eyebrows nearly fully grown back and a short stubble covering his head. His skin had finally recovered, and he'd judged he could withstand a scouring. He decided to leave his eyebrows and scour the rest of the hair on his head away. He recited the words of the Code, then envisioned the equation, calling the scouring down upon himself. The pain was startling, intense. Yet he felt clearer afterward, more focused. The fact that Isabelle had chosen to do the same added to his growing sense that they were perfect for each other.

The roads were busy with morning traffic and noise and smells. The air was dry here, and still, so that the dirt and odors seemed to hang in a pall, obscuring the pale green sky. Rather than the fresh scent of the sea, he smelled rotten food, waste. The buildings flashed one brilliant sign after the next, the messages of all lost in the chaos. Intelligent beings of several different species passed them: the native Wychad, Pak'ma'ra, Humans, Kinbotal. They avoided eye contact, looking down or into storefront windows.

Isabelle seemed invigorated by the activity, pointing out different places and hurrying ahead. Of course, this was her home, so she would have grown used to the congestion and turmoil, just as he was accustomed to the open plain and clean breezes on the mak.

Galen had visited cities before, and as they went, this one was particularly dirty and run-down. The lack of humidity made it seem colder, too, as if an extra layer of insulation had been taken away. He crossed his arms over his chest for warmth.

His senses felt as if they were under assault. He became aware again of the undercurrent of energy from the implants, the itchy agitation they generated. Perhaps that was why he felt so uncomfortable here. He determined to keep firm control of his tech at all times, to hold the restless energy in check, to cast a spell only with careful deliberation. He would not act on instinct. He would not fail the mages again.

Isabelle pointed out the crooked, glowing sign for the Strauss Hotel farther down the street. The hotel's seven-story facade was a grimy white, except immediately below the sign, where a row of whiter spots revealed where letters had once spelled out its old Wychad name. The entryway was modest, with a small black awning over the open doorway. "Quiet, Comfort, Convenience" was written in script across the awning in stained yellow.

They entered to loud, raucous chanting. The words—and the language itself—were lost in the sheer volume. Yet Galen recognized it immediately. He'd been up late into the night listening to it. The Narns were still at their drinking game. They seemed to have an endless capacity for alcohol.

The chanting came from the lounge, which was off the lobby to the right. Several Narns were packed in the doorway. Galen recognized two of the cargo techs from the *Khatkhata*.

They'd hoped that studying the Narns would give them

some idea how to proceed, how to uncover what kind of passengers the ship was carrying, who was paying the bill, and where their final destination lay. Galen and Isabelle had examined the records of the crew, searching for opportunities. They'd found precious little. Of the ten crew members, eight had no family, no ties. They were opportunists and criminals. Some had sold weapons to Earth during the Earth-Minbari War; many had been with the same captain, Ko'Vin, for a long time. They formed a solid group, doing almost everything together.

Tricking them to reveal a connection to the Shadows, when they might not even be aware of it, would be difficult. And if they did know of the connection, how could they possibly be coerced into betraying their wealthy, powerful employers? A simple deception would not work, and a complex deception was impossible, since Galen and Isabelle had so little knowledge of the Shadows and how they worked.

Galen began to realize how ill-prepared they were. Of the steps Elric had taught him—information, preparation, control—they had only superficial information, minimal preparation, and were in a position to control very little.

The lobby was modest in size, with worn furnishings and a dingy flower-patterned carpet. They approached the front desk, a long counter manned by Cadmus Wilcox himself. Cadmus had eyebrows that hung low over his eyes, which gave his face an expression of perpetual fear. His thin, receding hair was combed to the side, and a lock of it curled around onto his forehead. A shaggy, walrus-style moustache completely obscured his lips. He stood in the center of the area circumscribed by the front desk and looked out toward the lounge, as if caught in a position of lonely command behind frontline bunkers.

Galen had studied Cadmus' records and found that he had worked at the Strauss since it changed owners twelve years ago. He'd been manager for eight years and seemed to have little life outside work. His home was a modest apartment two blocks away, though he spent most of his time at the hotel. He ate his meals in his office behind the front desk, and kept a cot behind the door that he was using more and more frequently. He seemed very concerned about the hotel and its staff, though unable to do anything to alleviate those concerns.

Cadmus jerked back a step when he saw them. Then, as he recognized Isabelle, his mouth opened, and Galen caught a glimpse of a damp lower lip sticking out from the bottom of the moustache. "I'm so glad to see you," he said. He had a thin, nasal voice. "I thought you were away. This current crowd"—he stepped up to the desk and leaned toward her, lowering his voice—"they're completely out of control. In the last day they've had two knife fights. They offered one of my employees fifty credits to get married, another employee two hundred credits to run a cocktail straw all the way up his nose. They've made the most outrageous demands, throwing credits away like they were nothing. Their captain offered a thousand credits if we could produce authentic Narn breen from our kitchen, and then when we couldn't, threatened to disembowel our chef. The captain told me the manager at Hotel Ribisi displeased them the last time they were in port. I know that man. He's in the hospital still." He glanced nervously around the lobby. "I have a call button to the port authority, but by the time they arrive, it could be too late. I know your mother put a spell of protection on the hotel, and I can't tell you how much I appreciate that. But even if no one gets killed, I don't know if I can take this stress!"

Isabelle laid a hand on the counter, her voice measured, calming. "My mother understands. She is aware of your situation, and that is why she has sent us. I am a mage now in my own right, and this is Galen, a very skilled member of our order."

As Cadmus' nervous eyes took him in, Galen nodded, pleased at Isabelle's description.

"Is that"—he rolled his shoulders in an odd, jointless way—"what happened to your hair?"

"Yes, that is our custom. My mother thought we might spend some time here while the Narns remain, to help you get through this difficult period."

Cadmus' bottom lip peeked out again. "Oh, I would be grateful for that. Not—not that I can't take care of myself. I can be as rough as the next guy." Glancing nervously toward the lounge, he reached under the counter, lifted into view a PPG, which he held between thumb and forefinger. He returned it quickly to its hiding place. "But I worry about the rest of the employees."

Galen thought that if Cadmus ever tried to shoot anyone, he'd most likely shoot himself in the foot.

"Of course," Isabelle said. "We thought we might take a table in the lounge and tell fortunes, the way my mother used to do. Then we'll be nearby, if the need arises."

"That would be fine. That would be perfect. Anything you need, anything I can do, you let me know."

Isabelle leaned toward him, and Galen could tell Cadmus enjoyed being the confidant. "We would appreciate it if you could spread the word about our services being available. Particularly to the Narns, and particularly to the second-in-command, G'Leel. You know her?"

"She has the . . ." Cadmus ran his finger across his nose.

"Yes. Have you spoken with her at all?"

"Only to ask her to step aside so the cleaning tech could deal with a rather unpleasant mess she'd made after drinking too much." Cadmus adjusted his curl of hair with a careful index finger. "But I can tell you that she recorded a message to be sent to an address on the Narn homeworld, and then canceled it."

Isabelle put a hand on his arm. "That's very useful. You're managing the stress incredibly well. I'm sure you don't need our help at all. But we're glad to offer it."

Cadmus' moustache shifted, and Galen assumed he was smiling. "Isabelle, would you tell my future?"

"Hold my hands."

He took her hands. She bowed her head and closed her eyes. When her eyes opened, Galen could see the moment in Cadmus' face. She captured him completely. His nervous gaze fixed on her, and his face relaxed, losing its self-consciousness, its momentary concerns. All that remained was hope. It seemed a terribly intimate contact.

"You have always known that you are different, that others depend on you. You have difficult weeks ahead. You will face the most severe trial of your life. When you do, something will rise up within you that you never knew you had, a bravery and strength of character that have lain deep within you. You will stand up for what is right. You will defend your place and your people. You will behave with nobility. From that moment forward, your life will change. The bravery will remain with you, refusing again to be buried. It will bring you success, prosperity, and love."

Isabelle's voice was brilliantly modulated. Stress, rhythm, and repetition combined with striking power to create an almost hypnotic effect. Isabelle maintained eye contact for several more seconds, giving him that knowing smile. He smiled with her. Gently she released him and pulled slightly back.

"I couldn't ask for better than that, I suppose," Cadmus said, straightening self-consciously. His eyes resumed their nervous activity. "Let me show you to a table in the lounge."

Galen could never have done what she had done. Could never have reached out to someone so strongly, to have created such an intimate contact. He always held back. That was why, as Elric constantly reminded him, his presentation was weak. He didn't want to connect to other people. He didn't want them to know him.

The predictions, of course, were creations of Isabelle's imagination. But Cadmus seemed to believe them.

Cadmus squeezed his way into the lounge past the Narns, who had begun thinning out after a long night. Galen reached into his pocket, dipped his finger into a packet of what felt like fine dust. As he brushed past several Narns, he planted probes on their arms, jackets, whatever surface presented itself. Isabelle, he knew, did the same.

The lounge was modest in size, with a bar at one end and small tables crowding the rest of the room. The dingy flower-patterned rug clashed with green-and-gold striped wallpaper. The lighting was dim, and the lack of windows gave the feeling of perpetual night. In their dark leathers, the Narns clustered around the bar and nearby tables. The drinking contest seemed to have ended, although the drinking had not. The Narns had begun to look a bit fatigued, though, hanging on one another, swaying unsteadily, gold-and-black spotted heads drooping. One slid off the bar and thumped to the floor.

Cadmus jumped at the sound. "Oh." He showed them to a table in the corner, and after fussing over Isabelle for a few more minutes, retreated.

"An optimistic prediction," Galen said, "wasn't it? Cadmus doesn't quite seem the heroic type."

"If he believes it, then it will become reality. And I would much rather give him something positive to believe, and play a role in the creation of a positive reality, than be party to a negative one."

Galen stared into her mysterious grey eyes, hoping he might see a positive future for them. "What if he didn't believe?"

"A skeptic does not ask his fortune to be told. And if he does, he should be politely rebuffed."

"Have you any predictions regarding our success?"

She smiled. "Yes."

Suddenly Isabelle's head turned toward the bar, and she grabbed blindly at Galen's arm. "Galen, look. It's Tilar."

On a stool at the far end of the bar, sitting by himself, was Tilar, the Centauri apprentice who had been cast away three years earlier. Several Narns had been standing in front of him before, so Galen hadn't seen him.

He wore an ornately decorated vest and a brilliant white shirt. He took a long drink from his glass, his sharp nose nearly touching the alcohol. He didn't look much different than Galen remembered, though he'd cut his crest short, and his hair even shorter. It seemed so strange, running into him here, now. Techno-mages, as a rule, did not believe in coincidences, except for those they had arranged. Seeing Tilar made Galen think of an old mage trick: turn up unexpectedly in a place, as if you had arrived ahead of the person you were contriving to meet. Many times Galen had gone on a walk along the cliff only to find Elric already there, waiting for him. Of course, Tilar wasn't a mage. But he knew the tricks.

Tilar turned in their direction, and Galen saw surprise, puzzlement, and then pleasure on his face. Tilar slid off the stool and came toward them, his gait unsteady. Galen felt uncomfortable as he approached. It wasn't forbidden to talk to someone who had been cast away, though it was forbidden to maintain a relationship with such a one. Galen did not want to know what Tilar had been doing since he had been cast away, did not want thoughts of his own failure resurrected. If the Circle had voted differently, Galen would have been cast away. He would be the one at the bar in shirtsleeves and hair, living with his own failure.

"Galen! Isabelle? I barely recognized you without the . . ." He waved a hand over his head. "It's so great to see you!" He bent down, glass in hand, and hugged each of them, wrapping them in the smell of alcohol. "What are you doing on Zafran 8?" He pulled a chair from the table behind him and fell into it.

"I live here," Isabelle said. "Galen came for a visit."

Now that Tilar was closer, Galen could see some blotching of the skin on his forehead, a sign of heavy alcohol consumption in Centauri. Tilar's body slumped in the seat at an angle. Galen had never been close to Tilar, who was several years older, but he remembered watching Tilar train at the previous convocation, and had thought his skills impressive.

Galen glanced at Isabelle, not sure what to make of Tilar's presence. Had he learned of their arrival and sought them out in an attempt to renew some contact with the mages?

"I forgot you lived here," Tilar said. "Did you always live here?"

"Yes," Isabelle said. "With Burell."

"It's so great to see you." He looked from Isabelle to Galen. "When did you get . . ." He waved his hand again over his head.

"Just a few weeks ago," Galen said.

"A few weeks. That's right. Third anniversary of my casting away." He held up his glass with the word *casting*, then swallowed its contents. He squinted at them. "Shouldn't you be at—still be at—the convocation?"

Galen glanced toward some noise at the bar. The remaining Narns were staggering out. He and Isabelle were losing their opportunity to talk to them—until tonight, anyway.

He needed to track where they went, listen to what they said. The Narns might reveal something valuable. Remembering his resolution to cast spells only with caution, Galen focused on the blank screen in his mind's eye, visualized the equation to access Burell's probes. The tech strongly echoed the equation. The network of probes requested Burell's key, and he gave it. A menu appeared, and he selected two probes in the lobby, watching as the Narns stumbled toward the elevator. They all seemed headed toward their rooms.

Galen received a message from Isabelle. *I'll deal with him, if you track the Narns.*

Yes, he responded. He visualized the equation to send the message while observing the input of several of Burell's probes and simultaneously keeping track of the conversation at the table. He felt as if he were back in the training hall keeping four balls in the air.

"We left the convocation early because Burell was taken ill," Isabelle said. "She's been ill for some time now, and hasn't left her place of power in years. The strain was very hard on her. We thought it best to get her back at once. Galen came along in case I needed help caring for her."

Isabelle was right not to confide in Tilar, of course. Yet Galen wondered if he might have some information that could help them. If it had been Galen cast away, he would have liked to help.

"I'm sorry to hear that," Tilar said. "Can't she be healed?"

The Narns pushed into the elevator, one of them starting up a drinking song. Galen switched to the probe within the elevator.

"No," Isabelle said. Silence followed.

Keeping careful focus to maintain probe access, Galen roused himself to speak. "What brings you here, Tilar?" he asked. He cast the spell to activate his sensors, feeling wrong to distrust a former member of their order, but remembering Elric's caution to be wary. Another ball in the air.

Tilar waved his glass in circles. "Oh, I've been traveling a lot. Went to Centauri Prime for a bit but couldn't stand living with those self-important fools. I made some money in investments, using all the knowledge I'd gotten as an apprentice. Then I lost it all. I guess you could call me a con man these days. Nothing as exciting as being a techno-mage, I'm sure."

There had been an odd jump in his heart rate as he spoke the last sentence, but Galen thought it most likely arose from dissatisfaction with his own circumstance.

He's telling the truth, Isabelle wrote. *But then he knows we could detect a lie.*

"Would you care for a drink?" Tilar waved toward the waitress.

"No," Galen said. He followed the Narns to their various rooms, watched them go in. *They're all in bed—probably for a few hours, at least,* he wrote to Isabelle. And he hadn't let any of the balls drop. If he had been working with his chrysalis, he would have been breathless and dripping with sweat from the effort of casting so many spells. Now, the physical effort was minimal.

Yet the mental effort remained, and without the physical exhaustion to slow him down, he realized he was putting a greater stress on his mind, on his ability to remain focused and in control. He must not overestimate his abilities and risk a slip.

The waitress came over, and Tilar ordered another. When Isabelle declined as well, Tilar looked with curiosity at their empty table.

"We came as a favor to Burell," Isabelle explained. "She has a long-standing relationship with the manager, Cadmus Wilcox. He was nervous about some of the wilder elements"—she nodded toward the bar—"so we came to offer protection."

"They like to drink." Tilar straightened his vest. "Don't we all?" Though his head wavered back and forth, his eyes fixed on Galen. They were filled with longing. "What is it like, being a techno-mage?"

The agitating undercurrent of energy, the constant need for control, the ease of casting spells, the instantaneous echo of himself—none of these were things Galen would share with anyone. He shook his head. "It is—hard to describe."

Tilar snorted.

"We're still figuring it out," Isabelle said. "It's similar to having a chrysalis, but the connection is much clearer and stronger."

The waitress brought Tilar's drink.

He leaned onto the table, his hands on either side of the glass, and stared into its depths. "Tell me about the initiation. What was it like? What did you say when they asked 'Why are you a techno-mage?' "

Another awkward silence descended among them.

"I don't think we should talk about this," Isabelle said.

Tilar's eyes glistened. "I need to know. It was all I thought of every night for the first year. How I would have answered that question."

Galen could imagine himself doing the same thing. "I said I wanted to further the work of the ancients. To master control of the tech. To do good where I can."

"And you, Isabelle"—Tilar's head turned toward her—"what did you say?"

Isabelle's grey eyes met Galen's. *I don't like his questions,* she wrote. "I said I wanted to penetrate the mysteries of the tech. To understand how it works."

"And is that what you really want? More than anything else?" His heartbeat was rising.

"I'm not sure what you mean," Isabelle said.

He straightened, and Galen saw some of the old mage training in him, the authority of posture, the stern expression, the demand for answers. "I mean, if your powers were unlimited, if there were no restrictions, what would you want? What would you want the power to do?"

The conversation had turned from Tilar's regret and curiosity to something else, something Galen didn't understand.

"For a techno-mage," Galen said, "can there be anything greater than to master control of the tech?"

"That is what I asked you," Tilar said.

Isabelle's hands closed into fists. "I would heal my mother."

Tilar smiled, and he didn't seem half as drunk as he had before. "I always dreamed of ruling an empire, as did Kwa-kiri and Neldonic. Or at the least to be like Frazur, who gave his blessing to the first emperor of the Centauri Republic and became the power behind the throne. As he said, 'Magic enables clever men to dominate others, become kings, set up the first states, and become immortalized as gods after death.' " His gaze lingered on Galen, almost as if in challenge. Then he took a long drink from his glass. "Instead, I issue orders from a barstool."

Isabelle was staring down at her fists, preoccupied.

"We should be leaving," Galen said. "The hotel seems safe for now, and Burell will be waking up soon."

Isabelle stood. "Yes. We should get back to her."

"Perhaps I'll see you again," Tilar said.

"Will you be long on Zafran 8?" Galen asked.

"My schedule is unpredictable. But I would imagine a few days more at least."

Galen dipped his finger into the packet of probes. He realized he should have planted a probe on Tilar earlier, when Tilar had first come over. The Centauri would be suspicious of any body contact at this point. Elric always told him to plan ahead. But Galen had been so surprised, he hadn't thought to plant a probe.

"It was good to see you again," Galen said.

"You'll pardon me if I don't stand," Tilar said. "My legs no longer seem to be functioning."

Isabelle laid a hand on his shoulder. "Do you need assistance?"

"I'll be fine. I'll just sit here a while, lord of all I survey."

They said their good-byes. Outside, Galen turned to Isabelle. "That was—"

She gave him a stern look, eyebrows raised. He found he had received a message. *Check yourself for probes.*

Tilar could have enough knowledge to make probes of his own, as Galen did. Probes need not be coordinated through mage implants. They could as easily transmit their findings to a datasystem. Tilar had hugged them both when he'd first approached. Of course, he would know that any probes he planted would eventually be detected.

Galen scanned down his body, looking for foreign transmissions or electronic activity.

I don't find anything, he wrote.

"I don't either," she said. "But what was that all about?"

"I don't know. I believe he contrived to meet us. Perhaps to find some answers for himself?"

Isabelle nodded. "If not for himself, then for whom?"

— chapter 9 —

Elric closed the door behind him, glad to be home for once before midnight. The convocation had been running more smoothly since the initiation, though there were daily crises to be handled and changes to be accommodated. He'd given his presentation on additional hyperspace currents he'd discovered, solved a food shortage, and stopped a fight between two of the Kinetic Grimlis. He'd found a private site for Blaylock and his followers to perform a mortification ritual, shuffled meetings to keep feuding parties from running into each other, and ejected Jab twice from the proceedings.

Circe had been upset that he'd missed her lecture, but as much as could be expected, the mages seemed to be enjoying themselves. The young apprentices played and learned; those new to the chrysalis had their first awkward training sessions; the initiates worked with the Kinetic Grimlis to meld a piece of their chrysalis to their new ship and master its operation. The rest of them talked, bragged, laughed, and argued.

Elric had always enjoyed these meetings, but this convocation was different. Since Galen had left, Elric had felt detached. He seemed to pass through events like a holographic illusion; nothing could touch him. He felt as if he lived in a world of Shadows, and doom, and he was the only one who could see them coming. Blaylock, he knew, felt it too, but that was little comfort. It wasn't Blaylock's student who had been sent into danger.

Elric stood in the middle of the main room. The lights were dark, the fire cold. The house was quiet, empty. And perhaps it would remain so from this time forth.

Elric shook off his mood, turned on some lights, and conjured a magical fire on the hearth. He had given Galen a staff, had told Galen all that he could. The Circle had determined that Galen and Isabelle must complete this task themselves. Was there nothing more he might do?

He sat at the table, found himself accessing the probe recording of Galen's attack on Elizar. He had watched it many times the night of the attack, so much that he almost knew it by heart. But he hadn't watched it since.

The probe on the tent had been situated a bit behind Elizar, so Elric could see only Elizar's side and back, while Galen and Isabelle faced him. Beneath the light globes that illuminated the night, their features seemed flat, washed out.

Elizar brought his hands to his mouth and released a sustained syllable, casting a spell.

"No," Isabelle said. Her fingers moved to conjure a shield.

Galen's eyes widened, and Elric could see the moment he cast the spell, the instinctive flash from Galen's mind to the chrysalis, like the parry of a well-trained fencer. Such fights were not uncommon. What was uncommon was the strength of Galen's defense, a counterattack that could completely annihilate the opponent, and perhaps much more.

But did that mean he had to be sent, just out of the chrysalis, to face the Shadows, perhaps to die?

Almost instantly Galen's face tightened with concentration, and Elric could see him trying to alter the spell, to render it safe.

Suddenly Elric's attention was drawn away. Far behind Galen, in the shadows by the cliffs, someone was standing. Elric was amazed he had never seen the person before. He'd been so focused on Galen, he hadn't noticed anything else.

He cut away the rest of the image, enlarged the figure. The resolution was poor, the light dim, but he could tell that it was Human, male, of compact build. The man wore not black robes but a dark suit, and he had dark hair. The resolution was good enough that if the man had been a mage, Elric would have recognized him. But he was not a mage.

Elric remembered the man sent by the Rook of Tain, a special messenger with crates of pects. Morden. He looked like this man. Morden had arrived on the opening night of the convocation, though. This was the next night, the night of the Becoming, when all outsiders were banned. Yet here he was, watching.

Elric recalled that something about Morden had disturbed him, though the meeting had been so brief, the situation so chaotic, he had never determined what.

Elric accessed the probe archives in his place of power, returned to the opening night of the convocation. After some quick searching, there was Morden, with his smooth voice, his message from the Rook, and his crates of pects. As Elric looked at it now, the situation struck him as a sloppy attempt at misdirection: generate chaos to avoid scrutiny. He was ashamed that it had worked.

But why would Morden want to avoid scrutiny? His authorization from the Rook had been valid. What was he afraid Elric would find?

Elric labeled Morden's figure and did a search for it throughout the probes in the convocation area, from the moment of Morden's arrival through the present. Since he didn't have probes in the tents, out of respect for the mages' privacy, what he might find was limited.

Yet there were forty positive identifications, and many more possible ones. They began on the opening night and continued for the next two days. Apparently, by the morning of the initiation, Morden had left.

In his mind's eye, Elric went through the forty appearances. Morden arrived, entered the tents. He came back out in conversation with one of the Kinetic Grimlis. That one introduced him to the others. He mingled that first night with many of the mages, though Elric noticed Morden stayed away from the members of the Circle. Occasionally he would lead one mage away from the others, to talk in private, in the shadows. He did this with Circe, Djadjamonkh, Maskelyne, others. There was so much noise from the opening-night gathering that Elric couldn't hear any of these conversations.

Early in the morning of the second day, as most of the mages returned to their ships for a few hours' rest, Morden entered the tents. He didn't come out until nightfall, when he came upon Galen and the others. He observed the argument. He saw Galen strike, with overwhelming force. Then he withdrew.

Morden didn't appear again until the next afternoon, when he mingled again with mages outside the tents. Since the Becoming had been postponed until the Circle came to a decision regarding Galen, no one expelled the outsider. This time the one taken aside was Alwyn.

Now Elric would find out what Morden had been saying. Besides Galen, he trusted Alwyn more than anyone—trusted him to be sarcastic, outspoken, uncompromising, and honest. Tonight Elric had left him, half drunk, in the middle of a probe-spitting contest. At least, perhaps, he could get the part of the truth that Alwyn remembered.

He composed a message. *Alwyn, you spoke to this man.* He inserted Morden's image. *What did he say to you?*

Elric waited impatiently for a response, continuing through the recordings, finding an image of Morden leaving for Lok on the evening of the third day. He switched to the probe by the Lok wagon station, found Morden getting transportation back to Tain. Estimating the travel time, Elric accessed his probes in the Rook's office and home. Morden did not appear.

Instead, he arrived at the Tain spaceport. The spaceport was actually little more than a wide, flat field around which numerous shops and businesses had grown up, handling what little trade Tain had with other systems. A small building handled the processing of off-worlders and foreign goods—mainly charging fees and checking their names off a list. Elric maintained several probes inside and outside the building. Morden entered about half a day after leaving Lok, and headed out onto the field, where a small personal transport waited. Elric watched it lift off with a feeling of relief. He was gone.

He received a response from Alwyn. *In the middle of something IMPORTANT here, as you know. Three points ahead! Fed got a bull's-eye but vomited on it, so I had it disqualified. Youngster can't hold his liquor.*

I remember the man, vaguely. He was the representative of someone from . . . somewhere. Welcomed us here, said his—employer?—was curious about mages. Asked why do I do what I do? What do I want? I gave him the standard line about— Hold on a minute.

The message ended. Elric sighed, waiting for another. In a minute, it came.

Stiff competition here. Where—yes, I gave him some standard lines about knowing all that can be known, creating awe and wonder—the Circle would have been proud of me—but he didn't seem satisfied, I remember. Asked me again, what do I want? I can't remember exactly how the conversation went, but I ended up saying I wanted all hypocrites to have their sins broadcast on ISN and then be questioned in their underwear by a journalist. He was unamused. In fact, I think I actually upset him. That's it.

Now to put these rapscallions in their place.

The message ended.

Elric was becoming more and more concerned. Someone had come into their convocation, questioned them, observed them, and to what end? Morden had somehow gotten the Rook to lend his name and authority to the enterprise, though the questions Morden asked had not been for the Rook. His answers had been delivered elsewhere.

Elric retrieved the note from the Rook, grateful that instinct had made him keep it. On the envelope, his sensors isolated a Human thumbprint. It was not his own. Elric linked to Earth's databases, searched for any record of Morden. Luckily, it wasn't a common name. In the current taxpayer records, banking records, retirement account records, he found only 1,211 Mordens. Of those, 591 were male, 73 within the twenty-eight to thirty-eight age range, and only 19 with Morden's coloring, height, and weight. None of them matched the thumbprint or the face.

Elric decided to search farther back, looking at births within the likely period. Eliminating all the Mordens he had already checked, he found only one additional record of birth: May 25, 2223 in Summit, New Jersey. From there he traced the opening of a retirement security account when Morden was in his teens. The thumbprint matched, and the face—though much younger—belonged to the man he had met. His first job was at the Michigan State University bookstore. Elric checked the school's records, was surprised to find that Morden had earned his Ph.D. in archaeology, with a specialty in archaeolinguistics. After graduation, Morden had gone to work in EarthForce's New Technologies Division. His records there were closed. Elric would send a computer demon to breach the security and retrieve them.

Elric found an identicard photo of the adult Morden; it was definitely the same man. In June 2248, the retirement account records showed he was married. In October 2250, daughter Sarah born. Then in May 2256, both wife and daughter died. And at the beginning of last year, January 2257, Morden's retirement account had been closed. He was registered deceased.

Which did nothing to illuminate the situation. What was a dead archaeologist doing at their convocation?

Alwyn had said that Morden grew upset at the mention of ISN, the Interstellar News Network. Elric followed the hunch and accessed the ISN archives, which were open to the public. He searched under *Morden*, found a cluster of dates around May 2256. He called up the first news story. The anchorwoman announced that the Io jumpgate had been destroyed in a terrorist bombing. At the moment of the explosion, a ship with over five hundred passengers had been entering the jumpgate. As she spoke of the grieving relatives, they showed a swarm of reporters surrounding Morden. As they yelled out questions—"How do you feel about the death of your wife and child?" "What would you like to say to the terrorists?"—Morden struck out at them, shoving them back, turning in a circle as he did to clear some space for himself. "Stop it! Stop it! Stop it!" Morden yelled, his face red. The nervous reporters hastily backed into one another, but continued to shout questions. In the middle of the empty space he had cleared, Morden turned slowly, brought his hands to his ears, and screamed.

Alwyn had written, *I ended up saying I wanted all hypocrites to have their sins broadcast on ISN and then be questioned in their underwear by a journalist.*

Could this be Morden's sin? Could he have had his wife and five-year-old daughter killed, along with a ship full of other people? If so, what powerful allies could have helped an archaeologist destroy a jumpgate?

When they had met, Morden's voice, his body, were carefully controlled. He had used misdirection to avoid scrutiny.

What was he hiding?

Elric removed the image from his mind's eye. All his questions were merely ways to avoid the one question he feared to ask, the one he feared to answer, and the one he believed he now could.

He knew they worked behind the scenes. He knew they found others to do their bidding, dark servants seduced by their own desires. And he knew those servants constantly searched for more.

Had Morden been sent by the Shadows?

And from that question inevitably came the next. Did the Shadows now know of Galen's power?

Elric found he had received a new message. It was from Galen. He opened it eagerly, realizing it was what he had hoped for since arriving home. He needed to know that Galen was safe, especially now that he'd discovered this new danger.

We have more to tell you, Galen's message read. *Would you like to do an electron incantation?*

Yes, Elric responded immediately. *I will do it now.*

A message was sent by means he well understood. Their network of relays monitored the location of every mage whose energy was within range and channeled each message to its recipient. But the electron incantation worked through a much more mysterious process. Instead of his message traveling to Galen, Elric felt as if he himself traveled to Galen. It was like a dream.

He closed his eyes, focusing, centering. In his mind's eye, he visualized himself stepping from his body, visualized the long journey: up out of the atmosphere of Soom, past the brilliant orange outer planets and out of the solar system, into the vast blackness of space, which cradled him like a bed of black velvet. He passed the star systems and nebulae that marked his way. He saw the Zafran star, a shining beacon in the night, the eighth planet of brown and green, the sprawl of the port city, Burell's building, her penthouse apartment. In his mind's eye, the apartment was empty. Yet, as in a dream, he knew Galen and Isabelle were there. He searched for the mage energy characteristic of Galen, felt a vibration as he came close to it. He visualized his hand reaching out to grasp the energy, drawing it inside him. Then he searched for Isabelle and did the same.

For the location of their meeting he chose his circle of standing stones on a warm, bright day. The brilliant mist, the breeze, the ocean's sharp tang usually served to lighten his heart. Everything within the incantation had a sense of heightened intensity and significance. He ran a hand down the moss-covered stone beside him. Velvety, damp, it was a part of the planet, and a part of him.

Galen and Isabelle stood a few feet away. What he saw was not them, but their self-images, the way they imagined themselves to be. He was pleased to see that their heads were scoured. Their commitment to the Code had become part of their identity. Typically, their self-images looked a few years younger than they did. Galen's image was a little fuller in the cheeks, carrying the baby fat he'd had when he was eighteen. Elric remembered him then, just into the chrysalis, so eager, at last, to do what he'd studied for so long.

They looked well, and he took comfort in that. If something horrible had happened, he believed it would be revealed somehow in the self-image.

"You are well?" Elric asked.

"Yes," Galen said. "We've met the manager of the Strauss

Hotel, and we've begun watching the Narn crew of the *Khatkhata*."

Elric's anxiety allowed him to wait no longer. He extended his arm and conjured an image of Morden standing beside him. "Have you seen this man?"

"No," Isabelle said.

But Galen nodded, and Elric's heart jumped. "I saw him in the tents at the convocation. Just for a minute."

"Did you speak with him?"

"In passing. I thought he might be lost. I asked if he needed help. He asked if I needed help. It was strange. I was in a hurry, so I left him behind." Galen's hungry eyes absorbed the image. "Who is he?"

"His name is Morden. I believe he is a servant of the Shadows. If you ever see him, you must inform me at once. Do not approach him."

"What was he doing at the convocation?" Isabelle asked.

"He was observing us, searching for allies, searching for ways to divide us. He asked questions of many of us. He asked, 'Why are you a techno-mage?' and 'What do you want?' " Elric hoped that Morden's search had been fruitless. The techno-mages must remain united, or they would fall.

Galen and Isabelle exchanged a look, and in that look Elric saw that they had grown closer. Unfortunately, there was nothing to be done about that now. That was the least of his concerns.

"We just had a conversation like that," Galen said.

The Shadows knew that Galen could be their greatest enemy, or their greatest ally. He was in a position of grave danger. And there was nothing more Elric could do to help. Galen must face his trial.

"This conversation was with Morden?" Elric asked.

"No." Galen's hesitation told Elric the answer was not one he would want to hear. "With Tilar."

For the better part of two days, Galen and Isabelle had sat at the table in the Strauss lounge, telling fortunes, monitoring probes, and searching for information. They had told many fortunes, they had witnessed incredible feats of drinking and dexterity, but none of the Narns had approached them. Galen thought that he and Elizar had been all too right in their fear that people had lost their respect for the mages.

He and Isabelle had adopted some of the trappings common to Narn fortune-tellers in an attempt to lure the crew over. The table was covered in black lace. A short pedestal in the center of the table was draped with a white cloth. A deck of Narn fortune cards sat on top of it.

The Narns laughed, and sang, and drank, and fought, and spent outrageous amounts of money. But they did not approach.

Through the probes in the hotel, they had heard other guests speak of money to be made, power to be had. But nothing of Shadows. They had learned of illegal operations, of traffic to the rim. They had traced leads, made connections. But none to Shadows.

They had seen nothing of Tilar since their initial encounter. Isabelle's probe had ended up in the garbage, either because it had failed to attach itself properly, which was unlikely, or because he had deduced it was there and disposed of it.

Elric had been alarmed when they'd told him of their meeting. He believed that Tilar, like Morden, had become a servant of the Shadows. If it was true, then agents of the Shadows were all around them. Galen was shocked to think that Tilar could have so fallen since being cast away. Tilar had almost become a techno-mage. He knew the mages, and he knew their ways. If he was a servant of the Shadows, then the Shadows would know much.

Burell had determined to trace Tilar's movements, but found no record of his arrival or departure, no record of housing or expenditures, no record, in fact, of any activity, on planet or off, for almost a year and a half.

One thing they had accomplished was planting probes on all the Narns without arousing their suspicion. The Narns' private conversations hadn't turned out to be any more illuminating than their public ones, though. They argued about sexual conquests, discussed the best ways of spending large amounts of money, and compared the most disgusting things they had ever seen.

The visuals from the probes, however, provided plenty of views of the exterior of the ship, as the crew rotated in the guarding of it, and even a few glimpses of the interior. Hopefully, soon, they would get a view of those passengers who seemed to have been left to their own devices in the hold. And eventually, if all else failed, they would discover where the ship was bound, once it reached the end of the jumpgate line, and to whom its contents would be delivered.

The microelectronic probes weren't powerful enough to transmit over such vast distances, but the mages commonly employed faster-than-light relays, about two feet square and a few inches thick. These were usually put into orbit around a planet they wished to observe. In the case of a ship, the relay was often planted onboard or attached to the hull. It would collect the data from the probes and hold the information until a mage signaled for retrieval.

But how to plant the relay? As he and Isabelle had considered different methods, Galen had recalled a classic case where Maju had planted a relay in a gift for an important passenger on a ship. From there, it had taken Isabelle only seconds to apply the idea to their own situation. The gift would be given by Cadmus Wilcox to the Narn captain, Ko'Vin. The gift would be of great value. The gift would inspire great desire. The gift would be breen.

Which led to Galen's current predicament.

"Quit pretending you're busy and come over here and taste this," Isabelle said. Across the kitchen, she held out a small plate with a single spherical brown lump covered in gravy.

Galen stuck his spoon into his bowl, which contained a foul-smelling brownish paste. It was his latest attempt at mixing up something that tasted like breen. The spoon stood upright in the curdled mass.

He approached Isabelle's plate with more dread than he'd ever faced a training session. He'd eaten at least a dozen of the greasy, pungent orbs by now, each worse than the one before.

The gravy looked a bit thicker on this one, as if it had begun to coagulate, and as he tilted his head he saw it had a kind of jellied sheen. The sphere below was shrouded in mystery. He tried to remember if this was the batch in which they'd done the extra protein processing for added texture, or where they'd replaced the artificial proteins with some local mealworms. Did it really matter, though?

Her thin brows raised, Isabelle handed him the fork, handle first. He wished now he'd learned how Blaylock turned off the taste center in his brain. He stabbed the ball, swirled it in the gravy, and jammed the breen into his mouth. He closed his eyes, focusing on the texture they were trying so hard to reproduce. Narn cooking literature spoke of the texture of breen in great depth and complexity, praising the sensation of the teeth sinking into the perfectly cooked breen, "the playful hint of a crunch followed by the incomparable juicy meaty moistness." The literature cautioned that "Breen should be neither too loose and crumbly, nor too firm and stodgy."

Galen just tried not to gag. After an incomparable amount of time, his mouth was finally empty. Though the taste lingered. "I think I felt it that time." Galen opened his eyes. "The crunch. The juicy meaty moistness."

"Really? You think that's it?" She ran the back of her hand across her forehead, leaving a brown smudge there. Her robe was covered with powders and stains, as was his.

"I think I felt it. You try it."

Dread filled her face, then resignation. She jabbed a ball in the frying pan, swirled it in the gravy, inserted it into her mouth. As her face contorted, down the hall a door opened. Burell floated out on her yellow armchair.

Her jaw frozen in midchew, Isabelle exchanged a worried glance with Galen. Burell had not been sleeping well since they returned, and though she hid it well, Galen sensed that her condition was worsening. Isabelle's concern confirmed it.

Burell wore an elegant golden robe, her hair and makeup fixed immaculately in the illusion. Galen wished they had not awakened her. It was 4 A.M. They'd left the lounge at 1 A.M. to begin working on the breen project. The *Khatkhata* was scheduled to leave port at 4 P.M.

"What's going on out here?" She swirled around the counter into the kitchen. "I smell"—her face wrinkled up—"something."

Galen explained the situation while Isabelle chewed.

Burell took a look into the frying pan, then retreated several feet. "So you're using chemical equivalents to the Narn ingredients, and trying to reproduce the texture through processing."

Isabelle nodded, a lump still visible in her cheek.

"But how do you know if you've got it right?"

"We've found descriptions in the foremost Narn culinary texts," Galen said. "We're matching appearance and consistency with them."

Burell took in the mess that they had made. "I hate to be the bearer of bad tidings, but a book is not going to tell you if you've made good breen. Narns are fanatical about it. They've written love poems to their breen. If it's not exactly right, they won't touch it. The only way to know if you've got it right is to have a Narn test it."

As soon as she'd said it, Galen knew she was right. They'd been fooling themselves into thinking they could do it on their own.

Isabelle looked from Burell to Galen, bent over the sink, and spit out the last remaining chunk. She grimaced. "Why didn't we think of that two hours ago?"

"As mages you should know," Burell said. "If the execution is not absolutely perfect, the deception will not work."

After a few minutes of consulting and staring at the breen with a kind of repulsed fascination, Burell returned to bed.

Galen and Isabelle had only a few more hours to get this right. Yesterday, they had devised a container for the breen, with a false bottom in which the relay could be hidden. Isabelle had decorated the container with ornate engraving to minimize the chance that it would be thrown away after the breen was eaten. Yet if the breen was bad, the Narns would likely jettison the container out of anger. They needed to make sure their breen was good. And to do that, they needed a Narn close by, but not too close, one without ties to the port or the Narns on the *Khatkhata*.

Narns were rare on Zafran 8, and even more rare outside the port city. As Galen searched for one, Isabelle formulated their plan.

Within an hour, they were outside a high-priced apartment in a town to the west of the port. The inhabitant was Ko'Dan, a retired engineer who had moved from the Narn homeworld to Zafran 8 three years earlier. He had traveled extensively for his career, including a long stay on Earth, so no translation would be necessary. While his choice of retirement spots was unusual, he seemed perfect for their needs.

"Ready?" Isabelle asked.

They were surrounded by bags of ingredients and cooking equipment. Behind them floated the illusion of a camera, a saucer the size of a dinner plate. The promise of appearing on the newsfeeds might encourage Ko'Dan to cooperate. Both Galen and Isabelle had conjured full-body illusions to disguise themselves as chefs, with the traditional white shirts and pants, and white chef's hats. They had both restored their hair as part of the illusion, Isabelle's pulled back in a neat braid. It was strange seeing Isabelle in white after she had been so long in black. Her face seemed to glow. Galen held the certificate and a stay-warm container with the last batch of breen they'd made. He held his breath, removed the cover, and nodded.

Isabelle pressed the bell. After a minute, she pressed it again. This was the first time either of them had truly tried a deception. For his part, Galen was nervous. Isabelle jumped as a voice bellowed over the speaker.

"Who's there?"

"This is Isabelle from the new Chemical Culinary Institute." Her voice was strong, assured, though her hands were clenched together. "I'm excited to inform you that you have just won our grand prize in the Great Breen Eat-Off Sweepstakes. For the—"

"I'm sleeping. Go . . . Did you say *breen*?"

"Yes, sir, I did. We are at your door with a huge bowlful of breen and the makings for much, much more. For the next three hours, we'll make you as much breen as you can eat. It's all—"

"I'll be right there."

Isabelle shot Galen a nervous smile, then straightened before the door, putting her hands to her sides.

The door opened. Ko'Dan stood there in a robe and pants.

"Congratulations!" Galen and Isabelle yelled. The camera zoomed up to Ko'Dan's face, and he jerked a step back.

Isabelle took the certificate from Galen and presented it to Ko'Dan. "You have won our grand prize in the Great Breen Eat-Off Sweepstakes. For the next three hours, we will make you as much breen as you can eat, using our new patented process."

Ko'Dan looked from the certificate to Isabelle to the camera. "This is all— I must say— Thank you so much. I'm overwhelmed." He shook his head. "I didn't even know I was in the running."

Galen extended the breen and a fork, and Ko'Dan eagerly stabbed a piece and closed his mouth around it. Galen imagined his teeth entering the orb, the hint of crispiness followed by the juicy meaty moistness. Ko'Dan's jaw made only one chewing motion, then stopped, allowing him to savor the taste.

"Oh that's terrible. Truly terrible."

Isabelle attributed the bad breen to the travel time and offered to make a fresh batch. Soon they were setting up in Ko'Dan's spacious, state-of-the-art kitchen. A large photograph of Ko'Dan's deceased mate, Na'Rad, hung over the table. Aside from the rather dim lighting, the apartment seemed more Human than Narn in style. Perhaps he'd become accustomed to that during his time on Earth.

Age had paled the spots on Ko'Dan's head and chest, but he seemed in good health and good spirits. He watched with curiosity as they unpacked their ingredients.

"What are these powders? You can't expect to make breen out of powders. Where is the meat?"

Isabelle unpacked their pans and bowls. "The goal of the Chemical Culinary Institute is to re-create culinary delicacies without the original ingredients. We use these chemical equivalents and process them for appropriate texturing."

"Why?"

"So that people like yourself, far from home, can enjoy the delicacies of home."

Ko'Dan put his hands on his hips and surveyed the ingredients, frowning.

It wasn't long after he'd gagged on their second batch that he'd taken over the cooking. Although the ingredients were strange to him, he quickly began adjusting and improvising to get the result he desired. The mealworms, when he discovered them in an overlooked bag, excited him the most. "Real meat!" he said, pinching one between his fingers.

Ko'Dan had a great passion for breen, and he lectured them as he worked. "The exterior of the ball must be firm but not too firm. The interior needs to have a certain . . . chunkiness."

Galen stood on one side and Isabelle on the other, and over the cooking breen their eyes met. Isabelle smiled.

Batch after batch failed to meet Ko'Dan's standards. But he was determined, now that he had begun, to unlock the secret of the perfect breen. Under his direction, Galen stirred up another batch, while Isabelle cooked the previous one. Ko'Dan stuck a spoon into Galen's batter and tasted a sample, his tongue flicking in and out of his mouth. "That, I think, is our finest mix yet." He reached into the frying pan and removed one of the cooking balls with his fingers. He squeezed it between thumb and forefinger. "Better. We are getting closer to that perfect composition—soggy but meaty."

Galen stopped stirring. "But I thought the perfect texture was a hint of a crunch followed by juicy meaty moistness."

"No, no." Ko'Dan shook his head. "No. No. You want no crunch. No crunch at all. Soggy but meaty. That's the key. Soggy but meaty." He waved his batter-covered spoon for emphasis, and a lump of the moist mixture flipped onto Galen's cheek. Galen started. The lump stayed in place. Ko'Dan scraped it off with a finger, studied it. "Soggy but meaty."

Isabelle broke out in silent laughter, her body shaking. Her face and ears turned a bright red, and at last the sound burst from her, light, breathless. Galen felt the irrepressible urge rise up in himself, this sense of lightness, and he started laughing. It felt as if his internal organs were convulsing, about to rupture. Yet he couldn't stop. He doubled over. Ko'Dan looked from one of them to the other, shrugged, and returned to his cooking.

Galen and Isabelle would just get their laughing under control when something new would set them off: a glob of gravy so thick it jiggled on the plate, a new breen to be tested for that "soggy but meaty" quality, Ko'Dan urging Isabelle to try "just a bite." Galen had never laughed so hard in his life. He attributed it to sleep deprivation.

At 7:10 A.M., Ko'Dan declared victory. He had created the "perfect breen, one unparalleled in the annals of culinary history." As he sat down at the table with a bottle of wine to treat himself, Galen and Isabelle broke again into laughter, for no particular reason. Just looking at her made him laugh now. He rested his elbows on the counter, gasping for air, and Isabelle did the same beside him. Her arm touched his as it shook. After a few moments, her hand closed around his.

The laughs dropped away as he turned toward her, and she turned toward him as well, her grey eyes alight, mouth caught between gasping and laughing. He drew in a deep breath, feeling a connection to her he had never felt with anyone else. The lightness inside him again swelled, and as she gasped for air so did he, shocked with the intensity of his love for her.

"You must try a piece," Ko'Dan called. "I can't take all of this incredible breen for myself."

They began to laugh again. She squeezed his hand and released it, and they sat with Ko'Dan at the table.

Ko'Dan asked them to join him in a toast. As they raised

their glasses he said, "To new love and old love." He nodded toward the portrait of his mate and drank. "I moved here to get away from all memory of her. Yet it is in my memory of her that I find the most joy."

As Ko'Dan's gaze lingered on the portrait, Galen wondered what he would do if he ever lost Isabelle. He wouldn't, he decided. They would die together, as his parents had. He wouldn't let her leave him alone.

By 8 A.M., Ko'Dan had made enough of his "perfect breen" to satisfy his appetite, with plenty remaining to comprise the gift for the Narn captain. He gave them the excess as "samples," reminding them again of the keys to making great breen.

They left the remaining ingredients for Ko'Dan, and he bid them happiness and long life.

At the door, Isabelle hesitated. "Have you ever been to a fortune-teller?"

"A strange question," Ko'Dan said. "I went only once, the night I met Na'Rad. I asked if she might ever love me. The fortune-teller said yes, if I bathed more often! I was bathing three and four times a day until she agreed to mate with me."

Isabelle smiled. "Was there a reason you chose that particular fortune-teller?"

Ko'Dan's eyes narrowed in curiosity. "This teller was not well known, but I passed her table every day in the market. It was unadorned with the trappings used by so many—the lace, the cards, the nonsense. Those things came from the Centauri influence. Because of that, I suppose, I felt she could be trusted."

Galen exchanged embarrassed glances with Isabelle. They should have researched the tradition more thoroughly.

"I know of no fortune-tellers here," Ko'Dan said. "Did you want to consult one?"

"I was curious," Isabelle said.

"One look and I can tell you two will be very happy together," he said.

"Thank you," she said.

When he closed the door, they both laughed again, for no particular reason, then began racing toward the tube with their precious gift of breen. Morning had come, and as they dodged through the cold, busy streets, Galen found he could not stop smiling.

— chapter 10 —

In four hours, the *Khatkhata* would continue its journey to the rim.

Sitting again at the table in the hotel lounge, this time without the lace, the pedestal, or the fortune cards, Galen watched through the lobby probe as two more Narns checked out and left for the ship. Only two now remained in the hotel, Captain Ko'Vin and the second-in-command, G'Leel. Only two more chances to pull information from the Narns before they left.

The container of breen was now with Cadmus, who was nervous about the gift and afraid he'd be blamed for whatever it contained. Yet he was so relieved to see the Narns leave, that his complaints had been only halfhearted.

An overweight woman in a brightly colored top and pants wove among the scattered lunch patrons, heading toward their table. She wasn't a guest of the hotel, though Galen had seen her in the lounge the day before, also at lunch.

Isabelle was preoccupied, watching G'Leel through the probe in her hotel room. Galen knew Isabelle still hoped the second-in-command with the knife scar across her nose would stop to have her fortune told. *She often looks toward us when she's in the bar,* Isabelle had said. *But she won't come over with the others around.* Isabelle's hands were folded tightly, her thumbs tapping a nervous rhythm against each other.

The overweight woman stopped at their table. "Do you tell fortunes?"

Isabelle had done all the fortune-telling thus far. She

stopped her thumb tapping to shoot a pointed look at him, raising her eyebrows.

"Yes," Galen said. "We do. Please sit down."

The woman remained standing. "How much does it cost?"

Burell had told them that most people would not believe a fortune-teller unless they had to pay. A fee too low encouraged doubt.

"Five credits," Galen said.

She nodded and opened her small handbag, pressing it into her stomach as she searched carefully through the ragged papers inside.

Galen studied her anxiously. He understood the mechanics of gathering information on people, but he often drew the wrong conclusions from that information. At least, his conclusions were often contrary to Isabelle's. Her "predictions" seemed to come out of the blue, yet her customers invariably expressed amazement at their accuracy.

Of course, Galen knew that if people expected to find a relationship between two things—between their lives and the predictions of a fortune-teller, for example—then they would find a relationship. They would ignore ten off-base statements and focus on the one that most connected to their concerns, astonished by the accuracy of the fortune-teller. But he wondered if he would be able to make that one correct statement.

He had practiced fortune-telling only a handful of times in the past, preferring to focus on the tech and its abilities rather than on a performance talent that even a nonmage could develop. Since the main qualities needed for fortune-telling were showmanship and an understanding of Human nature, Galen wasn't terribly good at it.

The woman handed her credit chit to him. He pushed it into the credit reader on the table, watched as her name and account number came up on the display. He visualized the equation for information access, then ran her name and number through various databases.

She sat. He deducted five credits from her card and returned it. She slipped it carefully into her handbag.

Her name was Mary Stein. She was married, forty-six years old. Galen quickly retrieved her financial records. She had 117 credits in her account.

"I'd like you to take a deep breath. Clear your mind. That's it." In his mind, Elric berated him for weak presentation. Galen took a moment, focused on his voice. "Look"—he extended his hand, conjuring a sphere—"into this globe of light. In it, time lines converge. The past, the present, the future." His hands made a flourish around the globe. She stared into it.

Galen was going to skip over the rest of her financial information when he found that she'd had twelve thousand credits in her account up until two weeks ago. The money had been withdrawn in one lump sum. The next day, her husband's name had been removed from the account. He searched for marriage and divorce records.

"You are troubled," he said. "You have a difficult decision to make." Most people were troubled, and those who sought out fortune-tellers, even more so. It was a safe opening.

"Yes," she said, surprised. "I don't know what to do."

She'd been a citizen of Zafran 8 for the last nineteen years. Records showed three marriages, the first two ending in divorce.

"You are troubled financially, and you are troubled in love."

"It's not the money I care so much about." She turned from the globe to him. "It's my husband." Her face puffed out, and she burst out sobbing.

Galen snatched a napkin from a neighboring table and madly searched for records on the husband. Albert Stein was a bartender at a restaurant just down the street. He had been married three times as well, though Galen found no record of divorces. There was a warrant for his arrest on Earth. He had stolen money from his second wife and left the planet.

Mary delicately blotted her eyes.

Galen found that Albert had purchased passage off-world on a ship that had left yesterday. He had taken her money and abandoned her. Galen could see why Mary was angry with him.

"Your husband has stolen from you and mistreated you. Now he is far from here. He should pay for what he has done, but it will be a difficult struggle for you to obtain justice."

Now Mary was shaking her head. "I don't want justice. I want my husband back. Can I get him back?" She seized his hand. "Please, can I get him back?"

Galen wished her attention would return to the globe. He was uneasy with the intensity of her need, and didn't know what to say. Getting her husband back was obviously the worst thing that could happen to her. He did quick checks on her previous two husbands, found that they too had criminal records. The divorce proceedings revealed that they had been unfaithful to her, had stolen from her.

"You will not get him back. He cares more for money than for you, and now that he has yours, he has moved on."

Her sobbing returned with renewed force, her hand hot and tight about his. Galen noticed that Isabelle's attention was focused now on him.

"Why does this keep happening to me?" Mary said.

What could he say? His tone came out more distant than he intended. "You fall in love with men who do not love you. You will continue to fall in love, and men will continue to break your heart. Your life will not change."

She released his hand and shot to her feet, knocking her chair over. "He did love me. Who are you to say? Who are you?" She staggered out of the lounge, her arm with the handbag extended, searching for balance. The other patrons stared at her.

Galen berated himself. She had enough problems as it was. He would have gone after her, except he knew he would only make things worse. He didn't understand people. He never had.

Isabelle continued to stare at him.

"I know," Galen said. "I'm terrible with people. I should be locked away in a laboratory somewhere."

"How do you know," Isabelle said, "that she cannot change?"

"People are what they are." Galen took the crumpled napkin, looked toward the door. "She has married three husbands who abused her trust. She will not change. I am bad with people. I will not change."

"You don't believe people can transcend themselves? That they can learn and grow and become greater than they once were?"

"I believe we can learn. But I believe, at base, we will always be the same."

"I believe that people can transcend themselves," Isabelle said. "In fact, I believe the universe is designed for the express purpose of helping them do so."

Galen turned to her. "Are you saying you believe in God?"

"If God is what we call the mind who designed the universe, yes."

The death of his parents had taught him that there was no God. "But how can you believe in God? We simulate miracles. We create the appearance of magic. We, more than any others, know that no true magic exists."

"The true magic," Isabelle said, "is science. Science reveals a consistency, a design underlying all things. I see evidence of God every day, in every thing. This universe did not arise by chance. There is a pattern. It is a pattern I would like to learn to weave."

"But the existence of scientific laws doesn't mean there has to be a God. Matter itself dictates them."

"What is matter but an expression of God?"

Debating the existence of God with Isabelle—as doing anything with her—carried an element of pleasure. But the topic was one that had always made him uncomfortable. Even angry. Had God then killed his parents to fulfill some cosmic pattern? The tech within him echoed his anger, surging with agitating energy. He enunciated harshly. "Would you admit that perhaps you *see* a pattern to events because you *believe* there is a pattern to events, just as the customer of the fortune-teller sees truth in the telling?"

She smiled. "I see a pattern, dear Galen, because there is one. That woman keeps meeting men who would take advantage of her because the universe is trying to help her see and overcome her problem. Just as the universe sent her to you to help you overcome your problem."

"The universe is some sort of vast dating service, then?"

She raised her eyebrows, considering the idea. "Perhaps."

"What problem?" Galen asked, catching up with her. "Are you saying I need to transcend myself?"

Isabelle's eyes shifted to the door. "She's here."

G'Leel stood in the doorway of the lounge, looking back into the lobby. Galen could see, through the lobby probes, that it was empty except for Cadmus Wilcox. The lounge had a handful of patrons still eating lunch, but no Narns. G'Leel approached.

She wore a sleeveless tunic, pants, and gloves all of black leather, with a gun case fastened at her waist. Her gold-and-black spotted arms were sharply defined with muscle. As she walked, each shoulder moved forward in turn. Her posture was stiff, erect. Her knuckles came down on the edge of the table.

"I hear you read futures."

"Yes," Isabelle said. "Please have a seat."

G'Leel righted the chair that had been knocked over by Mary Stein, turning it so the back faced the table. "A satisfied customer, I see." She straddled it, the back forming a short wall between them and her.

"We tell the truth," Isabelle said, "rather than what people want to hear. Some do not wish to know the truth."

"Most, in my experience," G'Leel said, and Galen realized Isabelle had said exactly the right thing. "Are you techno-mages?"

"Yes. We devote our lives to knowing everything that can be known."

"And how do you know all that?" The scar across her nose was a line of white interrupting the golden tan of her skin.

"Through methods secret to our order. Methods of science, and technomancy."

G'Leel pulled her credit chit from a black leather armband around her biceps and handed it to Isabelle. "I liked you better the first day you came, before you brought all that silliness." She flicked her fingers at the table. "I'm glad you've gotten rid of it."

"Some people require the trappings to believe. Just as some need to pay to believe." Isabelle handed back the card without deducting any credits.

An expression passed over G'Leel's face that Galen couldn't identify. "Let's get on with it, then. Tell me my future." Galen set his sensors to record, so that any information they received could be passed on to the Circle.

"I can tell you only your possible futures. You must decide which one you will choose."

"So that's how you get out of it."

"You are at a moral crossroads, as we both know, G'Leel."

G'Leel's lips tightened. Isabelle did not take her hands, since G'Leel would likely see that as silliness. Her head tilted slightly down, Isabelle fixed G'Leel with her gaze.

"You profit by bringing materials and people to the rim. These resources are being used to build a huge war machine, a war machine that will take the lives of billions if not stopped. You do your work and collect your generous pay, and you tell yourself that it has nothing to do with you. But you know that is not true. You hear whispers of what is being done. You see hints of what is to come. You see the materials you bring; you know to what use they might be put. You see forces gathering, and you know that at some point the gathering must stop, and the movement must begin."

G'Leel's gloved hands were clenching the back of the chair.

"You have two choices. You can continue to support those who seek the deaths of billions. You are then as responsible for what happens as they are. That blood is on your hands. Or instead, you can fight them, do what you can to stop this before it is too late."

The back of the chair broke off in G'Leel's hands. She looked down at it in shock, as if it were some alien artifact that had appeared out of nowhere. She stood and slammed it down on the table. Hunching over them, she spat whispers at Isabelle. "And what am *I* supposed to do? How can *I* stop this great movement?"

"You can stop it," Isabelle said, "with the help of others. You can stop it by telling us everything you know."

G'Leel's red eyes widened, and for a few moments she remained over them, breathing hard. Then she sat. "Why is he staring at me that way?" G'Leel jerked her chin in Galen's direction. "With those big eyes. Doesn't he ever blink?"

"He looks that way at everyone," Isabelle said. "He examines everything as if his life depends on it."

Galen, mystified at this turn in the conversation, averted his gaze. He felt the familiar discomfort that others saw in him things of which he was unaware. "I don't mean to offend."

"He can talk as well," G'Leel said.

Galen stared back at her. "And you can delay with foolishness." Galen raised his hands, conjured a globe of light between them. "The last time these dark forces moved across the galaxy, scores of intelligent species were exterminated; tens of billions died. Narn itself came under attack, and all the Narn mindwalkers were killed. How long will it be before the Narn homeworld is again under attack?" Within the globe, Galen conjured an image he had previously designed: the city of Ka'Pul on the Narn homeworld, its massive, plain stone structures tinted copper by the red sun. Narns moved between the buildings, going about their business. Yet as the vision drew closer, some of the Narns stopped, looked up at the sky. One let out a cry. A shadow spread across their faces. The vision focused on two figures within the crowd. They were G'Leel's parents, their faces filled with terror.

With a wave of his hand he made the image vanish.

G'Leel took a deep breath. "Is that the future?" she asked Isabelle.

"It's a possible future."

"Is it too late to ask for the version where you just tell me what I want to hear?"

Isabelle smiled. "Take the step. You're a good person. You want to do it."

G'Leel lowered her head. Her gloved hands closed around the broken chair back. "I've been to the Thenothk system on the rim three times. That name appears on none of our charts. Only our captain knows the system's coordinates. I have no idea which of the thousands of systems on the rim it might be.

"When we reach the last jumpgate on the line, he sends us all to our quarters. We travel four days, until we're far from everything, and then another ship meets us. It forms a jump point, and we travel with it through hyperspace to the Thenothk system. I figured that much from the sounds of the ship. But I had to see what Captain Ko'Vin was hiding from us. On our last run, I left my quarters. The ship that came for us—I could swear it screamed, though I know that's impossible. It was black as space, and bristled with arms."

Galen held up his hands, visualized the equation to create an image between them. He made the image black with many arms.

G'Leel looked up, saw it. "No. The arms to the side and back, not to the front. Long, and tapering to points. The central shape more flattened. Yes. That's it. And it had a way of moving—I can't really explain it. It seemed alive."

The image between his hands was sleek, alien, disturbing. Yet familiar. The ancient Narn holy book, the Book of G'Quan, contained a drawing of a similar shape, which it associated with a darkness that had fallen upon the land. If these were the Shadows' ships, then they had acquired an important piece of information. Galen dissolved the illusion.

"You don't recognize the image?" Isabelle asked.

G'Leel frowned. "Recognize it? No." Her red eyes flicked between Galen and Isabelle. "A huge city is growing on the fourth planet of the Thenothk system. Each time we go, it's fifty times the size it was. Millions are migrating there. A race called the Drakh are going in great numbers. And some are being brought against their will. Our hold carries twenty sleeper tubes, each one containing a Human mindwalker. A telepath. I don't know why they're being taken. But I don't like it.

"On the planet, I see a few Humans, Narns, Drazi. But most are species I've never seen before. In the bars—where we spend most of our time—I've overheard talk of war. And I've heard a name—I don't know if it means anything. The Shadows."

Galen's eyes met Isabelle's. *We have a piece of evidence,* he wrote. *At last.*

It is as Burell feared.

"What is it?" G'Leel asked. "Who are the Shadows?"

"They are an ancient race," Isabelle said. "At rest for a thousand years. They have powers far beyond ours, and a thirst for warfare. Now they have awakened again. They are spoken of in the Book of G'Quan, and the very ship you described is pictured there."

"You take those religious myths seriously?"

"Myth begins in history."

G'Leel rubbed a finger across her lip. "I'm not a reader. But if I'd known it had pictures . . ."

Through Burell's probes, Galen saw Captain Ko'Vin step out from the elevator into the lobby. He knew they had only another minute or two with G'Leel. "Have you heard of a planet called Z'ha'dum? It is the legendary home of the Shadows."

"I've heard that word. I didn't know it was a place."

"Do you have any idea when the Shadows will be ready for war?"

G'Leel shook her head. She heard the captain's voice and looked toward the lobby. Cadmus was giving the captain his present. There was still time.

"Who would know?" Isabelle asked. "Who gives your captain his directions?"

"There's a Drakh here, in the port. The Drakh sets up our shipments and schedules. The captain told me once how much he hates working with this Drakh. I think the Drakh frightens him."

All Galen knew of the Drakh was that, according to legend,

they were allies of the Shadows. "Where is this Drakh?" he asked.

"I don't know. He stays out of sight. But Ko'Vin will meet with him before we leave. He owes us pay, and the captain never forgets pay." G'Leel looked over her shoulder, then back. "Have you ever met a Drakh?"

"No," Isabelle said.

"There's something *off* about them. They're different. Be careful." She looked from Isabelle to Galen, shook her head. "You're too young for this." G'Leel stood, and Isabelle laid a hand over hers.

"You are a good person. You're going to make an important contribution in the conflict ahead. You have already been a great help."

G'Leel's mouth tightened, and she drew in a breath. When she let it out, her stiff posture relaxed a bit. She was relieved to have told them. Isabelle had known she would be.

Captain Ko'Vin stepped into the lounge. He called out in Narn, and the program translated. *G'Leel, there you are. I need you to carry something back to the ship for me. You aren't going to believe it!*

Coming, G'Leel responded.

The captain stepped out of the doorway, then leaned back in. *Getting your fortune told? G'Leel, if you crave my love, you can just tell me directly.*

G'Leel rolled her eyes. "I hope I helped," she said under her breath. She turned and strode across the room to her captain.

As G'Leel and Ko'Vin went into the lobby, Galen picked up their words through the lobby probe, and they were translated. *The manager has given us some breen. We'll have to stay here every time we come, just to get more. Unless it's bad. Then we'll stay here to punish him.*

They laughed.

Galen took Isabelle's hand. "We've got our first proof! Finally, something concrete to report to Elric."

Isabelle smiled, and this wasn't the mysterious lips-pressed-together smile; it was a big grin. "I knew we could do it."

"Another positive prediction?"

"I told you, I'm always right. Except for the times I'm not."

They made an odd group. Isabelle sat in a large armchair, her legs tucked beneath her, fingers intertwined in her lap. She was wearing a brown gown she seemed to like to wear around the house, its hem embroidered with runes. Though she was staring straight at him, she did not see him. She was monitoring the Drakh.

Galen sat beside her on a small area of the sofa he had managed to clear. He was searching again through the records Johnny had spirited from the Drakh's system. Johnny was an extremely sophisticated demon, though Galen had yet to get used to his scantily clad appearance, even if he was just an artificial intelligence.

Burell hovered nearby in her yellow armchair. She was doing an experiment that had been occupying her for the last three days, involving a microscopic transceiver. Galen was dying of curiosity about what she was doing, but so far, she'd waved off any questions.

Burell's health hadn't improved since they'd returned to her place of power. She continued to hide her true condition as much as she could, yet she was spending more and more hours in bed, and when she was up, he could see that she was in great pain. Isabelle had grown reluctant in the last few days to leave the apartment. When Burell was sleeping, Isabelle checked on her regularly. And when Burell was up, Isabelle's attention constantly turned to her.

Galen felt they should do something, but he didn't know what. Burell's organelles were failing to heal her, and Isabelle had said she refused healing from anyone else. Healing did not work well on chronic illness, but still, why would she refuse even to try? Did Burell have something to hide?

As if reading his thoughts, she shot him a pointed look, raising her eyebrows. At times her expressions were strikingly like Isabelle's.

He returned his attention to the Drakh's records in his mind's eye. They had to get more information somehow, information that would reveal the hand of the Shadows. He feared they had gotten as far as they could without taking a much greater risk.

Three days earlier, they'd watched, through the probe they'd planted on Captain Ko'Vin, as the captain sent G'Leel off toward the ship, and headed in the opposite direction himself. The probe was right in the center of Ko'Vin's forehead—he'd been so drunk, Isabelle said, she could have put it anywhere. So as the view swiveled back and forth, they could tell the captain was glancing nervously over his shoulder.

Only a few doors down from the hotel, the captain turned down a long, dark alley. Off the main streets, which had been constructed to attract off-world business and were occupied mainly by foreigners, any sense of prosperity vanished.

The probe revealed a neighborhood occupied by the native Wychad, a species that, in the port city at least, had been overwhelmed and relegated to a subservient position. On the right side of the alley, two- and three-story buildings stood abandoned, windows broken, facades cracked and discolored. On the left side, ramshackle structures made of fiberboard and tin leaned against one another for support. Wastewater ran into the street. The entries to underground maintenance access ways had been pried open and cables fed downward for illegal power splices. Some Wychad moved up and down the alley; others loitered outside their houses. What was strange, Galen realized, was that they all kept to the left side of the alley.

After traveling some distance, Captain Ko'Vin approached one of the abandoned buildings on the right. As he drew nearer, Galen realized this one was intact, windows sealed and opaqued, door secured with a sophisticated security device.

When Ko'Vin pressed the bell, the door opened for him, and he stepped inside. He went down a flight of stairs, and then he was in a small, dimly lit room. Galen could make out the light-colored walls and some dark shapes of furniture.

A man's voice spoke. The word it spoke, Galen thought, was Narn. The program translated it. *Sit.*

Ko'Vin found a seat near the only light in the room. He scanned the dim room nervously.

You have the cargo as we agreed. Galen caught movement in the darkness. It was the speaker. Galen altered the display in his mind's eye to show longer wavelengths of light. As it did, objects that generated heat became visible. The probe displayed these infrared wavelengths as shades of red. Out of the dull background arose two brighter spots, one more intense, one less so. In front of Ko'Vin was the less intense body of red, a silhouette in Human form. The man moved as he spoke in Narn.

We have your next payment.

In the corner was a more brilliant red silhouette. The body was humanoid, but the head was striking, unlike anything he'd seen before. That must be the Drakh. The back of the head had two protuberances that extended back and up in two craggy peaks, one above the other. He wondered what kind of brain structure it must have.

Ko'Vin's head turned toward the corner, perhaps sensing the presence of the Drakh lurking in the darkness. The business between the Human and the Narn captain was done quickly. Ko'Vin presented a credit chit, and the man inserted it into his machine, transferring credits onto it.

Ko'Vin seemed to have lost all his bluster. In fact, he hadn't spoken a word since entering the building.

You've done an exemplary job, as usual, the man said, returning the credit chit to the captain.

Ko'Vin stood quickly.

Then, from the corner, the Drakh's voice came like an arid breeze. *Secrecy.*

The view from the probe shook as Ko'Vin nodded his head rapidly, then retreated hastily up the stairs.

They had connected the traffic to the rim with the Shadows' legendary allies, the Drakh. Now they must discover whether the Drakh were the masterminds of this activity, or whether they themselves had masters.

As the *Khatkhata* had resumed its journey to the rim, Galen and Isabelle had visited the Drakh's neighborhood, disguised as maintenance workers. They had taken the appearances of two workers who were often sent to disconnect the illegal splices and check the houses for dangerous power use. In the underground maintenance access way, they spliced a small device into the power lines that would allow them to cut off power to the neighborhood when they wanted.

As they passed from house to house, stopping briefly at the locked building to knock and move on, they managed to assess the structure. All the windows were intact and sealed, and there was only one door. A high-end alarm system secured all possible entries. Monitors had been placed on either side of the front door, which was controlled with a sophisticated card-locking system.

They planted a huge number of Circe's mobile probes on the door and in the doorway of the building. Larger and more complex than Galen's probes, each was still no larger than a speck of dust. Yet they were microscopic robots, with a great degree of flexibility—and unpredictability. These probes would stick to an object for a time, then pry themselves free at certain signs. Drawn to rapidly changing light or sound, they could move on their own—albeit very slowly—to improve their positions. Someone coming into the house might then pick up a probe on the bottom of his shoe and track it inside, where it would drop off and search out activity. Galen had adjusted the probes to be drawn to dimmer light than usual, which the Drakh seemed to favor, and he had even input the silhouette of the Drakh's head as a target.

Two days later, they had eleven probes inside the building. All but one were gathered in a cluster on the floor of the dim room where Ko'Vin had been. The other had made it into a different room, a windowless chamber with low light and a thin mat in one corner. A stack of identical brown robes were folded against the wall. This was where the Drakh slept.

While waiting for their probes to penetrate the building, they'd sent Johnny to infiltrate the Drakh's datasystem. Johnny had said it was heavily protected, and "strange." It had taken him a full day to access. When Johnny had finally penetrated it, he'd not only found shipping records but financial statements, communications with various shipping companies, and other records. These were written in Narn, presumably to mask the participation of the Drakh in case of a security breach.

The Human who had met with Ko'Vin—Brown was his name—maintained the records. All communications were channeled through him. Over the last six months, the Drakh and Brown had coordinated the movement of millions of intelligent beings and massive amounts of materials. By the numbers, it seemed as if entire species were on the move: Drakh, Streib, Wurt, and others whose names Galen did not recognize. In other cases, only small groups or individuals were involved. The materials being transported included great engines of fabrication and construction. But products of every kind were being shipped as well, in quantities that revealed a huge demand.

The shipping records listed no final destination for all these shipments except the word *kiva*, which translated as *fortunate planet*. Not something he'd find on the charts.

Galen visualized the equation to close the file of shipping information. The oddest thing about what Johnny had found in the Drakh's datasystem was what he had not found. There were no records of communications with the rim.

To establish a link to the Shadows, they had to take a more personal approach. They had hoped at first that Brown would be the one to lead them to the Shadows. They had followed him and planted a probe on him. For the last three days, it had revealed nothing beyond his preferences for personal recreation. Watching Brown and the Drakh at work, Galen and Isabelle had deduced that Brown was just a front man. He seemed to spend only a few hours each afternoon in the building. He followed orders, was paid well, and actively cultivated a lack of curiosity. Between him and the Drakh there was no talk of Shadows.

"I'm getting more of that interference," Isabelle said.

Galen accessed the probes in the Drakh's building. The Drakh was in the same dim room where he'd met with Ko'Vin.

Brown had left for the day. In the long-wavelength light, the Drakh was a bright red figure against a dimmer red background. The angle was disorienting, since the probe was on the floor. It felt as if Galen were lying on the ground, looking up at the Drakh. Bursts of static interrupted the picture irregularly, sometimes affecting all of the image, sometimes just part of it.

They'd been getting the interference off and on since the probes had been planted. They'd tried various things to eliminate it, but it seemed to come and go of its own accord. They could find no power source, radiation, or object that corresponded to it.

The Drakh went into his sleeping chamber, and as Galen transferred to the probe in that room, the interference vanished. The Drakh took off his robe, folding it neatly on top of the pile of identical robes, and lay down on the mat. It was only 6 P.M., but the Drakh seemed to be on his own schedule. If the last day and a half was typical, he went to sleep around this time and woke up around 1 A.M. With no windows on the basement level, he wasn't tied to the sun's cycle.

"Why does he do it?" Galen asked, ending contact with the probe and picking up a conversation they'd begun earlier in the day.

With a quick motion of her fingers, Isabelle broke contact as well, and she unfolded her legs and stretched. "He's working with the Narns on the *Khatkhata*, and probably others like them, but he couldn't be more different from them. No alcohol, no sex, no gourmet foods, no wild expenditures."

"He's got over five million credits in his account. Brown draws a generous salary, but the Drakh doesn't pay himself anything. As a middleman, he's in a perfect position to capitalize on this."

"All he does is work, eat, and sleep," Isabelle said.

"You're describing a monk," Burell said, her face pressed to the viewer on the image processor. They both turned to her. "The behaviors and motivations are the same. He's devoted to this work. It is his holy cause. No pleasures, no distractions. He's acting just like a monk. Or Blaylock."

Galen wondered how he had failed to see it. All the signs were there.

"How can helping the Shadows spread war and chaos across the galaxy be his holy cause?" Isabelle asked.

"Because he is a Drakh. Because the Shadows are their lords."

Galen was astonished. "How do you know that?"

Burell raised her head from the viewer. "To be a good techno-mage," she said, "you have to know everything about everything." She looked from Galen to Isabelle. "I just love the looks on your faces."

"What is your source?" Isabelle asked.

"You know the mage Osiyrin?"

"Was he a contemporary of Wierden?" Galen asked.

"A little before her time, but yes, they did overlap. Osiyrin took an interest in the Drakh, who were figures of mystery even then. He studied them—surreptitiously, of course—and collected some fascinating data. His records are available."

"How did you come to know his work?" Isabelle asked.

"Aside from my quest to know everything about everything?"

"Aside from that," said Isabelle, "which we accept without question."

"Late in life, he became the first mage ever to be reprimanded by the Circle, soon after it was formed by Wierden. There was a time, after my first reprimand, that I was consumed with knowing who else had been so blessed, and for what reason. I didn't quite make it through the whole long and ignominious list—to which I welcome Galen, our latest esteemed member—but I did get to Osiyrin, since he was first.

"The records of the Circle's proceedings are closed, though. When I couldn't find the reason he was reprimanded, I looked at some of his research, thinking perhaps that was it. The study of the Drakh seemed his most unusual piece of work. I don't know why the Circle would reprimand him for it, but then I don't know why the Circle does anything it does. I imagine they were afraid the Drakh would discover his work and call down the wrath of the Shadows upon the techno-mages."

"Can we read his work?" Galen asked. He realized he had a message.

"There it is. And let that be a lesson to you. Know everything." Isabelle said the last sentence with her, and Burell gave her a crooked smile.

Burell returned to the experiment, yet Isabelle's gaze lingered on her mother, her face falling into lines of worry. After a few seconds she seemed to become aware that Galen was watching her. "You take the first half of Osiyrin's research and I'll take the second," she said. "Meet you at the end."

Galen nodded, opening the document in his mind's eye. It was written in the ancient runic language of the Taratimude, of which he had a basic understanding from studying the work of Wierden. It would take him far too long to read the work in that language, though, so he used his Taratimude program to translate it.

He first scanned quickly through the text. It was short, only thirty-eight pages in length, but seemed to contain a wealth of information: images of Drakh, anatomical scans, descriptions of their language, their culture, their beliefs.

"Let me do it!" Isabelle cried. "I've got you."

Isabelle had her arm around Burell's shoulders. The yellow armchair was flashing between opacity and transparency, and Burell's full-body illusion was flickering on and off, her figure alternating in a crazy strobe between red silk dress and black robe, elaborate coif and bare head, youthful healthy face and . . . something else—a face that was off, that was not right. . . .

Galen stood, unsure how to help. Isabelle was trying to replace Burell's conjured chair with one of her own.

"Wait." Burell's face—healthy, distorted, healthy, distorted, a Jekyll and Hyde caught between its two identities—closed its eyes, concentrating. "I can get"—healthy—"it"—distorted—"back."

The yellow armchair faded toward transparency. The flickering slowed, black robe bare head lasting longer and longer with each cycle, red dress coiffed hair flashing ever more briefly, the cycle running down like the last spurts of a windup toy, or the final contractions of an exhausted heart. Finally the armchair dissolved, and Burell dropped an inch or so into the transparent chair created by Isabelle.

"No!" Burell cried.

Isabelle seized her in a fierce embrace. A sound came from Burell then, a sound Galen never wanted to hear again. A high, hollow cry, it was the sound of someone who had lost part of her body, part of herself; a person who was now partly dead and yet still partly alive.

Galen stood with his hands at his sides. He had known Burell was weakening, worsening, but he had never dreamed she would lose her powers.

He had felt at odds with the implants at first, yet already, he realized, he had begun to use them automatically, like he used his eyes or his hands. For someone who had lived with them and used them for twenty-five years, he couldn't imagine what it would be like to lose them.

"Get off," Burell said, pushing Isabelle away. "Get off."

Isabelle stepped back, revealing Burell's slumped, twisted body.

"There are things I must tell you," Burell said, her face broken, misshapen, "if you will hear them."

— chapter 11 —

Burell's hands were emaciated, her skin yellow, almost translucent. Within her robe, her body was hunched, her left shoulder poking upward. Her face looked like it had been broken into pieces. Her lips cut across her face at an odd angle, no longer quite able to close. Her right eye was twisted, drooping down to the side. Her left eyebrow stretched high on her forehead. The skin of her cheeks hung flat and papery. Galen thought it looked almost like the results of a stroke. Was that the condition Burell had been hiding?

"You should rest," Isabelle said.

"No, I can keep silent no longer." Burell's voice had lost its depth, its power. Yet she somehow managed to enunciate clearly through uneven lips. She rubbed one hand over the other, her head hanging. "I've kept my work from you these many years because I didn't want for you the life that has come to me—a life of reprimand, condemnation, and isolation. But I have taught you too well—to question, to examine, and to continue until you find an answer. And I have, perhaps, told you bits of my work when I should have remained silent. It was hard for me not to tell you everything.

"I know that you have managed to access some of my findings. I know that you have conducted experiments on your own. And I know now that your curiosity will not be turned to a safer subject, though this has been a bittersweet truth for me to accept."

Burell paused, her uneven shoulders rising and falling with her tired breaths. She raised her gaze to Isabelle, though her head remained hanging. "If you are to study the tech, then I must tell you everything I know. Then perhaps you can succeed where I have failed. Then I can save you from what has happened to me."

Isabelle took her hand. "We will carry on your work together."

Burell gave her a crooked smile. "I can't pretend to understand it. All I can do is point to some pieces that seem similar to things I understand, and ignore the pieces that don't." Her uneven eyes flicked to Galen. "As my resourceful daughter has discovered, a large part of the tech is made up of stem cells. These stem cells develop into different types of cells, growing into an additional system within each of our bodies, like a second nervous system. It connects itself intricately with all our systems, and in part becomes almost a mirror of our brain, something that echoes our processes, yet also enhances them. Our DNA comprises about half of the genetic material within these cells. The other half, I can't identify. It may be from species we don't know, or it may be engineered.

"The cells also carry what we would think of as nonbiological elements. Some very sophisticated microcircuitry is in the cytoplasm, and more is on the cell membrane itself. On the membrane, this microcircuitry looks almost like"—she lifted an emaciated hand and pointed over her shoulder, where the implants would have discolored the skin around her spine—"on a much smaller scale. The microcircuitry seems to direct the growth and functioning of the implants, to impose control on each cell."

Galen remembered his initial discomfort with the implants, his feeling that they had a will, that they had desires. Perhaps it was the microcircuitry he had been responding to.

Burell's research seemed important and valid, yet Galen couldn't imagine how she'd been able to obtain samples for study. "Burell," Galen said, "how have you been able to examine the tech in such depth?"

"Another mage used to live in the next system over. Do you remember Craiselnek? Sour old woman. She died about eight years ago. I arrived to pay my respects before any of the members of the Circle. By the time they arrived to oversee the burning and disposal of her remains, there were a few pieces missing."

"You flayed her?" Galen was appalled.

"I took a few small samples. I wish now I'd taken more." A spasm passed over her broken face, and her breath caught in her throat. Her hand squeezed tightly around Isabelle's.

After a few moments, the hand relaxed, her breathing resumed. She continued as if nothing had happened. "There are many other elements in the implants. Clumps of microcircuitry, like ganglia, that are interconnected with the neurons. Transceivers, relays, capacitors. Biochips that work as sensors. Some of the stem cells develop into specialized cells that are actually tiny manufacturing plants, building our organelles. Others develop into types of cells I've never seen before. Cells whose purpose I can't even guess." Burell took her hand from Isabelle and pressed her palms flat against the arms of the chair, shifting her weight. They slipped off, too weak. She slumped to one side.

Isabelle made the arms on the chair higher to hold Burell upright. "You can finish later," Isabelle said. "Or just give us access to your files. You need to rest."

Burell's head hung against her shoulder. She raised one eye to them. "There's one more thing I have to tell you." She clenched her teeth, and with great effort brought her head erect. As she continued, her voice was softer than before, but still clear, steady. "About the transceivers. The tech has several of them. They allow us to communicate with other mages, connect to our places of power, access signals. All of these transceivers are connected with the neuron-heavy areas of the tech, so they can respond to our directions. They're in the brain, neck, shoulders, and upper spinal column. All but one.

"This one transceiver seems the same as the others, but it sits near the base of the spinal column, away from the most developed areas of the tech. It's still connected, but doesn't seem to be in the best place to receive our directions. I wondered what sort of signals it might be set up to receive. One of the pieces I took from Craiselnek included this transceiver. I tried sending it signals from my place of power, from probes—various signals, but it didn't pick up any of them. It seemed to be listening for one particular signal.

"As I failed to get any response, I fed more and more exotic signals into it. One day, the transceiver finally responded. The signal I had sent was an elaborate and intense one, in the radio band. Craiselnek's transceiver responded by sending out a complex answer. But the tech itself didn't seem to do anything or be affected in any way. If that had been a normal signal, like one sent from Craiselnek's place of power to her, then the signal would have traveled into her brain, to pass information to her.

"I sent the radio signal again, but the transceiver didn't respond the second time. And after that, Craiselnek's implants refused to work consistently. Some of the pieces had become inert, while others worked fine. I thought perhaps it was the long-term effects of having implants outside the body. I'd had the tech about three years by then.

"I fought my curiosity for as long as I could. I think I lasted almost a year. Then I had to try it. I sent the radio signal to my own transceiver."

Isabelle's head turned slightly back and forth.

"The rest, as they say, is stupidity. The first time I sent the signal, my implants sent the answering signal. The second time—and I held off a month before trying it again—about a third of my implants went inert. That's when I sent you off on that silly research project. I was a bit panicked. I couldn't use any of the implants for a while. Although some were still active, I had to relearn how to access them.

"The control has not come naturally, though. And it is not without cost. Some of my own systems have had to carry signals meant for the tech. My body isn't equipped to do that. It's been getting harder and harder to make the tech respond."

Galen realized his first impression of her condition had not been far off. Like a stroke patient, she'd been partially paralyzed, and had regained some ability only by relearning how to use her body, how to bypass those pathways that had become inert.

He remembered the sickening feeling of paralysis when

Elric overrode his control of the chrysalis. That must reflect only a small hint of what Burell suffered. "There must be some way to undo the effect of the signal," he said.

Burell's head rose and fell with each breath. "I've experimented with Craiselnek's implants for the past four years. Nothing works. I must have overloaded the transceiver with that signal. It froze up the system. There's no way now to unfreeze it."

"Will you give us access to your work?" Galen asked. "Perhaps we can find some way to help."

"Get me a screen." The last word was slurred. Burell was exhausted. Her body had slumped further in the chair. She no longer tried to look up at them. "I will give you the key to all my work. Which I keep in my place of power. But I do not give it for you to help me. I am beyond help. I give it to aid in your own work."

Isabelle laid a screen in her lap and pressed a stylus into her hand. Burell jerked it onto the screen, so she could draw the diagram that was the key to her most secret places. Her emaciated hand shook as she labored to form the symbols precisely. Her breath sounded heavily in the silence.

At the top she rendered a simple drawing of a solar system, and below wrote several lines of text. Galen recognized the letters from the alphabet of the native Wychad.

As Burell finished, Isabelle expelled a short breath.

"What does it mean?" he asked.

Isabelle recited the words. " 'I do not believe that the same God who has endowed us with sense, reason, and intellect has intended us to forgo their use.' "

Galen recognized the quote. It was Galileo.

Isabelle took the screen and stylus from her, and as she turned to put them down, Burell began to crumble forward. Galen rushed up and grabbed her shoulders, holding her upright.

"I'm all right," Burell said.

"That's it! I don't care what you say." Isabelle snatched something from her pocket and grabbed Burell's head in her hands. A crystal on a chain dangled from between her fingers.

"I have to try to heal you." Isabelle closed her eyes, and her fingers moved slightly against Burell's skin.

"Galen, stop her!" Burell batted an arm at Isabelle. "If she connects with my implants, hers may become inert too." Burell's uneven green eyes pleaded with him.

Panic welling up, Galen grabbed Isabelle, driving her back into a table covered with equipment. "Wait!" he said. "Stop!"

"We have to try it! I have to try!" Isabelle ripped her arms free. The blue tinge of a defensive shield snapped over her body. With a flash of her fingers she conjured a fireball in one hand. Her eyes shone with reflected flames, and her lips articulated with fierce precision. "Don't stand in my way."

Galen's body raced with the instinctive need to defend itself, just as it had with Elizar. He had no talent for shields. The only defense was a counterattack. Galen fought the urge, the sudden surge of energy driving through him like a cataract.

"You would invade me against my wishes?" Burell said.

"I can't let you die. I have to heal you. I've waited too long already." Isabelle's face was flushed.

The fireball's heat burned into Galen's skin. He held tightly to the racing energy searching for outlet. He must keep control.

Anger rose within him, anger that she would dare to threaten him. She knew what he could do. Her shield would be no defense against it. Why would she tempt him?

"You can't heal me, Isabelle. This is no disease of the body. If you try to heal my implants, if your tech connects to mine, yours will become inert as well."

"You don't know that," Isabelle pleaded. "You have to let me try."

"I can't. I couldn't stand to lose you. You are the one beautiful thing that has come out of my life. The one thing that tells me why I was here at all. I'm so proud of you.

"My time is passing. But yours is to come. That is my great joy. Please don't take it from me."

Isabelle shut her eyes, and tears ran down a face hard with

anger. She closed her hand over the fireball, extinguishing it. Her shield dissolved.

The danger was over.

The energy inside Galen slowed, quieted. Galen realized the pain she must be in, watching her teacher and mother dying. He was shocked at the anger he'd felt only a few seconds earlier. How could he have been so close to attacking her?

Galen stepped aside, and Isabelle returned to Burell. She grasped the shimmering arm of the chair. Burell stroked her hand. "You're my dearest Isabelle."

Isabelle bowed her head. "What if I don't try to heal you," she said softly. "What if I just give you some of my organelles, in case they can do any good." She glanced back at him, and the hardness had gone from her face. "Galen could give some too."

Galen moved to Isabelle's side. "If part of your tech is inert," he said to Burell, "then you're probably producing fewer organelles than usual. They may be overtaxed. Perhaps more could help. Not cure you, but help you cope with the stresses."

From the set of Burell's crooked lips, Galen could see she believed it would do no good. Yet her gaze lingered long on Isabelle, and at last she said, "Perhaps you're right. Perhaps it can help."

Isabelle wiped her tears. "Yes. Maybe it will help. Maybe it will. Galen?"

Isabelle pulled back Burell's sleeve and laid one hand on her arm, the other on the back of her head. Galen went around Burell to the other side and did the same. Her forearm felt like a cold stick in his hand. He visualized the spell to trigger the release of organelles.

His hands tingled, and there was an odd sense of a shift in his body, as when he got out of bed in the morning and his blood redistributed itself. In a moment it passed, and he removed his hands.

A tentative smile had appeared on Isabelle's face. "You need rest now."

Burell took a deep breath. "Yes."

Isabelle followed Burell into the bedroom. While they were both gone, Galen tried to study the research of Osiyrin, but instead found himself worrying about his earlier anger toward Isabelle. They had turned on each other in a moment. Between their work and Burell's deteriorating health, Isabelle was exhausted. But what was his excuse?

The restless energy of the tech—he had already become so accustomed to the constant, irritating undercurrent that it seemed part of him. Could he blame it for his flash of anger? Or did the impulse to anger begin with him? In either case, how could he better control it?

Isabelle returned from the bedroom looking much better. She had washed the tears from her face, and a sense of peace that he hadn't realized was missing had returned to her features.

"She went right to sleep," Isabelle said. "Usually she can't, because of the pain. I think that's a good sign."

Galen followed a path through the boxes and piles to Isabelle. He took her hand. "I pulled you away from her because I was worried what would happen to you."

"I know. Sorry about the fireball."

He nodded.

"I guess we've had our first fight," she said.

He released her hand.

"Now it's time to share something more pleasant." She took a breath, composing herself, pushing herself ahead. "Our first Winter Solstice."

"What?"

"You may have lost track of time, dear Galen, but I have not. Today is December twenty-second on Earth, the time when the sun reaches its farthest point south of the equator, a time of turning, changing. Our ancestors considered this a day of power, the day when the sun stopped its journey away and began its return. From then on, every day grew longer, and light pushed back darkness, hope pushed back despair. It is a day Burell and I—always celebrate."

"How do we celebrate?"

"First, I have a present for you." She went around the counter into the kitchen area, reached into a cupboard and pulled out a brightly wrapped box.

"I don't have anything for you."

"That's the best time to get a present, isn't it? When you aren't expecting one?" She led him toward the sofa, squeezed into the small cleared area beside him. He liked the feeling of her body next to his. She handed him the box.

He opened it. Inside was something tan-colored, woven. He pulled it out. A scarf.

"To keep you warm." She grabbed it and wrapped it around his neck, her subtle essence enveloping him. She leaned back, biting her lip. "Quite handsome."

"Did you weave this yourself?" It had an odd texture, with bumps spaced irregularly over its surface.

She rested her head against his shoulder. "Of course."

"Does that mean there's a spell woven into it?" He ran his hand over the bumps as if reading Braille.

"That's for you to unravel."

They sat in silence for a few minutes as Galen puzzled over the gift. Isabelle's ribs pressed into him as she breathed. "Are there any more parts to this celebration?" he asked.

"Just one more. A toast." As she put a hand on his chest and pushed herself up from the sofa, he regretted asking the question. He followed her into the kitchen, where she poured two glasses of wine. Her head was bent, a line of muscle in her neck revealing tension. "I first read of the Well of Forever when I was nine years old. I knew Burell was having trouble getting tech to study, and I suggested to her that we go to the Well. When she told me that it had been lost, this burial place of the earliest techno-mages, this great repository of tech and knowledge, I became obsessed with finding it." She handed him a glass. "Every Winter Solstice, Burell and I toast, and say 'Next year, we find it.' You'll have to stand in—" Isabelle's voice broke, and she turned away. "If the Circle had only given her tech to study, she wouldn't have had to experiment on herself. She wouldn't"—she ground out the words—"be dying." She picked up her glass and turned back to him with a fixed, despairing smile on her face.

She raised her glass and, with a pointed look, told him he should do the same. He hated to see the pain on her face. Yet Isabelle would not give up the quest, he realized, feeling another moment of connection with her. Her failure to find the Well in time to help Burell would make her more determined to find it, just as Galen's failure to live up to the Code made him more determined to prove himself. Perhaps he could help her, and in their success, in recovering this lost piece of the mages' past, he could erase that expression of despair from her face.

They spoke together. "Next year, we find it."

"Have you done this before?" Isabelle asked.

"You're asking now?" Galen jammed the thing in, shaking it up and down.

"It seems the question of the moment. Well?"

"No." He pulled it out, cursed, jammed it in again. "Have you?"

"No. Maybe we should have thought this out a bit more."

"Alwyn told me it always works." He pulled the card out of the lock system. The door remained stubbornly closed.

"Nothing *always* works." Isabelle's back shifted against his as she spoke, and the full-body shield she had conjured around herself tingled over his skin like an electrostatic charge. She was keeping watch while he worked on the lock to the Drakh's building.

The neighborhood was dark, since they'd cut off the power supply, and that had knocked out the Drakh's monitors and alarms. But locks always had a battery backup. "We've got to try something else. Force?"

"That will ruin our plan." Galen's mind was racing. He felt like an idiot. He strove for calm, control.

"Heat? Electrical surge?" Isabelle suggested.

"Will that open it?"

"No idea," she said.

Galen turned the card upside down, jammed it in again. The door clicked open. Isabelle turned at the sound. "Brilliant!"

They hurried inside, closed the door gently behind them, sealing themselves into blackness. Isabelle's shield gave her silhouette a faint blue glow. She had urged Galen to conjure a shield as well, but he'd told her that if he tried to sustain one, he'd be unable to concentrate on anything else. Anyway, if all went to plan, they'd be in and out without anyone knowing they were there, just as Elric taught.

The plan was a bit crazy, but they'd been able to come up with nothing better. The Drakh was likely the only one on Zafran 8 who knew whether or not the Shadows were involved. But he never left the building, and their probes had detected no communications to the rim that they might intercept. The only way to discover the truth was from the Drakh's own lips.

In his mind's eye, Galen looked out through the probe on the outside of the front door. Using the infrared band, he watched a Wychad across the alley wander toward the main street and the lights. No one had observed their entrance.

The probe in the Drakh's bedchamber showed that he was still asleep. It was five after ten. He was the only one in the building.

Galen put his sensors on the infrared band, so he could find his way. Isabelle preceded him down the stairs. He checked that the door would open from the inside without any trouble when they were ready to leave. Then he followed.

The location—underground with no ready exit—wasn't a good one. But as far as he and Isabelle had been able to discover, the Drakh had no weapons. Although the Drakh was physically quite large, Galen felt certain they could handle him if he became violent. He wondered why Captain Ko'Vin, who was always armed, had been so afraid.

Isabelle stood outside the Drakh's room, her hands weaving mist. It appeared as granular red wisps in his mind's eye. With her dark robe and pale red skin, she seemed to float like a spirit.

The mist quickly filled the Drakh's bedchamber. Galen

waded carefully through it. He breathed deeply, repeating to himself his vow to uphold the Code and the directives of the Circle. He would conjure nothing by instinct, but consider carefully before visualizing any spell. He touched his pocket and felt the special tranq tab they'd made. They would use it after they'd gotten all the answers they wanted, or earlier, if the plan began to fail. Galen found the brilliant red of the Drakh's body, knelt beside the Drakh's head.

Isabelle came into the room and stood to one side of the door. She nodded to him. She would record whatever the Drakh said and did. She moved her fingers, and a dim light suffused the mist. Galen turned off his sensors, his regular vision now sufficient.

The Drakh lay on his back, arms straight down beside him, his face turned upward. He slept with a thick cylindrical pillow beneath his neck, which kept the back of his head from touching the mat. He seemed larger in person, and somehow more real. A subtle scent hung around him, like mold. His skin was a striated brown and black, looking more like rock than flesh. The two craggy outcroppings on the back of the head were striped with more fluid lines, making Galen think of cooled lava.

He called up Osiyrin's scans of the Drakh brain, with the area Osiyrin believed corresponded to the temporal lobe highlighted. According to Osiyrin, the Drakh brain wasn't that different from the brains of other intelligent species; the temporal lobe was supposed to be located within the upper outcropping. It was the lower outcropping that really distinguished the Drakh, serving no purpose that Osiyrin had been able to identify.

Galen circled his hands around the upper outcropping, bringing them as close as they could without touching the Drakh. If Osiyrin was right, this should work.

Galen closed his eyes and visualized the equation to stimulate the temporal lobes. Kell had done the same to Galen when he had challenged Galen with a hallucination. Stimulating the temporal lobes turned an illusion into an extremely intense emotional experience, disorienting and striking, each moment weighted with great import. Galen wanted that for the Drakh.

The corner of the Drakh's mouth began to twitch.

Galen glanced up. Isabelle was a gray shape in the mist. He couldn't see her hands, but he knew they must be moving, for a darkness began to gather within the dim curtains of mist. Over the Drakh's bed, a shadowy figure formed. It was vague, shifting, a black form with spiky limbs poking out in various directions. They had decided to keep it vague, since Osiyrin's description of the Drakh god had been a bit uncertain. The effect was rather like a black sun with a shifting, spiky black corona. In the center of that dark sun were four piercing points of light, the one detail that seemed certain. According to Osiyrin, the god wasn't exactly a Shadow; he was the source of Shadows. The Shadows were his highest servants. And the Drakh served the Shadows.

The Drakh stirred.

The god spoke, in a dry voice that carried a faint echo. Isabelle had worked hard on the voice, which was similar to the Drakh's own, but more resonant. It spoke in the limited vocabulary of Drakh that Osiyrin had provided. The words were translated in Galen's mind's eye.

You have earned my wrath.

The Drakh jerked awake. His arms shot out to the sides, pressing against the mat as if he were desperate for balance. His mouth fell open in what Galen hoped was awe.

You have not prepared the way. You have not furthered my cause. You are not fit.

The Drakh's head wavered back and forth as he fought disorientation. Galen struggled not to make contact with his skin, though he doubted the Drakh would notice if he did.

The Drakh's lips moved, though no sound came out. Then, the Drakh whispered. Osiyrin's dictionary translated. *I have tried. I am devoted to your cause.*

The god's voice grew louder. *You are too slow. You are too cautious. It is time I stretched forth my hand.*

I am working toward the great conquest, the Drakh whispered. *The plans are [words unavailable in program].*

You are too slow.

Your high servants are cautious, but they will bring us victory.

Too late.

No, the Drakh said, flailing a hand in agitation. *We are gathering the resources. We are gathering allies. We have made great progress. Within weeks, our provocations will begin. Within a year, the galaxy will be consumed with war. Chaos will ascend.*

The Drakh pushed himself into a sitting position, his head slipping out from Galen's hands. Galen's heart jumped, and the tech echoed his panic. He reached for the tranq tab, glanced at Isabelle. He couldn't make out her expression, but the illusion continued.

I see no allies, the god said. *Where are they?*

The Drakh, seeing the image now without distortion, looked around the room, puzzled. He uttered a word then in his dry voice, a long, intricate word that sounded like the rustling of papers in the wind.

[Word unavailable in program.]

If they were to continue, they couldn't let the Drakh get his bearings. Galen jerked to his feet and seized the Drakh's outcropping, nervous energy swelling within him. He kept a fierce focus on the single equation he was visualizing. He would let nothing else slip through.

The Drakh threw his arms out, trying to fight off the attack, but overcome again with disorientation and awe.

Who are these allies? the god asked.

The Drakh continued to flail about, elbowing Galen in the side. He repeated the long, intricate word.

What of the magic workers? Isabelle had jumped ahead to their final question.

But Galen realized the Drakh would answer no more. Galen visualized the equation to stop the temporal stimulation, snatched the tranq tab from his pocket, and slapped it onto the Drakh's neck just as the Drakh turned to look up into his face.

Galen stepped back, and within seconds, the Drakh fell

over onto the mat, asleep. He would be unconscious for hours. Galen's pounding heart began to slow. He turned to find Isabelle beside him.

There's something near the door, her message read. *My sensors are picking up—something. The interference we detected earlier.*

He focused his sensors on the area near the door, ran through different frequency bands. At the upper end of the infrared band he caught the static. His sensors showed him more precisely what the probes had only crudely transmitted. The static wasn't due to some energy in the area. If that were the case, the static would be widespread. But the mist that floated in front of the doorway showed clearly on his sensors, with no interference. Something within the doorway, some shape within the mist, was a source of static.

The Drakh sat up. "You have been most clever," he said in his arid voice. He spoke English. "I commend you." The Drakh's eyes were in shadow; Galen couldn't tell if they were open or not. But the Drakh couldn't be awake. The tranq had been strong enough—they thought—to keep him out half the day.

"I told you what I thought you wanted to hear," the Drakh said. "I hope you don't mind. I found your questions intriguing. I wanted to see what you would ask. And now I will ask. Why do you come here? Why do you ask me this?"

Except for his mouth, the Drakh did not move at all. His head hung downward, his arms limp. He looked like a marionette held up by a single string. *You must follow the strings from puppet to puppet master,* Elric had said.

"It was a prank," Isabelle said in a wavering voice.

Heart pounding, Galen scanned higher frequencies, searching for any kind of energy that could be holding the Drakh up, that could be making him speak. Galen almost ran past it, the energy was in such a focused, narrow band. It was exciting the lower outcropping of the Drakh's brain, the area whose purpose Osiyrin had been unable to explain.

"You are young," the Drakh said. "Forget this matter, and it will be forgotten. Or if you truly seek knowledge, join me.

My associates can offer you great knowledge. The secrets of the universe. Is that not what every techno-mage seeks?"

Isabelle's blue-tinged shield suddenly unfolded and extended to form a barrier across the room, between them and the doorway. The static-filled silhouette was moving through the dim mist toward them. Isabelle's fingers worked furiously.

The shimmering static reached the shield and, with only a slight hesitation, passed through it.

Galen grabbed Isabelle's hand. The shield vanished. With single-minded focus, he visualized the equation to conjure a flying platform beneath them. He seized her about the waist. He formed an equation of motion, then another, then another. The platform swerved around the static shape, snaked out the doorway, and shot up the stairs. They slammed into the front door and fell to the floor.

Isabelle grabbed the door handle and pulled it open, knocking Galen in the head. He dissolved the platform, stumbled to his feet. They raced out into the darkness.

They fled down the long alley to the lights and activity of the main street, ran several more blocks, dodging pedestrians, before finally slowing, walking. Galen looked back. The streets were busy as those in port sought out late-night entertainment.

Energy surged through him, refusing to be calmed. Danger seemed close, imminent. He couldn't believe they had gotten away.

That was a Shadow, wasn't it? Isabelle wrote. Somewhere along the way they had taken each other's hands, and Galen didn't want to release her.

I don't know, he replied. *I never saw anything like it.*

Did they let us go? Why would they let us go?

I don't know.

Too shaken up to do more conjuring, they decided to take the tube home. Isabelle said she wanted some time to calm down before facing Burell, and Galen hoped the nervous energy within him would begin to dissipate. With all the spells he had cast, his energy showed no sign of declining. He hadn't even grown breathless. Yet his mind felt exhausted.

They went down into the tube station, ran their credit chits through the reader. A train must have just left, because the station was empty. They stood near one end of the platform, silent, caught in the memory of what had happened.

The lights in the station dimmed. A blue sphere of energy appeared in front of them, perhaps a yard across. It was the work of a techno-mage. Galen turned quickly, certain he would see Elric or Burell or someone who had come to help them.

But the platform was empty.

Isabelle's face appeared inside the sphere, then Galen's. "We know your ways." The voice from the sphere was artificial, and not very skillfully created. What was clearly meant to be deep and powerful had a tinny undertone. Elric would never have let him get away with it.

Isabelle conjured a full-body shield.

"You seek knowledge," the voice continued. "We have knowledge." Within the sphere, diagrams and equations flashed by one after another. "We are far ahead of you in technology. But of all the younger races, your group is closest to ours in knowledge. We find you worthy to share in what we know."

The jumble of images resolved itself into an image of the galaxy. "A firestorm is coming. We have no ill intentions toward you. That is why you were allowed to leave. We should be allies."

At the mouth of the tunnel, Isabelle wrote. *Look.*

Galen glanced toward the end of the platform. There, inside the tunnel, a dark figure stood in shadow.

"Who are you?" Isabelle demanded.

"We are friends," the sphere said.

"We prefer to keep to ourselves," Galen said. "When we do form alliances, it is in our own time and at our own whim."

"Galen, you seek to understand the secret you have uncovered. We can help you."

Galen's breath stuck in his throat. "What secret?"

"The others of your kind fear you and your power, and even now hope for your destruction. That is why they have sent you to us. You show them what they should be, and are not. We also show the universe what it should be, and is not. Many prefer to destroy those who are superior, rather than face the knowledge that they are inferior."

"I don't know what you're talking about," Galen said, but at the same time he wondered if it could be true. Elric had thought him unable to perform the task set by the Circle. Had the Circle sent him in the hope that he would be killed? Had they made him a mage only to use him as cannon fodder? He couldn't believe it.

"We praise your discovery instead of condemning it. And we would aid you in your work, opening repositories of knowledge to you that you can barely imagine."

Elric had told Galen that the Shadows found others to do their bidding, that they worked behind the scenes, creating disputes and inciting war. "You seek to divide the techno-mages," Galen said, "as you seek to divide the galaxy, to pit us against each other in war and chaos. But we will not be divided. The Code unites us."

"You are already divided," the sphere said.

A sense of dread filled Galen, and he felt a driving need to act, to strike back at this threat. He held it tightly, scanned the figure in the mouth of the tunnel. Energy characteristic of a techno-mage emanated from it, but some of the normal traits were missing. Then he realized that this was not a full mage; the figure was wearing a chrysalis. Had one of the new chrysalis-stage apprentices joined with the Shadows? Was that the division he meant? Or was it something deeper?

"Isabelle," the sphere said, "you struggle to find answers that were already found long ago. You seek samples of the great tech for study. You look for an ancient place of power, the Well of Forever. We know where this place is. We can take you there. Today. Tomorrow. At your will. There you will find the ancient knowledge of the techno-mages. There you will find the materials you need to complete your studies. And there you will find the way to save your mother."

Inside the sphere, Burell's image appeared, her face broken, deformed.

Isabelle gasped. "You bastards!" Before Galen knew what

was happening, she had conjured a fireball and hurled it at the figure in the mouth of the tunnel.

A dim blue glow enveloped the dark figure just before the fireball hit. Fire splashed out, and at the site of the impact the flames sank into the shield, interacting with the top layers, spreading outward in a yellow-red wave. In the illumination of that fleeting circle of light, the face of the figure flashed into stark relief.

Mouth open in startled terror, eyes wide—it was Tilar. On his head was fastened a chrysalis. The yellow-red wave overran his face, growing dimmer as it diffused. At last only the blue remained. Tilar's shield had held. The dim blue glow vanished, and Tilar faded into the blackness.

Isabelle conjured a flying platform and shot off after him. Galen quickly followed. In the mouth of the tunnel they conjured globes of light, but there was no sign of Tilar. They used sensors in case he was disguising himself, but still nothing.

Galen didn't understand how this could have happened. How had Tilar acquired a chrysalis? And how had he known of Galen's secret, and Isabelle's dream? They hadn't told him.

Isabelle prowled deeper into the tunnel, shaking her head. "That bastard. That bastard. That bastard."

Galen turned. A breeze was blowing down the tunnel. "Isabelle. The train is coming."

"That bastard," Isabelle said again. "That bastard!"

Galen formulated the equation of motion, sped to her side. The breeze gained strength. "We should go back. We need to tell Elric all we've discovered."

Isabelle was shaking her head, scanning ahead.

"We need to check on Burell."

She turned sharply, her face flushed and hard with anger. For a moment Galen thought she might attack him. The wind whipped through their robes. Then her eyebrows rose, and he saw, in an instant, her anger turn from Tilar to herself. "What have I done?" she said.

She had rejected the only chance to save Burell. She had made the right decision. But what could he say? Galen reached for her hand, but it was encased in her shield. With a slight tingling, his fingers slipped away.

They flew back to the station. Only when the tube came did Isabelle dissolve her shield. Then she took his hand.

She remained silent on the ride home, her hand in his. Twice he heard her release a heavy breath. She was trying to calm herself to face Burell. Galen needed to do the same, to still that wild energy. He began a mind-focusing exercise, but found he could not concentrate.

The tech was closely guarded by the Circle, the secret of its creation held only by them. How, then, could one cast away by the Circle, one found unfit, still have access to it? How did Tilar have a chrysalis?

You are already divided.

The Shadow had let them go. Tilar, speaking for the Shadows, had offered them alliance. Did the Shadows think that Galen and Isabelle would join them because Tilar had? Or were other mages involved?

Tilar had known their secrets, had known just what to say. Galen had thought he and Isabelle were investigating the Shadows. But now it seemed the Shadows were investigating them. The mages were not safe.

And the Drakh had said it would be only a few weeks before the Shadows took the first steps toward war.

— chapter 12 —

"You are well?" Elric asked.

They stood again in Elric's circle, among the vibrant green stones and the sharp sea breeze. In the dreamlike strangeness of the electron incantation, Galen thought, Elric's sharp-edged figure looked almost like a flat paper cutout against the hazy background of mist.

"Yes," Galen said. "Our plan was poorly conceived and poorly executed, but we managed to survive it." Isabelle had sent Elric the recording she'd made. Galen felt ashamed, thinking of Elric watching it, seeing how quickly their plan had fallen apart.

"It would have been difficult to prepare for what happened," Elric said. "You have gathered valuable information. And you have handled yourselves well under unexpected and difficult circumstances."

The praise shocked Galen into silence.

"Thank you," Isabelle said.

Elric approached them, his figure becoming more three-dimensional. "Have you tried to locate Tilar since he left you?"

Galen nodded. "We detected the characteristic mage energy while he was in the tube station. But later, when we searched for it, we found no trace. He could have dissociated to hide."

"How could Tilar know so much?" Isabelle's face still carried some of the hardness he had seen in the tube station. She was still angry at Tilar, and herself. "I never knew him well, and we told him little in our meeting. If he has no continuing relationships with mages, then what is his source?"

"Some," Elric said, "may have come from Morden. Whether that accounts for all, I am not certain."

Galen suddenly saw the symmetry. "The Shadows sent Morden to investigate us, just as the Circle sent Isabelle and me to investigate the Shadows."

"Yes," Elric said. "Each side has sent its scouts. Now the time has come for the next step."

Morden had searched the convocation for allies, just as he and Isabelle had searched the port city. They had found G'Leel to provide information. Had Morden found anyone?

The situation had seemed much simpler when they had been sent to Zafran 8. The threat had been from without, not within. Yet now, everything had changed. "How could Tilar possess a chrysalis?" Galen asked.

Elric's lips formed a thin, grim line. "That is the most troubling," he said. "The Circle must launch an investigation at once."

But where could Tilar have gotten the chrysalis, except from one of the Circle? Galen believed in the Circle, trusted them. He knew that Tilar's accusation could not be true, that Elric and the rest could not possibly hope for his death. Tilar had planted the lie among truths, as mages were taught to do. It failed to convince.

Yet Galen also knew that Elric had not believed he could succeed. And he remembered Elric's anger toward the Circle when he'd left for Zafran 8. Why had Elric been angry? And why had Galen been chosen?

Elric had refused to explain. The Circle might even have forbidden him to do so. Yet Galen felt as if he needed some explanation, some certainty to hold to.

Isabelle was looking at him curiously. She turned to Elric. "Do you think the information we have gathered is sufficient to convince the Circle that the Shadows have returned?"

"That," said Elric, "is difficult to say. I believe your evidence leaves no room for doubt. This time, I think, they must accept the truth."

"I trust in the Circle," Galen said. "But I require something. A reason. You never told me why I was sent to Zafran 8.

I know that I was not the best choice. I know that you were unhappy with my selection. So why then was I sent?"

Two frown lines appeared between Elric's brows. His voice turned hard. "We have spoken of this. What more would you have me say?"

Galen pushed a bit further, hoping Elric might understand his need. "Tilar said the Circle feared my power. He said they hoped for my destruction. He said that is why I was sent."

Elric spoke through clenched teeth. "What the members of the Circle fear, and what they hope, is private to each. You were chosen, and you went willingly." Elric fixed Galen with his stern gaze, forcing Galen to linger over that truth. "You have proven yourself skilled and in control of your powers. If any doubted the wisdom of your initiation, you have begun to put those doubts to rest."

They did doubt him. That's what Elric was telling him, without telling him. He had been sent on the task as a test. Although they had initiated him, they did not believe in him. They feared he would again act on instinct, that he would do what they had forbidden, that he would unleash the power that could not be unleashed.

Galen's uncertainty evaporated, replaced by shame. They should fear him. They should doubt him. Perhaps, even, they should hope for his destruction. The tech was subtle and restless, and if his control wavered for a moment, he could conjure destruction on reflex.

Galen met Elric's harsh gaze. "I will not betray their trust. I am sworn to that purpose."

"As it should be," Elric said. "For now, you have done enough. I wish you had not found what you have found. But we choose to live in knowledge, not ignorance. And we now know that the situation is grave. I will recommend that the Circle declare your task completed and call for your immediate return. You should hear from me soon." Elric hesitated, looking to Isabelle. "Your mother?"

"Is not well," Isabelle said.

"Does your home remain protected?"

Galen hadn't even thought of it. Tilar knew Isabelle, could

find the apartment. Most mages had extensive protections warding their homes and places of power, but Galen didn't know how Burell's had been set up, or whether they would remain operational despite her illness.

"Yes," Isabelle said. "If any changes are required, she has given me full access."

Elric nodded. "Be wary. You are vulnerable. I am here if needed."

The circle of standing stones suddenly lost its depth, becoming washed out and pale, like a projection. Then everything went black, and there was a horrible vertiginous moment where he received no sensory input of any kind, where he was cut off from everything. At last Galen found himself back on the sofa in Burell's apartment, Isabelle beside him. Outside the incantation, only an instant had passed.

She pushed to the edge of the sofa and turned toward him, speaking gently. "Why the Circle sent you is irrelevant. Whether they hoped for your success or failure is irrelevant. You shouldn't worry about the Circle stopping you from what you need to do. You should worry about you stopping yourself from what you need to do."

Galen felt a flash of understanding. "You've faced the same problem."

"I saw Burell struggle with it for many years, and I determined to handle it differently." She threw an arm across him and squeezed. She had released him and stood before he had a chance to react. "Let me check on her."

As she left, Galen looked toward the front door. Whatever warding Burell had designed, he doubted it could protect against a Shadow. That one had passed easily through Isabelle's shield.

Deciding that the answer to worry was action, Galen studied the recording Isabelle had made that night. When the Drakh had awoken to the image of his god, he had seemed convinced of the illusion's reality. Galen believed his answers were true, despite his later claims. Once the Drakh had been tranquilized, though, things had changed. The Shadow had manipulated the unconscious Drakh like a puppet, trying to repair the damage. The Shadow had controlled him through some sort of transmission.

Galen thought back to the times they'd picked up static on the probes—a Shadow in the room, somehow hidden, yet watching the Drakh, directing him.

Isabelle came out of the bedroom, closing the door softly behind her. "She's not asleep, but she's resting. She looks better." Isabelle flashed him a small, hopeful smile.

"Good." Galen smiled back, glad to see that the hard anger had finally left her face. "I was just thinking of those times we saw static through the probes. The Drakh never spoke to the Shadow."

Isabelle nodded. "Except that word—that untranslatable word he said when he was coming out of the illusion. I think he was calling for it."

"I think so too. But he was disoriented then. What if their normal method of communication is through that transmission I detected, a transmission that involves the lower protuberance of the Drakh's brain?"

Isabelle brought her hands together and her fingers moved. He knew she was calling up her recording. "Then if we could intercept and decode those transmissions," she said, "we would have access to some of their most private communications." She drifted to the armchair beside the sofa. "If you work on intercepting, I'll take decoding."

He returned to the recording, focusing on the excitation he had sensed in the Drakh's brain. The energy producing the excitation was in a narrow band. He studied the breakdown of frequencies, amplitudes. The signal was compressed, so that what had at first seemed simple was impossibly complex, a snarl of chaotic impulses that resembled nothing so much as random noise. It seemed impossible to decode. But he would leave that to Isabelle.

She was already engrossed in the work. It was late, and they should have gone to bed, but Galen was far too wound up to sleep. Elric had said he would get back to them soon, anyway. And Galen felt better keeping an eye on the door.

Meanwhile, perhaps he could find a way to intercept the

transmissions. In his mind's eye, he manipulated the recording. He searched the Drakh's room. If the Shadow broadcast the signal in all directions, it should be easy to pick up from anywhere in the room. If the signal was strong, it could even be picked up at a great distance, like a radio broadcast. They could stay safe in the apartment and listen in on the Shadows.

Yet he did not find the energy radiating throughout the room. It must be sent in a narrow directional beam from the Shadow to the Drakh. Unless he scanned the sender or the receiver, or stood directly in the beam's path, he would be unable to detect it.

Standing between the Drakh and the Shadow didn't seem like a good idea. Scanning the Drakh would probably be the easiest method. He'd already picked up the signal once. Yet he'd been only a few feet away. Could the signal be detected from a greater distance?

Galen accessed the recordings of the probes in the Drakh's building, searched for those times when static was present. Then he scanned for the narrow frequency of the transmission. He searched through several hours of records without finding anything. Then it was there—a pulse.

It wasn't an extended transmission, as they had detected when the Shadow controlled the Drakh, but just a millisecond-long signal. Galen pulled it out of the record, sent it to Isabelle. Even if she could find some pattern in the extended transmission, it couldn't be decoded without other examples for comparison. So he searched further.

Going through all the material they had recorded thus far, he found eighteen of the transmissions, all short, all in the same narrow band. In all cases, the Drakh was within three feet of a probe when that probe picked up the signal. When the Drakh was farther away, the probes picked up no hint of the signal. That made life more difficult.

Galen was eager to acquire more samples, so he directly accessed the probes in the building to find out what they were recording now. But none of them responded to his signal. They had been either deactivated or destroyed. Tilar could have helped with that.

Burell's door opened, and she came out, riding in her yellow armchair.

Galen jumped up. "Burell!"

The chair rotated in a slow circle. "How do I look?"

"Very well." The chair looked solid. Yet Burell hadn't resumed her full-body illusion. She was conserving her energy. Galen turned to Isabelle. She seemed busy at work, her fingers moving in spurts, her shoulders making tiny movements as if she were threading her way through the signal. Yet a smile had appeared on her face.

"Don't try to get her attention when she's like that," Burell said. "She's impossible."

"I heard that," Isabelle responded.

Galen returned his attention to Burell. Though her appearance was unchanged, she seemed stronger, sitting upright in the chair, holding her head erect. Apparently the additional organelles had brought her some benefit and allowed her to access at least some of her tech. He wondered how long it would last.

"You two are miracle workers," Burell said. "I haven't felt like this in months."

As she went into the kitchen and started coffee, Galen checked the clock. It was 4 A.M. They were all on odd schedules.

Galen followed her into the kitchen, filling her in on all that had happened. The presence of a Shadow on Zafran 8 shocked her. But Tilar's offer to cure her outraged Burell. "How dare he tempt Isabelle with my health. That bastard."

A short laugh escaped Galen. "That was Isabelle's reaction."

Burell's uneven green eyes fixed on him. "I raised her to do good, Galen, even if that good sometimes clashes with the views of the Circle. She is the most precious thing in my life."

Galen felt as if the conversation had taken a sudden turn. It wasn't last night they were talking about; it was the future. "I know." *She is precious to me too,* he thought, but couldn't say the words aloud.

"I've got it!" Isabelle cried. She shot up from the chair, arms upraised. "I'm brilliant! I'm brilliant!" She bounced over to them, stopping on the opposite side of the counter. She slammed her hand down. "Eureka!" She gave them a huge grin.

"You couldn't," Galen said.

"I did! I've figured it out—well, except for a couple of things, but I know this will work. I know how to understand the transmissions.

"Those probe recordings you sent me helped me figure it out. They were missing some of the harmonics—the probes didn't record the transmissions fully. That helped me start breaking the signal down into different components.

"The only full transmission we have is the one we were in the room to record. My sensors were able to pick up the whole thing, I guess. Or at least enough to work with. I was even able to decode part of it. I realized that the Drakh's words, after he was tranquilized, must have come from the Shadow. So I searched for correspondences between the words he spoke and the signal, and I found them in part of the transmission. It's a voice speaking, saying those same words to the Drakh that the Drakh said to us.

"There are other parts of the transmission going on simultaneously. I haven't figured those out yet."

Galen felt a smile form on his face. "You're brilliant."

Isabelle smiled in return, that mysterious, lips-pressed-together smile that seemed meant only for him. She came around the counter and hugged Burell. "I'm so glad you're feeling better." They held each other, and Galen remembered her quick embrace of him earlier. He wished he had put his arms around her.

She released Burell and poured herself a cup of coffee. "Now we need more transmissions to decode. We need to find out what they're planning."

It was basic to all mage strategy to know more than one's opponent. "Now is the time they're likely talking about us," Galen said. "If they have any plans involving the mages, they may come out."

"To go back to a place after you have once been discovered," Burell said, "is never wise. In fact, if I were the

Circle—which of course I'm not—I would have already ordered you two to leave the system, at least until things calm down."

Isabelle ran a hand down Burell's head. "I'm not going anywhere."

Galen knew Burell was right: going back to the Drakh's building was not wise. But there were so many unanswered questions, and who knew when they would have this opportunity again? The Circle could stop the investigation; the Drakh could move his operation elsewhere, now that it had been discovered. It would take time to locate another Shadow, and meanwhile what might the Shadows do?

They had said the mages were already divided. Perhaps he and Isabelle could learn what that meant, could discover the source of Tilar's chrysalis. The Drakh had said it was only a matter of weeks before their provocations began. If he and Isabelle could uncover the Shadows' plan, perhaps they could stop the war before it started. Besides, the Circle had not yet declared their task completed, so wasn't it their responsibility to continue?

"They've destroyed all our probes," Galen said. "We can't see what's going on in there."

"The probes won't record the complete transmissions anyway," Isabelle said. "We have to go there in person. We have to get close enough that our sensors can pick it up."

"Close enough," Galen said, "is three feet."

Isabelle's gaze met his, intent, and he could see her already trying to figure out a way to make it work.

"If Tilar is there," Burell said, "he may be able to sense your presence."

The sensors on a chrysalis weren't nearly as good as those on a mage, but if they were close, he might detect them.

"If Tilar is there," Isabelle said, "he will regret it."

Galen remembered Elric saying the Circle needed evidence beyond doubt. Elric believed they had gotten that, yet he had still seemed uncertain that the rest of the Circle would be convinced. Some might believe the Drakh's claim that he had been lying. They might doubt whether war was truly coming. They might even doubt that the Drakh's words had been forced into his mouth by a Shadow, which appeared only as static on their recording. *If doubt remains an option,* Elric had said, *some will stubbornly cling to it.*

Galen had vowed not to fail the Circle, or Elric. He and Isabelle could secure absolute proof now, and perhaps gather intelligence that would help the mages fight the Shadows. With Isabelle's discovery, they had an incredible opportunity. Could they let it go?

"We need a plan," Galen said. "And this time, a really good one."

"That is the final piece of evidence gathered by Galen and Isabelle thus far," Elric said, dissolving the last image of the recordings. He stood before his chair in the great amphitheater. "My recommendations are as follows. Commend the two mages on their work and remove them from danger. Begin an investigation into the source of Tilar's chrysalis. And create an expanded intelligence-gathering network to follow the movements of the Shadows. If you have any questions, I would be happy to address them."

Elric remained standing, looking over the others in the semicircle. Ing-Radi, Kell, Blaylock, Herazade—they all were silent, shocked.

They had discounted his suspicions about Morden. The shipping and bank records secured by Galen and Isabelle had made little impact. The statement by the Narn, G'Leel, and her description of a Shadow ship had moved some, though others had remained skeptical. And after viewing the recording of the Narn captain and the Drakh, Herazade had been eager to jump to the conclusion that "It is the Drakh behind all of this, not the Shadows."

Yet the next recording, in which Galen and Isabelle questioned the Drakh, made that theory hard to sustain. It was clear to Elric that a Shadow had actually entered the room and taken control of the Drakh's body. He didn't know how else the events could be interpreted, though he assumed he would find out shortly. The confrontation with the static-filled shape had led directly to Tilar's appearance. Though Tilar had been careful not to name the Shadows, his comments about the "younger races" and a firestorm strongly suggested he was speaking for the Shadows.

And then there was the most distressing piece of evidence: Tilar had a chrysalis. This fact had shaken them to the core. Even Kell.

Now Elric waited impatiently. Nearly five hours had passed since his conversation with Galen and Isabelle. He'd been unable to gather the Circle any sooner. Every moment that passed increased the possibility of danger.

At last, Blaylock stood, a dark specter. "I commend Galen and Isabelle for their success in this difficult task. They have found definitive evidence that the Shadows have returned." His voice, usually so harsh and certain, was hesitant. "Before we take any other action, though, we must discover the source of Tilar's chrysalis." His voice picked up speed, strength. "To have a rogue—someone we have cast away—practicing technomancy is an outrage and an abomination. If each chrysalis is under our control and carefully accounted for, then how could such a thing happen?"

"Yes," Herazade said, "how could this happen?"

Kell extended a placating hand. Blaylock, reluctantly, sat. "I, too, am extremely disturbed by this development," Kell said. "The most disturbing part of it is that each chrysalis is accounted for. The chrysalis Tilar trained with, along with the implants he was meant to receive, were destroyed in the casting-away ceremony three years ago, in which we all participated. This year, we had twelve new chrysalises, for the twelve new chrysalis-stage apprentices. All twelve apprentices are still here; all were in training this morning, each with his own chrysalis."

A new chrysalis was really the only possible answer. Each chrysalis developed in accordance with its user, taking on specific traits that made it incompatible with any other user. Older chrysalises, retained by the initiates and other mages, were far too specialized to be used by another. The further complication was that Tilar was Centauri, and so could use only a chrysalis designed for a Centauri.

"What of Carvin?" Herazade asked.

"What of her?" Elric said, angry that the name of Alwyn's fine student would come up, frustrated because he had known it would.

"She is the only Centauri we have initiated in some years. She received her chrysalis at the same time Tilar's was taken from him. Perhaps, somehow, they made an agreement of some kind . . ."

"That seems impossible," Kell said. "But we will check. We will check all initiates; we will again check all chrysalis-stage apprentices. And when we find nothing, we will be faced with the same unacceptable answer." He sat back, his shoulders hunched, face tensed. He seemed weary, as if he had suffered a loss in a war he had long been fighting. Whatever he knew of the Shadows, Elric thought, and however he hoped to fight them, clearly this was not part of his plan.

The rest fell into silence, as if afraid to give their thoughts the power of utterance. Elric felt as if he alone was dealing in reality, as if he alone realized what was at risk.

"If an investigation into the chrysalis is our next step," Elric said, "let us declare Galen and Isabelle's task completed. They are in great danger on Zafran 8 and should be recalled to report in person and be questioned on their findings."

"Yes," Ing-Radi said, distracted. "Let them be recalled."

Herazade glanced her way with dissatisfaction. At last, Elric thought, they would hear Herazade's opinion on the evidence. "Could they not bring us information that more certainly establishes whether the Drakh or the Shadows are behind this current activity? I am not yet convinced that the Shadows have returned. I see a patch of static, and I see a Drakh speak who has supposedly been tranquilized. We know little of these Drakh. Their brain structure is peculiar, and the fact that a part of the brain seems to vibrate as if it is picking up a signal does not mean that it is, in fact, picking up a signal. Perhaps this section of the brain is activated in sleep.

Perhaps the Drakh himself spoke, or his subconscious did so. Perhaps the tranquilizer was not appropriately designed for a Drakh. I am not ready to reach any conclusion without definitive proof."

Blaylock had been tapping his hand through her entire speech. Yet when she finished, he said nothing. He had no doubts, but he would let Galen and Isabelle remain. A further test of Galen's control.

"Let them be recalled," Kell said. "They have done well. And their position, now that they have been discovered, is untenable." Kell would protect his weapon and keep him close.

"I will do so at once." Elric sat, instantly composing the message he had been waiting to send. *The Circle commends you on your work and requests you return at once. Leave as quickly as possible. Bring Burell if you can. If not, let her stay. She will be safer without you than with you. Respond at once.* He sent it to both Galen and Isabelle.

While Elric waited impatiently for a response, the Circle finalized details of the chrysalis investigation, and agreed to meet again the next day. Sufficient time passed, but there was no response.

The members of the Circle filed out, Blaylock casting a backward glance. The illusion of the grand amphitheater dissolved around Elric. He sat alone in a small tent chamber. He closed his eyes, took a deep breath, and began the electron incantation. He had never pulled a mage into the incantation without first obtaining permission. But he had to find out why Galen and Isabelle had not responded.

He again visualized himself traveling the vast distances, reaching Zafran 8, the spaceport, Burell's penthouse apartment. Galen's energy was not there, nor Isabelle's. He could look for them elsewhere on the planet, but it would take time.

Within the apartment he sensed a weaker energy: Burell's. She would know where they had gone. He plucked up her energy, drew it inside him.

The circle of stones took on definition around him. He had no time for its comfort. Burell stood a few feet away. Her self-image was not the illusion of beauty she projected for others, nor the illness-ravaged truth she hid. It reflected what she had looked like several years ago, before the illness had taken her. She was beautiful, yes, but more than that, strong. The dark slanting lines of her brows, the brilliant green of her eyes reflected a will that would not be beaten, a curiosity that would not be satisfied, and a personality that demanded truth. Her spirit had not been crippled, and Elric was glad for that.

"Elric. I think I was asleep. If you wanted to jump into my bed, you could have asked first."

"I'm sorry," Elric said. "My concern for Galen and Isabelle has overruled my manners."

She came toward him, a startled smile crossing her face as her legs responded. The sea breeze blew past them. "What of Galen and Isabelle?"

"The Circle has recalled them. I sent them a message but have received no response. Where are they?"

Burell's eyes narrowed. "Damn the Circle. Isabelle and Galen should have been recalled sooner. They went back to obtain more information from the Drakh. Isabelle discovered—"

"Can you go to them?" They were not reading his message. Even if they did, they would finish what they had begun. Galen was feeling unworthy, particularly after his last conversation with Elric. He wanted more evidence for the Circle. "Can you find them and convince them to leave at once? Or bring them away yourself?"

Burell hesitated only a moment. "Yes. I can do that." Something in the steady control of her features told him how difficult this would be for her.

He regretted asking, but knew of no other way. He took her hand, kissed it. "Thank you. My queen."

As she smiled he dissolved the image, returned her energy to the place from which he had taken it. Then there was nothing for him to do but return to his body, to the lone chair in the empty room. And wait.

— chapter 13 —

They found the neighborhood still in darkness when they returned. They had forgotten to end their earlier blackout of the local power grid, and if any maintenance workers had come to solve the problem, it had proven beyond their abilities. The alarms in the Drakh's building would still be deactivated. They flew directly to a back window in the top story of the building. Galen was wearing Isabelle's scarf tied tightly and tucked into his robe, and he was glad for its extra warmth. The predawn darkness was dry and chill. Her shielded form glowed beside him.

I wish you would use a shield, she wrote.

I would if I could, really. I have a much better chance of dodging a threat, though, than shielding against one.

Her face lingered on him in the darkness, and he had the sense that she felt his failure to use a shield somehow repudiated her use of one.

I wish I had the skill you have, he added.

She turned toward the window, and he did as well. Galen scanned the interior for mage energy.

I don't sense Tilar, Isabelle wrote. They had agreed that if he was there, they would turn back.

Galen had brought his staff this time, and he took it in both hands. Vaguely warm, filled with potential, it felt like nothing so much as a sleeping snake. It was a snake he must learn to control, a snake that was part of him. Taking a calming breath, he visualized the equation to associate.

It awoke, echoing his equation. Its energy slipped into him. Galen braced himself for the intense parallelism he had felt before, and the staff echoed his apprehension. His anxiety increased; the increased anxiety echoed back. The echoes reflected back and forth, faster and faster, swelling in intensity, driving Galen toward fear.

He performed a mind-focusing exercise, pushing down the surge of energy and adrenaline. To his surprise, the staff's energy calmed easily. Galen realized that it was not so much the energy of the staff that caused the instability but the sudden linking, the parallelism that created the sense of an additional echo. The implants were much more powerful than the staff. Living with their restless, energetic undercurrent had made dealing with the staff easier.

The staff's menu of options appeared in his mind's eye. If the staff was like an additional arm, then the menu was like an array of tools available within reach of that arm. He held the end of the staff to the window, selected a narrow, low-energy beam. The staff echoed the command, and a narrow, yellow beam emerged. It cut quietly through the metaglass.

As it did so, Galen realized he had a message. It was from Elric. He left it. Whatever the news, it could wait until they had finished their task.

He conjured a flying platform inside the window, eased the glass onto it, and directed it gently to one side. Then he climbed in, and Isabelle followed. Galen activated his full array of sensors, alert for anything. The tech resonated with his concern. Carefully, he visualized the equation to record, so any evidence they found could be passed to the Circle.

The interior was even darker than the night outside, so he switched to the infrared band.

I don't sense anyone on this floor, Isabelle's message read. Her full-body shield glowed a pale red against a darker red background.

They were on the third floor. The Drakh, if previous activities were any indication, would be in the basement. They used flying platforms to skim the stairs silently down to the second floor.

No one here, Isabelle wrote.

They descended slowly to the first floor. Galen began to

pick up some readings. Faint light, leaking up the staircase from the basement. With the power grid off, the light must use an alternate power source. A voice. Galen activated Osiyrin's dictionary.

They located the vent they wanted, near the ceiling in the central wall. By studying the probe recordings, they had found a corresponding vent in the basement, directly below this one. Galen leaned his staff against the wall, and they levitated themselves to reach the vent. Isabelle conjured a soundproof shield while they pried off the grid.

She dissolved the soundproof shield, leaving her normal defensive one, and removed the amulet from her pocket. Faint voices echoed up the shaft. The amulet radiated a slight heat, appearing dull red in Galen's mind's eye. In the center was a great eye, surrounded by the curving flames of a corona. They had tied a cord to the back of it. Isabelle brought her fingers together and made a quick movement, associating with the piece of chrysalis inside the amulet.

Her eyes flared wide, and Galen knew the contact had been made. It was a piece of her now, a piece that could be sent somewhere she could not go, a piece that could get within three feet of the Drakh without his knowing it.

Galen lowered the amulet by the cord down through the vent, careful to keep it in the center of the shaft, where it would make no sound. A dim red light bled into the shaft from below. They had brought about twelve feet of cord. He was near the end when Isabelle held up her hand.

Tilar. He's there. He's not wearing his chrysalis. Isabelle closed her eyes, concentrating. A muscle stood out on her neck. *Brown too. And the Drakh.* Her red eyes opened, and they stared silently at each other for a moment. They had resolved to leave if the situation looked too dangerous. Yet they were here, so close to accomplishing what they had been sent to accomplish. She raised her eyebrows and gave a short nod.

He nodded back.

She closed her eyes again. *No interference. Wait. There it is.*

Galen gently rested his arm on the edge of the opening, his

shallow breathing sounding loud through his sensors. The Shadow had let them go the first time. What would it do if it caught them again?

"They attacked me." Tilar's voice traveled up the vent. "They aren't going to join you. Why don't you kill them?"

The Drakh is receiving a transmission, Isabelle wrote. *I'm picking it up. I'll try to decode it.*

Isabelle's fingers moved again, in a long, complex pattern. With a rush her breath tightened into a gasp, and the faint red glow of her full-body shield vanished. Her head jerked back. Her mouth stretched wide, so wide that her head began to quiver. And then, as if worms moved beneath her skin, the muscles on her neck writhed.

As he reached out, her platform dissolved and she dropped to the ground with a thump. Her body was rigid, seized in a twisted paroxysm. Her chest heaved in a quick gasp, and her wide-open mouth undulated. From her sinuous lips, her voice emerged, rich, booming. She spoke in Drakh. The program translated automatically.

Tell Tilar they will join with us or they will die.

Galen dropped the cord and swooped down beside Isabelle. With fierce focus, he visualized the equation, extended his platform beneath her. He clamped his arms around her rigid shoulders, grabbed his staff, formed the equation of motion, raced for the front door. Her mouth moved against him, strange words driving out of her with the force of possession. The Shadow's secret words to the Drakh.

Who speaks? The magic workers are upstairs!

Galen stopped the platform and grabbed for the door handle, while the pounding of footsteps sounded behind him. The menu for the staff remained in his mind's eye. He selected a high-intensity shock wave, slammed the staff against the floor. A rumble roared through the building, and the walls began to shake. Galen heard someone fall on the stairs below. He ripped the door open, fled into the alley. Isabelle yelled a single Drakh word.

Kill them.

Dawn was breaking, and the dim light overloaded the infrared. He sped down the long alley, switching back to his regular vision. He hadn't gotten more than a dozen yards when his sensors read multiple energy bursts behind him. Guns. They were shooting.

He raced for the main street, furiously forming one equation of motion after the next to jig the platform up and down and throw off their aim. But the street was still several seconds away, and Tilar had somehow associated with his chrysalis, conjured a platform, and now several of them were on it, rushing in pursuit.

The road to Galen's right exploded, throwing his platform to the left, and Galen barely managed to straighten it before he and Isabelle fell off. The time it took to regain his balance allowed Tilar and the others to come close. Galen was using all his concentration to visualize the equations of motion and keep hold of Isabelle; he had nothing left to try to conjure a shield. He surged ahead, his back tensed, expecting to be hit.

Then something swooped down over him, a great black-and-yellow shape coming fast and traveling in the opposite direction. Galen glanced back. It was Burell in her yellow armchair. Or rather, it was six Burells, all swooping down from different directions, forming a line across the alley between Galen and Isabelle and their pursuers. The six Burells raised their right hands, conjuring fireballs.

Go, Burell's message read.

Isabelle cried out in Drakh.

The one on the left, the program translated.

His sensors flashed with the burst of a plasma weapon behind him. He shot a look back, saw the Burell over his left shoulder lurch with the impact of the blast, her arms flying out like a rag doll's. The other Burells winked out. The chair beneath Burell's limp body vanished and she collapsed to the street. Her body jumped as they shot her again. And again.

Then they raced after Galen and Isabelle.

Galen reached the main street and swerved to the right, his body aflame with energy and panic and grief. He clutched desperately to control. The streets had become busy with people going to work. He shot above the pedestrians as they stopped and pointed.

A fight in the open was too dangerous. But there was no time to hide; they were just seconds behind, and at this short range, Tilar could track them. The black awning of the Strauss Hotel appeared on his right. Galen focused, formed the equation of motion, and darted through the doorway. He prayed that Isabelle had been right and Cadmus Wilcox did have bravery lurking somewhere within his cowardly soul.

Cadmus was standing behind the front desk, patrolling his lonely command. He jumped at the sight of Galen and Isabelle rushing toward him.

"Some people are about to come through that door," Galen said, swooping over the counter and down behind it. He dissolved the platform, left Isabelle's rigid form on the dingy carpet along with his staff. "Wait until they are all inside," he said to Cadmus. "Then fire your gun. Fire it anywhere."

Cadmus stared at him as if he were speaking Drakh, his damp lower lip sticking out the bottom of that shaggy walrus moustache.

Galen spotted Cadmus' PPG under the counter, grabbed it and shoved it into his hand. He tried to imbue his words with power. "This is the moment Isabelle spoke of. The moment when you will save her and everyone here."

Galen crouched below the counter with Isabelle, closed his eyes, gathered his energy, and visualized the equation to conjure a soundproof shield over both of them. His sensors told him he had been successful, at least temporarily. It wouldn't hold off high-energy weapons, but it was strong enough to block out sound waves. No sound from within would pass into the lobby; no sound from the lobby would penetrate within. He accessed the lobby probes to see and hear what was happening.

Cadmus stood frozen behind the counter, his low brows giving his face that expression of perpetual fear. He swiped nervously at the lock of hair curling onto his forehead. The probe outside the front doorway showed that Tilar had dissolved his flying platform. He was breathing heavily with the effort of using his chrysalis, his face red. He, the Drakh, and Brown approached the doorway warily, on foot, their weapons at the ready. Galen had no time to search through frequencies for static, but he felt certain the Shadow would be with them.

The Drakh and Brown entered, but Tilar held back, looking up at the hotel with suspicion. He was probably accessing the sensors in his chrysalis to search for anything unusual. Isabelle had told him that Burell had a long-standing relationship with the manager.

Back in the lobby, Cadmus had begun to shake. "Can I help you?" he asked the Drakh and Brown.

Isabelle's voice boomed within the confined shield, echoing and reechoing. It was another message from the Shadow to the Drakh.

They are hiding beside this Human.

The Drakh was no longer within three feet of the amulet. He wasn't even within three feet of Isabelle. Yet still the transmission held her.

The Drakh approached the desk, his weapon aimed at Cadmus. His brown-and-black striated body was massive, and he walked with an odd stiffness, as if movement were not his natural condition. Cadmus glanced nervously toward the doorway. Tilar stood just outside the threshold, watching the others.

Brown turned toward him. "Afraid of some *real* techno-mages?"

Tilar straightened. "Only an idiot wouldn't be," he said, yet he stepped inside. Galen cut off the audio signal from the probes.

The Drakh leaned over the counter. Finding his quarry, he pointed his weapon toward Galen and Isabelle.

Galen forced his mind to focus only on the equation for the shield, to conjure nothing else.

Cadmus' shaggy moustache spread as the face beneath it grimaced. He raised the PPG to the Drakh's head at point-blank range, closed his eyes, and fired.

Being Cadmus, of course, he missed.

Detecting the high-energy discharge, Burell's probes instantly activated her spell of protection. Throughout the hotel, sonic generators blasted out sound waves so intense they vibrated the internal organs of patrons, stunning them, causing spasms, or liquefying their bowels.

Tilar grabbed his stomach and doubled over. His lips spat out a curse. Then he collapsed. Brown followed a moment later. The Drakh jerked erect, twitching. He fired into the ceiling and chunks of plaster rained around him. His body spasming, he dropped to the floor.

Cadmus' head rolled back and he slid below the counter.

The signal continued for thirty seconds. Then the spell was deactivated. Galen had no idea how long the effect would last. Burell had never said. He dissolved his shield. The lobby was quiet.

Isabelle was rigid in his arms, her eyes and mouth wide, oblivious to anything but the Shadow signal. He laid her on the carpet and stood up from behind the counter. The Drakh was twitching. The others were still. Galen moved quickly, remembering how the Shadow had used the Drakh's body before. He snatched the weapon from the Drakh's twitching fingers, took the guns from Brown and Tilar as well. He put them all on the shelf where Cadmus had kept his PPG. To one side he saw the call button that linked to the port authority. He pressed it.

Then Galen pulled up a stool and propped Cadmus' unpleasant-smelling body on it, molded his hand around the PPG. Hopefully the others would have learned their lesson when they woke, and would flee.

The Drakh grunted and drew his legs in, attempting to climb to his feet. Galen had no more time. He knelt beside Isabelle, wrapped his arm around her, and snatched up his staff. He visualized the equation, conjured a platform.

As they rose up from behind the counter, Isabelle's chest heaved, and the words seized her again, driving out of her. This time, they were in English. "YOU WILL JOIN WITH US. ALL OF YOU. OR YOU WILL DIE."

Galen clutched her tightly and formed the equation of motion. They raced from the hotel. He swerved to avoid hitting two pedestrians, then swooped up, over them, up to the level of the rooftops. The sun had risen over the horizon, illuminating everything in a harsh light.

Isabelle's body suddenly relaxed, slumping against him. He couldn't see her face. The scarf she had made for him had come out of his robe and fallen across her. He tossed the end over his shoulder. Her face was slack, eyes closed. Yet her respiration, her heartbeat, were normal. The Shadow transmission had finally released her.

Are you all right? he wrote.

No answer.

They had to leave the planet. He had to get her safely away. But they couldn't leave Burell's body. It was bad enough that Tilar had a chrysalis. Galen couldn't let Tilar and the Shadows get their hands on a sample of the tech.

He formulated the equation, dove down into the alley, landing beside Burell's body. She lay on her back, her large robe blanketing thin, fragile limbs. Several great black burns had blossomed across her chest and leg where her robe had been burned into the skin. Her head was turned toward him, the side of her neck and ear burned black. Her uneven green eyes stared at him.

He had not prepared sufficiently for their invasion of the Drakh's building. He had not aborted the plan when he learned the Drakh was not alone. He had not controlled the situation. Burell had paid for that failure with her life.

And Isabelle—she lay limp in his arms.

Galen realized he was inhaling in quick, shallow breaths. He was exhausted and surging with energy at the same time, his control unsteady. He forced himself to focus, carefully extended his platform below Burell. He put his arm across her and pulled her in close.

Isabelle started at the touch of Burell's body, pushed herself up. His relief at seeing her well was countered by the growing realization on her face. "What? No. No."

Galen remembered Elric walking out of the fire of the spaceship crash, the remains of his parents floating behind.

Holding desperately to control, Galen visualized the equation of motion, shot them up into the pale green sky.

Isabelle seized Burell. The tendons stood out on the back of her hand. Her head turned slightly back and forth as she mouthed the words. *No. No.* Her lips turned out, revealing clenched teeth. Her pain seemed horribly private, but he couldn't look away.

As she drew Burell to her, Isabelle discovered the burned ear. She cried out, then, hesitantly, brought her fingers to it.

Galen headed toward the port, not sure what they should do next, but knowing his ability to focus was rapidly deteriorating. He remembered the message from Elric, opened it.

The Circle commends you on your work and requests you return at once. Leave as quickly as possible. Bring Burell if you can. If not, let her stay. She will be safer without you than with you. Respond at once.

Galen expelled a sharp breath. She would have been safer without them, that was certain. She would have been alive.

Isabelle laid Burell's body on the platform, and her hand slowly explored each wound.

"Isabelle, I need your help."

She continued her inspection, unhearing.

"Isabelle. I need your help."

She dragged a finger through one of the wounds, bringing it out covered in ash. She rubbed it between her index finger and thumb, getting a chemical analysis through her sensors. "What type of guns did they have?" she asked, her voice light, dreamy.

"Tilar and Brown had PPGs. The Drakh had a plasma weapon I've never seen before."

"It was the Drakh who killed her then." She turned to him absently, eyebrows raised, face covered in tears. "I *will* kill him."

"I will help you," Galen said. "But we must escape now. Escape now, to fight later."

Isabelle's gaze wandered. "Burell's place of power must be destroyed. Our home, the samples of the tech she has. We cannot let them fall to Tilar or the Shadows."

"Has she set up a system to do that?"

"Yes. I must contact Johnny." She brought her hands together, made a lazy motion with her fingers.

In a conjured globe above Burell's body, Johnny appeared. He fell to one knee, bowed his head. "Greetings, Daughter of Enchantress." He stood, smiling, wearing only his red bathing suit.

"Your enchantress is dead," Isabelle said.

Johnny looked down, saw Burell there. The smile fell from his face. "She told me she was going to die. Oh, hell."

"Did she tell you what must be done?"

He raised his head, his jaw firm, like the EarthForce captain on whom he had been modeled. "All of her places, all of her belongings must be destroyed. That power has to be kept out of the wrong hands."

"And as for yourself?"

"I have to die too."

"I'm sorry, Johnny."

Johnny shook his head. "I lived to serve her. I'm happy to die with her."

"First, give me a copy of all her files." She closed her eyes, and Galen knew she was visualizing Burell's key. She turned to Galen, and there was an expression on her face he couldn't identify. "Give Galen a copy as well."

She was afraid that something might happen to her. Galen closed his eyes, visualized the key. He received the files—files of research for which Burell had been reprimanded.

"It is time," Isabelle said. "It must be done at once. Goodbye, Johnny."

Johnny dropped to one knee. "It is my great pleasure, Daughter of Enchantress." He vanished, and Isabelle dissolved the globe.

Galen realized there was one more piece of tech that had to be destroyed. "Your amulet," he said to Isabelle. "I left it behind." It was a piece of Isabelle, a limb that she now must sever.

She nodded absently, closed her eyes.

Galen looked toward Burell's apartment building, which

stood out against the skyline in the harsh light of the sun. The apartment was on the top floor. Galen used his sensors to magnify the view, but found no peculiar activity or energy in the apartment, until he reached the right corner window. Something flashed inside: an intense blue, churning energy. Then the window exploded outward, and blue flames whirled and diffused into the pale green sky. Galen directed his gaze inside, magnifying further. A great maelstrom whirled within those walls, consuming all.

The apartment seemed to shift, and as Galen removed his magnification, he saw that the building was swaying slightly. He looked over the city and watched the swaying pass in a wave from one building to the next, radiating outward. As it approached them, a low rumble grew out of the ground. Then it passed by, moving toward the outskirts of the port. Burell had said her place of power was underground. It must have been destroyed.

Ahead of them, the hangars of the spaceport came into view. When they had arrived, Burell had parked her ship in a private hangar, which was protected against intruders. Now it, too, was consumed in a whirlwind of blue flame.

Galen found an empty alley near the spaceport, formulated the equation, brought them down. He dissolved the platform too soon. They dropped a few inches to the ground. Galen caught himself on hands and knees on the dirty, wet pavement. His scarf dangled into a brown puddle.

He had energy; he had boundless, surging energy inside of him. But his body was exhausted. His limbs quivered with the effort of keeping balance on the platform. And more than that, his mind was tired, tired of the endless, ferocious focus required to maintain control.

The alley stank. Isabelle was pulling Burell away from the puddle, straightening her limbs. Galen wanted only to sit here with her, to be still and try to forget how his foolishness and failure had led to Burell's death. Yet he had a duty, a duty to the Circle.

He tried to concentrate. "We need passage out of here. We need false identification. We need to disguise Burell's body."

Isabelle straightened Burell's head as if she hadn't heard. Galen seized her wrist.

She looked up and it seemed as if she really saw him for the first time since she had discovered Burell's body. She pulled in a breath, and her face tightened, regaining its focus. He was shocked at how relieved he was to have her back. He needed her.

She nodded, and her strong fingers threaded decisively through each other. "There's a ship leaving for the Brensil system in an hour."

"Sending them was a mistake. We might as well admit that to begin with." Herazade seemed finally to have grasped the gravity of the situation, Elric thought. After watching the latest recording sent by Galen, she even seemed willing to acknowledge at last that the Shadows had returned.

The evidence allowed no further room for doubt. The messages Isabelle had ingeniously intercepted and decoded came from a being whose orders the Drakh followed without question, a being who could make itself invisible, a being who could penetrate their shields and illusions. It had penetrated the illusions of Burell, and so she had been killed.

No techno-mage had been killed in their lifetimes. Even Ing-Radi, almost two hundred years old, could remember nothing like it. Burell's death had stunned them. *You will join with us. All of you. Or you will die,* the Shadow had said. Burell's death proved it could fulfill that threat.

She had sacrificed herself to save Galen and Isabelle. Elric had sent her to that death, and he would have to live with it. If he had not sent her, perhaps Galen and Isabelle would be dead. Or perhaps they would have escaped, and Burell would still live. He would never know.

Galen's last message, with the new recording attached, troubled Elric with what it did not say.

Burell is dead. We have her body. We will arrive in the Brensil system in two days. Perhaps someone could meet us.

Galen blamed himself, of course. That was how Elric had raised him. They were two of a kind. Yet when Galen was very upset, he succumbed to an odd quietness, a disconnection quite unlike Elric's stubborn movement forward.

Elric imagined Galen as he had been in the days following his parents' funeral, sitting on a stool by the fire with his hands folded, not moving for hours. Elric could sense the stillness in the words of Galen's message. As if any movement would trigger another catastrophe.

When he'd received Galen's message, Elric had wanted to take to his ship and abandon the convocation for the Brensil system. Elric needed to see with his own eyes that Galen was all right.

But instead, he had called this emergency meeting of the Circle. He had his duties, and may they be damned to hell.

Herazade continued her endless speech. "Our intelligence-gathering activities have invaded the privacy of the Shadows and angered them. My suggestion is that before hostilities escalate further, we arrange a meeting with the Shadows, apologize for our intrusion, and lay out our position of neutrality in any coming conflict. We can explain—"

Blaylock's tapping hand slammed against the arm of his chair. "How long is this nonsense to be allowed to continue?"

"If we explain," Herazade continued, "that we have taken no side in any war in the last three hundred years, they will have to understand. That is our way."

Blaylock stood, scowling down on Herazade, and flung the words at her. "They will not understand. That is their way." He seemed ready to continue, but stopped and turned his back to her, facing the other members of the Circle. "The time has come to decide on a course of action. The Shadows' intentions are clear. Now we must make clear our own. We have three choices. We may join the Shadows. We may fight the Shadows. We may seek a place of safety to wait out this threat.

"I find the first two options unacceptable. If we join with the Shadows, we must abandon the Code. If we fight the Shadows, then we are making ourselves into something we were never meant to be: soldiers. We carry a special blessing. We have a special destiny. We are not meant for war. That would be moving in the wrong direction. If we are to survive, I believe we must create a special place of hiding, where none can find us until we see fit."

Blaylock sat.

Herazade was staring at him with her mouth open, amazed at this grim piece of advice. Kell and Ing-Radi were less surprised, but still seemed unhappy with Blaylock's suggestion.

Kell pushed himself to his feet. "Your proposal, Blaylock, seems premature. Just as Elric's proposal to forge alliances and prepare to fight the Shadows seems premature. Isabelle has given us the promise of a weapon to use against the Shadows: the ability to hear their communications. What other weapons we may have against them, we do not know. And what weapons they may have against us, we do not know. Our illusions seem easily penetrated by them." He hesitated, looking down toward the well of the amphitheater. Kell never hesitated.

He was considering telling them, Elric realized, telling them the secret he'd been keeping, his knowledge of the Shadows. Kell lifted his gaze to scan the members of the Circle through squinting eyes, Herazade and Blaylock to his right, Ing-Radi and Elric to his left. Did he no longer trust them? Tilar had said the mages were divided. Morden had sought allies during his visit. Had he found any?

Kell cleared his throat and continued. "Now that we know the Shadows are abroad, I believe we may acquire more information shortly. We should at least question Galen and Isabelle personally, before we take any further actions."

Again he was delaying. But this time Kell had revealed more than he had planned. He was expecting information. His plan, whatever it was, would bring them further intelligence on the Shadows. And none too soon. Burell had already died while he delayed.

Ing-Radi bowed her head. "I agree. Let us first send Burell to the other side. Let us second speak with Isabelle and Galen. Then a better decision can be made."

Elric stood. "We have not yet resolved the immediate

issue. Who is to bring Galen and Isabelle from the Brensil system? I volunteer myself."

Ing-Radi extended an orange hand toward him. "You are needed here, Elric. Besides, Brensil is three days' journey. Galen and Isabelle will arrive there in less than two days, and would be safer picked up as soon as they arrive, in case they are pursued. Can we not hire a ship to bring them?"

"A hired ship would also take time to arrive there," Elric said. He had prepared for this. "Brensil has little traffic. It has no ships ready for hire. Those who owned ships left the system when the mine closed."

Kell ran his index finger over his white goatee, revealing his anxiety. "Perhaps we could send Elizar." His words were slow, reluctant. "In his ship, he can travel from Zafran to Brensil quickly enough to arrive before Galen and Isabelle. They could leave immediately."

"He is well?" Blaylock asked, the question an accusation. The implication was clear: if Elizar could heal so quickly, then he should not have left the convocation.

"He recovers."

Blaylock held them for a moment in the silence of his disapproval before responding. "Very well."

"It is best to have them picked up quickly," Ing-Radi said.

Kell turned to Elric. "Have Galen contact Elizar at once. See if they can make arrangements." Kell seemed more positive about the plan now.

Elric nodded. If Elizar was involved in Kell's attempt to gather information about the Shadows, that could explain why Kell was reluctant to interrupt him with this task. But Elizar was in the best position to go to Brensil, and despite his arrogance, Elizar was a skilled initiate. He could help Galen through any trouble that might occur.

Elric composed the message. *The Circle would have you contact Elizar. He is on Zafran 7 and could reach Brensil most quickly. See if you can make arrangements and advise us.* He sent the message.

Kell nodded. "This is for the good. They can mend any ill feelings between the three of them."

As Ing-Radi began to discuss changes in the convocation schedule to allow for Burell's funeral, Elric found himself waiting anxiously for Galen's reply. If Elizar was available, Galen would soon be safe at home. Right now, that mattered more to him than the Shadows, more than fighting the Shadows, more than discovering whether the Shadows had allies among the mages. All of that would be easy to face, once Galen was safe at home.

At last a response came. *I have contacted Elizar. He is fit and can meet us at Brensil. He says he can be there even before we arrive, so we can leave for Soom at once.*

Elric found his heart pounding and slowed it.

The news was good; Galen would soon be home. And Galen's new message carried less of the sense of stillness. He was coming back to himself. In five days, Elric could see for himself that Galen was all right.

Across the room, Blaylock's unyielding gaze was fixed on him. As the message arrived, Blaylock gave a slight nod. *Your student has performed well.*

— chapter 14 —

Inside the freighter's cabin, Galen read Elric's message. "The Circle wants us to contact Elizar. He's the closest."

"Of course," Isabelle said. "I should have thought of it. If he's well enough to make the trip." She knelt beside a vent in the wall, her brown gown pooling around her feet. She flipped the switch on the vent and a blast of dust came out, followed by a stream of fresh air.

From the look of it, no one had used this cabin in years. It was tiny, meant for crew not passengers, with two bunk beds on the left, a small desk and cubbyhole for clothes on the right. Everything was coated with a thick layer of dust. A single harsh ceiling lamp glared down on the neglect.

The ship ran food and sundries once a month to the mining colonies on Brensil 4 and other settlements on the verge of abandonment. It carried much less cargo than it had been built to hold, and the captain seemed to have compensated for this lost revenue by cutting expenses. Though it was meant to have a larger crew, the captain made do with three. That left one empty cabin in the narrow section rotating about the center of the ship. From the dull, unsteady vibration that ran through the superstructure, Galen judged he also saved money on engine maintenance.

Galen finished making the upper bunk with the clean sheets the captain had given them. "I'll contact Elizar then." He was reluctant to ask Elizar to put aside his convalescence. But if they were somehow tracked to this slow-moving freighter, Tilar, Brown, and the Drakh could easily be on Brensil 4 waiting for them.

They had disguised themselves with hastily bought clothes and wigs. They hadn't wanted to conjure full-body illusions in case the Shadow was monitoring the port. The energy might draw it to them, and it could easily penetrate those disguises.

Isabelle wore a becoming brown gown, Galen an uncomfortable brown turtleneck and pants. The wigs, it turned out, were infested with bugs, and they'd thrown them out as soon as they'd boarded.

Even if the disguises had worked, though, they might not be sufficient. This ship, one of the first to leave after their confrontation, would be a logical choice for the Shadows to suspect. Galen didn't want to be trapped on Brensil 4, virtually a barren rock, waiting for a ride. He would study the layout of the planet's domed settlement in case of emergency, but he hoped they would not be forced into a fight there. Brensil 4 wasn't an ideal destination; aside from this monthly delivery, it had little other traffic. A much busier port would have been better. But the ship had been leaving when they needed to leave, and its captain asked no questions.

Galen realized he was delaying when he should be contacting Elizar. He knew that Elizar would want to help them if he was able. Perhaps it was the reminder of his failure he did not want to face.

He composed the message. *Elizar, the Circle has suggested I contact you. Isabelle and I were sent to Zafran 8 on a task. We did not fare well. Burell was killed, and Isabelle and I escaped on a freighter bound for Brensil 4. We may be pursued. We will arrive in two days and require transportation back to Soom. I do not know the state of your health. If you are not well, by no means should you come. But if it will not endanger your recovery, we would be grateful for your help.* He visualized the equation to send the message.

Isabelle had been watching him. "Elizar knew there was a danger facing the mages. He warned me. It was not the danger of decay, as he claimed before the Circle."

" 'A threat not only to us, but to everyone,' that's what he told me. Perhaps he saw signs of it, as Burell did."

She moved toward the desk and chair, which required that she squeeze past Galen. Galen tried to move out of her way, but the room was so narrow his hip grazed her stomach. The touch was electric.

Isabelle pulled out the chair and sat, seemingly unaffected. "Why would he lie to the Circle?"

Galen sat on the lower bunk. Their knees touched. "He told me Kell was not willing or able to fight this threat."

"He said that?"

Galen nodded. "If that is true, if Kell and the Circle cannot fight the Shadows, then none of us can."

"The Circle," Isabelle said, "is not the answer to all things." Her chest hitched with a quick breath, and she looked away.

She was thinking of Burell, he knew. Every few minutes it would come back to her, the realization that Burell was dead. He would see it in a slackness to her face, an emptiness in her eyes. Then the loss would turn to anger, her jaw clenching and a muscle in her neck gaining prominence. Gradually, as they spoke, the anger would fade, and she would become more like her old self.

He was amazed at how well he could tell what she was thinking. He'd never felt such an awareness of another's feelings, not even Elric's.

Even with that knowledge, though, he didn't know what to say to make her feel better. Burell was in a stasis crate in the hold. If he had read Elric's message when it had first arrived, if they had left immediately, Burell would still be alive.

A reply arrived from Elizar. *It grieves me to hear of Burell's passing. Please convey my condolences to Isabelle. Of course I will come to Brensil, my good friend. I am well enough. I will be there as quickly as speed allows, which will be much sooner than you. Perhaps then you can tell me something of what you encountered.*

Galen composed a quick message to Elric, letting him know. "Elizar will come," he told Isabelle.

She nodded absently. "She must have a grand funeral."

"Yes?" Galen said.

"She spoke of it often, even more so right before we left for the convocation. I tried to make her stop. I thought it morbid." She gave a short laugh, and Galen took her hand. " 'Five hundred naked slave men,' she would say, 'all weeping and ripping at their hair. A shower of red poppies from the sky. My body in the perfect bloom of health.' She had it all planned, down to the toasts to be made afterward. She wanted to be sure to leave with a last spit in the eye at the Circle." She squeezed his hand. "I have to do everything as she planned. That would please her."

"I will help you."

"How do you get used to it, Galen? That someone who has always been there, who has been part of the fundament underlying everything you do, everything you think, is there no longer."

He realized with surprise that she was asking him about his parents. She didn't know that he never spoke of it. And although he knew he was hiding from himself, he never wanted to speak of it.

Galen pulled his hand away. "You get used to it. You have no choice."

She gave him that penetrating look that made him think she knew everything about him. "You are still angry at the universe for killing them."

"Aren't you?"

Her slender eyebrows rose. "No. I'm angry at Tilar. I'm angry at the Drakh. But I'm not angry at the universe. Why would I be?"

"I'm not angry," Galen said, pushing down the emotions. "I am disappointed. I am disappointed that we live in a universe of random joy and random despair. I am disappointed that what we do is ultimately lost in the vacuum fluctuations of a heartless cosmos. I am disappointed that there is not some greater meaning to it all."

"But the death of your parents doesn't prove that there is no greater meaning. Burell's death convinces me more than ever that there is meaning, there is a design."

"How can you believe that? How can you believe in a god that would kill her to fulfill some abstract purpose?"

She laid a hand on his knee. "Burell has been in agony for the last four years. She wanted to see me through my training, and so she did, traveling to the convocation when she knew the horrible cost it would exact. That she died now, rather than hanging on through more months of pain, I see as an act of mercy. That she died saving us, I believe, gave her great satisfaction. That she had the strength to reach us, to use her powers one last time, reveals our capacity to transcend our limitations."

He bit out the words. "And if she had died in an accident, saving no one, what would that show? That she lacked the capacity to transcend her limitations?"

"No, Galen. No. I don't pretend to understand it all, but I believe God works through patterns, patterns that intersect with other patterns, patterns that occur in different variations. And I believe one of these patterns is to provide opportunities for transcendence."

Galen found his voice control uncertain. He lowered his head, unwilling to speak.

"You could just admit I'm right. I always am, except for the times when I'm not." She leaned forward, resting her forehead against his.

Galen felt his mouth turn up in a slight smile. "You were right about Cadmus. He was ready to defend that hotel to the death."

"A man of great loyalty."

Galen remembered Mary Stein, the woman whose fortune he had told, who kept marrying men who didn't love her. Isabelle had said the universe sent Mary that sort of man so she would recognize her own problem. And that the universe had sent Mary to Galen to help him overcome his problem. He raised his head. Her face was inches from his. "You said that I had some problem to transcend."

Her lips pressed together in a smile.

"Must I guess?"

"Problem is not the right word." Her rich voice wrapped around him. "But if I were telling your fortune, I would tell you that you must transcend yourself in three ways."

"So I have *three* problems?"

"First, you must open yourself to others." Her head darted forward, and her lips met his. The touch was soft, her heat and nearness intoxicating. She pulled back, her face flushed, searching for his reaction.

"What is second?" he asked breathlessly.

She shook her head. Her lips came to him again, and he brought his hand this time to the side of her face. His finger traced a line down her scalp, along the curve of her ear. He drank in the chemical composition of the subtle oils and perspiration sheening her skin, her unique formula of attraction. He inhaled and captured her essence. He had never wanted anything so much.

She drew his hand down to her neck, to the artery there. Her pulse pounded in time with his.

First things first, her message read.

It was magic.

"That shirt is definitely you, Mr. Wilcox," Isabelle said.

"Why thank you, Mrs. Wilcox," Galen replied. "And may I say that's a lovely frock you're wearing."

"You may."

Packing up their few belongings, they prepared to disembark on Brensil 4. They had spent the last two days being extremely silly, and extremely happy. They had put everything aside for the duration of the trip, knowing that they would have to deal with reality soon enough, when they returned to the Circle.

Galen felt strange. His face seemed caught in a constant smile, and the undercurrent of energy from his implants no longer felt restless or irritating. It had subsided over the last two days into a deep, secure channel, making him feel rich and suddenly alive.

He closed up the two shopping bags filled with their robes and the meager belongings they'd purchased before leaving Zafran 8. They were back in their street clothes, Isabelle looking bright and beautiful in her brown gown, a white-and-brown patterned scarf around her neck. Galen tugged at the brown synthesuede turtleneck, unused to the feeling of the soft, rich material against his skin. He had wrapped the scarf Isabelle had made him around his neck. They had joked about being husband and wife like regular Humans, both with their scarves.

In the absence of the wigs, they created the illusion of hair on their heads. Galen's was short and dark. Isabelle's long strawberry-blond hair looked much as it had before she'd been initiated. She'd included in the illusion some locks that were twisted back and clipped, adding to the semblance of reality.

If Elizar was there to meet them, then the disguises would hardly be necessary. But they were being cautious, now. Galen conjured an illusion to disguise his staff as a packing tube, then picked up the shopping bags.

"Shall we go, Mrs. Wilcox?" He offered her his arm, and she took it.

"Certainly, Mr. Wilcox."

They headed down the narrow corridor to the air lock, walking easily in step. The brush of Isabelle's body against his felt right. Galen knew Elric would not approve, but he and Isabelle were meant to be together. Their feelings would not burn away after time.

Since the ship was still being guided into dock, the captain and his crew were occupied. The area around the air lock was empty, but for the stasis crate with Burell's body. It had been left on a wheeled cart.

The sight of it sent a restless surge of energy through Galen.

Isabelle laid her hands on the crate. Galen realized that their time alone was ending, that they must resume care and caution. He swore again to himself to maintain strict control, to conjure nothing by instinct.

The air lock doors opened, and they pushed Burell's stasis crate out onto the passenger promenade. The ship's freight would be unloaded one floor below. The promenade was a vast area, a shiny green malachite floor highlighting the former richness of the mines. The settlement's domed ceiling stretched high overhead, its darkness dotted with stars. When the mines had been open, the promenade had probably been crowded with new arrivals, those eager for work, those searching for opportunity, or those seeking easy money. But now, with the mines closed, the settlement had turned into a backwater's backwater, little more than a jumpgate, a planet, and a handful of nearly abandoned domed settlements. The only inhabitants who remained were those who couldn't afford to leave.

Galen had found Zafran 8's dirt and congestion unpleasant, but somehow this was worse. The vast emptiness of the dome seemed to reflect the coldness of the universe.

He searched for the energy characteristic of a mage, found it in a figure approaching them from across the promenade. Galen recognized the long stride and maroon velvet coat of Elizar. Surprisingly, he detected the energy of another mage, at a greater distance. Could Elric have somehow managed to arrive so quickly?

They pushed the stasis crate toward Elizar. He looked well, his angular face tilted upward. Since the initiation, he'd grown back his dark goatee scoured into the shape of the rune for magic. His scalp he kept bare. As he walked, his arms swung, and Galen could find no difference between the movement of the left and the right. He hoped that meant Elizar's recuperation was progressing quickly.

They met, and Elizar embraced Isabelle. Galen recognized the same anxious intensity that he had noticed in Elizar at the convocation. Elizar released her and took her hands, staring into her eyes. "Isabelle. I am truly sorry for your loss. I know that in the past I've been critical of Burell. I apologize. That was Kell's influence. I realize now how brave she was to defy the Circle and carry on her work, at all costs. And I realize how brave you are for continuing that work."

Isabelle looked shaken. "Thank you."

"Galen, good friend." Both of Elizar's arms rose to encircle him. "I wish the circumstances of our meeting were better."

"Your arm," Galen said, amazed.

Elizar flexed it. "Yes, I am much improved. Ing-Radi did better than she knew."

Seeing Elizar whole again lifted a great burden from Galen. He smiled. "It's good to see you well."

"And so our friendship need not be clouded by anger or guilt."

"Are you alone?" Isabelle asked.

"Razeel accompanied me. She's preparing the ship for departure. It's waiting at the next promenade." He pointed the way, toward a wide passage that connected the promenades, and they headed toward it. "I've seen no suspicious offworlders. The port records show no ship has arrived in the last eight days. You picked a place with very little activity, so anything unusual would be apparent. I think Razeel is the strangest thing they've seen here in some time."

Galen remained vigilant anyway, but few people walked the passage, and those who did wore workers' coveralls and had the weary step of locals. The passage was lined on one side by shops, but they were all closed.

"How is it you were chosen for this ill-fated task?" Elizar asked.

"The Circle wanted to send two of us to Zafran 8 to investigate unusual activity," Galen said. "They wanted two who would draw no suspicion."

"And this unusual activity, it involved traffic to the rim?"

Galen looked at his friend with surprise. "Yes."

"You warned us of a threat," Isabelle said. "You knew of the Shadows."

"And now you know," Elizar said. "It will be a relief to finally speak of it."

"But how—" Isabelle began.

"We should stop for something to eat," Elizar said, pointing to the one open storefront along the passage. It was a tavern, small and dark. "I don't have much food on the ship. When I got your message, I pretty much jumped in and took off."

Galen glanced up and down the passage. Just beyond

where they stood, it opened into another promenade. There would be Elizar's ship. He saw nothing out of the ordinary.

"I'll call for Razeel," Elizar said. "She can take Burell's body onto the ship and then join us."

Isabelle's gaze was directed at the tavern.

Galen activated his sensors and joined her examination. The restaurant seemed perfectly unremarkable—no odd energy sources or unusual readings. There were two Humans inside.

"Thank you for coming for us," Galen said. "I hope we didn't interrupt your recovery, or your quest."

"You remember I said I must undertake it alone," Elizar said. "I hope that I was wrong."

Razeel came from the promenade, pale and petite, her thin, inch-short dark hair drifting like the fibers of a seed-puff around her head. Galen was sure that the dress she wore—this one of blue velvet—was different than the ones he had seen before, yet it, too, hung on her as if it were much too large. Without her hair to obscure her face, he saw that her eyes were huge, the skin around them darkened as if with lack of sleep. She looked from Isabelle to Galen.

My condolences, her message read.

"Do you want her to take any of those other things?" Elizar asked.

Galen put the two shopping bags on top of the crate, but kept his staff. Razeel took the cart with the stasis crate and wheeled it away toward the promenade.

Elizar put his arm across Galen's shoulders. "Let us go in. Then we can talk at last."

Galen entered with Elizar, Isabelle following. The interior was decorated in dark stone and dim light, with tables on the right side and a bar along the left wall. A man stood behind the bar. "Sit where you like," he said.

They chose a table against the right wall. Galen leaned his staff against the wall, and the bartender approached. "Planning on eating or just drinking?"

"Since this is a restaurant, we were planning to eat," Elizar said. "Unless it's too much of an inconvenience."

The bartender frowned, handed them menus. They ordered quickly, and the bartender apparently committed their order to memory. "I'll go wake up the cook," he said, and disappeared into the back.

"How did you learn of the Shadows?" Isabelle asked Elizar.

"Kell knew that they were returning," Elizar said, speaking in a low voice. "Kell has known for some time. You were sent on a needless task. To discover what he already knew."

Elizar stopped, waiting for them to absorb the implications. If it were true, Galen thought, then Burell had died for nothing. He could see the same thought on Isabelle's face.

"Did Kell tell you this?" she asked, intent.

"No," Elizar said.

"Then what is your source?"

"About a year ago, Kell mentioned to me that Carvin had discovered Alwyn's key and accessed his place of power. It was just one of those tricks that Alwyn encourages Carvin to play on him. But I wondered if I had the ability to do the same to Kell. And so I tried, and gained partial access to Kell's place of power. There I discovered information about the Shadows, evidence gathered by Kell that revealed their power was once again growing . . . and much more." Elizar looked from Galen to Isabelle. "If he had shared this knowledge . . . But at least with your work, the information is no longer Kell's to control. Now that you know, all the mages must be told." Elizar leaned toward them. "But how did you discover that this traffic to the rim was connected to the Shadows?"

"We tracked the shipments to a Drakh," Galen said. "And with the Drakh we saw a Shadow, as static on our sensors. Then we picked up transmissions the Shadow was sending, and Isabelle discovered a way to decode them. I have no idea how she does it, but it's potentially a great weapon, the weapon we need to defeat the Shadows."

Elizar's hand curled inward, and his thumb began its restless course around his fingertips. "You can really understand what they say?"

"The method is far from perfect," Isabelle said.

"But it is a weapon." Elizar glanced toward the back of the restaurant, leaned in closer. "You must listen to me, quickly."

The message arrived as he spoke. Elizar must have composed it earlier. *I know much, much more than I have said, things that, if I were to tell you, would turn your understanding of the universe on its head. There is a reason Kell has kept his knowledge secret for so long. There is a reason you were sent on this task, rather than mages with more experience. You should never have been involved. Burell should never have been involved.*

Galen found his energy surging in response to Elizar's words. What was he implying? That Kell was in league with the Shadows? Elric had clearly indicated that Galen had been chosen for the task to test his control. Could there be more to it? Could Kell have had another reason? Could Kell have sent them hoping they would find nothing? Galen held tightly to the anxious energy, trying to calm himself.

I respect and trust you two more than any others. And I tell you that the Circle has led us astray. They have lied to us, again and again. They have so constricted our powers that we are now only a shadow of what we once were. If we are to restore the techno-mages to greatness, this coming war is the time to do it. But it cannot be done without risk. It cannot be done by supporting the Circle.

I want to share with you what I know. We three, working together, can explain to the rest what is really happening. We three can rally them to fight, no matter what the Circle says. We three can learn the secrets of power needed to break free, to start again with no masters to suppress us.

But I cannot tell what I know to mages who have sworn loyalty to Kell and the Circle. I have held my silence this long because I fear what might happen if I speak out alone. Kell is old, but he is still a formidable opponent. We may have only one chance to reveal the truth, and I need allies of whom I can be sure. I need you to swear loyalty to me, now, and to our common cause: truth, freedom, and glory.

The message ended.

Galen sat in shock. He could not believe the Circle—and

Elric—capable of such things. How could Elizar accuse the Circle and expect them to accept the charges without proof? Kell was their greatest leader since Wierden. He would not keep such secrets from them, would not have sent them into danger for nothing.

Yet at the same time, Galen realized that Elizar had been right before, in his warning about a threat. What if his accusations now were true? Galen's heart pounded.

"Where is your proof?" Isabelle hissed. "Where is the proof that the Circle sent us—and let Burell die—all for nothing? To secure evidence of something they already knew?" Isabelle had said before that the Circle's reason for sending them was irrelevant. They had agreed to go. Yet if sending them had been unnecessary, if they had agreed because they had been lied to, if Burell was dead for nothing—it would change everything.

"The proof is in Kell's own files, which I can show you. All you need do is swear allegiance to me. I dare not show you without that, for you could take the evidence to Kell and he could hide everything he has done."

This part of Elizar's argument didn't ring true. If Elizar had the evidence, why not just show it? Why not show it to all the mages? The more who knew, the harder it would be for Kell to deny it. Yet once Elizar released the information to all, then he, the source of it, would become unimportant. In keeping the information to himself, and perhaps a few others sworn to him, Elizar retained power. He could use the information as a base of power, gaining allies for a coming contest with Kell.

Yet all this supposed that Elizar spoke the truth, that he held evidence against Kell and the Circle. And if that was so, should they not support him?

"I have disagreed with some of the Circle's actions in the past," Isabelle said, "yet I cannot believe them guilty of what you claim. They are conservative, stubborn, and secretive. But to send us without need, hoping we would fail—I must see the evidence. Show me that. Show me that, and if it proves what you claim, I will swear allegiance to you to my dying breath."

Elizar wiped the back of his hand across his mouth. "The allegiance must come first. You know you can trust me. I gain nothing by lying. If I have no evidence, you will forswear me soon enough. You must trust me. Else you will never know the true cause behind Burell's death."

Below the table, Galen reached for her hand. It was clenched into a fist. *Don't do it,* Galen wrote to her. Whatever information Elizar had found, he must be misinterpreting it. The Circle could not be guilty of what he claimed.

"Kell has been the greatest of us for many years," Galen said. "He is of the line of Wierden. He has brought us peace and encouraged learning. Even if I could believe what you say of him, I can't believe it of the whole Circle. I know Elric"—*better than I knew my own father*—"and he would not willingly have sent Isabelle and me into needless danger. He would not lie. He lives by the Code. I know that more than I know anything."

Elizar extended a placating hand. "Perhaps I am wrong about Elric. Perhaps he knows as little as the rest of us."

"Then come back with us and present your evidence to him."

Elizar shook his head tightly. "You must join me. This is your only alternative. Without me, you will never know the truth."

Galen suddenly had the feeling that his friend had made a horrible mistake.

He knows something, Isabelle wrote. *And I will know what it is, if there is any way it can be known. But I will not swear allegiance to Elizar. I trust him less than I trust the Circle. I fear if you told him how to conjure your weapon, and I told him how to listen to the Shadows, he would have no further use for us.*

"I know you've uncovered something important," Galen said. "Show us what it is. Come with us before the Circle and confront them with it. I will support you. I will stand beside you and demand the truth. Give them the chance to answer your charges. You should not forswear them without giving them that chance; I know I cannot. They have made me everything I am. They have given me all I have. I have sworn to live up to their faith in me."

Elizar slammed his fist against the table. "No. It's not possible. I tell you that Burell is *dead* because of the Circle. They valued secrets more than they valued her. You must join me. It is the only way the mages can survive." Elizar's dark blue gaze fixed on him. "Galen, you and I share a dream. We want the same things. We want the mages to do good, not putter away their lives with petty magic tricks. You and Isabelle and I can stand together in the new Circle. I told you there would come a time when I would need your support. This is the time. And you need mine. I am your only salvation."

"I cannot do what you ask. Come with us back to the Circle. Together, we can uncover the truth. And with Isabelle's weapon, we can convince them to fight the Shadows."

Elizar turned to Isabelle. "It is your own mother who lies dead. Isabelle, surely you?"

She brought her hands together under Galen's. "No."

Elizar's mouth hung open at a crooked angle. He seemed at a loss. Then his mouth wrinkled shut, and his gaze flicked between them. His confidence, which seemed to underlie everything he did, had vanished. He whispered. "You don't understand. You can hear what they say. They can't let you share that power with—" Elizar bolted upright. "No! No! Not yet!"

Galen jerked to his feet, Isabelle with him. Something slipped over Galen's body, and a blast of plasma bloomed yellow across his chest, rippling through the shield Isabelle had conjured around both of them.

In the doorway to the tavern stood a dark shape, its head a distinctive outline, rising in the back into two craggy peaks, one above the other. Within its dark silhouette, a small spot flared repeatedly with brilliant yellow light as it fired at them. Across their chests, plasma blasts sank into the upper layer of the shield like a series of brilliant yellow stones thrown into a pond, radiating ripples over their bodies.

Frantic energy welled up in Galen, desperate to defend, to counter with deadly force. He grabbed his staff and with fierce focus forced his mind to be still, to be blank. He would not endanger Isabelle and everyone else in this settlement—everyone else everywhere—by unleashing some uncontrollable power. He would not violate the Code. He would not make the same mistake he had made before.

"You gave them every chance," a voice said from the back of the tavern. "They are fools." In the doorway to the kitchen stood Tilar, the chrysalis affixed to his head, a subtle blue glow around him, and a PPG in his hand. Behind him, Galen saw one, perhaps two more.

In the tube station, Tilar had known all about them, had known Galen's failure, Isabelle's dream, because Elizar had told him.

Tilar began to fire, and Elizar stumbled away, a shield shimmering around his own body. Plasma blasts now sprayed over Isabelle's shield from two directions. Her eyes had closed and her fingers were working rapidly.

The answer was escape, Galen realized. Too many to fight. Tilar edged farther into the room, and taking his place in the doorway was Razeel.

Galen took the staff in both hands. The shield made it feel slippery. Clenching it tightly, he visualized the equation, associated with it. He had to create an opening in the wall. He selected a high-intensity shock wave, brought the staff back over his shoulder, and slammed it into the wall.

The effect was instantaneous. The wall itself seemed to throw him back, blasting out a great wave of energy that tossed him up, spun him through the air. He slammed into the table, banged against the floor. As the wave spread outward, the room shook as if seized by an earthquake. Pictures jumped from the walls. Tables overturned. The bottles over the bar shattered, spraying their contents.

Galen tried to rise, but his body seemed unable to respond to his commands. He couldn't tell if the room was still shaking or if he was shaking, but gradually the shaking stopped.

He lifted his head. Isabelle was already standing, her fingers moving to maintain the shield. Behind her, the wall was intact. It had completely repelled the blast. As Galen struggled to his knees, he focused his sensors on it. Though there had been nothing unusual about the wall when they'd entered, there was now. It was reinforced with a containment spell, just as Elric reinforced the walls of the training hall to prevent wild energies from escaping. It now formed an impenetrable barrier.

Galen climbed unsteadily to his feet, looking quickly to the other walls, the floor, the ceiling. All were reinforced.

They were sealed inside.

— chapter 15 —

"The room is sealed," Galen said.

Isabelle's face was tight with concentration as she maintained the shield around both of them. She gave no reaction. Plasma blasts continued to splash over the faint blue covering.

The two doorways were the only ways out. The front was defended by the Drakh, the back by Tilar. His mind racing, Galen desperately focused, visualized the equation to conjure a mist. It rose from the floor around Isabelle's shield and spread outward. They would have to make an attempt on one of the exits, and this would help hide their escape. But it would take a few minutes to fill the tavern. In the meantime, he had to clear the way.

He visualized the equation to create a translucent sphere, packing it with as much energy as he could without threatening its coherence. The ball coruscated with blue brilliance. He formed an equation of motion, fired the ball at the Drakh.

The Drakh had no time to react. Perhaps he had not expected them to fight back. Perhaps he had simply been foolish to expose himself. Perhaps he wasn't a fighter. Galen didn't know.

The ball hit him in the chest and slammed him onto his back. As his dry voice screamed, the sphere of blue burned down into him. The light gained intensity until a brilliant incandescence shone up out of his chest. Then the Drakh's scream faded like a dying breeze. The sphere finished burning its way through his body, and the light slowly died.

The mist was beginning to obscure things now. Behind the Drakh's fallen body, Galen saw a dark figure peek through the doorway, fire off a shot before ducking again behind the door frame. He conjured another ball. Equation of motion. Fired it at the figure. It shot through the doorway, curved back to hit the spot where he believed the attacker hid. Galen couldn't tell if he'd hit his target or not.

Elizar took up a position in the doorway. Would he help them to escape? He made a quick motion to someone outside. The figure hidden behind the door frame stood; it was Brown. Elizar extended his shield to protect the man. Brown smiled and aimed his PPG at Galen, fired off a series of blasts in quick succession.

Galen turned toward the back door. It was obscured now in the haze, but he could make out Tilar and Razeel. Tilar was firing burst after burst at them. Razeel's lips were moving, vague forms of darkness taking shape in the mist around her.

Galen conjured another ball of energy. Another equation of motion. He hurled the ball at Tilar. It struck the center of Tilar's chest, and he stumbled back in alarm, waves of red and yellow spreading from the impact as the shield struggled to absorb the attack. After a few seconds, the shield returned to its normal blue. With a few more attacks, Galen thought he could penetrate it. Yet while he did that, how many more blasts would Isabelle's shield be forced to withstand?

He didn't know, but he could think of nothing better. He had to drive away Tilar. He visualized the blank screen in his mind's eye. With ferocious focus he imposed equation after equation on it. A ball of energy. Motion to hurl it at Tilar. Another ball. More motion. Ball. Motion. Elric's voice drove into him, stressing control, control.

A flashing red-and-yellow shape in the mist, Tilar pushed past Razeel, retreated into the kitchen.

Razeel was barely visible, a faint blue form. Galen conjured a ball, hurled it at her. Then another. The play of light over her shield vanished almost instantly after each impact. Galen found himself racing with energy, his control growing shaky.

I can't last much longer, Isabelle's message read. Her body was stiff, face flushed, teeth clenched. Her fingers moved rapidly.

Galen put an arm across her back. They should make a run at Razeel and Tilar. Tilar might now be too weak to fight, and Razeel hadn't yet mounted a serious attack. "Come on," he said, pulling at her. Then he stopped, looked back over his shoulder.

Something was buzzing.

Out of the mist came a swarm of spikes, thin, dark, sharp. Elizar was attacking them directly.

Although the mist should have made it difficult for him to aim the spikes accurately, they seemed to know exactly where to go, homing in on Galen and Isabelle's mage energy. They drove into Isabelle's shield in a hundred places, striking at heads, arms, chests. They began to drill their way through.

Isabelle had been able to hold off Elizar's attack in the training hall, but now she was tired. Galen tried to remember what they had said. Her weave was tight; that was how she had held out the spikes. She would need all her concentration to maintain the shield. He couldn't move her now, or the spikes would break through.

Clutching desperately to the tech's wild energy, Galen conjured ball after ball, hurling them against Elizar's shield. His shield had never been terribly strong, but now it showed no sign of weakening.

They needed a plan. They needed another way out.

They needed to break through the wall. Perhaps Elizar's reinforcement of the walls wasn't as strong as it should be. If the weave of his energies wasn't as tight as Isabelle's, perhaps something small could break through, could create a tiny breach that could then be expanded.

Galen grabbed his staff from where he had dropped it, aimed its end at the wall. The spikes drilled up and down his arms, over his body, searching for any weakness.

He conjured a narrow beam, similar to the one he'd used to cut through the Drakh's window, but even smaller in diameter and higher in intensity. The brilliant thread of light shot out at the wall, cut straight through it. He tried expanding the diameter of the beam. He was able to enlarge the hole a tiny bit; then the reinforcement stopped any further progress. He terminated the beam. The hole was perhaps an eighth of an inch across.

He sent a quick message to Isabelle. *I've made a tiny hole in the wall. If you can push your shield through it, you might be able to break open a larger hole.*

Her eyes flew wide and she turned to him. Her face was flushed and shiny with sweat, and the muscles in her neck stood out with tension. Spikes skated over the surface of her shield. She looked to the wall. The shimmering blue of her shield extended to the hole there, pouring itself through.

The buzzing of the spikes intensified. Then suddenly they broke off their attack, unsuccessful, and flew back into the mist. Galen aimed his staff toward the front door. If its fine beam could break through the reinforced wall, perhaps it could also break through Elizar's shield. There was so much energy and activity in the room, Galen's sensors were of little use, but he believed Elizar was still there.

He fired the beam.

Something slid over Galen, like a scarf slipping over his face. It was Isabelle's shield, he realized. It no longer protected him. A rumble grew in the wall behind him. The floor shook. As Galen looked over his shoulder, the wall exploded in a great hail. He jerked his head back around, raising an arm to protect himself. Something heavy slammed into him.

He found himself again on the floor, which now seemed to be tilting beneath him. His ears were ringing, and the air was heavy with dust. The fine beam still shot out of his staff. He stopped it, grabbed the staff, and dragged himself out from under the rubble.

Isabelle, he wrote.

She, too, was pulling herself free. In the dim light, he saw a trickle of blood running down beside her eye. He pushed the debris away from her, glanced toward the wall. The hole was about a foot above the floor, big enough to crawl through. *Go,* he wrote.

He pushed her toward the hole and crawled after, looking back over his shoulder.

The mist and the dust were clearing. Galen could see Elizar standing near the doorway, a shimmering skin of blue protecting him. His cheeks had grown taut, his mouth turned down. His eyes met Galen's, and for a moment Galen thought he saw in them regret.

Elizar bent forward, cupping his hands to his mouth. With a jerk of his body he cried out, releasing a harsh, sustained syllable. A single thin spike emerged from his hands, not short as the others had been, but stretching out and out, over two feet long before its end appeared. It buzzed with high, oscillating intensity. Elizar removed his hands from his mouth, straightened. He blew on the spike. It shot toward them.

Suddenly Galen remembered explaining to Elizar why his spikes had been held off by Isabelle's shield. *Your strategy would have worked well on most shields, but with Isabelle's, the best attack would be one with all the energy concentrated at a single point. If that energy is greater than the energy of the shield, it will have to fail.*

Galen spun on his knees to face Elizar, conjured a ball of energy, hurled it at the spike. The spike passed through it, unaffected.

The spell of destruction. It could stop the spike. He forced his mind's eye blank. The spell was too dangerous. And he had sworn himself to the Circle, sworn not to use it. He would not let them down again.

Galen threw himself at Isabelle, pushing her flat beneath him. His hands slipped off her. She'd been able to restore a shield around herself, he realized. Her strength was not completely gone. The spike would drive into him, but she could escape before Elizar conjured another.

He pressed his arms against the floor on each side of her, blocking off any opening the spike might find. But something was wrong. His hands were slippery against the floor.

His hands had slipped from Isabelle. The shield did not encompass both of them; it was between them.

As he realized what she had done, the spike struck him. It

skipped over the surface of the shield as it spun, sensing unprotected mage energy. Galen squeezed his body tight around her.

No, he thought. *How could she do this? It couldn't happen. It couldn't happen.*

The spike danced up to his shoulder, then down, burrowing between his arm and his body, sensing Isabelle below, Isabelle who had shielded him at the expense of herself. Galen crushed her to him, knowing there was no way to stop it.

With a tickle against his arm the spike slipped into her. Her body convulsed, and she released a ragged cry. He cried with her. As she spasmed against him, her breath accelerated into harsh, quick pants. Then the slipperiness of his body vanished, and there was nothing separating them, nothing except that she had been wounded, and he had not.

Galen's body was on fire now—with rage, and grief, the need to kill them all, to destroy everything. He felt the equation forming in his mind. It took everything he had to force it away.

Isabelle was still alive. Isabelle could still be saved. He must take her away.

He became fire. On the blank screen in his mind's eye he conjured equation after equation in symbols of flame. Fireball. Motion. Fireball. Motion. Fireball. Motion. He fired out one after another. The direction was unimportant, as long as they stayed clear of Isabelle.

He wanted to be surrounded by flame. Burn the place down, create chaos so they could not be pursued. The alcohol behind the bar exploded in a wall of fire. The tables, the curtains, all began to burn. The tavern filled with flame.

As the fiery equations blazed one after the next, he conjured a platform beneath Isabelle, slid her out through the hole. To follow her, he had to stop the flow of fire, but he found his body inflamed with it, racing.

He forced the pace of the equations, little by little, to slow, creating the fireballs, hurling them, creating them, hurling them, with longer and longer intervals between. He focused on Isabelle. She needed help. He could not help her with fire. He must go with her, now.

At last he stopped the fiery equations. His control had turned shaky, uncertain. He grabbed his staff and crawled out after her on quivering limbs.

On the other side of the wall he found a dark, empty room. In the dim glow of the fire, Isabelle was panting, her body curled up on the platform. Galen didn't allow his gaze to linger on her. They had to move quickly, before they were trapped again. Elizar was probably waiting in the passage outside. Galen extended the platform and stood over her on it.

His message to Elric was brief. *Isabelle is wounded. Elizar and Razeel have betrayed us.*

Then he brought his staff down against the stone floor, and the building shook. The great slabs of stone cracked, split. Fractures radiated outward, spread across the room, widened into fissures. The floor buckled, and huge chunks rained onto the level below.

The only chance for escape was to get back to the freighter. He could force them to take off immediately, to call for medical help. Isabelle had to have help. Elizar could destroy the freighter easily with his ship, but Galen hoped he would not attack so openly. Elizar's new partners, he thought, would not like that. The Shadows preferred to work more quietly.

Galen guided the platform down through the largest of the fissures and found himself in a vast storage area. The area directly below him was unoccupied. Farther away, workers in coveralls drove lifts filled with crates. The workers were looking up, afraid that the spaceport was collapsing.

Galen skimmed past them, following the trail of lifts and workers backward, toward the promenade that lay below the one where they had disembarked. That was where the freighter was being unloaded.

He came out of the storage area onto the promenade. The captain was standing beside the large cargo air lock as a lift drove out filled with supplies. Galen scanned the promenade for any sign of Elizar or the others. Nothing. He formed an equation of motion, raced toward the captain.

As the lift moved out of the air lock, a tongue of fire licked out after it. Galen thought he must have seen incorrectly. Then a huge concussion rumbled out from the ship across the promenade. Galen's ears popped, and across the floor one ring of stone tiles after another jumped up in a rapidly expanding wave. The air was sucked out of him, and for a strange moment the walls seemed to undulate.

The air lock belched a stream of fire. It shot out across the promenade, instantly incinerating the lift. Galen wheeled the platform to the left, crouched to cover Isabelle's body with his own. How could it be? Would they kill all these people, just to make sure he and Isabelle did not escape? Just to make sure she died?

As he sped away from the ship, a second concussion spewed huge pieces of metal and fiberboard out across the promenade. The platform surged ahead on the shock wave, and shrapnel peppered Galen's back. A flap of metal slammed into a worker ahead of them and swept him into Galen's path. Equation of motion. Equation of motion. Galen jigged around the worker. Something stung him in the cheek.

He crouched lower over Isabelle and flew away from the promenade. Her back fluttered with rapid breaths. Galen's body surged with frantic, desperate energy.

He was losing his ability to focus. He could feel it slipping away. He could find no help. He could find no escape.

He would hide them, hide them where Elizar could not find them.

Galen sent more organelles into Isabelle's body, feeling them tingle through his fingertips.

"It's no use," Isabelle said. "This is not a wound you can heal. It is a weapon inside me."

Galen ignored her. He was shaky, his body fighting shock, his mind exhausted from the constant, single-minded focus required to control the tech. But he could not give up. He could not lose her.

He picked up his staff from the cold stone floor where he knelt and held it over her. He had no crystal to aid in directing the organelles. He was trying to make his staff serve the same purpose. He remembered again Ing-Radi's words: *You must understand the damage. You must find the shape of what needs to be done. And you must become that shape.*

He understood the damage. In fact, when he had first seen it through his sensors, it had done more to make him still, and clear, than any mind-focusing exercise. The spike had penetrated her side and worked its way inward, puncturing the small intestine as it entered, puncturing it again as it left. It had found its way to the spine, its head slipping between a vertebra and a disk into the spinal cord itself, where it had begun to work its way upward, severing nerve roots and artery branches along the way.

The perforations of the small intestine had caused a rapid onset of peritonitis. Isabelle's temperature had shot up, and despite her attempt to manage the pain, Galen knew it had been terrible. Once the spike had reached the spinal cord, she had gained some relief from the pain, as she lost all movement and feeling below the spike. Now, with the spike, the paralysis was ascending. She had lost all sensation in her body from the chest down.

From his sensors, it looked as if the entry wound had already healed. The cut that had run down the right side of her forehead into her eyebrow was healing as well. But the spike was causing damage much faster than the organelles could heal it. And more important than that, the spike continued to work its way upward, the organelles seemingly powerless to stop it.

The spike had reached the sixth cervical vertebra, C6, just above the shoulders. When it reached C5, she would lose control of her hands. Worse, the spike would begin to cut off the phrenic nerves, which stimulated the movement of the diaphragm. The diaphragm's regular contraction and relaxation caused the lungs to fill and empty. When the spike reached C3, the phrenic nerves would be completely severed. The movement of the diaphragm would stop; the lungs would fail.

If he had access to medical equipment, he could keep the lungs operating, could keep Isabelle alive. Yet even then, the ultimate goal of the spike seemed clear. Once it passed C1, it would enter the brain. And there would be no saving her from that.

The spike was a much more sophisticated weapon than he had ever imagined. He would have thought it far beyond Elizar's capability. Yet Elizar's skills had rapidly improved. He had found secrets of power.

You must find the shape of what needs to be done. And you must become that shape.

As he held the staff over her, Galen visualized the spike winding up her spinal cord. He imagined the organelles forming a wall against it, stopping its forward progress. He imagined the organelles turning the spike out from her spinal cord, driving it out of her body.

But the spike slid slowly, steadily upward.

"Talk to me, Galen. Please."

Galen put aside the staff, visualized the equation, dissociated. He could not look at her. She lay on a narrow bunk, in one of the rooms meant to house miners. A few worthless possessions had been left behind: some blankets rotten with moisture, a sheer white curtain of insect netting, two rickety tables, a few candles.

He had lit the candles rather than conjure magical light; he wanted to focus all of his powers on Isabelle. For all the good they did. He was no healer.

They were far, far below ground here, over two miles. Elizar could not find them here; at least, Galen had stopped sensing Elizar and Razeel on the surface after he had descended a half mile. That meant, too, that the nearest relay of mage signals could not detect him here either, so he could neither send nor receive messages. Only someone who ran a focused scan on each cubic foot of the interior, one at a time, would be able to find him. They were well hidden. Yet what was the point of it all? Had he brought her here just to watch her die?

He received a message from her. Attached were her files: her work, her spells. He didn't want them. He wanted her.

"Thank you for killing the Drakh for me," she said. "I was—occupied."

He should not have trusted Elizar. He should have discovered the way to escape sooner. And she should not have protected him with her shield.

"You are angry with me."

He had to look up at her then. Isabelle's hands were clamped together, her neck muscles taut. The illusion of hair remained even now, she was so focused on maintaining control, on not giving in to the pain.

"No. Not at you. Never at you."

"You are angry with the universe, then. With God."

If God showed his face, Galen would gladly burn it to cinders. "Will you say that this, too, is part of his plan?"

Her grey eyes fixed on him, intent. "Yes."

Galen looked out toward the dark hallway, restless energy pushing through him. This was not part of *his* plan. He had planned that they would die many years hence, and when they did pass, it would be together, not one leaving the other behind.

"Do you know what I most wanted to conjure since I was a child?" she said. Her neck was straining to see him where he knelt.

He sat on the bunk beside her and shook his head.

"A shield. I have been fascinated since I can remember, with creating a barrier that could protect me from anything, that could keep me safe, beyond touching." Her voice was brittle, and she paused irregularly with the effort of holding back the pain. Her eyebrows were raised, adding the emphasis to her words that her body could not. And still she strained to lift her head, as if she must be as close as possible to him to convey the importance of her words. He couldn't imagine what could possibly be important in the face of the one all-encompassing fact: she was dying.

"When I received my chrysalis, the first thing I conjured was a shield to cover my body. I felt safe in its cocoon. Whenever I wore my chrysalis, I always wore a shield. I suppose I was frightened of Burell's illness, and the shield brought me security. Yet it was more than that, a basic mind-set that said 'Protect yourself first, above all. Keep yourself safely away from others.' Eventually I realized that was not the way I wanted to live my life. That was not who I wanted to be. I had to transcend myself.

"And so I began to step out of my cocoon. When you sat beside me in the hall, you, whom I had long watched and admired, I knew that we should be together. I quickly came to love you—more than I knew I could."

And I love you, he thought, but could not say the words. How had she invaded his hiding place? How had she made him feel these feelings?

"When I had the ability to protect only one of us, I knew it must be you. My first thought was no longer for myself. I could not have lived, knowing that I did not protect you."

And how am I *to live?* he thought. He bit out the words. "Does transcending oneself mean that one has to die, then?"

She gave a weak smile. "I was merely—unlucky." Her neck muscles tightened with pain, and she closed her eyes and let her head fall back. Galen's gaze was drawn to her clenched hands. Against his will, her fingers one by one released their tight grip, grew slack. She had lost control over them. Her inhalations became shallower, more labored. The spike had reached C5.

At last the pain seemed to fade and her neck relaxed, her lips parted. He wanted her eyes to open.

"You said I had to transcend myself in three ways," he said.

She gazed upon him. "Yes. You have opened yourself to another. That was the first. Next you will open yourself to yourself. Finally, you will open yourself to God. To his design."

Galen shook his head. The only design or pattern he could see was one of his own failure. He had wanted to become a healer. Instead, he had discovered a weapon, a weapon that had not even helped him to save Isabelle. If this was God's design, he wanted no part of it. "I don't think that I can," he said.

"I was right about Cadmus. And I am right about you. I know that you can, Galen. That is why I was put in your life."

Galen heard something from the hall, a faint whisper of sound. He used his sensors to increase his sensitivity. Hard, measured footsteps echoed through the passageway. Isabelle didn't hear them yet.

He stood. "I'm going to the mine shaft. See if I can reach Elric from there." He saw the dismay on her face. "I'll be gone only a few minutes. Rest, and I'll return quickly."

Before she could respond, he drew the sheer white insect netting across the bunk. He unwrapped her scarf from about his neck, let it fall to the floor. He stepped out into the hall, closed the door behind him.

The hall wasn't completely dark, as it had been before. A light shone from a corridor that branched off farther down. A figure reached the end of that corridor and stepped into the dark hall. Lights flashed on up and down the hall. Galen remembered the vision Kell had sent him, in which he'd searched through a grey maze for himself, for the part of himself from which he hid.

It was a Human, a man, of compact build and dark hair. He was the man Galen had seen in the tents of the convocation. *His name is Morden,* Elric had said. *I believe he is a servant of the Shadows. If you ever see him, you must inform me at once. Do not approach him.*

Morden walked toward him, and Galen mirrored the action. Perhaps he and Isabelle would die together. Energy gathered within him, eager to be used.

They met under the harsh lights of the bland metal-grey corridor, two miles beneath the surface.

Morden folded his hands in front of him. "She can still be saved." His smooth voice echoed down the passage.

Galen had expected an attack, not an offer. He found he could not respond. It was what he wanted, more than anything else, wanted with an intensity that made everything else irrelevant. And perhaps they could do it; Elric had said their powers were great. He imagined Isabelle restored to health, walking with him hand in hand, giving him that private, knowing smile.

It was another offer for his allegiance, as Tilar had made.

Turning down Tilar's offer had been easy, since Tilar had offered only knowledge, which Galen believed he could acquire himself. But this . . . was not something he could do himself.

Morden stood with a mild smile of curiosity on his face. "Isn't that what you want?"

The Shadows had done this to her. And now they offered to undo it. His energy grew hot with rage. "You offer to heal her, after you have Elizar . . ."

"Elizar said you would swear loyalty to him. That's what we wanted. But he is a fool."

"And what do you ask in return?" Galen couldn't believe the words had come from his mouth. He was negotiating with the Shadows, the same who had killed Burell.

"Just that at some point in the future, we may come to you and ask you for a favor of equal magnitude."

And what would that favor be? Fighting for the Shadows? Killing another mage? Overthrowing the Circle? They could ask him to destroy the universe, and it would still be of lesser magnitude than what they offered him.

And what did he owe the Circle? If they had knowingly sent Isabelle and him to fail and die, he would kill them anyway, one at a time, down even to Elric. The rage raced through him, urging him to act. He held tightly to it, refusing to let it free.

Morden's face grew serious, shadows pooling beneath his eyes. "Choose carefully, Galen. Many would give all they have for such an opportunity."

Galen had been able to turn down Tilar easily. It was Isabelle who had been tormented with the hope of saving Burell. Now he was in the same position she had been.

But she had known what to choose, and with that realization, now so did he. She had chosen death for Burell, and he must choose death for her. She would never forgive him if he chose otherwise. Besides, if she were here, he knew what she would say. If he accepted Morden's offer, it would ruin the entire plan of the universe.

But perhaps the plan could include his death as well.

"I decline the offer."

Morden regarded him with a slight frown, and Galen waited for the attack to come. He would not defend himself. He would not fight.

"I wonder," Morden said, "whether you'll be able to live with that decision." He turned and began to walk back down the hall with those same hard, measured footsteps.

Galen called after him. "Why don't you kill me?" The rage, the heat, began to spread out from him, no longer able to be contained. How could he be left here, left with nothing?

He conjured a fireball, hurled it at the wall to Morden's left. It exploded in flame.

Morden flinched and kept walking.

"Why don't you kill me?" he yelled. He conjured another. It burst into flames to Morden's right.

Morden continued.

"Why don't you kill me?" Fire blazed across the ceiling above Morden's head.

Morden stopped, turned, his body silhouetted in flame. Though he spoke in a normal tone, the words carried down the empty passage to Galen.

"Because you are already one of us."

With that, he turned and continued down the passage, eventually turning at the branch in the corridor, disappearing. The lights up and down the hall went out, leaving Galen with darkness and flames.

The heat left him. He panted, suddenly feeling he had made a horrible error in attacking Morden.

What had Morden meant?

As the flames slowly died, he turned back toward Isabelle. Candlelight flickered beneath the door to her room, the room in which she lay dying, and he was struck with the reality of what he had done. He slapped his hands to his mouth to muffle a cry. How could he live with his decision? How could he live, knowing that he could have saved her, and had not?

He had to go back to her. He had to do something. He had to save her. Things could not end like this. He clenched his jaw, desperately calming himself. He must go in.

He willed himself into movement. He opened the door, went to the bed, drew back the netting.

Her eyes flew open. "Were you able to get through?" The last two words were a breathy exhalation. Her chest heaved with the effort of drawing air. Reluctantly, he used his sensors on her. Even in the short time he had been gone, the spike had reached C4.

He sat at her side. "We can't call out. We're stuck on this miserable rock until the others come looking for us." He drew the netting across the bed, cocooning them both inside. Perhaps it would keep out the burned smell from the hallway.

The urge to do something was overwhelming. "I'm going to walk to the next settlement. With any luck they won't have heard about the trouble here yet." The mines had grown extensive before they'd been closed down. In studying this place, he had learned that some tunnels led as far as the next dome. Perhaps there he could find help.

She argued with him, of course. She would die soon; they both knew that. The next settlement would take him hours to reach.

He clung desperately to his control, not wanting to break in front of her. He had refused her only chance. Yet he continued to protest, as if there were still some way to save her.

"I'm dying," she said. "The wound is too deep. It's my time."

"Stop saying that. I refuse to accept a universe that would choose to take you away from me now that we have found each other."

She raised her head again, her eyes straining upward for him. "How improbable was it that we should meet, and fall in love, and spend even this short time together, Galen? There is a design. And we are as much a part of it as my love for you."

He was part of no design. There was only randomness and chaos and despair.

Her voice rose in intensity. "No one here can undo what has been done. Don't leave me to die alone."

Why did he fight her, when he knew she spoke the truth? "I

won't," Galen said. "I won't." He knelt, cradling her head in his arm, hoping that she would be reassured and lie back.

"I'm cold. Hold my hand."

He pulled her limp hands apart, inserted his between, closed her slender fingers in his.

Her neck remained tense, holding her head up ever so slightly. She raised her eyebrows. "Listen to me, Galen, my dearest love. You have made me happy, and proud, and I regret nothing. My only regret would be . . . if the fire that I see in your eyes now were to burn your soul to ash in the future. Your soul is too beautiful for that." She ran out of breath, gasped. "You must learn, one day, to forgive God for His decisions." Again, her words ran out of air. She closed her eyes, and her words were soft, breathy. "I'm sure it will greatly relieve Him."

Her breaths were shallow, rapid. Within her, the spike reached C3, where the last phrenic nerves branched from the spinal cord to the diaphragm. He willed her eyes to open, and they did. All her energy was focused in that fierce gaze, on her struggle to stay with him.

"If there is a purpose, if there is a design, if there is a way, after I am gone, I will call to you—say your name—send you a message—and you will know I was right." Again her eyes closed. "As usual." Her lips pressed together in the slightest of smiles. Then she looked up at him, and he realized her gasping had stopped.

He could see her failing, the intensity in her grey eyes fading. The words were a whisper of breath. "Kiss me good night."

He leaned down and kissed her soft, precious lips. Her final breath seeped into him, and he tried to tell himself that it was her soul entering him, that she would always be with him. But when he pulled away, her head drifted to the side, her eyes blank, her face slack, and he knew that she was gone. The spike had reached her brain.

Her heart beat a short time more, then slowed, stumbled, stopped. The hair faded from her head. All that she was, all that she would ever be, was gone. There would be no message.

He cried out.

Galen closed his eyes against the light. The candles had burned out long ago, and he had grown accustomed to the darkness. He had sat there, beside her, for hours, for days, for years, forever—it made no difference. There was nowhere to go. There was nothing to be done.

Yet the light. And the breeze. He flicked his eyes open and closed. He sat on a bench, outside. His left hand was extended. Isabelle's hand was not in it.

He squinted his eyes open. The air smelled of the sea, and home. Beneath his feet was the mak, around him ranged Elric's circle of stones. Elric stood a few feet away, watching him.

Galen did not want to be pulled away. Galen did not want to see, do, or say anything ever again. He wanted to be dead, dead with Isabelle in that vast tomb of rock. He folded his hands in his lap, prepared to wait.

"Isabelle is dead," Elric deduced.

Galen said nothing.

Elric's lips compressed into a thin straight line, and he was silent for a time. At last he spoke. "Her loss is a great tragedy. These are dark times. I am sorry, Galen, for all you have endured. I would have spared you. If I could."

Galen lowered his head. He didn't want to hear. It comforted him more to be angry at Elric than to know the truth.

Elric took a step closer. "Carvin is on Brensil 4. She has come to bring you and Isabelle home. But she cannot find you. I have searched for you since receiving your last message—almost three days now. You hid yourself well. It is time, now, to come out. Elizar and Razeel have gone."

Elric took another step forward, crouched down before Galen. "It is time to send Isabelle to the other side."

Galen met his gaze.

"And I have much to tell you."

Galen waited.

"And you have much to tell us. We must know what happened with Elizar and Razeel and the Shadows. Only you can tell us. Only then can we decide what is to be done."

Galen understood Elric's words, in a distant, intellectual sense. Elizar and Razeel's treachery must be exposed. The hand of the Shadows must be revealed. Wasn't that what he had sworn to do? Yet he could not find the will within himself to move. His eyes drifted to the hands folded in his lap. They were limp, as hers had been.

"I need you back."

The voice did not even sound like Elric's. It was soft, weak. Galen looked at him. Elric's lips hung open, uncertain, and the lines of disapproval between his eyebrows had vanished, leaving a horrible vulnerability. Suddenly Galen found the will to move. He had to erase that expression from Elric's face. That, above all.

He stood.

"Thank you," Elric said, and his voice, and the stone circle, faded into silent blackness.

Isabelle's hand was back in his.

Galen stroked the cold, stiff fingers. It was not Isabelle. She was gone. She had left him.

Galen conjured a dim globe of light within the cocoon of insect netting. Her face was slack, waxy. He released the hand, pushed the arm down against her body. He yanked back the insect netting, stood on unfamiliar legs.

He took a deep breath, released it. He picked up his staff, the scarf made by Isabelle. They hung uselessly in his hands. Then the platform was conjured beneath Isabelle and he was moving forward, the globe of light brightening, taking the lead. Isabelle followed like a shadow.

And so he found himself emerging from the mine.

Carvin rushed up to him. "Galen, it's so good—" Her hands fell away from him as she saw Isabelle. "Oh. They told me, but I couldn't . . ." She burst out sobbing.

Galen assumed her ship was at the spaceport. He headed in that direction, Isabelle following.

— chapter 16 —

Anna rippled out of hyperspace into the blackness of Quadrant 37. She loved the feeling of the transition, leaping out of roiling red chaos and pushing through the shimmering membrane into vast black stillness. She surveyed her surroundings quickly, hungry for challenge.

The Eye had told her there would be Narns here, Narns to be destroyed. She had waited long for this day, training, providing stealthy transport, gathering reconnaissance. She had listened eagerly as the Eye had told her the thrill of battle, the exhilarating chaos of conflict, the ecstasy of victory.

She found three heavy cruisers and ten fighters in unimaginative formation around the outpost on the grey-blue planet below. A petal-shaped sensor array moved in geosynchronous orbit. It was irrelevant. Farther from the planet, a probe lurked in the darkness, watching.

Puttering through a defensive patrol, one of the fighters crossed right into her path. Excitement gathered in her throat. The slow, clumsy ship barely registered her presence before she attacked. She shrieked out her war cry, the energy blasting from her mouth. The beam impaled the ship, killing it.

Her sister shimmered into space beside her. She spun, crying out victory at her first kill. Together they fell upon the Narn ships, their mouths screaming destruction, their bodies cutting through the invigorating vacuum, swirling in a dizzying dance of death.

Soon the Narn ships and the probe were in pieces, and Anna and her sister rejoiced in their power. The Eye showed Anna what she must do next: the outpost below, covered in flames, every building destroyed. Anna cried out to her sister and wheeled closer to the planet, and to the outpost on the grey continent below.

She held her body in perfect control. Neurons fired in harmony. Cleansing and circulation were synchronized in sublime synergy. The complex, multileveled systems beat out a flawless march. The skin of the machine was her skin; its bones and blood, her bones and blood. She and the machine were one. She felt tireless, invulnerable.

The outpost was far below, yet she could sense its buildings, its generators, its Narns—more than ten thousand of them. She calculated the most efficient targets within the widespread outpost for maximum destruction, coordinated her speed, course. There must be no survivors.

A weak energy beam shot past her from behind. One short-range fighter had survived. It was unworthy of her attention. She and her sister spread over the outpost like a shadow, shrieking in exultation as they delivered great balls of destruction. Their shrieks sang an oratorio of evolution through bloodshed. The balls plummeted through the atmosphere, and far below, structures exploded in great waves of annihilation.

One of the fighter's beams passed across her underside, its touch a brief, startling caress. Anna's war shriek stilled. Her body, which she had almost forgotten, lay at the heart of the machine, cold, longing for touch. She wanted to turn back, to feel the beam's caress again.

The march of the machine's beat stumbled, and the machine seized her. It was so beautiful, so elegant. Perfect grace, perfect control, form and function integrated into the circuitry of the unbroken loop, the closed universe. All systems of the machine passed through her; she was its heart; she was its brain; she was the machine. She kept the neurons firing in harmony. She synchronized the cleansing and circulation in sublime synergy. She beat out a flawless march with the complex, multileveled systems. The skin of the machine was her skin; its bones and blood, her bones and blood. She and the machine were one: a great engine of chaos and destruction.

She spun to face the fighter, gathering energy in her throat.

Her shriek sliced it in two. More energy boiled up into her mouth, and she carved through the sensor array, slicing it into pieces. At last she felt satisfied.

She and her sister crisscrossed the outpost. The destruction was pure, absolute. Not a single structure stood, not a single Narn lived. They danced among the nighttime clouds, and Anna reveled in the ecstasy of victory. The battle was a complete triumph, and it was but the first of many.

For now the war had begun.

On the cliff's edge, against the fading light of the sunset, Isabelle burned. The blue, magical flames roiled with fierce intensity, roaring like a living beast, consuming all.

He could see her no longer, though he knew she was there. She lay on a simple flat rock, in a robe of Carvin's with sleeves too short. Her hands lay together, fingers intertwined. Her scalp was bare. Some wisps of hair had grown during the journey back, and Galen had scoured them from her with a gentle caress, knowing she would want it that way. She had lived for the Code, and she had died for it.

Around her the mages stood like phantoms in the thin mist, their faces lit irregularly by the flames. The roar drowned out any sound, but Galen could see that a few, like Carvin, shook with tears. Most of them looked more afraid than anything else.

Elric stood beside Galen, as he had at the deaths of Galen's parents. Though they did not touch, Galen felt Elric's presence like a wall of strength and necessity beside him. With Elric beside him, Galen would stand tall; Galen would continue.

There were no naked slave men, no shower of red poppies from the sky. But those were Burell's wishes, and Burell had received no funeral. Burell's body had been taken by Elizar.

Galen tried to lose himself in the hypnotizing movement of the flames, to think of nothing, to be nothing. When his parents had died, there had been two fires, side by side. Galen had always thought there should have been one, that they should have been burned together, their bodies joining at last as they crumbled to ash.

The flames billowed high, filled with new energy as they reached the tech in Isabelle's body. The brilliant fire curled downward, swirled in tight eddies around where her body must lay.

He could walk into those flames, climb onto the rock and lay beside her. They could be joined in fire. Yet he knew that what lay on that rock was not Isabelle. There was no way to join with her now. She was gone.

He found that the flames had died, and most of the mages had gone. He had at last been successful in losing himself, for a time. The blackness was lit only by scattered globes shrouded in mist. Elric stood beside him, as he had all night.

Elric turned to him. "We must go to the Circle now. You must tell them what happened. Do you need to prepare?"

Galen vaguely remembered Elric asking him that question this afternoon, as he and Carvin had readied Isabelle's body. Yet his only thought had been to stay with Isabelle, to spend every moment with her until he brought her to rest on the stone. Then, at last, he had separated from her, going with Elric instead.

Gradually Galen realized the point of Elric's question. He looked down at himself. He wore the same "Mr. Wilcox" clothes he and Isabelle had joked about a million years ago. Her tan scarf was wrapped around his neck, specks of gray dirt now trapped within the weave. The brown turtleneck was streaked with gray as well, where he had brushed against the rock. His body was unwashed, his head and face unscoured. He should not want to appear before the Circle this way. Yet he had no energy to do otherwise.

With the thought that they might find his appearance disrespectful, a small ember of his anger reawakened. If they had sent him and Isabelle on this task, they should see the results of it. "Let them see me as I am," he said, and headed toward the tents. Elric followed.

He passed a few mages—Alwyn, Fed, Gowen. They looked at him with expressions he did not want to read.

In the shadow of the tent entrance, Fa crouched in her

orange jumper, her fists jammed up beneath her chin. Her eyes sought him out, and she gave him a meek wave.

Galen passed her in silence.

Within the tents, he stood unmoving outside the chamber where the Circle met, waiting until they called for him. His mind was as blank as the white tent that surrounded him.

At last he was summoned, and he entered the great stone amphitheater to face those mages he had considered the best of them: Herazade, Blaylock, Kell, Ing-Radi, Elric. Yet his awe was tempered now by a shadow of doubt. Elizar had made many accusations against Kell and the Circle. Galen knew in his heart that they must be false, yet something within him clung stubbornly to those accusations. All techno-mages knew the best deceptions were those intertwined with truth. Would Elizar have created the entire story from falsehoods?

Kell gazed down on him from above, his intense, dark eyes studying Galen. Galen remembered Kell's wisdom in the challenge imposed on him, remembered Kell's generosity in allowing him to become a mage, even after his transgression. During his leadership, Kell had turned the mages from a group who spoke the words of the Code into a group who actually believed and followed them. Galen could not believe Kell would hide his knowledge of the Shadows while he sent Galen and Isabelle to search for them. Galen could not believe that he would lead the mages astray.

Kell used his carved ivory staff to push himself to his feet. He seemed fatigued, yet still he carried his large frame with the bearing of a great leader. The short white fur cape over his robe added to his stature.

"We are sorry, Galen," Kell said, "for the trials you have suffered in the performance of our task. We did not know the full danger of the situation, else we would not have sent you into it." He paused, running an index finger over his goatee, and Galen got the strange impression that Kell was afraid.

Then Kell continued, and the moment passed. "Tell us all that has happened since the death of Burell." He extended two fingers toward Galen in a precise gesture, then sat, hunched forward, his attention fixed.

Galen did not want to be there, did not want to think of it, did not want to speak of it. Yet he found himself recounting the events in an even, unemotional voice. Inside, quietly, the restless energy stirred, his anger and grief growing as he recited the actions that had led to Isabelle's death. Did Kell not carry some responsibility for the actions of his students?

The Circle listened without reaction until Galen began to repeat Elizar's accusations toward Kell.

"Elizar said that Kell had known the Shadows were returning for over a year. Elizar said there was a reason Kell kept his knowledge secret."

Kell's face remained impassive. Yet the other mages looked now from Galen to Kell.

Galen found the intensity of his voice growing. "Elizar said there was a reason the Circle had sent Isabelle and me on this task, rather than mages with more experience. He said we should never have been involved."

Elric turned toward him, gave a sharp, encouraging nod.

"Elizar said that we must forswear the Circle and swear loyalty to him, before he would show us the evidence he had obtained from Kell's place of power."

Blaylock grunted.

"When we refused, Elizar told us we could not be allowed to live, not with Isabelle able to decode the Shadow signals. We were attacked by the three from Zafran 8—Tilar, the Drakh, and Brown. Elizar told them no, not yet, but they attacked anyway."

Kell's shoulders straightened, as if he were relieved to hear of Elizar's action. Galen would end that soon enough.

"At first Elizar and Razeel did not attack. Yet they had reinforced the walls of the tavern with their power, so we could not escape. After I killed the Drakh and drove off Tilar, Elizar and Razeel took over the fight. Isabelle's shield had been so bombarded that she could not protect us both. She chose—to protect me." Galen remembered Elizar cupping his hands in front of his mouth, jerking as he released the long, deadly syllable. Anger flashed through Galen. He bit out the words. "It was Elizar's spike"—in his mind he hurled the word at Kell—"that killed Isabelle."

Kell's eyes flared wide, and they were filled with flames. He swept to his feet, bringing his staff to bear on Galen. "That is a damnable lie! Elizar is innocent. He could not—"

Energy surged through Galen at the threat of an attack. Yet as he held to it, watching avidly for a strike, Kell faltered. Kell's gestures, his words, his expressions were always perfectly formulated. But now he was at a loss.

Kell spread his arms to appeal to the Circle. "This is impossible. Elizar would not—" He whipped his fiery gaze back to Galen, as if his eyes could burn the lies out. Galen glared back, willing the truth to brand itself onto Kell's soul.

Slowly, Kell's arms lowered, forgotten, to his sides. The flames faded from his eyes. And then something in his dark, lined face shifted, some underlying structure that could no longer support itself. Galen thought of the image Elizar had conjured long ago, of Elric's circle of standing stones, crumbling. Kell's face had crumbled.

Kell shook his head. "You must be mistaken. That cannot be so. Elizar would never—could never—" The staff slipped from his hand, dropped silently away.

He collapsed to his knees with a great, anguished howl. "No! No. Have I been such a fool?" Kell looked up at the Circle, his mouth open in despair. His platform with the great stone chair sank to the ground, dissolved.

Galen stood unmoving as the others swooped down around Kell. Anger raced through him now, threatening to overwhelm him. He must turn his back on it, he must not feel it, for it carried too much pain. He would lose all control. He must not speak, he must not move. He must hold himself in stillness. He must feel nothing. He must be nothing.

Kell was on his knees, his fists curled on his legs. Although the rest of the Circle clustered around him, he looked broken and alone.

"You have been trying to protect us from the Shadows," Elric said. "Tell us what went wrong."

Kell looked up at Galen, held out a hand. "I am so sorry, boy. I have misjudged. I have misjudged. I am a foolish old man."

Galen did not move.

"Tell us all," Blaylock demanded.

Ing-Radi handed Kell his staff, and Kell braced it on the floor, climbed to his feet. The weight of his body seemed a horrible burden. His gaze swept over them all, pained yet still powerful. As he spoke, no gestures enhanced his words. One hand held to the staff; the other hung at his side. Although his voice retained its resonance, the certainty had gone out of it.

"It began exactly as Elizar said. It was nearly two years ago that I found the first indication of the Shadows' return. With that, I launched a search and found more. I knew what this would mean for us, and what it would mean for everyone. We have all read the ancient texts. I realized that we had no chance of fighting the Shadows unless we knew their secrets, their powers, their defenses."

Elizar had said he knew things that would turn Galen's understanding of the universe on its head. He had told the truth. Their task had been needless. Burell had died, and Isabelle had died, in the attempt to know what was already known.

Galen wanted to curse Kell, to burn him with eyes of fire, to break him. Yet Kell was already broken. Elizar's betrayal had broken him. And Galen had to remain still, or the pain would find him.

Kell continued. "The only way to discover their secrets was to have one of our number pretend to ally with the Shadows. The time to act was immediately, while the Shadows still believed their presence secret. But this deception could not be designed with planning and consultation. I feared that if our agent was discovered, our hand would be revealed, and the Shadows would turn against all of us. The best one to send, as always, is the one who does not know he is sent. Then if he is discovered, he will say he went alone, of his own free will. And we cannot be held to account."

Blaylock's eyes narrowed. "You manipulated Elizar, your own apprentice, as you would an outsider?"

Kell gave a single nod. "I baited Elizar with the story of Carvin invading Alwyn's place of power. I knew he could not resist the challenge." Kell's eyes narrowed with pride at the memory. "I allowed him to gain access to certain of my files, so that he would discover on his own the return of the Shadows and"—his gaze flicked toward Galen—"what this would mean to the techno-mages. He was angry at what I had hidden from him, though he said nothing. Yet I never doubted that he would work for the good of the techno-mages, that he would come to the same conclusion I had and do what was necessary to gain information for all of us. He has always dreamed of fighting for right, of regaining our glory.

"I left him clues, hints so that he could make contact with the minions of the Shadows. And soon he did. He began to gather information from them, which I would access secretly from his files. They did not tell him much, always promising more after he was initiated."

Again Elizar had spoken the truth, though only the truth as far as he knew it. Galen had studied the various methods of manipulation, and Kell's technique was one of the classics. Yet applied to Kell's own apprentice, it was a violation of trust. Galen could not imagine Elric manipulating him this way.

"I know that his alliance with the Shadows was feigned—at least at first. We all heard Galen and—Isabelle—say that he had warned them about a threat, that he was anxious to learn their spells to gain power to fight the threat."

"Or power for himself and the Shadows," Blaylock said.

Kell's hand tightened about his staff. "When Blaylock questioned Elizar about this threat, I turned the questioning to other issues. If the truth had come out, Elizar would have become contaminated and useless as our tool. When Burell brought her evidence before us, I suggested we send two inexperienced initiates, hoping they would find nothing. Once the Circle had clear evidence of the Shadows' presence, the mages would be forced to act, and we were not ready to act. We did not have enough information about the Shadows. We still do not. And yet now we are forced to act."

So Elizar had told the truth about that as well. Kell had sent them to fail. Kell had thought he could manipulate them all, could acquire information from one, could keep information from the rest. He had thought he could control all, control the Shadows, control chaos. He had thought he could impose his design upon the universe. And his arrogance had cost the lives of Isabelle and Burell.

"It was also important that the task fail," Kell said, "because once other mages came in direct contact with the Shadows, the Shadows themselves would have to act. Then Elizar would be forced to take one side or the other, and his ability to gather information would end."

"He did choose a side," Ing-Radi said. "But it was not the one you expected."

Kell cast his gaze upward, his face in lines of despair. "Even now I cannot believe it."

What Elizar's original intentions had been, or whether they had changed, Galen could not say. His faith in his friend, and his confidence that he knew that friend, had been destroyed.

And what did it matter? If Elizar ever had planned to betray the Shadows and bring his knowledge back to the mages, somewhere along the way—perhaps as he read Kell's files, perhaps as he sat at that table in the tavern, acting like their friend—he had decided instead to use that knowledge for himself. Among the truths he had told them was hidden that one lie—the lie that he did what he did for the good of the mages.

Galen believed that good, at least, had been Kell's true goal, as wrong as his methods had been. Galen and Isabelle had been caught between them, between the lies of one and the lies of the other. Meanwhile, the Shadows had remained in the background, protected. They were the true enemy—they, and Elizar, their servant. Galen focused on that, a subject that satisfied the anger without releasing the pain. The mages would now dedicate themselves to fighting the Shadows, to stopping their war. And they would hunt down Elizar and flay him.

"What of Tilar's chrysalis?" Blaylock asked.

"I know nothing of that," Kell said.

Blaylock's voice was harsh and certain. "Your deception of Elizar violated solidarity, and more, the bond between teacher and apprentice. Your deception of the rest of us not only violated the Code, but undermined the Circle."

"I believed I acted for the benefit of all," Kell said, "and I believed secrecy was best. Elizar is not the only mage whose allegiance the Shadows have tried to secure."

Kell was right, Galen thought. Elric had said Morden approached many at the convocation. If any of them turned to the Shadows, they too would be hunted down, destroyed.

"Perhaps it was arrogance," Kell said. "I believed that Elizar and I could save the mages."

"It is arrogance indeed," Blaylock said, "to doubt the allegiance of the Circle and trust in your student who consorts with Shadows."

Elric stepped forward, and Galen noticed an odd hesitance in the action. His voice, though, was at its most powerful and frightening. "You played a chess game with the lives of those who put their trust in us. You sent two fresh out of the chrysalis into danger to protect your secret. You sent them to face the Shadows when there was no need. And as we stood here and voted to send them, you withheld information so that your plan would prevail." Elric's lips formed a grim line. "That was the moment when you had to tell us. You had to stop it."

Kell bowed his head, his shoulders hunched. "You speak wisely. Yet I never—never imagined . . ." He straightened, and his gaze took in each of them in turn. As his dark eyes met Galen's, Galen realized that something was about to be lost, something fundamental to the mages, and something that could never be recovered. "At this most desperate time, I have made matters even worse. Two mages are dead, and two others have joined with the Shadows. I have brought tragedy upon us, and how much more will follow, I cannot say. I am no longer one of the Circle. I do not deserve to be." With that, Kell strode from the chamber.

Elric started after him, and Blaylock seized his arm. "He spoke the truth," Blaylock said. "Let him go."

Elric turned on Blaylock, eyes narrowed, three lines of tension between his brows. "Release me."

Blaylock let go and inclined his head. "My apologies."

Elric looked after Kell, but did not follow.

Despite all Kell had done, Galen couldn't believe he had resigned from the Circle. He had led them for nearly fifty years, all of Galen's life and nearly all of Elric's. Without him, and without Elizar and Razeel, they had lost the line of Wierden.

"We must—" Herazade looked stunned. "We must decide on a course of action."

"There is only one option," Blaylock said. "We must flee."

Elric turned from the stone archway that marked the exit. "We have not yet heard all of Galen's account. It is the best information we have. Should we not hear it before deciding our future?"

The meeting resumed, but now there was an empty space in the semicircle of seats, an emptiness at the center. Staring into that emptiness, Galen returned to that day, to that place, to that spike, to the fragile body spasming beneath his. He strove for the calm with which he had begun. In the absence of that, he imagined driving the spike down Elizar's own throat.

Yet even that did not protect him from the pain. He had to separate himself from his words, from his body. He had to go elsewhere, to that place deep inside where he hid from himself.

He told them of the escape from the tavern, the explosion of the ship, Morden's offer, Isabelle's death. When he spoke of her death, it seemed as if surely the tents must collapse, the rocky cliffside crumble. Yet all continued as before, except that she was gone. And so he was supposed to continue.

They dismissed him, and he wandered from the tents into

the night, watching absently as a mage ship rose off of the mak. Using his sensors, he located the three frequencies high in the ultraviolet. This ship was marked with Kell's rune. It shot into the sky. He was leaving them.

Galen found his legs had stopped a few yards from the tents. Everything was about to change. Perhaps the tents had not collapsed, the cliffs had not crumbled. But the mages would never be the same again. Isabelle and Burell were lost. The Circle was missing its leader. The Shadows had returned, and Morden had moved among them searching for allies. Galen felt that if he took another step, it would all collapse.

Carvin approached him, her eyes wide with caution. She looked different without the ponytail of hair bouncing behind her. It seemed as if something was missing. He hadn't noticed when she'd come to Brensil.

"Is the Circle finished with you?" she asked.

"Yes." She was a few inches shorter than Isabelle. That was why Isabelle's wrists had stuck out from the sleeves of her robe. Carvin had one hand clenched in the other. Isabelle's fingers were longer, stronger.

"Circe believes that the convocation may not end in the morning, as scheduled. Have you heard anything like that?"

"No." He realized it was New Year's Eve on Earth, the last night of the convocation.

She was regarding him oddly, eyes wide, lips sucked inward, as if she didn't know whether she should speak. A question came to him.

"Do you know why you were chosen to go to Brensil?" he asked.

"Alwyn sent me on a scavenger hunt as a way of getting me used to my new ship. It happened I was about half a day closer to Brensil than anyone else when your message came." She hesitated. "I'm glad I was able to pick you up."

His curiosity satisfied, Galen said nothing more. Carvin remained before him, and her lips once again retracted inward. He could not imagine what else there was to say.

At last her lips parted. "You know the custom among us." She spoke slowly, as if to someone who must be led carefully to the truth. "When an elderly mage passes, his wishes are followed. Or if no wishes are specified, the place of power is often used, or it is left to any who have been his students . . ." Her twisted hands came apart. She reached with one into the pocket of her robe, came out with a small vial.

It lay on her palm, the final, crushing reality.

He and Elric had released his parents' ashes around their adjoining places of power. Galen had thrown their ashes into the winds hoping he could lose his memories of them as well, consign them to oblivion. Yet still they haunted him.

And now, what was he to do with Isabelle? He would cherish his memories of her for as long as he could hold them. But her memories were not held in this vial of ash.

She had died too young for students, too young for a place of power. Her home had been destroyed.

Then he realized that she did have a special place, a place of power that would have been hers, had she lived. The Well of Forever. He would find that place for her, that source of tech and of knowledge, and when he did, he would pour her ashes on that sacred ground, where so many of their kind had been brought before. And he would use the knowledge left by her and Burell to try to find the answers she had so desired.

He took the vial from Carvin. "Thank you."

"You're welcome." She retreated hastily.

He had told no one that he carried pieces of their knowledge, not even the Circle. He had inherited them, and although they were just bits of what they had thought, what they had known, they were his.

Galen opened the vial, touched his fingertip to the top layer of ash. He vaguely remembered Isabelle saying she didn't want his soul to burn to ash. Yet here it was. He turned his finger over. A few grains clung to the skin. He rubbed them between thumb and forefinger, accessing their chemical composition. He remembered running his finger down her temple, collecting the elegant chemical compounds that comprised her essence. None of the compounds he had detected then survived in these dry grains of ash. There was the calcium phosphate of bone, a trace of phosphorus, a bit of carbon residue that had refused to completely burn. The compounds were jumbled together. They had lost the order, the pattern they had held in life. All was reduced to chaos. She was gone.

The Circle had lost its center. Kell had been the one whose wisdom moderated their extremes, whose achievements commanded their respect, and whose vision illuminated their proceedings. They had been like planets revolving about a sun, held to it through the attraction of gravity. Now that sun, Kell, had removed itself. What remained to keep the planets together? Without him, they threatened to fly off in different directions.

Elric wished he had deduced Kell's plan weeks ago. He'd had all the pieces; it simply had not occurred to him that Kell was using Elizar as an unwitting pawn. To use one's apprentice in such a way was a horrible violation of the bond between apprentice and teacher, as Blaylock had said. And to send one's apprentice alone to face the Shadows, expecting him to be the salvation of the mages, was folly. Knowing Kell, though, it made perfect sense. Kell had pinned such hopes on Elizar. He was blind to Elizar's flaws.

Kell's folly had sent Galen and Isabelle into unnecessary danger. It had killed Burell and Isabelle. It had provided the Shadows with two mages who could reveal much about their order and their ways.

As much as Kell's actions angered Elric, a future without Kell frightened him much more. Without their leader, Elric didn't know if the mages could remain intact. Kell had held them all together. Now they faced the threat of the Shadows without that unifying force, and with a weakened Circle. If the authority of the Circle and the Code was lost, they would fall to chaos.

Elric tried to focus on the Circle's debate, but Galen's face haunted him. Since Galen had arrived that afternoon with Isabelle's body, he had seemed stunned, his huge eyes unblinking, as if struggling to absorb something that could not be absorbed.

He had shown great skill in fighting Elizar and the Shadows, and most important, he had maintained control. He had not succumbed to the impulse for destruction he had surely felt. He had borne his burden well. Any wounds he had suffered seemed to have healed, though the back of his shirt was peppered with small holes and dark splotches of dried blood. Yet his mind was far from healed. He had retreated to some distant hiding place, as he had when his parents were killed, but that distance was threatening to collapse. As Galen had spoken before the Circle, Elric had seen him struggling to remain detached. The raw vulnerability on his face was almost too much to bear.

Galen had taken years to recover from his parents' deaths—if he had ever truly recovered. Elric didn't know how long this wound would take to heal. Galen had come to love her; that Elric had known from the moment he'd seen Galen in the last electron incantation.

Now, with the Shadows, there would be more trauma, and likely more death. Elric feared how Galen would cope.

"We must elect a new member to the Circle," Ing-Radi said. "Before we do anything else. There must be five. There must always be five. Five is the number of balance."

"We have no time." Herazade was sitting on the edge of her seat, her hands in constant, emphatic motion. "Even now, Elizar could be leading the Shadows to attack us. And he will tell them everything." She believed in the Shadows now. And she was in a panic.

"That is not the way of the Shadows." Blaylock seemed to be permanently standing, as if his unyielding figure could hold the Circle together by force of will. His harsh enunciation revealed that his patience was at the breaking point. "They do not attack directly. And as Galen revealed to us, they still hope to gain us as allies. The Shadows' message to us was that we shall join with them or die. We still have some time, I think, before the alternatives narrow to only one."

Elric stood, hoping to slow the frantic pace of the discussion. "I agree that we may have some time while the Shadows continue to gather their forces, though we cannot be sure how much. We must use this precious time to its fullest advantage. We must formulate a plan, now. Postponing any decision until after an election would cripple us.

"I again propose that we take an active stance against the Shadows, gathering information, forming alliances, sharing what we know with others, and preparing for war." Fighting the Shadows would mean the death of many mages, Elric knew, and likely even the end of the mages altogether, yet he could see no other alternative. Perhaps this was their destiny.

Herazade shook her head. "Kell said that we are not ready to act. We do not know enough about the Shadows. If they can penetrate our illusions so easily, as they did with Burell, if they can conceal themselves, if their powers are greater than ours, how can we fight them?"

It was easy to be brave and bold and do good when they were the most powerful beings in the galaxy—save only the Vorlons, who hid their power so well and used it so sparingly, it was described only in legend. Now that the mages were threatened with a greater power, many of them would collapse, as Herazade was doing. Her vision of a benevolent universe in which superior mages did good for the less fortunate ceased to make sense when the mages were no longer superior, and the universe no longer benevolent.

Blaylock, Elric knew, would vote only to find a place of safety and wait out the war. He did not believe they should become warriors. He felt it went against their destiny. Blaylock had long supported the idea that the mages should remove themselves from others altogether. His belief was so strong, Elric knew, that he was willing to leave his place of power permanently. The coming of the Shadows merely added strength to his conviction.

That meant Elric had to convince both Herazade and Ing-Radi to fight, which would require extreme measures. Herazade was terrified because she was not prepared. She had not believed in a universe where Shadows existed. Ing-Radi, though, was well prepared. She knew the threat they faced, and knew well that they might all die fighting it. She would be convinced only if she thought they had a chance. Elric used the only argument he thought might convince them. It was a desperate gambit.

"We could form an alliance with the Vorlons," he said. "Legend tells that they are the ancient enemy of the Shadows."

Blaylock's face soured. "The Vorlons cannot be trusted. Throughout our history they have treated the techno-mages with nothing but contempt. We need information, not impenetrable pronouncements."

"I met a Vorlon once," Ing-Radi said, and for the first time since Elric had known her, her slit pupils narrowed in anger. "Do you know what they call us? Fabulists. Tellers of tales. Liars."

Herazade waved off his suggestion. "If we ally ourselves with the Vorlons, that will simply give the Shadows another reason to attack us. They will be hesitant to attack the great forces of the Vorlons directly. Instead they will attack the Vorlons through us, the weaker link."

Elric felt the Code, all he had lived for and believed in, crumbling.

He found he had a message from Alwyn. He read it quickly and viewed the attached recording. At that, his hopes fell even further.

The Shadows had begun to show their hand. Anarchy was loosed upon the galaxy. "Then we can find other allies," he said. "There are good beings of many species who would stand beside us—Humans, Minbari, Narns. We have a responsibility to them. I have a responsibility to mine here, a responsibility to do good. Is that not the final and most important word of the Code?" He paused, forcing the Circle to linger over that point. "I have just been informed by Alwyn that the Narn outpost in Quadrant 37 has been destroyed. Ten thousand Narns are killed. Before Alwyn's probe there was destroyed, it detected this." He conjured the image from Alwyn's message, the same image the Narn G'Leel had described, a black shape out of legend. Against the grey-blue planet, the spiky silhouette wheeled and dove as if alive, blasting out great streams of energy. "What chance do the Narns and all the rest have if we leave them behind?"

The Circle fell silent, and Elric hoped that perhaps this new development would drive them to fight, hoped that the vision he had always held of the techno-mages was consistent with the reality. If they abandoned the galaxy in its time of greatest need, the order Elric had thought they were would cease to exist.

Blaylock had averted his eyes as Alwyn's recording played; now he looked up, and his gaunt face seemed shaken. He spoke slowly. "Elric, I understand your impulse. It is difficult to see a galaxy about to descend into war and chaos, and do nothing. I, too, have feelings for these beings. Yet war and chaos will come no matter what we do. They have come before, and they will come again. We have devoted ourselves to learning and understanding. If we abandon that now for war, then who is ever to bring greater understanding to the universe? Who is ever to break the cycle of war and death?"

Blaylock had great dreams, Elric thought, but the reality was that billions would die, and he would have the mages stand by and do nothing. "I do not think," Elric said, "that the cycle can ever be broken. Only that we must do good to the limit of our abilities. As for any understanding we may someday offer the universe"—Elric straightened, determined to say at last what none of them would say—"it seems likely to me now that all paths lead to our end."

Herazade brought her palms flat against each other, raised her praying hands to her lips. "I support Blaylock's plan. Create a place of safety, to which we can withdraw as soon as possible."

"I as well," said Ing-Radi. She extended a hand toward Elric. "I am sorry, Elric. We have a responsibility to our order, to keep them safe. I believe, against this enemy, we have no choice."

"Then it is decided," Elric said. They would hide and let the galaxy burn. His vision of the techno-mages, if it ever had been reality, was no longer. He felt himself drifting away from them, even while he knew he must not. The Circle must not be broken.

Blaylock's voice regained its harsh certainty. "The mages

will return home to gather their belongings and destroy the artifacts of their presence."

Ing-Radi's eyes were cast downward. She was thinking, no doubt, of her place of power. "Let none of the tech or our knowledge be left behind, so that it might be used for ill."

"We can leave tomorrow," Blaylock said, "as is normal, so that nothing will be suspected. We must then gather as quickly as possible in a secret place, where we can prepare for our migration in safety."

If Kell had stayed, Elric felt they would have come to a different conclusion. But Elric had failed to find the plan or the argument to convince them.

Their plans made, the Circle ended its meeting.

Elric brought his platform to the ground, dissolved it so that his boots sank once again into the soft, familiar mak. While the others huddled in conversation, Elric left the chamber. He accessed his place of power, pulled images from a number of probes. On the far side of the planet it was day. The wild tak had submerged themselves in the Lang River to escape the heat. The krit skittered over sun-baked rock. Across the continent, the desert city of Drel came to life as sunset approached, its colorfully dressed inhabitants filling the narrow streets and bazaars.

On this side of the planet it was night. The coastal city of Tain had grown quiet except for the neighborhood around the port, where sailors caroused and fought late into the night. The town of Lok had settled into a sense of stillness and expectation. Jab slept peacefully on Des' vast stomach. Some of the townspeople sat outside, waiting for the light show that had been promised at midnight, commemorating the final night of the convocation. The mages were already an hour late. Others of the townspeople waited down on the mak, staring skyward. Farmer Jae and Farmer Nee stood together, sharing a drink.

All around him, the planet lived and breathed. Magma circulated; volcanoes exhaled; water nourished; life grew. He could not imagine leaving Soom, walking without the soft carpet of moss beneath his feet, breathing without the smell of sea air. He could not imagine leaving the town and its people. He had sunk his bones deep into this planet. It was as much a part of him as his heart.

Yet how could he stay and defy the Circle?

Elric received a message from his computer demon. Attached was a file from the EarthForce New Technologies Division. The subject was Morden. Elric paused a moment to scan through it. The information seemed irrelevant at this point. He skipped to the end to see if the file contained any information about Morden's alleged death.

Morden had been on loan to Interplanetary Expeditions when he had been declared dead. While on the IPX-funded archaeological dig, his ship had exploded, leaving no survivors. Or so the file said. Explosions seemed to follow Morden like footprints. Had he arranged both the deaths of his colleagues and the deaths of his family? The file contained no details of the dig, only the location: Alpha Omega 3. It was a planet on the rim of known space—one among thousands on the rim, the legendary home of the Shadows.

Elric would continue his investigations later. For now, Morden's sins were not his concern. One of Morden's victims was.

As Elric left the tents, he saw Galen standing a few feet away, motionless in the night among the activity of others. Elric knew instinctively that Galen had been standing there since he'd been dismissed.

Elric stopped before him. Galen's face was blank, his brilliant blue eyes caught in a place far away. Elric was uncertain how Galen would react to the Circle's decision. He would no doubt be unhappy with it. But whether he would accept it with detachment or flash again with the anger he had shown Kell, Elric did not know. Elric wished he did not have this disappointment to add to Galen's burden.

"The Circle has come to a decision," Elric said. "We will create a hiding place and retreat into it. We will leave known space. We will flee."

Galen's eyes snapped into focus, fastened on him. Galen

had been in a hiding place of his own, and this had brought him from it. "What of the Shadows? And Elizar? We must fight them. We must destroy them."

"The Circle has decided we are in too much danger. We must preserve ourselves."

"They intend to let Elizar go?" Galen's breath was hard, and color rose in his stubbled cheeks. "What of the Shadow war? The Drakh said their provocations would begin within weeks."

Elric would have preferred to suffer what had happened to Galen one thousand times over, rather than watch Galen suffer it even once. "Their provocations have begun," he said. "And so the Circle believes we must leave as quickly as possible." Galen's face tightened, and Elric searched for the words that would bring him to acceptance. "Of us the Shadows know all. Of them we know nearly nothing. That is a situation rife with disaster."

Galen's lips bit out the words. "We will learn more, then."

Elric found himself echoing the arguments of the Circle. "They have given us a choice. We must join them. Or we must die."

"They try to frighten us. But we can fight them."

"The Shadows have great powers. We are few in number, and they could easily exterminate us all. They might even draw more of us to their side, through promises, threats, or even force."

"How can we run away and leave everyone behind? Where in the Code does it say that?"

"The Circle is afraid, Galen. Until a few days ago, no mage had been killed in our lifetimes. Now two have died, so quickly. And two lost to the Shadows. We are used to being the most powerful. We are used to being in control, to manipulating events. Now the Shadows have returned, and it is we who are being manipulated."

The anger seemed to abandon Galen. His face was bare. "Did you vote to flee?"

"No."

Galen's voice rose with desperate hope. "Could some of us

not stay behind, then? I would stay with you. And there must be others who would be willing to fight. We could—"

"No. Division would only serve the purpose of the Shadows. Above all, we must remain unified. Solidarity," he said, speaking one of the words of the Code. It resounded with years of history, years of devotion, and Elric realized Galen had pushed him into the commitment that he needed to make. "Obedience to the Circle and the Code has been our salvation. They are the only reasons we have survived as an order. The Circle is already weakened with Kell's resignation. The direct line of Wierden is no longer represented, for the first time in our history. We must support the Circle with all our energies, or it will not hold. And if it does not, the mages will fall to chaos. The Shadows will have triumphed."

Elric had given over Galen to the Circle's task when they asked it; now, he would give over his place of power. That was as it had to be. Galen must realize the same. "I know that you believe in the Circle, and the Code," Elric said. "You have followed their ways and obeyed their rulings, which I know could not have been easy. We must both trust in their wisdom now."

Galen moved closer, lowering his voice. Elric fought the urge to look away from the intensity of his gaze. "I nearly used my spell of destruction on Elizar, when he attacked us. I don't know what it would have done. I don't know if it would have killed him, or all of us." His lips parted with an odd eagerness, almost as if he wished it had killed them all.

Then Galen's gaze fell, and his mouth tightened in a way Elric recognized. He was doing a mind-focusing exercise, struggling to regain his detachment, his stillness.

"You did well not to use it. The dangers are too great. And it may be that Elizar hoped to provoke you into casting the spell. Perhaps he believed he could somehow survive it and discover its secret." Elric hesitated to go further, yet he realized Galen's commitment to the Circle then was the key to his acceptance now. "You followed the Circle and the Code in that most terrible hour. Do not fail them now."

When Galen looked up, his face was composed, still. Yet

his voice revealed the acute need behind his words. "Can there be no justice for Elizar, then?"

Fury rose up in Elric at the hurt that Galen had sustained, and he spoke through clenched teeth. "I vow to you, Galen, that if Elizar survives this war, we will find him, and we will kill him."

Blaylock stopped beside them, and Elric tried to hide his anger, nodding silently in greeting. Galen did not need this intrusion. Yet Blaylock would want to be certain of both Elric's and Galen's loyalty.

"You have done well, Galen," Blaylock said. "Elric has trained you to be a skilled mage. The information you brought may save us all. I hope you will rest now. We will depend upon your help to reach our hiding place safely."

Galen's voice had gained the stillness of his face. It was even, controlled. "I will help you," Galen said. "Though I wonder who will help everyone else."

January 2259

— chapter 17 —

In his residence on Babylon 5, Kosh watched and waited. By the Earth calendar, it was the close of one year and the beginning of the next. The Humans celebrated the new year while events cascaded toward war.

As the Vorlon buoys sang their perceptions to him, Kosh swam in the currents of history-in-making. Within their song, he slipped from planet to planet, observing, absorbing. On the rim, the forces of chaos gathered at the site of their ancient home, rapidly building their resources. They had spread now to the surrounding systems, a growing maelstrom that hungered to overrun all.

On Centauri Prime, the Centauri celebrated the destruction of the Narn outpost in Quadrant 37, not realizing who had struck down their enemy. The Narn defeat gave new energy to old dreams of conquest and glory, and they spoke of regaining Narn territory, of reconquering their old foe. The dream of the maelstrom infected them.

On Narn, horror at the deaths of ten thousand of their kind was turning to fury. They had suffered enough, and would suffer no more. They determined to exact revenge.

On Earth, a murdered president was mourned, his death believed an accident, and a new president was sworn in, one beholden to the darkness.

Even here on Babylon 5, the one named Morden moved freely, forming alliances and spreading chaos like a pestilence.

Yet order, too, had its strength. Sinclair was even now receiving the directive to step down as commander of Babylon 5 and accept the post as ambassador to Minbar. There, his development could continue under more controlled circumstances, and he could take charge of the Rangers, a source of light to fight the darkness.

Delenn was in the midst of a transformation, a fulfillment of prophecy that would reveal the connection between Human and Minbari, the order underlying the universe. This connection would encourage the Humans to ally with the Minbari, and so with the Vorlons. And the key to that new alliance would be the new captain of Babylon 5, Sheridan.

Slipping through the song of the buoys, Kosh reached at last those who hung precariously between order and chaos. Their great power could be the pivot on which the war turned. The images from the buoys were less clear here than elsewhere, since they needed to remain distant to escape detection. Yet the fabulists sent many messages to each other, and over one thousand years of watching them, Kosh had learned how to intercept these messages. Those the buoys had perceived clearly, as they had the movements of the fabulists and their ships.

Kosh slipped through the data streams, re-creating the song of the fabulists' assemblage. The pestilence called Morden had moved among them. Then a flash of great energy, as great as the energies commanded by the Vorlons. One among the fabulists now wielded immense power.

Two ships had left. Just a short time ago, one of those ships had arrived in a system on the rim marked by darkness. The symbol on the ship was that of the student of their accomplished leader, Kell.

Earlier this night at the assemblage, a burial fire had marked the death of one too young to die. After that, the assemblage had become quiet, their festivities subdued. Their leader had left, searching for his lost student. The remaining four who led the fabulists had met without him and decided upon a course of action. They had called all to gather and delivered the grave message. They would take no side in this war. They would leave known space.

Kosh slipped from the song and found himself alone again in his simple residence. Among the Vorlons, distrust of the fabulists ran deep, and some would doubt the truth of their decision, believing it a deception, a trick. Some even supported the destruction of all the fabulists, before they could join the ancient enemy. To assuage those doubts, Kosh would continue to watch the fabulists until they left for their hiding place.

Yet most of his kind would be relieved at the decision of the fabulists. Let them be gone. Let them be forgotten.

For his part, Kosh would mourn their passing.

It was the end of the convocation and the end of the Earth year 2258. Yet for Galen it felt as if this was the end of much more.

This last night was usually marked by raucous celebration, great displays of magic, passionate fights and hasty reconciliations. Yet tonight the mages stood in silence, their displays in the clear night sky mournful, somber. Elric coordinated them, incorporating Galen's suggestions. For Isabelle, glowing lines of warp and woof wove through the sky. For Burell, starbursts bloomed brilliant gold, and red poppies rained down. A few shooting stars fell like tears.

An hour ago, the Circle had gathered them all together, telling them of the return of the Shadows, of Kell's resignation, and of the betrayal by Elizar and Razeel. They had explained the necessity of retreating to a hiding place, had gone over the plan by which the mages would destroy their homes and places of power and gather at a safe site to prepare for their migration.

Galen sensed the mages were uncertain, but they were also afraid. The deaths of Isabelle and Burell terrified them. They would follow the plan. They would follow the Circle despite the absence of Kell.

As would Galen. He had no fear of death or the Shadows. Yet he had made a commitment to the mages. He had sworn loyalty to the Circle. He had spoken the words of the Code. Despite Kell's deception, and all it had brought, his commitment bound him. Elric had spoken truly. Galen had not broken the

Code when it might have saved Isabelle. How could he break it now?

He had planned to die with Isabelle, yet stubbornly he persisted. It was but the latest in a long string of failures—failures of skill, failures of planning, failures of character. Isabelle had told him he must transcend himself. She had said he'd completed the first step, opening himself to another. Yet even in that he had failed. He had never told Isabelle he loved her.

Galen remembered how they had laughed that morning at Ko'Dan's house when they'd made breen. He hadn't realized how happy he'd been. Now Galen had been left behind, as had Ko'Dan, who had moved to Zafran 8 to escape the memories of his wife. *Yet it is in my memory of her that I find the most joy.*

Galen found only pain in his memories of Isabelle, yet he would cherish each one of them.

Thinking of her smile that morning, Galen wondered what had happened to the breen, and whether the relay hidden inside the container was still aboard the *Khatkhata*. If so, he should be able to access the probes they'd planted on the Narn crew, even if they had reached the Thenothk system on the rim.

Galen closed his eyes to the glowing tapestry in the sky, visualized the equation to access the relay and the images it received and recorded from the probes. The relay responded, and Galen requested the images currently being transmitted by the probes. Since the ship had a crew of ten, ten images spread out before him in his mind's eye.

The images came from different angles—one probe planted on a forehead, another on a hand—and moved as the crew moved. It took him a short time to become acclimated to the views. The leather-clad crew seemed to be working in the hold, unloading the sleeper tubes G'Leel had told them about. Apparently the ship had arrived at Thenothk.

Galen requested coordinates, and discovered that the *Khatkhata* was in the Omega sector, on the rim of known space. The system was known as Tau Omega. If this wasn't the home of the Shadows, it must be close.

They were all working, even G'Leel and the captain. There was considerable grumbling among them; Galen translated and discovered they were complaining that they had to unload this cargo themselves.

This is not our job, one said.

We should never have agreed to take these damn mindwalkers, another said. He rapped on a tube. *She might know who I am. She could come after me when she wakes up. That's what they're going to do with her, isn't it? Wake her up?*

For what we're getting paid, Captain Ko'Vin said, *you should be selling them your mother. Now stop asking questions.*

One of the tubes dropped to the floor. *This one moved,* the first Narn said. *I swear.*

Don't be an idiot, Ko'Vin replied. *Let's get this done, and then we'll all go out and get drunk.*

The first Narn wrestled the tube back onto the wheeled cart, pushed it toward the air lock. A shadow fell over him, and the Narn jumped.

"Where is your captain?"

Galen shivered.

The Narn pointed over his shoulder.

"That doesn't do me much good if you don't get out of the way."

It was Elizar's voice.

The Narn backed up, and Elizar strode into the hold, marking his way with a platinum staff. Tilar followed. Somehow, beside Elizar, he looked like an anxious assistant.

"You are the captain?" Elizar said.

"Yes, sir," Ko'Vin said.

"You're loading this cargo into the wrong vehicle. It should be going into my lift, which is to the left here." With a precise gesture he extended two fingers toward the air lock.

"But, sir." Ko'Vin pointed to Tilar. "This man told us your lift was to receive only one tube."

"He made a mistake." Elizar turned on Tilar.

"Yes," said Tilar, "I made a mistake."

Elizar turned back to the captain. "One of these rejects"—he indicated the tubes with a flourish of his hand—"is to be my servant. My secret weapon. But to find one suitable servant, I must test them all. I'll be lucky to find one with the proper qualities in this small bunch. Could you carry no more?"

"This is all we were given," Ko'Vin said.

Elizar scanned the interior. "Very well then. Be quick about it."

"Yes, sir."

Elizar strode from the hold, Tilar following.

Get to it, Ko'Vin said, *unless you want to be turned into spoo. That was a techno-mage. And that one does not tell fortunes, he ruins them.*

Galen broke contact with the probes, keeping his eyes squeezed shut.

He hadn't been prepared to see Elizar again. The restless energy raced through him, and he realized his body was trembling. Elizar's life went on too, as if nothing had happened. He was across the galaxy, yet it felt as if he were in the next room. Galen wanted to go into that next room and crush Elizar in his own private universe.

How could Galen leave, knowing Elizar went on?

Galen opened his eyes to the sky. Isabelle had said she would show him a sign. It was a foolish promise; he was foolish even to think of it. The universe had no pattern, meaning, or justice. It cared not whether Elizar lived or Isabelle died. It cared not whether the Shadows triumphed or the mages were killed. All was chaos.

The energy within him gathered itself, ready for his command. Galen wanted to use his spell of destruction on the whole thing. Kill this damned uncaring universe. Kill himself. Kill Isabelle, who had sacrificed herself for him. How dare she?

Morden was right, Galen thought. He was just like the Shadows. All he wanted was destruction.

Something touched him, and Galen jerked away.

It was Fa. Her hand hung in midair, his father's ring on her smallest finger.

The energy was ready to erupt, if he gave it the slightest direction. "Go away," he whispered.

Fa backed away, regarding him with fearful eyes.

His father, his mother—both had died senselessly. There was no reason or pattern. People saw patterns because they wanted to see them, just as people believed he could tell fortunes because they wanted to believe he could tell fortunes.

If only he could have seen the future.

He knew the tricks, knew what to say or do to convince someone he could see the future, or change the present. But they were tricks, not magic. People liked to believe in magic, and so they saw magic.

Even the mages liked to fool themselves, disguising their abilities with flourishes and stage dressing to make acts of technology appear magical—to turn a simple hologram into a vision, a sound wave into a spell of protection.

Who were the mages, he thought, but mortals who wished to appear as gods?

He had wanted it just as much as the others. He had wanted to control events, to inspire awe and wonder, to perform acts that seemed miraculous. Yet something in him had changed. Those acts, once so captivating, now seemed pathetic and futile. There was no magic. They did not control events. They were not gods. They did not live forever.

Now he saw through the illusions and misdirection, through the manipulation and intelligence gathering, through the hocus-pocus and mumbo jumbo and staffs and cloaks and runes and circles of stone—to the simple power underlying it all. The power of the tech. The power of destruction.

He had aligned his thoughts and his spells into neat, regimented columns, and there, at the base of those columns, he had found it, the fundament upon which they were built, the power that allowed them to pose as gods. Elizar had known that power was important. With it, a mage could fly through the air. He could shower poppies from the sky. Or he could kill. Each made his own choice.

And so, as fire bloomed across the sky, Galen realized who he was. Kell had given him only part of the answer. Kell had made him realize that he was the techno-mage who carried the secret of destruction, the secret that must never be used. Yet there was more to it than that. Now he had found the rest, and knew truly who he was: he was the mage who carried the power of destruction, and who rather than use it, had let Isabelle die.

And now a sneak preview from SUMMONING LIGHT, the explosive second installment in the *Babylon 5* trilogy THE PASSING OF THE TECHNO-MAGES.

The ship sang of the beauty of order, the harmony of the spheres. The peace of its silent passage through space, the symmetry of its form, the unity of its functioning wove through its melody. But within the song, Kosh was disturbed.

The maelstrom was spreading.

Only a short time ago, the forces of chaos had been limited to their ancient home of Z'ha'dum. While that planet remained their stronghold, they had now spread to over a dozen worlds in the surrounding systems.

Kosh altered his ship's song, slowing its speed, drawing it carefully closer to the fourth planet orbiting the star called Thenothk. Near the end of the last war with the ancient enemy, Kosh had visited this place. It had been a sphere of red in the darkness of space, a frigid, barren desert, unable to sustain life. He had left a buoy nonetheless, and over time, it had perceived changes.

Soon after the buoy had begun its observations, a great ship had arrived, an engine of transformation sent by the ancient enemy. It was but one of many sent into the systems surrounding their home, designed to create habitable environments for them and their allies. Finally they had realized their vulnerability in remaining concentrated on a single planet.

Over the years, the great engine released many smaller

ones, in wave upon wave upon wave, each designed to perform a specific function. Some took up residence above, some burrowed below, some spread over the land. The planet warmed. Ice frozen for eons melted. Floods raced across the lowlands. The atmosphere thickened, and storms raged through it. Life forms were seeded and flourished, performing necessary chemical reactions. When their purpose was accomplished, they were replaced with others, one species after the next, until the work of transformation was complete. Gradually the storms lessened, conditions stabilized. From chaos, order came. As was inevitable.

Then other ships began to arrive, and a settlement was built. While the ancient enemy preferred to live underground, they built the majority of this settlement above, erecting structures that would feel comfortable and familiar to many of the younger races. It was to be a place where they could meet and interact with allies, where the maelstrom could present itself with a false face and draw others into its grasp.

The small settlement quickly grew, spreading its tentacles in chaotic form, until now over twelve million of various species lived there. Several other settlements appeared as well, where more secret work took place.

Now the planet was busy with activity, and Kosh took care to make sure his ship was not observed. He directed it to extrude several new buoys, which would take up positions around Thenothk 4 and provide more complete information about the activity occurring within the thick haze of the atmosphere. As the war cascaded from hidden attacks to outright aggression, the Vorlons would need to know their ancient enemies' actions.

A new harmonic entered the ship's song, alerting him to the presence of several other probes. They were small, nearly as small as Kosh's buoys, and they orbited a bit closer to the planet than the Vorlon buoys would. He recognized them immediately. He had come across the probes of the fabulists numerous times. They too observed many things in many places. Apparently, they too found the activity here of interest.

To Kosh, the probes held no negative significance. But

some among the Vorlons, he knew, would say the probes revealed a further connection between the fabulists and the forces of chaos, an interest that could perhaps lead to alliance.

Their position was precarious. They carried great power; they could be the pivot on which the war turned. The Vorlons would not allow that pivot to turn against them. Kosh feared that talk of destroying the fabulists would gain strength.

At the fabulists' recent assemblage, their leaders had decreed that they would go into hiding, that they would leave the coming war for others to fight. Although the plans of the fabulists were always difficult to decipher, Kosh believed this was their true intent. Yet others believed the plan a deception.

Kosh had watched as the fabulists left the assemblage and journeyed back to their homes. A few at a time, they destroyed those homes and set out for the place where they would gather in preparation for their migration. They gathered slowly to disguise their mass activity. Yet soon they must leave, or more among the Vorlons would doubt their intentions.

A dissonance entered the ship's song, and Kosh saw through one of his buoys that a jagged black silhouette was rising up out of the thick grayish atmosphere. If any would detect him, it would be this monstrosity created by the maelstrom. He would observe it through the currents of the buoy without revealing himself. Kosh directed his ship to withdraw to a safer distance. It obeyed eagerly. Obedience was its greatest joy.

The great black vessel screamed up out of the gravity well. It was an abomination, a failed technology that required at its center a living, intelligent being, enslaved to the needs of the ship and the directives of its masters.

Once beyond the atmosphere, the abomination stopped, waiting.

Kosh wondered if it carried any passengers within, but he could not look inside or he would be noticed. Instead, he too waited.

Shortly, another ship approached, a sleek dark triangle. It belonged to one of the fabulists. Kosh's concern increased. He located the hidden sign on the side of the ship. This ship belonged to the fabulists' former leader, Kell. Kell had left the fabulists after his students had joined with the forces of chaos. Since then, he had been searching for those students. Kosh had observed one of them arriving at Thenothk, not long ago. Perhaps Kell had discovered his student's location. Perhaps that student was even now within the enemy vessel.

Or perhaps Kell had decided to join with the enemy himself. Kosh had believed him an honorable leader, yet the fabulists were in a difficult position, caught between order and chaos. The ancient enemy could have made great promises; the dream of the maelstrom could infect any not Vorlon.

The underside of the black monstrosity stretched open like a hungry maw. Kell's ship entered the beast, and the darkness swallowed it.

Over the years, Kosh had observed Kell only from a distance, yet now he felt both loss and disappointment. Whatever Kell's intentions, the fabulist would not leave the vessel alive, unless he swore himself to chaos. He could have accomplished much more in the great war. Instead, with his actions, he might well condemn the rest of his kind.

Many among the Vorlons would believe this another fabulist defection, and would argue with new fervor that they must all be killed, before it was too late. Kosh knew he must take at least some action to placate the other Vorlons.

If indeed more fabulists did consider joining with the enemy, let him frighten them a little. He would destroy their probes. They would believe the forces of chaos had discovered their spying, and had been angered. That, perhaps, would help keep them away, keep them on the path to their migration.

It would also please the Vorlons. They liked to think of themselves as the ones who stood on high and watched, controlled. They did not like to think of others standing beside them, watching as well.

So he would destroy their probes. And then he, alone, would watch. If Kell emerged from the abomination, then Kosh would take the news back to the Vorlons. And it would very likely trigger the destruction of the fabulists.

He hoped it would not come to that.

The others would say Kosh spent too much time among the younger races. They would say he allowed sentimentality to weaken discipline. They would say he had forgotten his place.

But the destruction of the fabulists, he believed, would be a great tragedy.